A FALSE REFLECTION

Sarah Jones

Cinderhill Publishing

Copyright © 2025 Sarah Jones

All rights reserved

This is a work of fiction. Names, characters, organizations, places, events and incidents are either products of the author's imagination or used fictitiously. Any resemblance to actual persons, living or dead, or actual events is purely coincidental.

No part of this book may be reproduced, or stored in a retrieval system, or transmitted in any form or by any means, electronic, mechanical, photocopying, recording, or otherwise, without express written permission of the publisher.

ISBN-13: 978-1-0682405-0-8
eISBN: 978-1-0682405-1-5

Cover design by: Get Covers

*Dedicated to the memory of my mum,
Janet Elizabeth Burchnall (1937-2023).*

CONTENTS

Title Page
Copyright
Dedication
PROLOGUE — 3
PART ONE — 9
Lucy — 11
Lucy — 16
Cath — 25
Twenty Years Earlier — 27
Lucy — 30
Jon — 34
Twenty Years Earlier — 37
Lucy — 42
Twenty Years Earlier — 52
Lucy — 57
Cath — 63
Lucy — 66
Twenty Years Earlier — 74
Lucy — 77
Cath — 86
Twenty Years Earlier — 88

Lucy	92
Twenty Years Earlier	100
Lucy	104
Cath	111
Twenty Years Earlier	113
Lucy	116
Lucy	121
Cath	126
Twenty Years Earlier	129
Lucy	131
Twenty Years Earlier	135
Cath	139
Twenty Years Earlier	143
Lucy	145
Twenty Years Earlier	152
Cath	154
Lucy	158
Cath	163
Twenty Years Earlier	169
PART TWO	173
Lucy	175
Twenty Years Earlier	182
Jon	185
Lucy	187
Twenty Years Earlier	196
Cath	200
Twenty Years Earlier	203
Lucy	205

Twenty Years Earlier	212
Jon	215
Twenty Years Earlier	217
Lucy	219
Twenty Years Earlier	221
Rob	224
Cath	230
Lucy	232
Cath	236
Cath	238
Lucy	242
Cath	252
Rob	254
Lucy	258
Lucy	263
Cath	269
Lucy	273
Rob	278
Lucy	280
Cath	283
Rob	286
Cath	288
Twelve Months Later	290
PART THREE	291
Bella	293
Bella	297
Bella	300
Bella	307

Bella	310
Izzy	314
EPILOGUE	321
Izzy	323
Milly	324
Acknowledgement	327
About The Author	329
Books By This Author	331
	333

PROLOGUE
The end of the summer

The flashing blue lights almost danced in the darkness of the night. They had a festive feel, as if they were announcing the end of summer - just as the pretty twinkling fairy lights adorning the decking at Beach Cottage had saluted the start of that glorious sunny season. It was a day that had been looming all through the brightness of the holidays; just lurking in the shadows, a fleeting hint at the edge of their vision during those heady weeks that had started off with sunshine and the hope of new beginnings. Finally, the unwelcome guest had crashed the party. The thunder clouds that had been glimpsed in the distance finally broke and threatened to drown them all in the deluge.

    Whispers started in the early hours that there had been a death. Phones set to silent lit up the room as gradually the village spread the news of the tragedy. As kettles were boiled and the local police Facebook page was refreshed, shock waves reverberated through the small community. On this Monday morning, there was no groan of protest at the start of a new week as those who had known her (and those who hadn't) were eager to congregate at the school gates, united in grief and shock and a tiny thrill of involvement in this drama that was unfolding before them. Everyone dressed a little more carefully that morning, with just that extra bit of make-up. After all, you never knew if reporters would be there and no one wanted to be in the papers, never mind the television, looking anything less than their best.

    Before the funeral, the story was picked up by the local papers. Central to the narrative was an account attributed to 'a source close to the family who wishes to remain anonymous.' They spoke passionately about the devastation felt by the whole community, but plainly stated the truth that everyone recognised. This was an event that they should have seen coming and could have been prevented. No one wanted to say, 'I told you so' - after all that would imply that maybe they should take some responsibility for what had happened. Instead, they preferred to cast the blame on the 'someone.' The 'someone should have done something about this years ago.' There were numerous related articles over the days that followed: a blasting of the mental health support in the area, followed by advice from the local Community Constable of the steps you could take and the help you could access if you ever felt unsafe.

In the days after that, old friends emerged. People from years ago, many of whom hadn't thought about that school drama for years, happy now to tell the story of the events of twenty years ago, proclaiming with dramatic certainty that they always knew something like this would happen and how better action should have been taken at the time. After all, if it had been dealt with properly then, things could have been so very different. No fear there of getting the blame; after all they hadn't spoken to her in twenty years.

The family remained inside. Curtains drawn in a futile attempt to block out the reality. In contrast to the events of twenty years ago, the community formed a protective circle around them. After all, there was a child involved this time.

And Kate remained silent. A local reporter had tracked her down to the small farm where she had quietly lived for many years with her husband and children - hoping to seize the story that could be syndicated to the nationals. He was optimistic that his big break could be a good thing to come from the devastation, the story of the one who got away. But Kate remained elusive. Not even a 'no comment.' Rumours were that she was destroyed by the news, but this was based on gossip and imagination rather than any semblance of fact.

As the weeks passed, the flowers that had been laid at the spot slowly died and were removed, and the twinkling lights which intruded on the night sky were now those to herald the start of the season of goodwill to all men. The women at the school gate dampened down any niggle of guilt they might feel with a 'Pimm's and Party' night organised to raise funds for the local outdoor pool. They thought it would be what she would have wanted. After all, as far as they knew, that was where it had all started. There had been talk of another 'Pizza and Prosecco' event; after all that had been done once already - there was already a spreadsheet in place - and with the hectic season fast approaching it would make the organisation so much easier. But it was decided that, after the last time, it may be seen to be in rather poor taste.

The fundraiser was a very successful night, though the Chair of the PTA couldn't help but secretly feel a little aggrieved that the event rather hijacked the charitable donations that may have been spent on the school Christmas Hamper raffle. Predictably, a couple of the women drank too much and became very tearful. Thankfully the DJ had a great playlist: his Christmas party special. The tears were swiftly replaced by screams of delight, shoes flung to the side of the village hall and ABBA's Dancing Queen was shouted along with in your honour. You would have smiled at that.

Obviously there were strict instructions not to play any version of 'Lilac Wine'. The DJ thought it was a bit unnecessary to make that statement. After all it the song wasn't exactly high on his playlist, but it seemed the night needed to capture some of the drama. He nodded understandingly, reached out a reassuring hand to comfort a shaking shoulder and pretended to make a note on his phone.

As the party drew to a close and the DJ put on the slow songs that signalled it was time for people to start thinking about making a move, little groups formed around the edge of the hall, sharing their memories of the woman they were there to remember. Playing a medley of songs, the DJ made a dash for a much-needed toilet break, and on his way back attempted to listen in on a few of those conversations. After all, he knew he would be grilled by his wife when he got home, so it would be good if he could glean a juicy titbit that she could proudly share with her own circle. It was pretty dull stuff really -

nothing that hadn't already been splashed all over the local paper. Funny how death seems very black and white. You are either elevated to the sainthood or condemned as a thoroughly nasty piece of work. Memories that may show you in that murky grey light are simply erased, until you are reborn as a version that the majority have dictated is the version that will exist now that you no longer have a heart to beat or a voice to shout in protest.

Not long now and you will be consigned to a shiny plaque on a bench at the outdoor pool. The much longed for Splash and Play area will finally be made possible following the very well-attended fundraiser. The sun will shine again, and the delighted screams and laughter of the children will drown out the last little bit of guilt anyone else may feel. The plaque will slowly tarnish, the words becoming worn and increasingly unreadable, and gradually you will be forgotten, as if you never existed.

Soon it will be the start of another new year. A year that would no longer have you in it. Because, when it came down to it, if I couldn't have your life, then you couldn't either.

PART ONE
Holiday

LUCY

We had slowed to a near standstill just as we drew level with the Metro Centre. The A1 turned into a car park - mainly caravans and overloaded cars - with the eager faces of children grinning and waving from the back seat at their fellow prisoners. Milly, my four-year-old ('I'm five very soon, Mummy'), had started off in the same frenzy of excitement when we left home three hours ago, but the monotony of the journey had soon lulled her into a restless sleep. I was forever turning round and correcting her position in the car seat so she didn't get a crick in her neck.

'For God's sake, stop fussing with her, Luce,' snapped Rob, stressed by the current delay. I didn't bother to reply as I knew that once he was in this mood, whatever I said would be wrong. The day had not got off to the best of starts. It really is hard work packing for a holiday with a four-year-old at home, and despite my best efforts, this morning was all a mad rush. When we were half an hour into the journey, I realised I had forgotten to pack the coats, which were neatly folded on the bed in the spare room. I debated whether to mention it, but looking at the grey skies threatening rain, I had to confess the mistake. Rob sighed and turned the car round and had barely spoken since. In fact, I think the only time he had spoken to me was to tell me off for fretting over the McDonald's we were ordering for Milly. I still think the fruit pieces were the wise choice but, on this occasion, Milly got her own way and had the fries and then an ice cream as well. I made a mental note that I would need to adjust our evening meal for this, just to make sure she gets all the nutrients she needs. The last thing we needed was for her to be ill on holiday.

I sneaked a quick glance at Rob. He looked tense his eyes squinting against the sun, which had decided to finally make an appearance, after we had driven through torrential rain for the first part of the journey. I made a silent plea for the weather to be good to us - we all need this holiday. Finally, the traffic started to creep forward again, and I risked a look back at a sleeping Milly. She was due to start school in September and I can't really put into words how sad I felt about this. Her birth had been a difficult time but from the minute we were finally both safely home from the hospital, I was engulfed with this overwhelming love. The flip side of this was I was also overcome with pure panic and anxiety. *Was she feeding enough, was she feeding too much, was she going to the toilet properly, was that cry normal.* It was a never-ending anthem drumming through my mind, and I was a frequent visitor at the baby clinic, making frantic calls to the GP's surgery in between. Rob tried to be understanding, but his suggestion to try to relax just showed me how little he understood the dangers our Milly could be exposed to.

Eventually, Mum came to stay for a while and Mum understands me. Together we could work out a strategy to manage the overwhelming feelings and I have managed to do that, until New Year's Day when Rob mentioned that Milly would be starting school this year. Back then, it seemed such a long time away that it was just a low-level gnawing in the pit of my stomach that I could ease with some deep breaths and a phone call to Mum. But just before we came on holiday, we had the new parent visit from Milly's class teacher. They come and see you in the home and I had postponed and cancelled for as long as I could. In fact, the school secretary was starting to get quite short with me on the phone and I realised I needed to keep her on side if she was to help me keep an eye on my precious girl.

Rob always worried that my anxiety would spill over to Milly and that she would be afraid of starting school. After all, this would be the first time that she and I had been apart for any length of time. But Milly was beside herself with excitement at the prospect of proper school. I like to think that maybe she didn't quite grasp that I wouldn't be there with her for the day, but lately I had caught her curiously glancing at me as I hovered next to her at playgroup. I felt like she was noticing that the other mums were casually ignoring their children, whilst I was ever vigilant in case there was a choking hazard or toxic paint or stranger danger. I knew this wasn't completely rational, and I knew the other mums judged me, not particularly kindly, for it and I'd started to feel that maybe Milly was judging me in the same way.

Anyway, two days ago, Miss Murray arrived at the door. The teacher looked to be about fifteen with long straight hair in a plait, a ready smile and a soft-spoken hello. To be honest, she spent most of the visit chatting to Milly rather than me, and when I tried to share my fears, she smiled kindly and just brushed me off with a rather dismissive, 'Don't worry, Milly will be just fine. We are going to have a very exciting year.' Milly was smiling and clapping, obviously quite enamoured with the new lady in her life and I felt my stomach tighten a little more, and for a moment thought I wouldn't be able to breathe.

'Oh, how rude of me, I've not offered you a drink,' I managed to croak. When Miss Murray smiled and said *a glass of water would be lovely*, I was able to escape to the kitchen where I gripped on to the work surface as if I were on the juddering underground, my legs swaying to the motion that only I could feel. Just like the darkness of the snaking tunnels, I could feel the blackness starting behind my eyes, so I forced myself to concentrate on my breath work.

Breathe in for five - it's fine, she's here.
Breathe out for five - it's fine, she's safe.
Breathe in for five - all is as it should be.
Breathe out for five - it's fine, you've not lost her.

I ran through the pattern a few times and gradually I could feel my heart rate start to slow and my breathing become less ragged. I was back in daylight and could, for now, get off that runaway train of panic. With trembling hands, I was able to fill a glass with water and move back towards the lounge.

I stood for a moment in the doorway, watching my Milly chatting happily to the teacher.

Breathe, just breathe. You've not lost her.

'Here we go - sorry it took so long.'

'That's fine, we've been having a lovely chat, haven't we Milly? And to be honest, it's good to get some time together with the children on their own so we can get to know each other. OK Milly, I'm just going to have a chat with your mum now and see if there's anything she wants to ask me.'

'How long have you got?' I laughed, but I noticed Miss Murray was looking at me with some concern. I bet that witch of a school secretary has already branded me a troublemaker.

'It's funny, the little ones always find this easier than their mums,' she said with a reassuring smile. 'Now Milly wasn't at our nursery, did she go elsewhere?'

Later when I tell Mum about this, she sensibly offers that Miss Murray really wasn't judging me but was just assessing whether Milly was likely to know any of the other children in the class. But I felt judged - that already I was labelled as a neurotic parent and that I would have a special star against my name to mark me down as one to watch.

'I'm at home all day so Milly has stayed with me. We do a weekly playgroup session, but we have enjoyed our time at home together, haven't we Milly?'

Milly looked up at me and smiled. 'But I'm really looking forward to being a big girl and starting school.'

Miss Murray laughed. 'As I say, we always find the mums struggle much more than the children. I shall see you in a few weeks' time, Milly. Enjoy your summer.'

Milly watched her walk down the path and stood at the window waving for a long time after Miss Murray had got in her car and left. As soon as Rob got home - late again and looking tired - Milly ran to tell him all about Miss Murray. I tried to smile and look excited about it, but all evening I could sense that Rob was sending sideways glances of concern. Once we were in bed, he was brave enough to whisper, 'It will be alright, you know. This will be good for both of you, and it will only make your time together more special.'

I pretended to be asleep, tears sliding down the side of my nose, so he stopped before he could move into his usual patter about how maybe I could look for a part-time job, to allow me some independence and meet more people.

I don't need to meet more people. I have all that I need in Milly, and I just can't bear to lose her once the summer is over.

LUCY

Finally, we cleared the traffic jam around Newcastle and continued heading north until eventually we turned off to head towards the coast. Milly had woken up as we started on the winding country roads, and so we all started the competition of who would see the sea first. I knew the exact point in the road where the blue expanse of water stretched out to meet the sky, breaking away from the surrounding flat fields, but I held back my shout to allow Milly to exclaim, 'I see it, I can see the sea!'

I smiled at Rob and for the first time on the journey, he seemed to relax. We both feel the same about our holiday destination. We have been coming here for the last two weeks in July ever since Milly was born. We found out about it from Rob's best friend from university. Paul and Lou are Milly's godparents and their oldest is a year older than Milly. They discovered Dune Farm Holiday Cottages and raved on about how perfect it was with access to stunning sandy beaches, a children's playground and a couple of decent pubs within walking distance. They always visit the week before us, and we normally have a mini handover in the beautiful 'Beach Cottage'. But this year they had a family commitment they very reluctantly felt they had to attend and so, for the first time since we have been visiting, our friends wouldn't be passing on the baton of temporary ownership. I was not happy about this at all.

'It will be weird taking over the cottage from strangers.'

Rob frowned and cast that odd glance at me that I had noticed was becoming his frequent observation of me in recent weeks.

'Why weird? The cleaners will have been in and it's not like other people aren't using it for the rest of the year.' I bit my lip and said no more. I can't help it, I like routine, and Rob doesn't always understand how much I need that familiarity. It makes me feel safe that a family I know well have inhabited the space I am about to call my home. They have test-driven it for me - there have been no disasters during their stay, so it will be a suitable refuge for my precious family.

As we turned off the main road to the single-track lane that leads down to the sea, I once again experienced the profound sense of coming home. Of course, it would be no different the fact that Paul and Lou haven't been there before us. This place is familiar to me, it's safe, we are all safe.

Very little had changed as we approached the entrance to the farm complex. The lane was a little more bumpy than usual and Rob cursed as the car dropped in a particularly deep pothole; a rather ominous crunch made us both wince as the brambles scraped against the side of the shiny paintwork. And then we were on the smooth entrance to Dune Farm: a small complex of ten holiday cottages centred round a small communal green, with a grassy play area tucked away to the side.

We followed the signs to Beach Cottage and pulled into our designated parking spot, Rob tutting as he noted that the occupants of the cottage next door had taken up more than their fair share of the space. I could take a proper breath at last. Everything was as it should be. Outside the door of the cottage were two brand new buckets and spades - one pink and one blue, together with two green fishing nets, just waiting to be dangled in the gloopy depths of the rock pools that sit at the end of the cove. I can remember been so enchanted with this detail when we first visited the cottage, wondering initially if they had been left behind from the previous occupants, but then realising this was a nice welcome touch for every holiday maker. Milly ran ahead and opened the door, and I followed her in to the familiar bright, large kitchen with the wooden table around which I have spent many happy hours chatting, drinking, and eating. I find it incomprehensible that for fifty weeks of the year, other strangers inhabit this space that feels like only mine.

Milly skipped straight through to 'her' bedroom, and announced that she would sleep the first week in the bed by the window, before moving to the bed nearest the door. She exclaimed delightedly that the room had been decorated in her favourite colour of blue, as if the owners had made it pretty just for her.

I peeked round the corner to the double room opposite, which had been similarly redecorated, and wondered idly if they had a bargain offer on a bulk buy of the paint. I caught a glimpse of myself in the floor-length mirror and could almost hear my mother sighing, 'Lucy, you look tired.' My curly red hair looked a little wilder than normal where I had run my fingers absently through it as we sat in the traffic jam. My skin was pale, with a smattering of freckles that I hoped would take on more colour if we get the promised sunshine. I hoped the same every year. I am always disappointed.

I wandered back through the lounge towards the kitchen, pausing at the conservatory to open the windows as the small space was already stifling with the day's sunshine. I noticed with a shudder there are already a couple of dead flies languishing on the white sills. Moving back to the lounge, I sighed in contentment as I recognised nothing here had changed. The two leather sofas still framed the TV in the corner, with the squishy armchair, that I prefer, sat slightly to the side. I thumbed through the DVDs that were left, pleased to note there were no new choices. The coffee table still had the usual smattering of tourist information leaflets, menus from the local takeaways and the rather shabby guest book. Satisfied that all was as it should be, I went to help Rob bring the luggage in, and smiled in anticipation that he would be grumbling we have packed enough to stay for a month. But when I moved outside, I saw that Rob was chatting to the couple in the next-door cottage - the people who have 'parked their car like idiots'. I hesitated for a moment in the doorway, unsure what to do, when Rob turned and saw me and waved me over.

'Come and meet our holiday neighbours, Steve and...' he hesitated.

'Lydia,' filled in the rather glamorous blonde stood by the side of Steve, who appeared to be just heading off to the golf course. Though by the look of his ruddy cheeks, he spent most of his time in the clubhouse.

Reluctantly, I shuffled over to join the small group, noticing that the buckets and spades at the back door were identical to the ones that greeted our arrival, but had clearly been well-used. A couple of bodyboards - one blue with a shark, the other pink with a mermaid - were propped against the wall together with four wet suits hung to dry on the rotary line. Inwardly I groaned, anticipating Rob would later have a little sneer about what he thought of this stereotypical middle-class family. But as I reached the cluster, I noted that Rob was grinning in a way I hadn't seen him smile for a long time, and he seemed to be embracing the opportunity to make some holiday friends.

'Hi,' I smiled and raised a hand in greeting, 'I'm Lucy, seeing as Rob failed to mention that.' I meant it to come out as a light-hearted introduction, but I saw Rob stiffen and his mouth slip back to that hard line that had become all too familiar over the last few months. The other couple shifted uncomfortably and I was aware that somehow, I had dampened the atmosphere.

'Sorry, don't mind me.' I waved my hand and smiled ruefully. 'Long journey.'

'What you need is a large glass of wine,' was the suggestion of Lydia, who sounded like she may have already taken her own advice.

I started to say that I didn't really drink, not wanting to go into detail about how it didn't agree with me, or rather it didn't agree with the medication I was on, when I saw Rob looking at me impatiently, as if waiting for me to spoil things further.

'You are absolutely right, just got to wait for the grocery shop to be delivered in a couple of hours.'

'No need to worry about that,' grinned Lydia, 'You are my perfect excuse to start drinking - not that I need an excuse, it's holiday time.' I felt a bit smug that I had been correct in my assumption this woman had hit the bottle early, and then worried my face may have betrayed me, but Lydia was already heading indoors, reappearing seconds later with four glasses and a bottle of white, still glistening with condensation from the fridge.

'Not for me,' said Steve. 'I've got that tee-off time booked.'

He turned to Rob. 'I don't suppose you fancy joining me?'

I expected Rob to make his polite excuses, anticipating he would already be peeved by the fact we had somehow got dragged into having a drink with these strangers, but again he took me aback with his sudden grin. He hesitated and started to mumble about unpacking the car and not leaving me alone to sort the shopping, and I saw this was my chance to start the holiday on a positive note.

'You go, you know you're longing to get on the course. Milly and I will be just fine.'

I wasn't sure that we would be fine, but I was eager to give a better first impression than I had done with my earlier waspish comment. 'Speaking of which, I better go and check where Milly is.'

I smiled regretfully, impressed that I had managed to extricate myself from the glass of wine, when Lydia intervened. 'Oh lovely, get Milly and bring her over and she can join our two at the playground. There's quite a little gang congregating over there.'

I could feel the nerves start. 'She's only four.'

'Five at the end of the month,' stated Rob, who had

returned to the group sporting his golf clubs and was clearly eager to get away. As he joined Steve in the car, Lydia was calling to her two children, who I could now see across the grassy patch in the playground area. The older of the two, a boy, and presumably the owner of the shark bodyboard, skilfully unhooked the latch on the gate and raced towards his mum, whilst a younger girl trailed behind, casting wistful backwards glances at the swings still swaying in the breeze. Both children had mops of tousled blonde hair and the grubby look of a day spent playing outside. Lydia was looking at me curiously as the children approached and I could see she was expecting me to go and fetch Milly so we could settle down for our cosy chat. My mind was whirring to come up with an excuse - there was absolutely no way I was allowing this to happen. But then the decision was taken out of my hands as Milly emerged from the kitchen door, presumably bored of exploring the cottage and eager to get to the beach.

'Oh, hello,' she grinned happily. 'I'm Milly and I'm going to be five soon.'

I marvelled afresh at how relaxed this girl of mine was - how none of my anxieties had rubbed off on her - and realised I should embrace the fact that she had this confidence, that she was yearning to fly solo for a little while. Maybe this holiday was the time to do that.

'I'm Xander and this is Becca,' stated the boy.

'He's eight and bossy and I'm six and a better swimmer,' chipped in his sister.

And the two of them were off, bickering in a debate that was clearly a topic of frequent discussion.

Milly grinned and Lydia smoothed over the increasingly shrill bickering with the offering of ice creams and an instruction to take Milly over to the playground, introduce her to the rest of the gang and 'look after her.'

I began to protest but then I saw Milly's mouth start to fall in that same hard straight line that I had noticed earlier on Rob, and I heard the warning my mother had given me just the other week.

'I know you love that girl and I know you want to protect her, but you have to let her go a little bit, otherwise she will start to resent you. You'll end up losing her.'

In a huge effort of will I leant towards my girl and told her if she wanted to go that was fine, but she mustn't leave the playground, and I would keep checking. I sensed Lydia behind me rolling her eyes, but Milly eagerly grasped this first taste of freedom and ran across the green after Xander and Becca, giggling and waving her arms with the joy of release. I was consoled by the fact that as they reached the gate, she turned to wave at me; and then all three of them were engulfed by the little group of children playing there, and they disappeared off to the far side near the rope swings where there appeared to be a complicated game of tag in progress.

I wanted to stay and watch but Lydia was ushering me to their outside seating area, chatting about the holiday and how nice it was when the children made some friends. She was clearly delighted that Xander and Becca were keeping themselves occupied giving her 'me time,' so I was unable to explain that I didn't want 'me time.' That I wasn't me if I didn't have my girl by my side.

To my surprise, it turned out to be a rather pleasant afternoon. Lydia was easy to talk to. Well, more accurately, she did all the talking and didn't require much input from me other than a nod and a smile at the right place. I kept wandering over to the playground, just to check, but Milly was absorbed in her game and didn't notice me, and gradually I started to relax. I was shocked that when Lydia went to fill our glasses, the bottle was empty and despite my protestations, she went in to replenish supplies, returning with a new bottle and a bowl of crisps 'to keep us going until dinner.' I was a little concerned at this as Lydia sounded like it was assumed we would be spending the evening together, but as I took a sip of the ice-cold wine, I relaxed and decided it would be easy to make our excuses to leave once Rob got back from golf. I was certain he would not want to socialise for any longer than was polite.

But as the heat of the sun started to recede and families returned from the beach, another couple wandered over, waving their children off to the playground to join the happy shrieking game in progress.

'Quick, pour me a glass,' gasped the dark-haired woman who I had seen herding away what looked to be twin boys of around ten. She had a glowing tanned face that looked like it smiled a lot. I felt an instant warmth and wasn't sure if that came from the company or from the three large glasses of wine mixing with the medication. I sat, feeling shy, as introductions were made. The dark-haired smiling lady was Jen, her sunburnt, shirtless husband was Andy, who stayed to see his wife start on a glass of wine then raced over to join the children, waving a cricket bat and stumps in an effort to organise a friendly game. Jen smiled after him fondly and leaned towards me.

'He'll never get a match organised and will end up with the kids all wrestling him to the ground, but he loves it.'

I smiled, a little alarmed at Milly wrestling this large stranger to the floor, but stopped myself from saying anything and took a large gulp of wine instead.

As Lydia and Jen caught up on their day, I was content to idly listen, distracted by the shrieks of joy coming from the playground. This was not at all how I had envisaged our first afternoon to be. I had pictured the three of us wandering to the beach and discovering the rock pools before we headed home for fish and chips and board games. Everyone seemed to be settling down to make a night of it, and just as I decided I'd make a move, Steve's car pulled up. I noted that yet again he parked like an idiot, but clearly Rob wasn't going to say anything as he was still laughing at something Steve had said as they got out the car.

'Quick, a beer for the sporting hero, returning victorious!' Steve gasped, as he pulled Lydia in for a hug. Jen laughed and disappeared inside to collect the drinks. I was struggling to figure this out, as they seemed such close friends, yet from what I could gather, they had only met last week, on the first day of their two-week stay. I tried to catch Rob's eye as he plonked himself down, still laughing as Jen handed him a beer.

'Ah, victory will be mine tomorrow.'

I frowned at that; surely they hadn't arranged another game already. This wasn't like Rob at all. He always said the worst thing about golf was that you had to play it with other people, and I know his plan for the holiday was to practice at the driving range and play a few solitary rounds 'to get his head together'. Taking a large gulp of beer, he finally turned to me.

'Alright? Where's Milly?'

Lydia answered for me and smiled as she waved vaguely in the direction of the playground.

'Milly is over there being led astray by our assorted offspring and Andy!'

Jen grinned, 'Andy is the biggest kid of them all.'

Rob looked at me in surprise but then smiled at me warmly. The way he used to smile at me in the beginning. And it was this smile that took the 'Well, thank you for the drinks, but we really must get on now' from being uttered and instead I relaxed back in my chair, my hand resting on Rob's leg as I prepared to enjoy one last drink. After all, no harm ever came from enjoying oneself.

CATH

Cath looked anxiously at her mobile yet again as she waited for the kettle to boil. She had been uneasy all afternoon and knew she would feel like this for two weeks until Lucy, Rob and Milly were all safely back from holiday. Mentally, she corrected herself as she knew her anxiety was not for the whole family, which didn't mean she didn't love them all deeply. No, the butterflies in the pit of her stomach were fluttering for her daughter, Lucy, and had been in residence there since that dreadful time twenty years ago when Lucy was just sixteen.

Cath glanced at her mobile again - still no message to let them know the family had arrived safely at Beach Cottage. She would not allow her mind to go back to that time. It was twenty years ago, for God's sake. A dreadful time, but life had moved on, and they had all come out the other side relatively unscathed. If the constant nagging anxiety about Lucy was the price to pay, then she would happily pay it over and over with gratitude for getting her daughter back.

'Earth to Cath, earth to Cath.'

Cath became vaguely aware that someone was speaking her name and turned to see her husband Jon looking at her quizzically.

'Are you OK? You were miles away there.'

Cath wished she was miles away at that little cottage with Lucy and her family. She knows it's irrational, but she felt that as long as she was close at hand, no harm could come to them.

'No word from Lucy yet?' Jon realised straight away the cause of Cath's distraction. 'I'm sure they're fine and they will have been dragged straight to the beach by Milly. We will hear from them later.'

'I know. It's just I can't help but worry.'

Jon cut Cath off, 'Stop right there; it was such a long time ago and Lucy is doing just fine now. It was just one of those childish things that got a little out of hand, and to be honest I think it was wrongly blown out of all proportion. Now come on, how about I take you away from all this and we go to the pub for our tea.'

Cath smiled and agreed, though it did grate somewhat that Jon was able to brush off the past events as something that was a simple bump in the road. It was rather more than that and they both knew it, though Cath chose to fret about it silently and Jon chose to pretend it was a simple misunderstanding. However, the pub would be a welcome distraction and by the time they got home, they would have heard from Lucy, and they could sleep one more night knowing all was well. After all, lightening doesn't strike twice.

TWENTY YEARS EARLIER

Lucy was looking forward to the start of term. She had always enjoyed school and had a small but very close-knit group of friends. There were five of them, which - being an odd number - might have made it awkward, but they had been friends since they were all put in the same class when they moved to the High School at eleven years old. Lucy had moved there from her village school with her best friend Anna, and when they had arrived in the form room, they had been sat next to Lisa and Amy. They had swapped shy 'hello's' and from then on, the four of them stuck together as a group. That evening, Lucy's older cousin had dropped by to see how Lucy had got on, and she casually asked if there was a girl called Jill in her class. Lucy wasn't really sure (she thought that was the name of the quiet blonde girl sat a bit apart from the rest of the group of girls), and her cousin said she would be a good friend to have as she knew her older brother and they were a nice family.

So, the next day Lucy made a real effort to befriend Jill, who looked rather taken aback to be showered with attention from the girl who, just the day before, had struggled to say hello to her in the dinner queue. But from then on, the five of them came together as a package. Lucy's mum had named them the 'Fabulous Five' and that was how they jokingly referred to themselves. They had their arguments, as most groups do, and best friends changed and swapped through the years, driven by their favourite bands or boys they liked, but the five of them always ended up back together. The 'Fabulous Five' against the world. The years up to their GCSEs had flown by with no real drama, other than Jill breaking her ankle slipping on the ice rink on a youth club trip. None of the girls were interested in drinking or particularly serious about boys, preferring to spend their evenings hunkered down at each other's houses, listening to music and swapping clothes. Thankfully, they had all done well enough in their exams to be offered a place at the Sixth Form and so this morning Lucy waited for Anna at the bus stop, curiously watching the new batch of nervous eleven-year-olds waiting impatiently for the bus to arrive. She smiled to herself as she remembered her and Anna on their first day. They had sat together on the bus, both awkward in their brand new uniforms, ties neatly in position with the top button most definitely done up. Lucy remembered how quiet they had been that day, and how grateful she had been for the reassuring presence of the Sixth Form prefects. They had seemed so grown up as they organised the crowd onto the bus, then sat laughing and joking, looking so different now they were free of the constraints of wearing the school uniform. And now her and Anna were the transport prefects, and Lucy was wearing the first of many brand new outfits, purchased when her mum had whipped her off to Leeds for the day. Cath loved any excuse to shop.

Lucy spied Anna turn the corner and smiled at her as she joined her at the bus stop.

'Gosh, these little ones look so young and scared. Do you think we were ever like that?' laughed Anna.

'Absolutely, no doubt about it.' Lucy looked at the new pupils, who were looking at her and Anna with a mixture of nervousness and admiration.

'I'm looking forward to Sixth Form,' continued Anna. 'Just think - no waiting in line at the canteen now we can use the Sixth Form bistro.'

'The Sixth Form common room,' chipped in Lucy.

'And free periods and snogging in the study bays,'

interrupted Dan as he squeezed between them, slinging an arm round each girls' shoulders. The three of them laughed then got ready as the bus appeared round the corner.

'Positions, ladies,' instructed Dan, as the two girls rolled their eyes and started organising thirty noisy youngsters to board the bus.

Looking back at that morning, Lucy thinks that it was maybe the last time things were normal.

LUCY

When I opened my eyes, it took me a while to realise where I was. Stumbling and tumbling into bed last night, I hadn't bothered to pull the blinds on the VELUX window, figuring we didn't need to as it was dark and there was going to be no one on the roof peering in at us. However, at five in the morning, the sun was glaring in, and the brightness burned against my eyes, which were scratchy and sore. I lay still, hoping that the world would soon stop spinning and the accompanying sickness would start to recede. I was desperate for a drink of water, but I didn't want to wake Rob, who was sleeping soundly beside me. The screech of a cockerel pierced the headache that was already threatening to have me heading to meet the toilet bowl, as I tried to remember what time we had got back to the cottage last night.

Once Steve and Rob had arrived back from golf, Andy wandered over to join us and the night just slipped away from us. I do remember the Sainsbury's shop arriving and just dumping everything on the side and half-heartedly making an effort to put things in the fridge or freezer. I groaned again thinking of the mess that would meet me in the kitchen when I could eventually face the day. I know that when the shopping came, I saw this as the perfect cue to make our excuses to leave, but by this point Lydia was already sorting the kids with chicken nuggets and chips and Milly was looking as if she couldn't believe this day was actually happening for her. I remember I fussed a bit about how many additives were in the food and thought I really ought to insist she drank water rather than the can of fizzy pop that had been plonked in front of her. But as I watched her delightedly alternating between gulping down the sweet syrup and blowing bubbles in the can, copying the older children so it looked like a flow of alarming, coloured lava was erupting from the top, I just didn't have the heart.

The noise of everyone was overwhelming. Milly and Rob looked to be so happy and the effort to break the spell just seemed too hard. It was easier to sip my wine and console myself with the thought that this was just our first night and there were thirteen more nights ahead of us when we could have the holiday that I had planned for our little family. So I sat and, whilst I know I was quiet with little to offer as the night got more raucous, I was able to cope with the discomfort. A few times from the edge of my vision, I saw Rob looking at me, almost like you might examine a strange insect that had found its way into your room, and you were curious as to exactly what it was. I pretended I hadn't noticed his scrutiny, but I wanted to hiss at him 'See this is me as well, I can do spontaneous too'; but instead I laughed at some light-hearted ribbing of Andy's failed cricket tournament and tried not to fret that things were escaping from my control.

I know at some point Steve fired up the BBQ and we ate surprisingly good burgers with crispy onions, and I relished the greasy messiness of it all. Then we followed the single file track between the dunes, the children running ahead, chasing the moths and sand flies that had started to venture out as the sun dropped below the horizon. The three men and the children started a game of rounders, whilst the three women sat on the sand nursing warm glasses of wine. We cheered every time the bat made a satisfying *thwack* as it made contact with the ball that raced away across the beach, helped by the ever-present sea breeze.

Eventually Milly searched for me, and ran over and curled into my lap, reverting to sucking her thumb as she fell asleep within minutes. As the game petered out, largely due to drunk adults and tired children starting to argue about the rules, we gathered up our weary offspring and began the trudge back to the cottage. Rob offered to take Milly, but I was enjoying the feel of her soft breath against my cheek and her sticky arms wrapped tightly round my neck, so despite the ache in my back, I kept her with me.

There was a moment when we arrived back that I thought Rob was going to take Steve up on his offer of just one more, but then Becca cried to her mum that she thought she had cut her foot and in the commotion the moment was lost, and Rob reluctantly followed me to the cottage accompanied by the sounds of 'Goodnight, see you in the morning.'

And now the morning was here, and I was paying the price for letting my guard down. Softly moaning, I gingerly lifted my head and waited for the room to stop spinning. I was wearing last night's T-shirt and a pair of pants, so grabbed my fleece and walked quietly out to the hallway. The door to the room Milly was sleeping in was ajar and I cautiously peered in. My girl was fast asleep, wearing yesterday's clothes, her sandy shoes carelessly discarded in the doorway. Frustrated with myself for letting yesterday get away from me, I moved to the kitchen, wincing as bright sunshine flooded the space and highlighted the abandoned shopping. We hadn't even finished unpacking the car, but I saw my handbag in the corner, so once the kettle was on to boil I downed my second glass of water and hurriedly swallowed my morning's medication. I couldn't remember whether I had taken my pills last night but there was nothing I could do about that now. Once I had made myself a coffee and poured a large glass of orange juice, hoping for the vitamin C to work a miracle, I took some time to check out how I was feeling. Anxiety was there but at a level that I would accept as normal - no catastrophising thoughts, no urge to wake Rob to get him to check the electrics were safe and no compulsion to lay my hand on Milly's chest to feel her heartbeat. No harm done then if I had missed a tablet.

Once I put the box of medication back in my bag, I spied my mobile and my anxiety did increase as I saw all the missed calls from Mum together with a number of voice messages. *Shit*, I'd forgotten to let them know we had arrived and were safe. I couldn't face listening to voicemails which I knew would be purposefully causal, but no doubt each message would reflect the increasing panic in my mum's voice. I squinted at the time display and saw it was just after six - not too early to call, but then I didn't want to wake the rest of the house. I quickly typed out a message to the family WhatsApp group, which only consisted of Mum, Dad and me.

> *Oh my, I'm so sorry. I thought I'd messaged last night but I can see it hasn't sent. Signal here is shocking but all OK with us. Talk later. x*

Immediately, I saw two blue ticks appear and felt guilt with the knowledge that Mum and Dad would have been fretting all night. They try not to let it show, and we certainly never talk about that period twenty years ago, but the hurt and the anxiety that arose from that time is woven into the base fabric of our relationship. It's something only the three of us know, and we have an unspoken agreement that it is something that will never be shared with Rob. After all, it was such a long time ago - just a silly thing caused by a deluge of hormonal emotions - and there is no reason to think that I will ever go to that place again. My phone vibrates with a reply.

> *OK, no problem. Have a great time. Hope the weather stays nice for you. xxx*

It's a text that doesn't say anything that my mum wants to say, and I sigh with the knowledge that I don't think they will ever fully move on from that time.

JON

Jon was aware that Cath hadn't slept at all. And he only knew this because he hadn't slept a wink either. They'd had a decent evening at the pub. They had moved to the village nineteen years ago, when it became clear it wasn't the right thing for them to stay in the house they had started their married life in. It was a real time of new beginnings and both had thrown themselves into the local community in a bid to make this fresh start a good one. The village had just one pub, by a traditional village green, and it was popular most nights of the week. There were no spare tables outside in the evening sun, but as they walked in, their near neighbours were just leaving. Cath was able to grab a table inside and Jon went up to the bar to order their usual.

As he waited patiently for the customer in front of him to decide what sort of peas they wanted on the numerous fish and chips orders, he was vaguely aware that Cath was chatting to the couple at the next table, who were asking her if Milly was excited to be starting school. Jon smiled to himself. That was the nice thing about the village. Everyone knew everyone and knew most people's business. Mind you, it was that very community closeness that had caused such awkwardness in their last home. Giving his head a shake, Jon realised Andrea, serving behind the bar, was looking at him expectantly.

'Sorry, I was miles away.'

'Your usual?'

Jon confirmed and told himself to get a grip. He knew that Cath sometimes still thought back wistfully to their old home and friends they no longer saw. But Jon was much more given to making the best of living in the moment, and Cath relied on him to cheer her up if she got a bit glum. He knew why he was getting preoccupied. All because they were waiting for that text from Lucy to say all was well. For the most part, they were able to get on with their lives as if that episode had never happened, but as Jon carried the drinks over to Cath, he realised they lived their lives very close to the edge of a cliff. For a time, they both feared they would all fall from where they were teetering, crashing down to the rocks below where they would all be shattered. Would they ever feel they were far enough from the edge?

They stayed longer at the pub than they had intended. It seemed to be easier to be sat amidst the hustle and bustle than sat at home, where Jon had a sneaky suspicion that Cath would be asking him to drive her up to the coast 'just to check'. There was an impromptu music night on, and Jon found himself good-naturedly shaking a pair of maracas in a rhythm that bore no resemblance to the rest of the band. He was relieved to see that Cath was laughing, but could see that every few minutes she was checking her phone just in case she had missed that notification.

By the time they walked home it was close to midnight, and still no word.

'Honestly Cath, they will just have no signal or something daft. If there was a problem, we would have heard by now.' But they both lay awake for most of the night, not speaking but touching hands in a bid to anchor themselves to the new life they had built and not surrender to the fear that the past may repeat itself.

The vibration of the phone made them both jump, but Jon felt his heart slow as he saw the smile on Cath's face.

'They're all OK, just rubbish signal. Fry-up for breakfast?'

'For sure, I'll just nip in the shower.'

Jon heard Cath switch on Radio 2 in the kitchen and start on breakfast. He stood under the hot shower and, knowing the sound would be blocked by the music and the running water, he allowed the sobs to leave his body as he took great gulps of air. He wasn't sure if he was crying tears of relief, or still grieving for the life they had left behind. He hadn't cried in the last twenty years, since he had decided he needed to be the backbone for Cath and Lucy, and now he'd started he wasn't sure he would be able to stop.

'Please let her be OK, please let her be OK,' he whispered over and over, not sure who he was asking to help them make sure their world wasn't rocked again, before stepping out, drying his body and tears, and going downstairs to play his part.

TWENTY YEARS EARLIER

Making their way to the Sixth Form centre, Lucy couldn't help but feel some pride, along with a little nervousness. Lucy had always assumed that the 'Fabulous Five' would stick together until they departed for their chosen universities. However, Lisa had decided that nursing was the vocation for her, so she had opted for a college in town, that offered the course to allow her to follow that route. Lucy had been devastated and tried to persuade her to do her A-Levels as they'd always planned, but Lisa was adamant in her choice. There were long emotional conversations between the five of them, and Lucy felt the pain of separation deeply, as you can only do as a sixteen-year-old girl. And then, just as Lucy had reconciled herself to the idea that school would be different, but weekends and evenings would be just the same, Jill had dropped the bombshell that she wouldn't be attending the Sixth Form either. A talented linguist, she had been accepted on to a two-year course at an overseas programme near Paris. More tears followed, Lucy sobbing with her mum as she struggled to understand how her safe little world was changing so rapidly. Cath had been concerned at the strength of Lucy's emotions, but was reassured by talking to the other parents that all the girls were struggling with the speed of the changes.

As Lucy and Anna entered the side door and walked along the corridor to the common room, they giggled as they found their photos up on the wall, under the heading of

'Prefect Transport Team'. Dan caught them up and the three of them shyly entered the buzzing centre of the Sixth Form building. Amy was already sat chatting to a group of their fellow classmates and Lucy and Anna walked over to join her, leaving Dan to catch up with a group from the Upper Sixth he played football with. The girls hugged and soon Lucy and Anna were swallowed up into the group.

Lucy could still feel a knot of anxiety in the pit of her stomach as she waited for the bell to ring to signal it was time to make their way to their form room. *Would she be able to manage the work, was she good enough, had she picked the right subjects, would it be OK just the three of them?* These fears had been on a loop ever since she had joyously received her GCSE results and realised that her Sixth Form choice was now a reality.

The shriek of the bell pierced her thoughts and from then on, the day took on the reassuring familiarity that helped to calm Lucy's racing mind and quietened the continuous dialogue. Maybe it was going to be OK. Sure, things were different without Lisa and Jill, but in two years they would all be spreading their wings to different universities anyway, so maybe it was a good thing that they had this mini transition. By lunchtime, Lucy felt in control and was as excited as the others to avoid the jostling queue for the main school canteen as they made their way to the Sixth Form bistro. After they each chose a panini and a cold drink, they bagged a table by the window, where the September sunshine bathed them in a comfortable warmth.

'I meant to say,' spluttered Amy through a mouthful of string cheese, 'Those tights are just brilliant. Where are they from?'

Lucy glanced down, pleased that someone had taken the time to comment. Her mum had found the tights as they had wandered around the small independent shops clustered in the Victoria Quarter. At sixteen, Lucy was still finding her sense of who she was and preferred the safety of the chain store depiction of fashion, but Cath loved something a little different. The more colourful and flamboyant, the better. Lucy had sat on a little bench, choosing to look after the bags rather than be dragged into yet another quirky shop, where her mum insisted on chatting with the owner and normally trying to persuade Lucy to try on some item that would 'Look simply amazing on you.' When Cath finally emerged, blinking into the sunshine, she was clutching a bulging carrier bag and Lucy could see the clashing purple and yellow colours of her mum's latest find. Cath pushed a small brown paper bag at Lucy, grinning.

'Look, I've got you a present.'

'You shouldn't have,' protested Lucy, then laughing added, 'You really shouldn't have.' Seeing Cath's face drop, Lucy nudged her, 'Only kidding,' and opened the bag to see a pair of black opaque tights. Well, this was just fine.

'Go on, unfold them,' urged a grinning Cath.

Lucy did so and found that she was sporting a grin that matched her mum's. Snaking up the back of the tights were the most beautifully embroidered ladybirds.

'I couldn't resist,' giggled Cath, 'Ladybirds are a symbol of new beginnings, which seemed appropriate.'

Now in the bistro, Lucy was reminded of the safety net her mum always provided. 'Mum found them in one her little shops, you know what she's like.'

'Well, your mum did good with this one,' laughed Anna, and the girls shared a smile as they all remembered some of the flamboyant outfits they would giggle over back in the day, when Cath still thought it would be a nice surprise to buy Lucy clothes for Christmas.

That afternoon, Anna and Amy went off for their first free study period and Lucy made her way to the Humanities block for the first of her English Literature lessons. It felt strange to be going to a lesson on her own as Lisa had picked this option too, so she had fully expected to be sat with her friend. Still, she knew the teacher well and was friendly, if not friends, with others that she knew had picked this subject.

Peering round the door, she saw she was the last to arrive. The classroom was smaller than the traditional rooms she had spent the rest of her school life taking lessons in, and Mrs Pearson had arranged the desks in a square rather than the traditional facing-forward layout. She slipped into the last seat, smiling round at the others who were already seated, and looking at the text that had been placed on each desk. Mrs Pearson entered the room, and the class looked curiously at her and the person following her.

'Welcome to A-Level English. This is Miss Oxenham, who is completing her teacher training placement with us this year.' Lucy smiled a hello, the same as the rest of the class, but she was taken aback at the introduction. When Mrs Pearson had first walked in, Lucy had thought she was accompanied by another pupil for the class, maybe someone who had moved to the Sixth Form from one of the neighbouring schools. Miss Oxenham had the most striking black hair, cut in a jagged style that framed her face and contrasted with her quite startling blue eyes. Lucy knew she was staring but she couldn't help but drink in the sight of the girl, taking in every detail of her appearance, from the striped red, green and purple shirt which was tucked so casually into belted high-waisted black trousers, to the Doc Marten shoes. This was not what teachers looked like, and Miss Oxenham looked to be only a teenager herself.

On the introduction, Miss Oxenham grinned, and her hello was met with an eager response from the rest of the class. Lucy noted that the boy's response was particularly enthusiastic, and they were staring with open admiration, which Lucy feared her own face was replicating. The lesson passed in a haze for Lucy, who was unable to utter a single contribution to the discussion.

As she packed her bag at the end, Miss Oxenham smiled at her and said, 'Cool tights, I have some of those with bees on. I picked them as bees are a symbol of wealth, good luck and prosperity and being a student, I could do with any wealth there is coming my way.' Lucy found herself grinning back and managed a half-cheery, 'See you next time,' before leaving the room feeling like she had just been blessed by a goddess.

It's funny, but when you look back at people or events that have a fundamental effect on your life, the first meeting is often something innocuous. Something that, at the time, barely registers on your mind. It's only later when events have rushed towards their inevitable conclusion, that Lucy could look back and remember so clearly the exact moment her life was shoved onto a completely different path. And afterwards, all she could wish was, if only she had worn a different pair of tights, maybe none of the awfulness that followed would have ever happened.

LUCY

I took my coffee through to the conservatory and stretched out on the familiar wicker sofa, plumping up the faded cushions as I scrolled through my phone. I'm always declaring that I'm going to have a break from social media, but it seemed I was powerless against the urge to find out what people I barely knew were doing. With a sinking feeling, I saw there were new posts in the Reception children WhatsApp group. Miss Murray had mentioned this when she did her home visit. The parents in each year group set up a WhatsApp chat to swap tips, ask any questions or raise concerns. Apparently, the group tends to follow the children as they progress through the school and become 'quite sociable'. I wasn't sure how I felt about this and had been reluctant to add my details, but Rob reminded me I was always saying how hard it was to meet new people now I wasn't working. If I'm honest, a part of me felt a need to know as much as I could about the families of the children Milly would be spending more time with on a daily basis, than the hours I got to keep her.

 I saw that Heidi had posted. Heidi was Laura's mum and was the unofficial, self-appointed leader of the parents. She had an older girl in Year Four and was on the PTA, so had naturally taken the lead. She was reminding us all not to leave it too late to buy uniform and school shoes and that there was a Facebook group where second-hand uniform was available. I scrolled past it, with nothing to comment. Until recently, I hadn't even thought about shopping for the start of term, though Milly was so excited at the thought of a uniform and book bag. I had been putting it off, as if the act of not buying the uniform would stop September arriving. In the end, Mum had tentatively offered to take that job off my hands, which meant I no longer had to think about it. I could always trust Mum to know what I needed, to be a solid presence and keep me grounded.

I practiced some of the breathing exercises I had been taught all those years ago and felt my heart rate begin to slow and my skin lose the clammy feel of panic. I saw that my old work colleagues had been on a night out, and noted that a couple of people who left, both before and after me, had been invited. I felt momentarily aggrieved that I had not been asked. I know I wouldn't have gone anyway, but was that the point? Then my rational mind reminded me of the half-dozen or so invitations that had been extended my way after I had decided not to return after the end of my maternity leave. I had made excuses each time and had been relieved when they stopped asking. So it seemed petty to resent it now. I fired off a heart reaction and a *'You're all looking lovely, hope you had great time.'* The rest of my feed was 'things you might like' or 'because you followed' type things. I don't have many friends on social media; a few ex-work colleagues, my hairdresser (who seems to be friends with everyone), Heidi and one other mum, Rachel (who I had friend-requested accidentally when I was having a bit of a nosey one afternoon).

I keep my friends lists hidden. I'm hoping people will think it's because I'm a private person, but the truth is I'm embarrassed by the count tally, which has now reached the grand total of 22. For obvious reasons, I don't keep in touch with anyone from school. I continued to live at home when I went to university. It seemed the sensible thing to do after everything that had happened, and whilst Mum and Dad both said they would support wherever I chose to go, I could see the visible relief when I decided on Lancaster. To be fair to them, they did encourage me to look at student accommodation. I'm guessing they felt they were close enough to step in if there were any problems, or I needed extra support. But to be honest, all I wanted to do was to get my degree with as little fuss as possible, and living at home meant I wasn't under pressure to join in the social activities that my peers built their lives around. Every so often I search for names of old classmates from school - normally after a glass or two of wine - but it's my guilty secret and something I hide from Mum and Dad almost as if it's a heroin addiction. At times, when I'm feeling sorry for myself, I think they would have preferred that option to deal with.

I threw my phone down on the table by the neat piles of leaflets advertising castles, boat trips, horse riding on the beach and, bizarrely, the Metro Centre for shopping. That one always makes me laugh. I flick through, but it's the same stuff that has been there every time we have visited. I move on to the takeaway menus. Again, nothing different other than I note the pub at the bottom of the lane, which is always fully booked, has started to do a takeaway fish and chip option on a Friday and Saturday. I made a mental note to mention this to Rob as this might be a nice change to cooking.

Glancing at my watch, I saw it was still only just gone seven-thirty. There was no sound of movement from either Rob or Milly and I debate having a wander down to the beach. I love the sea - I find the sound and sight of the waves give me a new energy and sense of hope - but then I think that I want my first proper sight of 'our' beach to be the three of us. I'm ignoring the late evening trek there yesterday. That clearly doesn't count.

Bored, I reach for the guest book. I flick back through the pages to find our review from last year.

Fantastic time as usual. The cottage is clean and comfortable and truly is a home from home. So much to do. We can't wait to be back again same time next year!
Lucy, Rob and Milly (age 3, nearly 4)

I smile as I run my finger over Milly's name, that she had insisted on writing herself. She had also badgered me to include her age, with special reference to the fact she was nearly four. I remember so clearly writing that review and Rob pissing me off with his casual, 'Just think Milly, when we visit next year, you will be nearly five and getting ready to start big school.' I had thought it was unnecessary to mention this. I also detected a bit of a barb behind these words, as we had argued about whether Milly should start that year, for three mornings a week in the school nursery. I pointed out there really was no point in this, as I was at home anyway and that three mornings wouldn't give me any option to look for a job that fitted those hours. The truth was that I didn't want the inevitable to happen any sooner than it had to, and I think Rob realised this, as for once he didn't push his point of view.

As was my annual habit, I started to read through the other comments, certain that there would be something there to make me laugh. Nostalgically, I thought back to our first visit and Rob and I having the uncontrollable giggles over the review that criticised the holiday for there being too much sand, which got everywhere. Personally, I think the clue is in the name of the cottage. Beach Cottage tells you all you need to know really. I felt a pang of unease as I realise it had been a long time since Rob and I had giggled like that over anything.

I cast my mind back to last year. Things were a little tense between us as I know he thought I fussed over Milly too much and I did wonder if he was a little jealous of the love and attention that I heaped on her. After all, prior to her arrival in our lives, he was the absolute centre of my world. But we are still close, still affectionate. It was this last year, well probably since Christmas, that there had been a shift. I hadn't noticed at first, and then I decided I didn't want to think about it and decided I would tackle it another day. And before I knew it, seven months had passed and here we were on holiday.

Well, I certainly wasn't going to bring it up on this

holiday. If things were still a bit ropey once Milly started school, maybe I would have to confront it then - whatever it was. Locking that box firmly in my mind, I carried on idly flicking through the guest book, skim-reading some comments and taking in the detail of others. Unsurprisingly, I recognised a lot of the names. Beach Cottage - well the whole complex really - was the sort of place that people rebooked year after year. You were given first refusal on 'your' cottage for the same week the following year and there was very little availability for 'newcomers' in the peak months. I turned the pages on to see if the guests before us had left a review. Normally this would be Paul and Lou, but I was curious to see what the people who had snapped up this unexpected week had thought.

The first thing that struck me was the handwriting. All the reviews were in the normal blue or black ink, clearly written with one of the biros that were in the tray on the table by the side of the activity brochures. However, our predecessors had used their own pen and so the writing was in the most beautiful shade of ink I had ever seen. The light violet made me hold my breath for a second as my brain finally caught up with my eyes to tell me the colour was lilac. For a moment I felt that very particular lurch as my mind made the usual connotation to the colour. It threatened to take me right back there until, with a supreme effort of will, I forced myself back to the present, focusing on a few more deep breaths to bring myself back to where I was safe. I sniffed. How completely ridiculous, I mean who brings a fountain pen on holiday.

But there was no denying, the entry made a statement on the page before I could even focus on the words that had been written. The handwriting itself was all flowing loops, flamboyant and almost shouting from the page 'look at me'. Instead of starting a review under the last entry, the writer had christened a new page and filled it with the beautiful letters. It almost seemed unnecessary to read it; I was just in awe at the beauty of this coloured writing. I felt the same as if I had discovered a rare piece of art at a car boot sale, and I stared at it, the words out of focus, afraid to break the spell.

What if I started to read it and they complained that there were vital utensils missing from the kitchen or they had encountered dog dirt on the track to the beach (I had noted these comments in previous reviews). No, I refused to believe that such beautiful handwriting could convey such mundane trivia.

I felt ridiculously nervous as I brought the words into focus and even now, I'm not sure what I was expecting, but it was clearly going to be something very special.

> *Wow, just wow.*

I hesitated at this rather cliched start.

> *We were lucky enough to be offered the cottage at the last minute, when friends of ours were unable to take their planned holiday.*

I frowned at this. Rob had told me that Paul and Lou had been forced to cancel, but there had been no mention that friends of theirs had taken over the booking. Not that it mattered.

> *To be honest, we nearly didn't take up the offer as we have a trip to Crete booked for October half term.*

Yes, typical, I thought, already forming a picture of this family that had occupied our space before us.

> *What a gem we would have missed. The cottage is a pure joy to call home for the last week. Our days have been full and healing.*

I mean, who uses healing to describe a day at the beach, I thought to myself cynically, not sure what to make of the person at all. It seemed a bit over-the-top to me.

> *The beaches stretch out before you, as a blank canvas to paint wonderful memories.*

I snorted! *Really!*

> *And at the end of the day, we tumbled back to this cosy refuge where we could wile away the evenings. Evenings full of new friends, meaningful connections and laughter.*

Honestly, this person was just so completely over the top. But then I suppose, what did I expect from someone who carried a fountain pen with them on a beach holiday?

> *Thank you so much for providing this wonderful space. We are hoping we can secure a week next year as we are already dreaming of a new magical adventure.*

With a snort of derision, I slammed the book shut and took a gulp of my now stone-cold coffee. What complete and utter drivel. And clearly just written to try and get in the good books of the owners so they would be first in line for any future weeks that became available. They were obviously spoilt and used to getting their own way, I bet they only came so they could share with their friends that they had had a real 'Famous Five Summer'.

Determined to think no more about it, I opened the book one last time, just to see if they had left names. Of course they had.

Bella, Jules and Beth (aged 5)

I huffed again. Obviously Julian was far too plain for this family, or maybe Jules was a woman. I smiled at the stories my mind was weaving and then jumped as a voice from the doorway broke into my solitude.

'Morning, something rattled your cage already? Let me guess - someone has left a review saying the sea is too salty.'

I laughed and stood up to kiss Rob on the cheek. There was a time when he would have turned his head to kiss me on the mouth. Now he moved to the window to peer out at the sky, which was a clear, deep shade of blue. The sun was already starting to turn the conservatory pleasantly warm, though I knew from experience that by the afternoon it would be unbearable to sit in this small oven like space.

'Better get on with breakfast - I'm meeting Steve at nine for that round of golf. That's still OK, isn't it?'

I had noticed recently that when Rob wanted to do something that he thought was maybe not what I would like, he phased the question in such a way to imply it had been previously agreed, so that I felt it would be petty to disagree. And maybe I had agreed. I would be the first to admit my mind sometimes wandered and I didn't always take a lot of notice of the noise Rob made around me. But today I decided I wasn't going to make it that easy for him.

'This morning? I thought we would take Milly to the beach, you know she's going to be desperate to get down there as soon as she wakes up.'

'Well, she will be going down there, as you're meeting the rest of the gang at ten and Steve and I will join you for the big picnic we arranged last night. Don't tell me you'd forgotten? You were well up for it last night, and Milly will be so excited to spend time with the other children.'

I stared at Rob blankly. Did we really arrange this last night? It was possible I suppose, I might have got carried away, what with the wine that I wasn't used to drinking and the relief that Rob and Milly were no longer looking at me as if I were the Commander in Charge of the Fun Police. Rob turned to the kitchen, rolling up his sleeves as he declared he was going to do a fry-up to get us set up for another day of fun.

As he moved away, my stomach lurched. I wasn't sure if it was my hangover, the thought of a greasy fry-up or what the day of 'fun' was planned to look like. And since when had Rob started referring to people as 'the gang'? Especially as they were a bunch of strangers that we had just met, rather than lifelong friends that he seemed to be thinking they were.

'It's great that we've met Steve and Lydia and Jen and Andy, isn't it?' he called through, seemingly oblivious to my silence on the matter. 'It means we can all do our own thing a bit and Milly has lots of company, which will be great practice for her starting school in September. Besides, I think she would get bored if she was just stuck playing with her mum and dad. This will be so much fun for her.'

He poked his head back into the conservatory and tried a comedy lascivious wink, 'and us.' I responded with a weak smile. I had placed so many hopes on this holiday being the rescue package we all so desperately needed, and this was not in the plan at all. I was hurt that Rob thought that Milly found our company boring. He knew I was so afraid that I was becoming a little redundant in Milly's daily life, and it seemed thoughtless to refer to this after everything I had told him about the way I was feeling. I was also confused in the change in Rob towards 'the gang'. Rob had always mocked people who went away on holiday and came back with lifelong friends. He would sneer that he doubted the friendship would last past that year's Christmas cards and also queried why people would want to spend time with strangers on holiday, arguing that it was a precious time to spend with the people close to you that you loved. His eagerness to be a part of this group made me feel that maybe Milly and I were no longer enough for him.

As I trailed after him to the kitchen, I could see that

he was enjoying playing chef, though clearly he wouldn't be sorting the washing up after, as he seemed to be using every utensil in the cottage.

'Hmm... There doesn't seem as much cooking stuff as last year.' He broke into a grin, 'Maybe you should write a review!' He pulled me in for a hug and dropped a kiss on the top of my head. 'This is going to be a great holiday; I can just tell.'

At that point, Milly appeared in the door. Whilst she was wiping sleep from her eyes, she showed no sign of struggling after her late night the previous evening. 'Yay, family hug!' she cried, before throwing herself on the two of us. As I felt the warmth of Rob and Milly pressed against my body, I could feel some of the tension leave my shoulders. Whilst the holiday wasn't going the way I had hoped, maybe this change would be good for all of us. Thinking ironically of the review I had just read, I hoped that maybe the cottage would turn out to be magical for us too.

TWENTY YEARS EARLIER

The first week of Sixth Form flew by, and although Lucy looked out for her, she only caught a glimpse of Miss Oxenham as she moved down the corridor, usually surrounded by a bunch of admiring younger children. It seemed that it was not just Lucy who had been drawn to her. Friday night came around and a few of the people in Lucy's form were arranging to meet in town for pizza. Anna and Amy were excitedly planning what to wear and it was just expected that Lucy would be coming along. Lucy, however, had other plans. Friday night was the one time she could be sure to have the house to herself. Her parents religiously attended music night at their local pub, when they would come home giggling and shushing each other to be quiet, as they stumbled up the stairs. Usually, Lucy would dread been around to witness this reminder that her parents were maybe something other than just her mum and dad, but this week she had waited eagerly for the Friday night ritual to start.

As she peeped out the curtain to watch Cath and Jon walk down the street, chatting and holding hands, her phone was pinging on near repeat beside her with friends texting meet up arrangements and trying to persuade her to join them. Lucy hoped they would soon give up as, for once, she ignored them. As soon as she was certain that Cath and Jon were definitely out for the night and wouldn't be popping back for the one thing that her mum usually forgot, Lucy went downstairs and into the rarely used dining room.

    The room was dim, being at the back of the house, and her mum usually kept the slatted blinds down covering the patio doors 'to protect the furniture'. The room, in contrast to the rest of the house, was quite formally furnished with a mahogany table and sideboard that her mum and dad had been delighted to buy at the local furniture store. There were six fancy matching chairs, with a light blue cushioned seat which her mum kept under a plastic protective cover when guests weren't there. Her dad used to joke that if Cath had her way, the whole set would still be in its wrapping. It was a favourite family story about how, when they only went to browse, they spotted that there had been a mistake with the pricing on the display and the salesman had reluctantly agreed to honour the 'too good to miss' price. Lucy privately thought it just sounded like a bit of a sales tactic. After all, her parents came home after spending a decent chunk of money when they had only intended to browse; but Cath and Jon remained delighted with their bargain, so it seemed no harm had been done. The family congregated in the room for Christmas, birthdays and when they had visitors. Regular meals were eaten on laps in front of the television - or at Cath's insistence - at the Formica kitchen table that they kept meaning to replace but somehow never got round to. The rest of the time, the dining room was used when someone wanted to use the family computer, which sat on a padded mat to protect the mahogany table, until it was hidden away when the room was used for the purpose it was intended. Some of Lucy's friends had started to get laptops, but Lucy was told she would need to wait to see if she needed one when she started university. So, she was restricted to using the shared computer. She argued with herself that she wasn't doing anything wrong. After all, she was allowed to use the computer whenever and there were very few rules placed on her as to what she could use it for; but despite this, Lucy still managed to feel as if she was doing something she shouldn't.

    Shutting the door behind her, she didn't turn on the

light, preferring to skulk in the dull September evening light, as if semi-darkness would hide what she was doing. Fidgeting on the dining room chair, she patiently waited for the computer to come to life and then went through the painful waiting process whilst it attempted to connect to the internet. The familiar chirp and beep of the modem seemed to blast out through the machine, and Lucy almost expected her mum and dad to return home to demand what all the noise was about. She gave her head a shake. This was silly, she really wasn't doing anything wrong here. Finally, she was given the option to log on to Myspace, and clicking the search button, she found herself glancing over her shoulder one more time.

In the search bar she typed in 'Oxenham'. It wasn't a common name, so she was hoping she might find the student teacher fairly easily. It turned out her hunch was right and 'her' Miss Oxenham was the second result. Lucy clicked on the name and eagerly waited to see what information was available.

The first thing Lucy found out was Miss Oxenham's first name. Kate. Lucy rolled the name around her mouth. Kate. It sounded good. The name suited her. She wondered if Kate's parents had named her Catherine and still insisted on calling her that, and decided, in her own mind, that they did. Lucy leaned in closer to the computer screen to devour the picture posted there. It showed Kate sitting in the sunshine in a beer garden down by the river. She was laughing at the camera, her beautiful white teeth framed by perfectly applied red lipstick. Lucy didn't like her own teeth. They were a bit crooked and, even being kind, they looked a sort of off-white. Maybe it was the shade of lipstick that Kate had chosen that helped give her mouth that certain pop. Lucy wrote down 'lipstick' on the pad beside her, and then next to it 'bright red' in capital letters, and underlined the words. Lucy went back to studying the screen. Kate's ears were adorned with a pair of silver hoops and this picture showed her ears were pierced a second time. Lucy thought back to seeing Kate at school. Definitely no second set of earrings, but that was probably school rules. The same went for the tiny twinkling purple gem that graced Kate's perfect pixie nose. Yes, this was the real Kate, the Kate that Lucy would get to know, her special Kate, with the rest of her friends confined to 'Monday to Friday' Kate. Lucy felt a warm glow inside, knowing that Kate was becoming her best friend.

Lucy studied the clothes Kate was wearing. An all-black top was somehow lifted from the ordinary as it became the showcase for a colourful chunky necklace in various hues of purple. Lucy wrote a brief description of the necklace on her pad, along with details of the rest of Kate's clothes. She was pretty sure the jeans were Levi's 501s and she couldn't quite make out what Kate had on her feet, but it looked to be a pair of chunky boots. She already knew that Kate wore tights with bees on and Lucy made a careful note of the shop her and Cath had purchased the ladybird tights from. Finally, she could see on the table next to Kate was some sort of colourful bucket basket bag. Lucy recalled seeing other people around town with this style of bag, so she made a note of the colours - pinks and purples with a thread of silver woven between the blocks of colour - and sat back to read through her list. Had she missed anything? Peering closely once more, she noted a chunky silver ring on the middle finger of Kate's right hand, which further drew attention to her fingernails which were painted a flaming red to match her lipstick. Lucy made a note of both details and checked her watch. She still had more time.

Lucy read a few more entries, making a careful note of the names of Kate's friends that she seemed to interact with the most and trying to guess the locations of any photographs that were there - all the time recording the details. Clearly pink and purple were favourites of Kate, as she was always wearing something in those colours, even if it was just the flash of a scarf, the twinkle of jewellery or boldly painted nails. Looking out the window, Lucy noted it was now dark outside and shut down the computer, leaving the dining room and retreating to her own space.

For once, she didn't cringe when she heard her parents' stumbling entrance and theatrical 'shush'. She was too wrapped up in her new world with her absolute best friend, and as she whispered 'Kate' into the darkness, Lucy just knew great things were going to happen.

LUCY

Rob had left the cottage pretty much like I would imagine a tornado leaves its path of destruction. As we were sat round the breakfast table, he jumped to his feet with a decisive, 'Right, that's Steve loading the car. The conquering hero will see his two princesses later.' Milly giggled as he tickled her and planted a sloppy kiss on her cheek. I got pretty much the same but without the tickle. As I heard Rob shout a cheery greeting to Steve, I sat for a moment at the kitchen table, just to try and get a plan together for the day. I had an hour until we were meeting the others, so no time to sit around daydreaming. It's funny, when I'm at home I'm happy to leave the dishes all day, to live amongst crumbs and unmade beds. But the minute we arrive at a holiday cottage, I suddenly turn into Mrs House-Proud. I feel the people that stay there after us will be able to tell if we've not kept things neat and tidy and will talk about the slovenly family who inhabited the space before them. It doesn't matter how many times Rob tells me the cleaning company will blitz the place after we have gone, paying no heed to the fact I have already cleaned it; I worry we will leave behind an essence of ourselves, and I don't want that to be judged negatively.

    I went with Milly to her room and quickly unpacked her things and helped her pick out shorts and a t-shirt. I left her to wash her face and clean her teeth, telling her I would be back to check shortly. It didn't take long to load the dishwasher, and then I moved to our room to make the bed and quickly unpack my case. I took a petty delight in using most of the hanging space in the wardrobe and took most of the hangers as well, figuring that was a small price for Rob to pay for his morning of freedom.

As I moved through to our ensuite to arrange my toiletries, I spread out my basic face wash and moisturiser and debated whether to bother unpacking the small make up bag I had brought. Since I had been at home with Milly there didn't seem to be much point in bothering with makeup just to stay in the house, but I wondered if I should make a bit of an effort with 'the gang'. So, after I had run the brush through my hair and cleaned my teeth, I put on a mask I felt I could face the day with. The liquid foundation appeared to give my skin a yellow glow under the electric light and didn't seem to suit my colouring anymore. I shrugged; it would just be that I wasn't used to it. I added a coat of mascara to my pale lashes, noting that I probably needed a new one and, hesitating, I added a coat of lip gloss that had gone a bit dry and sticky since I'd last used it. Turning to leave the bathroom, I paused and turned back as I noticed the hand soap left on the side.

It wasn't unusual for there to be liquid hand soap left in the kitchen and bathrooms. I had never quite made up my mind whether these were left behind by previous visitors or if the cleaning company refilled the bottles similarly to the toiletries left in your hotel room. I know we always left condiments in the kitchen. Salt, pepper, dishwasher tablets, bin bags - it was a bit of 'play it forward'. We would use the things left by the previous guests and would play the favour forward to the people staying after us. I'm not sure, but I think it's pretty standard holiday cottage etiquette. But this bottle of hand soap was something different, and for a moment I stood quite captivated.

The first thing that struck me was the colour. It was the most beautiful pale green I had ever seen. It didn't look like the colour of soap, but rather looked like the clear ocean where the mermaids might swim. I shook my head and laughed self-consciously at this silly flight of fancy. Strangely, the name of the soap only registered once I had managed to drag my eyes from sinking in the green pool.

'Lucky'
Christian Dior
Paris

Well, no doubt about it - this wasn't something provided by the cleaning company. This must have been left behind by the previous occupants; what was the name in the guest book? The lady with the ostentatious lilac ink pen. This must belong to Bella. I wondered fleetingly if it was maybe some of that imitation stuff 'identical to the real thing' that you can buy off street traders for a fraction of the price. But as I gingerly pressed the dispenser and inhaled the scent of the soap, I was struck by the rich but so delicate scent of lily of the valley, and I intuitively knew this was the real deal. I ran my hands under the tap and enjoyed the smooth lather of the soap and noticed the scent seemed to fill the bathroom. Not overpowering, just subtly there, letting its presence be known and lingering in the air. It really was lovely, and immediately I just knew that this was something that reflected the character of Bella. I'm not sure how long I stood there. I was simply staring in the mirror but not looking at my own reflection. Instead, I was searching for the echo of a woman who had stood in this space the previous week. I felt that if I inhaled the scent and stared long enough, her image would appear, almost like summoning spirits from the dead. I was jolted out of my trance by Milly appearing in the doorway.

'Mummy, can you help me find my swimsuit?'

The scent was diminishing, and the moment was lost. I was back to me, Lucy, with a ridiculous face full of makeup for a day on the beach. 'Hang on, just a minute,' I instructed as I washed my face for the second time that morning, removing the painted mask so I could breathe as me once again.

Wriggling into my own swimsuit, I pulled on shorts and a t-shirt and hurried to help Milly. Finding my canvas bag,

I thew in towels, sunscreen and instructed Milly to get the bucket and spade and fishing net from the doorway. I ushered her out the house, locking the door, then stood awkwardly, unsure what to do. As I hesitated in the sunshine, I noticed it really was starting to look like the most gorgeous day; I could hear music pounding out through the windows of next door's kitchen. Should I go and knock? Before I could make a decision, I heard Milly give a delighted shriek next to me, and before I could stop her, she was happily running towards our neighbours' back door, calling out for Xander and Becca. Well, that was the decision made for me, and I had little choice other than to follow her down the path, through the open door to the source of the music.

I did that British thing of a soft tapping knock at the door and shouted what I hoped was a cheery 'Hello'. It was immediately obvious that there was no chance anyone was going to hear me. Milly had been swallowed up by the group of children milling around the patio doors at the back of the kitchen. She hadn't even glanced to see if I was following her. Lydia and Jen were in the final stages of packing up three enormous cool boxes, and I was disturbed to see they looked to be sipping from glasses with the tell-tale hue of a red-orange liquid and the garnish of plastic umbrellas. Surely not cocktails at this time of the morning!

I cleared my throat, feeling more out of place with every second that I stood there unnoticed. Unbidden, I thought 'I bet Bella wouldn't have faded into the background'; and before I had time to wonder where that had come from, Jen spun round laughing and noticed me standing there.

'Hello! Quick, come and get some Sex on the Beach - seeing as the men aren't here, we thought we would make our own entertainment.'

'It's a bit early for me.' I cringed as I heard my words. They sounded stilted and offhand even to my own ears. 'I bet Bella would have accepted a drink,' whispered a little voice in my ear. 'In fact, I bet Bella would have been the one making the cocktails.'

'Oh, go on,' I heard myself saying. 'After all, we are on holiday.'

'Hair of the dog,' agreed Lydia, moving towards me and enveloping me in a hug. 'And whilst admittedly there is vodka and a teeny bit of peach schnapps, it's nearly all orange and cranberry juice. Honest!'

'Yes, practically a breakfast fruit juice,' Jen laughingly agreed, though her eyes and the flamboyancy of her dancing to the music told a slightly different story.

I took a gulp from the glass Lydia gave me and my eyes watered. 'Flipping heck, that's a bit more than fruit juice,' I spluttered.

'Marvellous isn't it? We got the recipe from Jules, though I'm not sure we've made them quite as good as he used to.'

Jules, Jules - where did I know that name? Then it came to me. Of course, Jules was the husband of the lilac-penned, lily of the valley wearing Bella. They would have been staying next door to Lydia last week.

'Jules?' I queried anyway, following on innocently. 'Is he staying here too?'

'Oh no, Bella and Jules were staying in Beach Cottage last week. They were just marvellous and brought us all together. We were sad when they were only staying a week.' Seeing my face, Lydia continued. 'But we have you and Rob now, so every cloud and all that.'

I smiled the best I could, all the time thinking we were the dark cloud rather than the silver lining the group were clearly hoping for. 'Or rather,' I thought gloomily, and I confess a little self pityingly, 'I was.' My eyes drifted over to the cool boxes, stood to attention in the corner of the kitchen.

'Oh God, Rob mentioned something about a picnic, and I haven't brought a thing, not even drinks. I better go and sort something.' My mind started thinking through last night's delivery. I could make sandwiches, and we had crisps and...

Before I could do anything, Jen interrupted, 'There's

loads here for everyone. Besides, Rob volunteered that you would host the BBQ this evening.'

I could only stare at her. Rob very conveniently had failed to mention this when he slipped in the bombshell of his golf outing with Steve. What the bloody hell was I going to do to conjure up a BBQ for six adults and five children this evening? And we didn't have any booze in the cottage, which I guessed, as I took another desperate gulp of my cocktail, would not be what 'the gang' were expecting at all.

Seeing my face, Lydia put her arm round my shoulder. 'No need to panic, we placed the food and booze order at the click and collect this morning. Steve and Rob are picking it up after their game of golf and Andy is collecting the meat from the farm shop after he gets back from his bike ride. See, you don't need to worry about a thing.'

I took another gulp of my drink, feeling the panic starting to subside slightly as she continued. 'I hope you don't mind that we sort of invited ourselves - it's just that Bella and Jules always hosted the BBQ and the space at Beach Cottage is just so perfect for a party.'

I smiled weakly as she added, 'You can be our new Bella.'

CATH

Cath waved Jon off on his daily dog walk with Rufus, their much too fat Labrador. She stood watching as the pair of them walked sedately down the avenue, both secure in the rhythm of their partnership. Rufus had been a part of their family for eight years now, purchased once they felt some relief from the terror of looking out for Lucy. It was nice to have something so uncomplicated to look after. Rufus only wanted to be fed, walked and given a little bit of love and attention. The rest of the time he slept - a mainly peaceful sleep interspersed with yelps and twitching legs, which Cath liked to think meant he was dreaming of chasing the rabbits he was, in real life, far too lazy to pursue. She envied that restful sleep with what seemed to be only happy dreams. Cath had expected that at this stage in their lives, they would be travelling for extended periods to explore all those places they had fleetingly visited when Lucy was growing up. They had planned on spending some of their retirement with months in France, Italy, and Spain, pretending they were residents of these charming towns rather than the normal tourist. They had talked incessantly how they would buy their breakfast first thing and sit in the weak spring sunshine on the balcony of their yet undiscovered apartment. Their days would be spent exploring mountains and lakes, cooking with local produce, before falling exhausted into bed ready to repeat the day tomorrow. Cath used to spend her evenings googling apartments for a long-term rental, excitedly telling Jon that they could stay there for two months out of season for the same price as a two-week summer holiday. Of course, it was impossible now for them to even think of being away from Lucy, Rob and Milly for that amount of time; and so with that dream dashed, they had committed to getting a dog.

And whilst retirement was not looking how she had thought it would be, Cath was, on the whole, content with her life. She wished she could be more like Jon. He had always been the more relaxed of the two of them. Look at last night. He'd had a great time at the pub, able to compartmentalise his worries about the lack of a text from Lucy and lock it away in a separate part of his brain until he needed to take it out and deal with it. He'd eaten his dinner with obvious enjoyment, drank slightly more than he should have done and generally acted as the life and soul of the party with the friends that were drawn to their table.

Jon had always been like that, mused Cath, and hence he had found it so much easier when they had found it necessary to move to this village. Cath had hated the upheaval. Although she had lost most of her friends after the incident, she still felt so much more alone in their new village. It was one thing to know people when you walked down the street, even if they looked a little embarrassed and failed to acknowledge you. It was very different to walk down the street and be met by a sea of strangers. When she finally confessed this to Jon, he seemed surprised, saying that this was what she had said she wanted. To move to somewhere where they knew no one, and more importantly, where no one knew them. And Cath didn't have an answer for that because Jon was right. That was what she had wanted. But oh, how she hated it.

Of course, it was different now. They had lived here for nineteen years. Neighbours were now friends, they attended all the village functions and Cath could always find someone to chat to as she popped out to get the odd things she chose to buy in the village, liking to support the local shops to supplement her weekly supermarket delivery. And when they dropped in at the pub, it was very rare they wouldn't soon be joined by a small group of friends, swapping tales and laughter well into the evening. Last night had been no exception, except she was unable to concentrate. She may have been smiling and laughing and raising her glass in a toast to the band, but internally there was a constant beat of 'Oh God Lucy, not again, not again'. And at the same time, she recognised her panic, whilst not unfounded, was an extreme reaction.

She knew that she was on constant alert to something going wrong, when really the years that had passed should have reassured her that the normality was that things were just as they should be. When they had eventually got home last night, Jon fell quietly into bed, and she thought he maybe just simply fell asleep, until she nudged him to say that the longed-for text from Lucy had finally arrived. She, on the other hand, had watched the clock for every minute, wondering how long she needed to wait before she could call the police and not sound like an irrational lunatic.

When the text finally came, the first feeling was one of relief, but, to her shock, this was swiftly followed - at first - by resentment. She didn't like that she was 'that person', but she reluctantly acknowledged that she resented her only daughter, who had deprived her of a long-held dream. And then there was a simmering rage that gained force as she heard Jon humming in the shower and watched him devour the cooked breakfast. It was a relief when he announced he was off out with Rufus as she felt if he stayed much longer, she would ram the leftover sausage right down his throat. She recognised that part of this anger came from envy. Envy that he had been able to move on from those events twenty years ago, rebuild a new life that gave him everything he needed, and let the events of that summer just be a small diversion in the road - a diversion he'd rather not have taken, but little more than a nuisance in the grand scheme of things. 'Bloody lucky Jon,' mused Cath as she slammed the pots in the dishwasher and wished for the millionth time that she had never bought Lucy those flaming tights.

LUCY

Finally, they were ready to make their way down to the beach. I had finished the sweet cocktail and found that I felt quite relaxed about the whole thing. Normally the disorganisation would have been driving me quietly frantic - a serene smile hiding the inner turmoil associated with an unplanned day. I had barely seen Milly, who had been swallowed up in the giggling, wriggling group who had tumbled out to mess with the swingball which was set upon the grass square which the cottages bordered. The traditional toy reminded me of my five-year-old self and of the hot summer days spent in my own back garden, frantically swiping for the ball on a rope, with no idea if there were any rules to the game, and if there were, no care to try and follow them. Later that holiday, I was invited round to a friend's house, who also had a swingball set but they had an older sister, so they played the game according to the instructions. I remembered it hadn't been nearly as much fun as my own at home version, and I wondered fleetingly how I had become the person who lived her life according to the instructions, losing the flamboyancy of just seeing how it goes, what was fun.

    I don't know if it was the effect of the cocktail, gulped down so eagerly so early in the day, or just the novelty of mixing with these women who were so different to the normal groups I sought friendship with, but I couldn't help but feel not only excited, but hugely flattered that they had considered me worthy to be their Bella. I didn't know why I felt that way about a woman whom I had never met and only knew through her handwriting, scent and the odd spoken reference, but I gauged that 'being Bella' was a step up from being me.

As I walked with the noisy group on the sandy path that snaked through the dunes, I found myself lifting my face to the sun and opening my arms wide - as if inviting that brightness and heat to awaken me from whatever dull state I had been living in for the last twenty years. And I didn't walk once I saw the sand stretching down towards the rolling white topped waves, but dropped the bags and started running towards the sea, chased by a gang of screaming children. I felt that's just what Bella would have done, though I regretted my rather sensible black shorts and top as I was sure she would have been wearing some sort of tie dyed floaty dress. But as I ran across the beach, none of that mattered, because in my mind I could feel the soft fabric brushing my ankles; and as we reached the water's edge, I had to stop my hands from gathering the folds of the non-existent fabric to stop it getting wet.

I was shaken out of this fantasy by the rather plaintiff cry of, 'Mummy!' and with a jolt I realised that for the first time in my life, I had paid no heed to where Milly was in my mad dance to reach the sea. All thoughts of the pastel swirling fabric caressing my sun-tanned limbs (and OK, I knew I was still a typical redhead with freckles, but I was sure that Bella would be sporting a healthy honey-coloured glow) were dashed from my mind as I turned to see Milly lagging behind. Her chubby little legs were struggling to keep pace with the rest of us and I could see that her lip was trembling as she tried to hold back the tears that were threatening to show her up in front of her newfound friends. Immediately, I felt sick with guilt, but at the same time a wicked little voice whispered 'Ha, see you want your mummy now don't you, little Miss Independent'. Running back, I scooped her up with a smile and she was soon giggling as I pretended to dump her face down in the water, the rest of the children squealing as they fought to save her from the wicked monster.

Once I was certain that Milly was happily playing, I left the water to wander back to Jen and Lydia who were rather expertly setting up camp, securing the perimeter with the rainbow-coloured windbreaks that the older boys had carted down to the sand.

'Well done for getting the kids out from under our feet,' called Lydia. Jen nodded in agreement. 'Now that's something that Bella definitely wouldn't have done! She would have been too busy getting the next cocktail down her neck; speaking of which, where's the mummys' drink Lydia?'

The bright blue plastic bottle was soon located. I expect the manufacturers planned this to be filled with squash of some flavour, and I'm pretty sure their marketing photo wouldn't have included women eagerly holding out matching blue beakers for a taste of the good stuff.

'Here's to Sex on the Beach!' proclaimed Lydia. 'And may we all get some of the real stuff later!'

The two cackled whilst I looked round nervously to see if any of the children were within earshot. 'Relax Lucy, it's your holiday too.' Jen passed me a blue beaker and, closing my eyes, I allowed myself to take a sip and sink down onto the sand which had been warmed by the sun. Too late, I felt the dampness of the sand - that was hiding below the fluffy surface - seep through the towels into my shorts. Ignoring this vaguely uncomfortable feeling, I took another gulp and, whilst watching Milly, tried to appear nonchalant as I asked, 'So how did you come to know Bella again?'

And that was it. The two of them had just needed a little encouragement. It seemed that if Bella couldn't be there with them in person, the next best thing was to talk about her, almost as if trying to conjure back some of this magic that the woman seemed to sprinkle wherever she went. Lydia explained how her family and Lydia's had been taking the same two weeks for 'well, like forever', and they had noticed each other and would wave a hand in greeting or make a banal comment about the weather. You know, the usual thing, 'Gorgeous isn't it; who needs to go abroad when the weathers like this' or the more common 'Looks like another washout summer; feels more like autumn than August.'

'And then this year on our first night,' Lydia took up the story as she leaned over to top up my glass, 'there was a knock on the door, just as we had finished lugging the bags in and were debating whether to dash out to see if we could grab fish and chips before the pub closed. And there stood Bella, holding two glasses of fizz which she passed to me and Steve, and telling us the BBQ was nearly ready and would we join them in ten minutes.'

'And Bella is not the sort of person you would say no to,' laughed Jen. 'Not that you would ever want to turn down an invitation from her. We had already met her down on the beach, when she had lent Peter a boogie board after his split on the very first use. Crisis averted, and we bagged an invitation out too.'

'And the rest, as they say, is history. We had the most amazing week, I don't think we ever stopped laughing. We were just gutted that they were only here for the week. No offence.'

How could I respond, other than the standard, 'None taken,' whilst secretly noting that they never mentioned that they had seen us around the holiday cottages in previous years, and we had been there on their second week every year for the last five years. Sadly, I reflected that we were obviously the sort of family that just faded into non-recollection. Not beautiful enough or exciting enough or weird enough to make an impression. Just normal, quiet and nice. And as I took another sip of my cocktail, I realised I didn't want to be like that anymore. I wanted to be a part of this gang, and I wanted Jen and Lydia to be talking about me and saying, 'Oh yes, meeting Lucy and her lovely family just took the holiday to another level. I think we will be friends for life.'

I was happily weaving this fantasy as the sun warmed my skin, when there was a commotion as Andy arrived to join us, fresh from his bike ride.

'Any beers in that cooler?' He gratefully took one from

Jen's outstretched hand. 'I've just seen Steve and Rob pull into the cottages, so they will be down soon. I'm starving.' He gave a vague wave in my direction then took off across the beach to join the kids in the water.

Jen smiled after him. 'Honestly, I sometimes feel like I have three boys; Andy's just like a big kid. And takes nearly as much looking after!'

'And he doesn't like being with us women when the blokes aren't around,' laughed Lydia. 'Though he seemed much keener when Bella was still here.'

'Great', I thought. I knew they weren't doing it on purpose, but the conversation wasn't exactly doing anything to raise my self-esteem.

Sitting upright, I asked as casually as I could, 'Do you have any photos of Bella?' I hoped I sounded like I wasn't that bothered, but the truth was that curiosity was burning me up. I had such a vivid picture in my mind, and I was aware that I was building this woman up to be some sort of goddess. I was really hoping that I would be shown a picture of a dumpy, rather frumpy Earth Mother figure. Maybe they had loved her so much as she organised them and did all the cooking and tidying up, sort of like an unpaid nanny and housekeeper. Oh, I hoped that was it, though reluctantly I acknowledged that picture didn't really fit with the lilac ink in the fountain pen and the Christian Dior scented hand soap left behind in what was my ensuite for the week. Hmm, well I could always hope. Even better if she had spots and a bit of a moustache. OK, that was taking it too far.

Lydia looked delighted at my question, a bit like people do when you ask to see pictures of their new grandchild or show an interest in their dreaded holiday photos. She reached in her bag for her phone, which I idly noticed sported a pretty phone charm with a silver star.

Jen saw me looking at the sparkly pendant and proudly held her phone aloft which had the same trinket attached. 'Bella bought them for us and one for her as well, from the little art gallery in Alnmouth. Look, they are engraved on the back.' She held out her phone to me and on the back of the star, which was much heavier and of better quality than I had expected, were engraved the words, 'Each time we look up and see the same star, we are together in our hearts.'

Oh my word, this woman really was too much. I scanned Lydia and Jen's faces to see if there was any hint of a smirk at the sugar-coated sentimentality, but all I could see was admiration.

Lydia passed over her phone. 'Feel free to scroll, there's lots of pictures there and it's pretty obvious who Bella is.'

The first picture had clearly been taken outside the kitchen door of Beach Cottage. A woman, who quite simply must be Bella, was stood in the doorway, squinting slightly into the early evening sun, holding a pitcher of that enticing and by now familiar orange-red concoction and laughing at the camera. I took a sharp intake of breath, as such was the life and glow emanating from the photo; for a moment my mind expected the woman in the picture to spring to life out of the phone like those moving pictures famously depicted in the Harry Potter books. Bella was unlike anything in my imagination. She looked to be shorter than me and was definitely petite. She had that small frame that always makes men feel protective, but at the same time had, as the song goes 'curves in all the right places'. Her face was framed by a cloud of the most gorgeous dark brown curls that made her look like some sort of woodland nymph. Chocolate brown eyes twinkled with laughter, and she was displaying perfectly white teeth and a dimple in each cheek. It was a testament to the power of her joy that, despite myself, I could feel my own mouth curve into a smile. I was starting to see why Bella had proved such a focal point for the gang.

She was wearing a dusty pink vest top that showed off her golden, perfectly toned arms and, I noted dispiritedly, a hint of cleavage that, even as a woman, I found tantalisingly erotic, whilst not being trashy. She was wearing an amazing pair of patterned pink trousers, and they reminded me of the sort of thing my mother wore in her younger days. The picture was, overall, one of contagious happiness and I felt like someone had punched me in the stomach as I realised I was never going to be 'the new Bella'.

For a second, I did deliberate at that point just handing the phone back, but was unable to stop myself, even though I knew it wouldn't be good for me; my fingers started swiping through the rest of the photos. Bella on the beach in a perfect swimsuit, laughing with the children, unbothered by the salt water she was about to get a dunking in. Bella stood next to a tall, very tanned dark-haired man, looking beautifully casual in a white shirt and navy chino shorts, the pair of them laughing into each other's eyes, hands just touching but evidence of their attraction to each other burning through the screen of the phone.

Bella and the man - who I assumed must be Jules - sat on a boat with a picture-perfect child who I surmised must be Beth. On and on I swiped, faster and faster, greedily drinking in as many details as I could of this woman who seemed to be some sort of siren for me. The last photo was of 'the old gang' - that is, the gang before the sad departure of Bella and her perfect family and the arrival of what I now saw was a very disappointing replacement. I noted that this was indeed the last photo on Lydia's phone. Clearly our gathering last night had not been deemed worthy of recording. The six adults were all laughing at the camera, but I couldn't help but notice that without exception, each of them had angled their bodies towards Bella, who was stood in the centre. And her magnetism shone from the photo such that I looked, expecting to see some sort of spotlight angled above her, picking her out as the star of the group.

I was aware that there was silence around me and, dragging my eyes away from the screen, I caught the end of a look passing between Lydia and Jen, and noted that Lydia had her hand held out for the phone. I realised with some embarrassment that her hand had probably been like that for some time. I covered my awkwardness with some sort of gushing remark about how fabulous the photos were, and I think I tried to explain my intent scrutiny away by saying that I thought I recognised Bella from somewhere. And I did recognise her from somewhere; I recognised that she was the person I was absolutely meant to be.

TWENTY YEARS EARLIER

Lucy was not normally an early riser, so she could see her mum was surprised to see her already sat at the table, drinking a glass of orange juice and nibbling on a slice of toast as she studied the notebook on her lap. Hearing her mum come into the kitchen, Lucy hurriedly slipped the notebook into her bag and stood, giving her mum a hug as she announced she was off into town to get some bits, and she would be home for tea.

'Will the rest of 'Fabulous Five' be coming back here?' smiled Cath.

'Well, it's a bit far for Jill,' was the rather sarky reply, but seeing her Mum's face fall, Lucy relented and added, 'I don't think so, we all have a fair bit of homework to get on with - first week of Sixth Form and all that.'

As she walked down the road to the nearest bus stop, Lucy reflected that really, she had no idea what the others had planned for this weekend. No doubt they would still be in bed after being out last night, but Lucy reflected that in many ways they seemed a bit immature now, giggling over the quizzes in magazines and all dressing the same. As she saw the bus approaching, she reflected that it was probably because her and Kate were two of a kind. Two halves, who had finally found each other and become whole. Climbing the steps to the top deck, Lucy was lulled by the rock of the swaying bus as it negotiated the country lanes before it could turn out of the village to join the steady stream of traffic heading to town.

Exiting with the jostling crowd of other passengers onto the high street, Lucy stepped into the refuge of a doorway to consult her notebook once more and get a plan together. There was a lot to get through today. Satisfied she knew what had to be done, she stepped purposefully towards the main shopping area, feeling a bit like a superhero, disguised at the moment as 'Plain Lucy' but getting ready to stun and reveal her true self.

Lucy caught the six o'clock bus home, exhausted but buzzing with excitement at the same time. Coming through the front door, she was greeted by Cath with a cheery 'Hello,' followed by silence.

'Bloody hell! What on earth have you done to your hair Lucy?'

Lucy could see her reflection in the hallway mirror smiling back at her, and she could see in her smile a power that had not been there this morning. Gone were those silly red curls that blew into her face and took so much brushing and always ended up frizzy rather than curly. Staring back at her was a wonderful creature with a very short black bob. The hairdresser had tried to talk Lucy out of it, explaining that it was a major change, would need to be straightened every day and didn't really suit her skin tone, but Lucy was set on her path. The same hairdresser pierced her ears for a second time but refused the nose piercing as she was under eighteen. Not to worry, that could wait for another day. Her face was heavily made up with foundation - eyes blacked with Kohl and her lips still felt strange, coated in a glossy red lipstick which seemed to leave a mark on everything she touched.

For once, Cath had nothing to say, as Lucy casually informed her that she had felt like a change. Cath saw that Lucy was carrying a number of bulging bags, but rather than the normal logos of the shops she favoured such as River Island and Top Shop, it looked to be small boutiques of the sort that Cath liked to visit, and a selection of plain brown bags which likely had come from the market. That night in bed, Cath whispered to Jon how worried she was, and Jon reassured her that it was best not to make too big a thing of it and it was likely, 'just a phase,' that all her friends had probably done the same. Afterwards, they wondered if they had tackled it in a different way - told Lucy to scrub her face, take that jewellery off and return those clothes - things might have run differently. But they didn't, and so the stage was set.

LUCY

Rob and Steve finally joined us on the beach, both flushed from their game of golf, but I suspected the glow was more to do with a couple of quiet pints celebrating their escape from the madness. Rob dropped down on the sand by the side of me and gave my leg a squeeze, which was his way of checking all was OK. I loved him for that, for letting me know he did care without making it obvious to this group of relative strangers that I sometimes needed to be checked on. As predicted, as soon as Rob and Steve joined the group, Andy sprinted back up from the water's edge, where he had been helping his boys with their inflatable kayak, and flopped on the sand, accepting a cold bottle of beer from the cooler Steve had brought with him.

'That's our signal to open the wine,' declared Lydia, and produced sugary pink goblets that looked to have been dipped in glitter and would have been more at home in a nightclub than on a windswept beach in the Northeast.

I knew I was being judgemental, and I looked at Rob, expecting to see a reciprocal gleam of scorn in his eyes that hinted we would laugh about it all once we finally escaped the gang. But Rob was in deep conversation with Steve, discussing some difficult shot on the course and the best way to tackle it when they played again. I really hoped this was just a conversation and he wasn't planning to leave us on another morning. I gasped as ice cold wine dripped on my leg, which felt sticky from the suntan lotion I had smothered myself in, and looked to see Jen grinning at me and passing over a huge goblet of rosé. Of course, what else for the pretty pink glasses.

'Drink up, don't let it get warm.'

I took the glass and wondered how I could get out of drinking it all, but soon realised no one was really paying attention to what I was doing. Lydia and Jen had relaxed back onto the sand, seemingly content to let the older children act as babysitters for the younger ones. I could see the group, with my little Milly chasing to keep up with them, building some sort of complicated sand fortress in a game to keep the tide from reaching the castles, that were being crafted further up the beach. Milly, it seemed, had been given the job of filling the moat around the castle and I smiled to see the concentration and determination on her face as she ran back and forth to the sea with her little bucket, delighted to be given such an important task. As I watched the children playing, I was vaguely listening to the quiet chat of Jen and Lydia, and listened more intently when I heard Bella's name mentioned.

'Have you heard from Bella since they went home?' That was Jen asking; an uncertain tone in her voice hinted she rather hoped that Lydia hadn't, as that would mean that she had been left out somehow.

'Not a peep.' I smirked to myself as I could imagine Jen's feeling of relief, and then felt a bit mean. Yet again, I was being very judgemental about these women who had been nothing but friendly towards us since we had arrived. 'I've messaged her a few times, but I can see she's not been online.'

'Probably busy sorting out the new school for Beth. It's bound to have been a bit stressful for them all.'

My ears perked up at this. Stress and the vision I had of Bella did not go together at all. I couldn't help myself and blurted out, rather louder than I meant to, 'Why, what happened?'

For a moment Jen and Lydia both looked a bit shocked at the intrusion, but then realised they had a new audience to talk to about their obviously favourite subject, so settled into the tale. And what a story it was. Apparently, things weren't quite as rosy in lilac ink Bella land as I had first thought. Whilst they didn't know all the details, on the last night of the holiday, after a day of drinking on the beach, Bella had shared that there was some ongoing drama relating to Beth's new school. Lydia took over the telling of the story.

'Bella had her heart set on private school for Beth, but at the last minute Jules point-blankly refused. Bella was absolutely furious and in a complete panic about finding a decent school at such short notice.'

'Well, you would be, wouldn't you?' interrupted Jen, and I nodded in impatient agreement, eager to find out what had happened.

'Bella hinted that Jules felt that way because Beth was a girl and he didn't feel it was as important for a girl to get a good education, as they would only be getting married.'

I couldn't help it, I snorted with laughter - I mean surely this had to be a joke. Then I realised Lydia and Jen were looking at me with wide-eyed solemnity.

Jen nodded sadly. 'Honestly, Bella thought it was a joke at first but apparently not. I really think it made her see Jules in a different light. It certainly did me. I'd always really liked him up to that point.'

Lydia continued, 'Bella was so upset. I couldn't believe she had kept this to herself all holiday, acted so carefree. All the time shouldering the worry, and Jules doing nothing at all to help her find somewhere suitable for September.'

I was aware that I was listening open mouthed. 'So what happened?'

'Well,' Jen looked around conspiratorially, as if the beach wasn't deserted apart from our group. 'Bella shared she had pushed and pushed Jules to reconsider, but then it all came out that they simply couldn't afford the fees. Bella had no idea; thought they were rolling in it. She didn't want to share, but it seems Jules has some sort of gambling addiction.'

'And that was why he was always on his laptop,' declared Lydia triumphantly. 'We thought he was having to work but all the time he was checking on the winner of the three-thirty at

Chepstow!'

I was listening fascinated - I mean, how could Bella not know the state of their finances? But then on reflection, I realised I really had no idea of our outgoings. Rob took charge of all of that and whilst we had a joint bank account, I knew his salary was paid into a different account and then he split the money from there. It had never seemed odd to me before - it didn't really concern me now - but I did make a mental note to talk our finances through with Rob once we got home. After all, if something were to happen to him, I would be at rather a loss.

Jen continued. 'She had been looking round for schools in the area and found a primary school that gets a great Ofsted, and she liked the feel of. She's just waiting to see if there is a space for Beth, so we don't really know any more than that.'

Lydia laughed and added, 'I think she's rather hoping that Jules might die in an unfortunate accident so she can collect the life insurance and that will sort all the problems out.'

Seeing my face, Jen added, 'Don't worry, she was only joking.' Glancing at Lydia, she laughed, 'But then again, haven't we all felt like that!'

Well, this was something I hadn't expected at all. But in so many ways, it made Bella more likeable, more real. She was like a warrior battling against the unfairness of old-fashioned values and a man who had let her down. Clearly, she was the strength providing the backbone of the family unit.

'Is Milly going to private school?' asked Jen.

'Er no, Rob wanted to look at that route, but I don't really believe in the private school system. The schools around us are excellent and we have agreed that as long as she is happy and doing well, we will continue on that route.'

Jen and Lydia nodded in understanding but as I looked away, I caught yet another raised eyebrow glance pass between the two of them, and I realised they thought I was making up a tale as we couldn't afford the fees. Putting my annoyance aside,

I stood up and announced I was off to see what the children were doing and left them to no doubt whisper a bit about the state of our finances. Milly turned as I shouted out a greeting, but looked quite cross to see me.

'What do you want, Mummy?' was the only welcome I got. 'I'm fine here, you don't need to play with me.' I know this is all part of her growing up - that desire for independence and to not want her mother constantly fussing over her every move - but I can't pretend I am fine with it.

Thinking quickly, I turned to the rest of the group. 'Anyone fancy a trip to the rock pools?'

The best rock pools were tucked around the headland, away from the main stretch of beach. Only accessible at low tide, I figured we had just about timed it right to make a visit. The response was enthusiastic, and as they needed an adult to accompany them, I was suddenly the star of the show. We waved at the group of parents further up the beach and pointed with our nets and buckets to indicate where we were going, and I followed the shrieking group of children to hunt for the elusive crabs and other ocean delights. Milly hung back slightly, just long enough to squeeze my hand and whisper, 'This is the best holiday ever, love you Mummy.' But she was away before I could answer, and my 'Love you more' was snatched away by the wind and the screeching song of the seagulls.

We pottered by the pools for the rest of the morning. I had thought it would be stressful watching over five children - I was so used to just having Milly to concentrate on - but the group looked after themselves really. Milly was clearly in awe of the older children and shrieked with delight when they chased her laughing as they threatened her with the slimy seaweed, before sweeping her up to show her the crab they had found and kindly put in her bucket. I sat on a rock, enjoying the peace and the feel of the sun on my skin. This was what I loved about the Beach Cottage holiday; the simple joys of the beach, only leaving the sand to grab a melting ice cream, before collapsing, starving, in the cottage at night, falling asleep to the distant sound of the waves before doing it all again the next day. I didn't want parties on the beach with too much alcohol clouding the brightness of the day. And up until yesterday I would have said that Rob felt the same way, but now I wasn't so sure.

Speak of the devil, I was roused from my thoughts by Rob's warm hand on my back as he leant in and kissed me on the neck. As his hands dropped to my waist he shouted over to the children, 'Lunch is ready.' Rob hadn't touched me like this in months, and although I could smell the beer on his breath, I was still grateful for the attention. Leaning back into him, I felt myself relax before I reluctantly straightened up and urged the children to gather their things and head back. They eagerly ran towards the promised food delights, carefully carrying the buckets that housed the creatures they had found. I collected up the forgotten nets and empty buckets; Rob waited for me, and we held hands as we walked in the edge of the waves back to the rest of the gang. Maybe this wasn't so bad, maybe we could compromise a bit on this holiday; after all I couldn't see Milly being too keen to be ripped apart from her new friends.

The afternoon passed in a blur of pink goblets of wine, too much sun and the salt of the sea drying on my skin as the tide rushed back towards us and the children fought the battle against the waves to protect their castle. A fight we knew was doomed to fail, but still all leapt up to join in at the end as if we could make everything just right for our children. As the castle succumbed to the inevitability of the ocean, we packed up the bags, gathered the weary children and started the straggly march back to the cottages.

I was tired and ready for some time alone, and I realised I had forgotten to take my medication at lunchtime. A quick glance at my watch showed it was half five. Too late now to catch up. I would just have to miss that dose and get back to the normal routine this evening. Jen and Lydia called their respective children to come in for a shower and a promise of some time in the games room after, and we agreed to meet at Beach Cottage at seven. An hour and a half to wash the evidence of the day from us and get ready to host a BBQ. Great!

Milly and I went in the shower together. She would normally be asking for a bath, but she was eager to join her friends in the games room and try out all the delights that they had obviously been discussing on the beach. As she nagged me to hurry up, I threw clean clothes on us both and headed to the building across the green from our cottage whilst Rob had a much more relaxed shower. I tried not to begrudge him that time, but I couldn't help but feel a little martyred as I pushed open the door, wincing at the sign above it: 'Fun Cabin'. In all the years we had visited, we had never bothered with this building. Inside there was a pool table, what looked like an Xbox connected to a giant TV, a couple of arcade-type games and in the corner, an old-fashioned jukebox. Walking over, I scanned the list of songs and recognised a few from my school days. There were cans of various soft drinks in the corner fridge with an honesty box. But my eye was drawn to the far wall, on which there was a cork board plastered with photos of smiling faces whom had all holidayed at the beach. Glancing over at the children, who seemed to be ignoring the delights of the games room to organise some complicated game of their own imagination, I wandered over to the board and studied the pictures that had been pinned there.

Older photos had been covered over by the later arrivals. All showed happy faces, with the occasional sulky teenager, and I noted that the majority had been taken in the sunshine, which would suggest that it never rained on the Northeast coast. I suppose pictures of a sodden family in waterproofs on a grey beach wasn't the sort of thing you were so eager to share. I searched the board but there were no photos of the gang, or of Bella and her family, which a little voice told me was what I was really looking for.

Shaking my head at my own silliness, I whispered in Milly's ear that I was heading back to the cottage, but she was engrossed with Becca, who was showing her some game on her hand-held Nintendo. It felt weird to be stepping out of the room without her, but I knew that she was relishing the freedom and. I could do this. I had to learn to let her go, and hopefully this would make the whole thing of her starting school so much easier.

Glancing at my watch, I figured I had five minutes to make a quick call to Mum. I know how much she worries since I was so poorly, and I guiltily recognise that she won't settle for the evening if she hasn't heard from me. I could take the easy route and drop a quick text, but figure I need to make up for the tardiness of not contacting them yesterday when we arrived.

The phone barely registers a ring before Mum picks up, so I know she has probably been sat at the kitchen table, willing it to ring.

'Hello love, how are you?'

'Hi Mum, I haven't got long as we are hosting a BBQ, can you believe? But just wanted to check in and let you know all is OK.'

'A BBQ. I bet Rob is delighted about that!'

I laughed, knowing exactly what she meant. 'Well that's the funny thing - it was him that got chatting to the family next door and he has got quite swept up in the socialising thing. I'm not quite sure what's happened to him. Maybe it's something in the water!'

Mum gave a snort of laughter. 'I can barely believe it, but nice that he has surprised us.'

I'm never sure whether Mum and Dad really like Rob. They seemed very confused when I first brought him home to meet them, and Dad whispered a remark to Mum that Rob was not exactly what they were expecting, but Mum nudged and shushed him. But I think they saw that, on the whole, Rob was steady and good for me. You know what you're getting with Rob, and even though he can be a bit inconsiderate and grumpy, overall, I think I made a good choice.

'Where's Milly? Can I speak to her?'

'Well, that's the other thing Mum.' I grinned as I knew Mum would be so pleased about the next bit. 'Milly is in the games room, playing with the other children. We have spent the day at the beach with them. She is having a fantastic time and looking so grown up.'

There was a second of silence at the other end of the line followed by, 'Well, isn't that just fantastic. I am pleased.' And I knew that whilst Mum was pleased that Milly was enjoying her holiday, what she was really conveying was her relief that I had managed to let Milly go a little bit.

After that we chatted about nonsense. I told the tale of Bella and the ridiculous entry in the guest book in lilac pen. I was about to share the story of Bella and the private school fiasco when I saw Rob waving to me from the cottage, and realised I needed to get on with the BBQ preparation.

'Listen Mum, I've got to go. The others will be arriving soon and no doubt everyone will be starving after a day at the beach. Say hello to Dad. Love you.' I realised I was starving too, and actually quite looking forward to the evening. It would be a nice change from board games in front of one of Milly's films, followed by an evening of endless scrolling on our devices.

I don't have many friends and I thought I was happy like that, but with a jolt realised I was enjoying the company of adults other than Rob and my mum and dad. So I had a smile on my face as I reached Rob and greeted him with a kiss and whispered, (corny I know) 'Let's get this party started!'

CATH

As Cath put the phone down and shared with Jon the update on the holiday so far, she realised she should be feeling happy. Lucy had finally managed to give Milly some of the freedom which the little girl craved. Cath had been worried about Lucy's protectiveness of Milly, not allowing her to play on the slide or swings without hovering within reach just in case the little girl should fall. Cath had tried to explain that all children had bumps, and that by hovering Lucy was stopping Milly interacting with the other children. Their mums sat some distance away, cultivating their own friendships whilst keeping an eye on their children, which was exactly what Lucy should be doing. It was as if Lucy had forgotten herself and was living life through Milly, and Cath knew that behaviour was unlikely to result in a happy ending. She had fretted about this in the evenings, picturing Milly's first day at school and fearing it would be Lucy rather than Milly who shed tears at the school gates; and that would be the start of Milly being singled out because of her mother's behaviour. So, the news of the holiday freedom should have lightened Cath's heart. Certainly, Jon had taken this as a positive move forward and was humming as he opened a bottle of red wine to have with dinner, to celebrate 'Another step closer to life in the sunshine.'

 As they ate and chatted about their day, Jon even started to talk about making that extended trip driving through Europe.

 'Baby steps - I mean we won't go until next year, maybe the summer, but then we could consider chancing two or three weeks. I really do feel we are coming out of the other side.'

Cath smiled and nodded, only half listening. She was trying to remember the conversation with Lucy and what it was that had pulled at that part of her brain that put her on alert. She ran through the conversation again. Milly playing with friends - that was all good news, nothing off there. Rob being sociable - well that may be unusual, but it seemed to be working out well for them all, and it would be good for Lucy to make some friends, even just holiday friends; it was a start. Maybe it was just that she had been on high alert for so long that she was unable to relax, even when all the news was good.

She realised Jon was still talking about the possible trip to Europe.

'I thought we could drive down to Provence and see the lavender fields. You've always said that's what you want to do, and I saw you dreaming just the other night over that Provence Instagram account you follow. If we time it for June, apparently, it's an amazing sight of all the shades of purple and lilac. They even have a museum - right up your street.'

Cath had stopped listening. Shades of purple and lilac. Lilac, that was it! It was Lucy's story about the woman in the cottage before them and her lilac ink in the guest book that had tugged at some long-buried memory of past behaviour.

'Are you listening, Cath?'

Cath realised Jon was still talking, and she reluctantly tuned back in to the conversation. She was being silly. They had moved past all this. It had been twenty years. But as Jon spoke about the possible future they may still get, like the rhythm of a train on the tracks coming home, all she could hear was the past echo beat of 'purple and lilac, purple and lilac', and it drowned out everything in her present.

TWENTY YEARS EARLIER

The following Monday, Lucy was initially pleased that Anna was completely speechless as she watched Lucy approach the bus stop. Lucy had been up since five o'clock that morning to make sure that she looked just right. Her hair hadn't quite gone the way the hairdresser had styled it, and she worried she had put on too much foundation and eye liner in a bid to stop the harshness of the black dye making her look so diminished. The red lipstick was harder to apply than the girl on the make-up counter had made it look, and Lucy was aware that the shape of her mouth could be described as more clown like than the voluptuous pout that Kate had sported on her photo. She was pleased with the chunky jewellery she had found, rummaging through the baskets on the little stall she remembered seeing near the entrance to the market. The addition of this had transformed the black T-shirt she had spotted at the stall that sold replica Levi's 501s. The school had a no jeans policy, so she had settled for black cords and a pair of boots that had been in the Next sale. The boots had called her to them as they had a tiny bee painted on the heel, which matched the rather garish yellow laces. Lucy felt sure Kate would approve of these boots.

    The bag had been much harder to replicate, but a tiny shop near the canal sold something a bit similar. It had been rather more than Lucy was expecting to pay, and she hoped her Mum didn't go looking at her TSB bank book for any reason, as she had withdrawn a bigger chunk from her savings than anticipated. It would all be worth it though.

She was brought back to the present at the sound of a snort from Dan.

'Fucking hell, I didn't realise it was World Book Day. Have you come as the witch from the Wizard of Oz? Cos she has a green face not a white face.'

Lucy looked to Anna, expecting her to come to her defence, but Anna shrugged and looked awkward. Thankfully, the bus appeared round the corner and further conversation was unnecessary with the distraction of herding the younger pupils on the bus, far too many of whom seemed to be staring and then smiling at Lucy. Lucy noted that they were not good smiles like they had greeted her with the previous week. More of a smirk. And suddenly she didn't feel like a version of confident Kate, but more like little Lucy who had played dressing up and hadn't quite ended up looking like the character she had intended.

Lucy had felt dreadful all day. She was sure the eyes of the entire school followed her movements. Some of the teachers looked quite taken aback but didn't make any comment, and for that Lucy was grateful. She hid away in the library during lunch and break times, telling her friends she wasn't hungry when they asked if she was coming to the bistro. She had been so looking forward to the English lesson, but instead it was a horror that seemed to never end. Lucy could feel Kate looking at her with pity, so she kept her head bowed low and watched the clock as the seconds slowly ticked by, counting down the time to her release. Lucy intended to go straight to the library for the following study period, and then she just had to endure the bus and she would be home.

As the bell rang for the end of the period, Lucy scooped her belongings into her bag, which seemed so much smaller now she was trying to use it, and stood to make her escape, when she heard Miss Oxenham say, 'Lucy do you have a minute?' She nodded mutely and sank back down to her seat as the rest of the class shuffled reluctantly towards the door, throwing curious glances in her direction. There was a burst of laughter as they reached the corridor, which Lucy just knew was about her, and then silence as the door closed and there was just the two of them in the room.

For a while there was just an awkward silence, until Lucy could stand it no more and was forced to lift her head to meet the steady gaze of Kate. Lucy could feel the prickle of tears as Kate asked with concern, 'Lucy, is everything OK? It's just you don't seem your usual self?' With that the floodgates opened, and the distress Lucy had been holding inside all day poured from her eyes, with the too black Kohl leaving streaks like dirty exclamation marks on her cheeks. Hurriedly, she wiped her face with her sleeve, inadvertently smearing the lipstick away from the shape of her lips. Kate said nothing but moved round the desk to sit by Lucy and put a reassuring hand on her shoulder.

'Want to tell me about it?'

And, hesitantly at first, Lucy explained how she had wanted a change of image, but that somehow it had all gone horrendously wrong.

Kate didn't ask questions or interrupt, but was content to let Lucy speak. Looking back at this moment, as she did many times in the weeks that followed, Kate would curse her own inexperience at this point. Maybe if she had been in the job for a few more years, she would have recognised the signs that this was more than a change of image gone wrong. She would have maybe recognised the beginnings of an obsession and would have had the tools to take appropriate action - maybe getting the school counsellor involved or calling for assistance from a fellow teacher. But Kate did none of these things, being overwhelmed with sympathy for poor, quiet Lucy. And Lucy wasn't truthful about the impetus for her change of image.

Kate, remembering perhaps her own awkwardness at leaving home for the first time and starting university with other girls who seemed so much more confident and sophisticated, decided the best thing to do was to help Lucy make her new style work. It was an impulsive decision, done with the very best of intentions. After all, what harm could come of it?

LUCY

Oh, my head! I could hear the rooster shouting the start of a new day, and as I tentatively opened my eyes, the light was streaming through the VELUX window - testament to the fact that once again we had forgotten to close the blinds. My eyes felt gritty and as the room came into focus, I could see rather more clearly than I expected to, and I let out a groan as I realised I had slept in my contact lenses. I would pay for that later. Next to me, Rob snuffled in his sleep and rolled on his side, flinging his arm across his eyes to block out the invading sunlight. Repeating the pattern of yesterday, I slipped from beneath the covers and tiptoed into the ensuite where I prised off the contacts which seemed to be stuck to my eyeballs. I blinked a few times as I adjusted to the mornings blurred vision, before I groped for my glasses at the side of the sink. Reaching for the blister pack of tablets, I groaned again, realising I had forgotten my evening dose too. My head felt heavy and thick, and although I had been steadily drinking all the previous day, the majority of this liquid had been some sort of alcoholic concoction. I realised I was probably dehydrated after a day on the beach and a night of overindulgence. Not a good combination. But I pushed these thoughts aside quite easily. In fact, as easily as I had forgot to take the tablets, which I admit I hate.

I know they help me. They keep me on an even keel. But they slow down my thinking and make me feel numb. I have been on medication for my supposed bi-polar for a long time now. In quiet moments alone, I am consumed with anger that I have been landed with a diagnosis from other people telling me that there's something wrong with me. Whilst I have learnt to recognise the triggers and the signs of the depression and mania which can threaten to consume me, it seems Mum thinks she can do this better. She watches me like a hawk, so there really is no escape from this massive flaw I seem to have to live with. The advice of the mental health nurse is now nagging me, even though I haven't had to see her for a good few months. All she told me anyway was the obvious - reminding me that alongside the hated tablets, lifestyle can do so much to help. Exercise, diet and sleep, and of course sensibly limiting my alcohol intake. This holiday is not really ticking any of those boxes.

I vowed to do better. Mum would have a fit if she knew. I quickly popped out my morning dose of sanity and swallowed it with a gulp of water that threatened to make me gag. Staring at my reflection in the mirror, I was surprised to see that, apart from my tired, slightly bloodshot eyes, I looked the same as I always did. I don't know what I was expecting, but I felt so different inside that I felt sure it would be obvious in my outward appearance. Sneaking from the room, I paused to peek in at a peacefully sleeping Milly, who we had clearly put to bed in the pants and t-shirt she had been playing in last night. I groaned again. What on earth was I playing at.

As I waited for the kettle to boil, I half-heartedly started to clear away the bottles and cans from the night before. The kitchen surfaces were covered in a sticky residue that reminded me of the late-night cocktail making. Things had started out reasonably civilised. Jen gathered up the children on her way over and Andy had collected fish and chips for them from the pub. I saw Milly grinning in delight as she realised she would be eating her impromptu picnic whilst watching TV. She had eagerly consumed hot and greasy sausage and chips from the paper, being careful not to burn her fingers, and squirting the ketchup to her hearts content. All my pet hates. Food should be eaten at the table, as a family, with cutlery and conversation, rather than the screen. And I can never understand feeding the children different food to the adults. Just lazy in my opinion.

But last night I had felt free and reckless. I had rifled through my holiday clothes and picked out a cover-up-dress type thing I had bought on impulse that I had thought might be OK for the beach. It was a mixture of swirling greens and shocking pinks, the bright colours imitating the dancing fairy lights strung around the decking of the cottage. It was the most flamboyant thing I had with me; in fact it was the most outrageous thing I owned, which tells you everything you need to know about my wardrobe. As I slipped it over my head, a little voice reassured me this was the sort of thing that I could imagine Bella wearing. Bare feet and barely-there make up meant I felt like the sort of mum who allowed her child the freedom to act feral on holiday; and as I poured myself another large glass of wine, I decided it was about time I enjoyed myself too.

A little voice in my head nagged me that I really shouldn't be drinking alcohol with my medication. A few more gulps of wine silenced that irritation. As the evening went on, the volume of the music and conversation turned up a notch. Milly fell asleep on the sofa, and I remember Rob carrying her to bed. I think at that point I decided maybe I better switch to water, especially as I saw the disapproving looks from a couple of families returning to the farm after an evening stroll on the beach. But then I figured Bella wouldn't be switching to water, so I heard myself shouting brightly, 'Let's do cocktails!'

I don't remember a lot after that. I do know this morning that I'm pretty sure Bella never looked this rough the morning after the night before. Taking my tea, I opened the patio doors and flopped down on the bench outside. The cottages around us were mainly quiet, with just the odd keen surfer heading out to see if there were any waves worth catching. On impulse, I grabbed my swimsuit from where it had been abandoned on our return from the beach yesterday and headed back to the sound of the sea.

I loved the beach at this time of day. It felt like it was my own personal swimming pool, and the crash of the waves soothed my pounding head. It was high tide, so I only had to walk a few steps after I emerged from the pathway through the dunes before my feet hit the morning chill of the water. Gasping, I strode on and, taking a deep breath, suffered first my belly button, and then my shoulders being submerged in the salty chill. I swam towards Beadnell, enjoying the pull of the current taking me nearer and then further away from the shoreline. Spotting a jellyfish, I decided to turn back, finding the return journey was much tougher and took me longer. I was puffing when I strode, or rather stumbled, from the water and focused on the solitary male stood at the footpath leading back to the cottages. For a moment I thought Rob had come to find me, and I felt the familiar panic that something was wrong with Milly, but as I quickened my pace, I recognised Steve, engrossed on his phone.

As I walked towards the dune, he looked up and gave me an uneasy smile.

'Morning. For a moment I thought I had stumbled on the set of 'Dr No' when I saw you emerging from the sea.'

I grinned, delighted at the corny compliment. 'Morning! Looks like it's going to be another nice day. Just trying to wash away the hangover!'

'Well, you gave me a real sense of deja vu there. Bella never missed an early morning swim. She was a real water baby - apparently swam every day back home, said it kept her sane!'

I smiled. 'I get that.' I was surprised how normal I sounded, when inside I was fizzing with the idea that this was something else Bella and I had in common.

'No signal up at the house. I just like to check nothing urgent has cropped up.'

I smiled again in acknowledgement, not really knowing what to say, but then felt the smile fade as he shouted after me, 'Tell Rob I'll see him at ten.'

Clearly arrangements had been made last night which no doubt Rob would tell me I had been fine with, and I didn't have any recollection of the latter part of the night to argue with him. It also occurred to me that Steve had taken the time to explain to me why he was on his phone, early morning, on the beach, when as far as I knew there was never really an issue with reception up at the farm. It seems maybe Steve had been up to something he shouldn't have been, and I filed that suspicion away for future reference. You never know when little nuggets of knowledge like that can work in your favour.

By the time I made it back to the cottage, enjoying the early morning sun drying the salty water on my skin, Rob was making coffee in the kitchen and Milly was sleepily ensconced in front of the television, half watching some cartoon. As I walked in Rob smiled and leaned in for a kiss.

'Ah, there you are, I'll get on with breakfast. Great night last night. What a holiday this is turning out to be.' He was in such a good mood, I didn't want to rock this better place we had reached by making a fuss about his planned golf trip, so I decided to just fall in with the plans for the day. After all, 'the gang' would be leaving at the end of the week and then we would still have another week to have the holiday I had planned. Taking the coffee Rob offered to me, I left him to the cooking and flopped down on the sofa next to Milly. I considered looking at my phone, but decided that only caused me stress, so instead I reached for the guest book, telling myself I would have a look at some of the other reviews just in case I could find a 'corker' to laugh about with Rob. But inevitably my eye was drawn to the last page of the book, and my finger traced the flowing lilac ink that seemed to carry the essence of the woman who had written it.

I decided that she probably wrote it on the morning of departure, whilst Jules was loading the cases in the car. Rooting in her brightly coloured tasselled bag, she would have retrieved her fountain pen, which I also think would have been purple, and perched on the edge of the sofa to write the review. I imagined her smooth skin would hold the honey glow of a week spent outside on the beach, Birkenstocks on her feet showing off her pink painted toenails. I bet she has an ankle chain - something dainty and subtle highlighting the fine bones of her ankle. Whilst on holiday she has worn shorts every day - this morning she has on a flowing skirt in shades of blue and green, together with a simple white vest top. Three or four bracelets encircle her slim wrists, a mixture of silver bangles and colourful plaited bands in shades of the ocean as a nod to the beach holiday. A simple silver chain at her neck and hooped earrings complete the look. A look which screams freedom, happiness, confidence, youth and an effortless beauty. Bella may now be a mum, but she has not let this define her. Tracing the sloping letters of the review, it's almost as if I feel some of her life essence transferring from the page to me. For the rest of the holiday, I vow that my mantra will be 'Be more like Bella'.

Over breakfast, Rob dropped the bombshell of the golf thing, and I could see he was surprised when I nodded and said that I would pop into Alnmouth with Milly and then meet him lunchtime. He also casually mentioned that we were hosting the BBQ again tonight and that Andy was collecting provisions. In fact, it seemed that the plan for the day was to follow the pattern of yesterday. As I breathed deeply, I asked myself 'What would Bella do?' and I realised Bella would make the best of the holiday and throw herself into the unexpected treat of new friendships, new people to dazzle - and I vowed to do the same.

As I happily waved Rob off, I was just getting a grumbling Milly ready for our trip out when Lydia appeared, ready for the beach.

'I'm just nipping into Alnmouth so best get on,' was the excuse I gave, but Lydia spotted Milly's mutinous face and before I knew it, it had been agreed that Milly would stay with them on the beach, and I could join them when I had finished the few errands I had planned. In some ways this worked for me, as I knew exactly what I needed to get done and having Milly would only make me slower. Five minutes later, I surprised myself to be happily waving Milly off with her friends with a lot of 'Love you, see you soon' and heading off to Alnmouth, feeling an anticipation that had been missing from my life for many years. In fact, I acknowledged I felt free in a way I hadn't done since I was a teenager.

    I knew exactly where I was going - a little shop on the high street that in previous years I had spared little more than a cursory glance. Forty-five minutes later I was on my way back to Beach Cottage, laden down with carrier bags and fizzing with excitement. I'd known exactly what I wanted to buy, and I had found nearly everything. A colourful shoulder bag, a dress in swirls of pink and purple, a flowing skirt in the exact blue and green pattern that I had imagined Bella wearing on her last day, and a selection of vest tops that clung to my body in a way that made me smile, all complimented by various pieces of colourful jewellery. I'd nipped in the chemist and managed to find a nail varnish in an approximate shade of pink that fitted in with my Bella vision, but no luck with the Dior scent. I would need to be more creative with that.

    I confess I had toyed with the idea of travelling to the Metro Centre to source my missing purchases, grimly remembering how I had mocked the leaflets advertising shopping back at the holiday cottage. Then I realised there were the joys of internet shopping when, for a price, you can get pretty much anything you want without suffering the two hour round trip and fighting the crowds. So, on my return, before I got ready for the beach, I ordered the elusive scent, with a matching body lotion, and then found a rather nice purple fountain pen and added the lilac ink. Paying an arm and a leg for the next day delivery, I felt the satisfaction of a job well done and figured it was my reward for not kicking up a fuss about Rob's golfing escapes. Changing into my swimsuit and throwing on the kaftan from last night, I made my way down to the beach, where no doubt the gang was waiting for me to arrive so the fun could start properly.

TWENTY YEARS EARLIER

That evening after tea, there was a ring at the door, making Cath jump. She was just settling down to watch 'Coronation Street' and Jon had already left for his Parish Council meeting. What a nuisance! But before she could move to answer the door, she heard Lucy racing down the stairs, calling that it was for her. Cath happily settled back in her chair and dunked another digestive in her cup of tea, transfixed by the drama playing out at The Rovers Return.

    Afterwards, Cath would wish that she had taken a bit more interest in who was at the door. She had just assumed it would be one of the usual visitors, and she was so used to them being in her home that she barely noticed the chattering giggling that wafted downstairs. In fact, it was such a non-event at the time that Cath never even mentioned it to Jon when he came home, furious that his proposal to increase the budget for grass cutting at the local sports field had been turned down. It's hard to look back at things objectively, when you know what has taken place afterwards. Sometimes you see things that really weren't there at the time. Cath remembers her and Jon did briefly comment on Lucy's rather out of character shopping trip, and recalled they had both thought it best not to interfere as she was bound to grow out of it, and probably pretty quickly, judging how subdued she had been at teatime.

    When it was all over, Cath sometimes wondered if it

would have been different if she had wandered up to Lucy's room during the advertising break, instead of nipping to make another cup of tea and grab a couple of custard creams. She would have seen then that the visitor in Lucy's room was not one of the usual girls and she liked to think that, when finding out that Kate was in fact Miss Oxenham, she would have had the sense to realise that this was not really appropriate, and the whole thing would have ended there. No doubt there would have been a few days of grumpiness from Lucy, accusing her mother of interfering, but it would soon have blown over, and in very short time they would have found their old Lucy back with them. She would probably have been able to get a refund on some of the ridiculous things Lucy had bought, and life would have continued on as before. Miss Oxenham would have no doubt felt embarrassed, but would have learnt a valuable lesson in teacher-pupil boundaries and that would have been that. But Cath was suffering with her hormones. Jon had mentioned once that it could be hell at times living with a sixteen-year-old daughter and a peri-menopausal wife. He knew better than to ever mention that again!

The reality was that all evening Cath had been craving something. She needed a dose of magic to ease the niggle of anxiety and take her mind off the spots she was suddenly developing and the tightness of her work trousers. She did pause on her way to the kitchen, lulled by the faint echo of a version of 'Lilac Wine' she had not heard before. For a moment, Cath was transported back to her bedroom at her parents' house, getting ready for a date night with Jon, listening to Elkie Brooks sing those same haunting words, as her stomach fizzed with excitement at the evening to come. But feeling sad at the version of herself she had lost, she didn't walk upstairs, or even call out hello to their visitor, instead taking refuge in the biscuit tin. And later, she didn't know if she would ever forgive herself for that, and vowed to never eat another custard cream.

Lucy had had the most wonderful evening with Kate. She

felt like Cinderella being helped by her fairy godmother. Kate had brought with her a Katie Melua CD. Lucy had never been interested in this music, judging it to be more Radio Two than One, but Kate raved on about her 'namesake' as the haunting chords of 'Lilac Wine' played in the background. Kate had also showed her how to apply her make up so she didn't look like an extra from the horror movie. Lucy was delighted when Kate commented that she had a lipstick in a very similar colour and how much she loved Lucy's new jewellery, but suggested maybe not to wear it all at the same time. The two them went through Lucy's wardrobe - both her existing stuff and the new purchases - and Lucy watched as Kate put together outfit combinations which Lucy would have never considered. When Kate glanced at her watch and exclaimed it had gone nine and she needed to be off as she was meeting her friends for a cheeky school night drink, Lucy half expected to be invited along. When the invitation didn't materialise, Lucy watched Kate hurry towards the bus stop from her bedroom window.

That night in bed, Lucy ran over the perfect evening and decided that Kate had not been able to invite her to the pub as her friends wouldn't like the fact that she had a new best friend. Lucy wasn't sure how Kate's friends knew about her, but she was certain that they did and was equally certain they would see her as a threat and would do their best to keep the two of them apart. Obviously, they would fail at this - nothing could keep her and Kate apart - but it was something she needed to be cautious of. She debated whether she should warn Kate, but then realised she had no way of getting in touch with her, and understood with a jolt that Kate's friends probably monitored her phone, her post and her every move.

Oh, poor Kate. But, reflected Lucy as she drifted off to sleep, it just showed how much Kate wanted to be with her, that she had managed to give them the slip and risk everything to sneak some time with her love. It would be fine. Lucy didn't need anyone else but Kate, and she would make sure that

Kate realised that Lucy was all she needed in the world too. Everything was going to be just as it should be.

LUCY

After my shopping trip, the rest of the holiday fell into a happy routine. Rob and Steve would play golf in the morning, picking up the online shop on their way home. Andy cycled miles all over the county, before collecting our order from the Farm Shop for that night's BBQ. Jen and Lydia took turns to provide lunch, which the three of us carted to the beach, along with the children, who had also fallen into their designated places in the pecking order. The sun shone and the days were long and lazy before we returned to our cottages, sticky with suntan lotion and spilt cocktails, before partying late into the night, pretending we were young and carefree in Ibiza, rather than parents with mortgages in the Northeast. In fact, the only thing that didn't follow a predictable routine was me remembering to take my medication. I decided there was no point fretting about this - there were no real adverse effects, and I could get back to normal once I was back home.

Milly was blossoming, there was no doubt about it. Every day she gained in confidence and both her and Rob had found their smiles. I spent more time with the children than everyone else as I was first choice to accompany them to the better rock pools, supervise the bodyboarding in the sea, or laugh as they raced down the steep dunes a little further down the beach from where we typically set up camp for the day. And suddenly it was the last night.

I came up from the beach a little earlier that afternoon as I was planning to wear my new dress and bits of jewellery together with the scent which had arrived a few days before. I had it all planned in my head. Jen and Lydia had sneaked off on a mystery shopping trip the day before, and I was pretty certain they had got me the phone charm to match the ones I had almost scoffed at on the first day. That way, I would be firmly established as part of the foursome with Bella. I knew from eavesdropping to their conversation when they thought I was dozing in the sun, that Bella had broken radio silence, and the three were planning to meet up for a spa day. No doubt once the arrangements were finalised, I would be invited too. Rob had already pencilled in a golf weekend with Steve, and there were drunken chats about a long weekend in Portugal at a golf resort in the autumn, so it made sense that I would be making arrangements with Jen and Lydia. And Bella, I corrected myself. Definitely Bella, who I think was quite likely to be my best friend. I hugged that knowledge to myself, aware of the jealousy this close relationship would trigger in Lydia and Jen.

    After I had showered the residue of salt water and sand from my body, I swapped my normal utility moisturiser for the silky smoothness of the 'Lucky' scent body lotion. I felt lucky tonight. Milly and Rob were both happy, the gang adored me, and at last I had adult friends that I could be myself with. This holiday had allowed a new version of myself to emerge, one which had been hidden for far too long. When I had finished getting ready, I barely recognised myself in the mirror. I looked like the sort of woman who would swim naked in the sea by moonlight, who would paint pictures in her spare time, capturing the joyful things in life whilst caring little for what others thought of her. As I sprayed the perfume and moved my wrist towards my nose to lose myself in the lily of the valley imagery, the bracelets on my arm jangled - a mixture of silver bangles and plaited friendship threads. The purple and pink of the dress highlighted the warm glow of my skin and the soft fabric that fell down to my ankle made me feel as if my limbs were being lovingly caressed with every step I took. I decided to go barefooted as I had nothing else that matched the mood of my look.

At the last minute I remembered my medication and, cursing myself for forgetting the lunch time dose yet again, I decided to double up on the night-time tablet early and that way I wouldn't need to worry about remembering to take it when I'd had a few drinks. Or maybe I would be leading the charge to swim naked under the moonlight. Tonight was a night of possibilities, and I just knew it was going to be magical.

To be honest, the evening didn't get off to the best start. Rob was grumpy when he eventually returned from the beach, clearly annoyed he had been left with the childcare and also clearly choosing to forget that he had played golf every morning. I also suspected he was sulking that his friend was leaving in the morning, and I shrugged off the disconcerting thought that he wasn't looking forward to spending the second week just the three of us. He failed to really pass comment when he saw me stood in the bedroom doorway, other than a slight raise of his eyebrow and a muttered, 'Bit different from your usual look.' But as he brushed past me on his way to the shower, he stopped short and snapped, 'What's that smell? Is it something you're wearing?'

I was pleased he had noticed and held out my wrist. 'I fancied trying something new and I liked the smell of the hand soap left behind, so I thought I'd try the perfume. It's 'Lucky' by Christian Dior.'

For a moment I thought Rob hadn't heard what I said, so I started to repeat, 'It's 'Lucky' by...'

Rob interrupted me, 'I heard you the first time. I'm just not sure why you would go with that perfume. It doesn't suit you at all. In fact, it's making me feel a bit queasy. Maybe it will be better once it's worn off a bit. To be honest, I prefer your normal stuff.'

I was tempted to ask him what my normal stuff was, after all he bought me a bottle every birthday, but knowing my mum always did the shopping for him, I decided to let it go. Bella wouldn't care what Rob thought of her perfume because she didn't need approval from anyone, and neither did I.

Touching my new bangles for reassurance, I thought they were the same to me as the bangles were to Wonder Woman. They would unleash my inner power. Milly was itching to get over to the games room, so I stood in the open doorway of the kitchen and watched her run across to join the others, surprising even myself how relaxed I was, but noting how she was flourishing under the new me. I quickly snapped a selfie and sent it off to Mum and Dad. That would keep them happy for the night. I followed it with a quick message:

> *Last night with the gang so all dressed up and ready to party. Will talk tomorrow when we get some time to ourselves.*

Duty done, I waved to Lydia and Steve as they neared our cottage, and was delighted to see they were bringing champagne. I also saw peeking from the top of Lydia's bag, a small, gift-wrapped package and my eyes fell to my phone, looking forward to attaching the charm later. Lydia greeted me with a kiss. 'Love the dress darling, Bella had one very similar. Just fabulous!'

'What a coincidence, I saw it in Alnmouth and just fell in love with it. Come on, I have champagne in the fridge; let's celebrate a fabulous week with friends.'

After that the evening flew by, and as the light faded Andy lined us all up so he could take a photo of 'the gang version two'. I jostled my way to take centre stage, just as I'd noticed Bella had placed herself on all the photos. In the distance I could hear the rumble of thunder, and as we stood giggling outside, the first drops of rain started to fall. The children ran squealing and giggling towards the games room and the adults followed, making a similar amount of noise. Once there, I just expected we would carry on socialising for a few more hours, and I wandered over to the jukebox and found the song that had caught my attention on the first day.

The whirr of the machine was hypnotic as the disc dropped into place and the haunting plea of 'Lilac Wine' filled the room. There's something about this song, though I haven't listened to it for nearly twenty years.

For a moment I was oblivious of the packed games room with the bickering children and loud drunk adults and was transported to a different world with my best friend Bella. Maybe we were on one of our short breaks to Ibiza. The Old Town of course, where we would soak up the sun and drink sparkling bubbles of fun whilst we shared our innermost thoughts. 'Oh Lucy,' Bella would whisper in my ear. 'How did I ever exist before I found you?'

Swaying to the music with my eyes closed, I was completely lost in this world I craved so much, until I felt Lydia tap me on the shoulder. It took me some time to bring myself back to the rather less serene reality. In truth, a large part of me didn't want to leave that other world I had created in my head. Somehow it seemed a much nicer place. A kinder place. Then I noticed that Jen had started making noises about needing to finish off the packing as they had an early start in the morning and Lydia agreed, telling Steve to round up Xander and Becca. Rob and I both stood there, and I'm sure I wasn't the only one feeling bereft. I could feel tears starting to prick behind my eyes and I blinked furiously, cross that the evening wasn't going the way I had planned.

As everyone stood awkwardly waiting for a break in the rain to dash back to their respective cottages, Andy suddenly exclaimed, 'The photo! I nearly forgot to add the photo to the wall of fame!' Suddenly everyone was chattering and smiling again and crowding round the board I had noticed on my first visit to the room, where Andy was ceremoniously pinning a photo of the gang to join the other smiling faces pinned for posterity. I was stood near the back, and I had to squint even with my contact lenses in, but I could see the pink and purple swirl of my dress in the middle of the photo, and I felt warm inside again as I realised that the night had turned out just fine after all. Before I had the chance to inspect the photo further, Lydia and Jen both hugged me and said they had a little gift for me. I made the appropriate noises to show surprise and the normal 'Oh, you really shouldn't have' and tore open the packaging to reveal the box beneath. For a moment, the feeling of deja vu almost took my breath away as I opened the box, remembering another carefully wrapped gift that had been shrouded in heartache. Smiling, I prepared the exclamation of, 'I love it,' but the words were stolen from my mouth as I opened the box to see, not the silver phone charm that should be there, but a coaster with cartoon-like bees and the corny caption 'Thank you for bee-ing there'.

'I really don't know what to say,' I stuttered, and I really didn't. What the hell was going on? Why hadn't I been given the phone charm to show that I had earned my place in the club?

'Well, we so appreciate everything you did this holiday,' gushed Jen. 'It meant we could drink cocktails all day without worrying about the children, although it did mean my hangovers were worse!'

'We might see you next year,' continued Lydia as she gave me a goodbye kiss. 'Though we are looking to see if we can arrange something with Bella and Jules, so it's all bit up in the air.'

At this point I could only nod as I knew if I tried to speak, the tears would start to flow. Milly was already starting to cry as she said goodbye to each of her new friends, so I took the opportunity to scoop her in my arms and bury my flushed face in her neck as I made the pretence of consoling her.

And then suddenly, with a bang of the door, the games room was empty apart from the three of us. I turned to see Rob, but he was stood staring at the photo on the wall and as I moved to join him, I gave an involuntary gasp. For the photo of the gang wasn't the picture that we had posed for tonight, and the woman in the centre in the striking pink and purple dress wasn't me, but was Bella. I couldn't help it - a sob escaped me -

and Rob was startled out of his trance and looked at me with a mixture of concern and irritation.

'What's the matter now? Don't tell me you're sad that they're leaving. You spent the first part of the holiday complaining that we were stuck with them, so at least now you've got what you wanted.'

'It's the photo,' I confessed miserably.

Rob's face closed off. 'What about the photo?'

'Well, we're not in it. I thought from a distance that was me in the middle, but it's the couple who stayed here last week. Bella and Jules.'

Rob clearly shared my disappointment as his mouth was set in a firm straight line and he snapped, 'Well it's obviously not you and whilst the dress may be similar colours, I would say that the lady there is wearing some designer garment that looks like it was made for her, rather than a cheap bit of market tat that doesn't fit.' As he watched me stare at him in silence, it was as if he was suddenly free from whatever spell he was under and he pulled me in for a hug. 'I'm sorry, I didn't mean that, you look lovely. I'm just a bit shocked the same as you that they didn't include us in the photo after we've had such a good week. Come on, my two girls.' He scooped Milly up in his arms and grabbed my hand. 'Let's get hot chocolate and ice cream before bed.' As we ran through the rain, I stood on the hem of my dress and heard a tear as the thin fabric ripped, but I didn't care. I never wanted to see the dress again.

CATH

Cath was just putting on her lipstick, ready for a wander down to the pub for tea, when the message came through from Lucy. They had exchanged messages each day and Lucy had sent some lovely photos through of Milly. Cath and Jon both marvelled at seeing the freedom that Milly had gained on this holiday, and Cath had started to think that maybe things were going to work out after all. Jon certainly thought so and spent his afternoons route planning for their grand tour and browsing hotels on the booking sites. His excitement was contagious, and Cath was starting to allow herself to dream, figuring she was being silly to get so worked up simply based on a feeling. She reminded herself that things had been just fine for the last twenty years, and now it's their time to relax and enjoy retirement like they had always planned. This holiday was just what Lucy had needed, and it couldn't have worked out better with them meeting the other families. It seemed that this group of strangers had succeeded where Cath had failed and had shown Lucy she could let Milly go just a little bit.

Smiling at her reflection in the mirror, Cath thought she didn't look at all bad. Her eyes had started to regain some of their sparkle, and for the first time in a long time she had rooted in a box shoved at the bottom of the wardrobe for a pair of colourful ladybird earrings that she had bought all those years ago from the shop she had loved so much before all the trouble started. As Jon walked into the room to see if she was ready, she caught his eye in the mirror and smiled as he came to hold her from behind and dropped a kiss on her neck. She squeezed his hand, then clicked on the WhatsApp message to access the photo so they could look at it together. At first Cath wasn't sure what she was looking at. She was expecting a photo of Milly playing in the waves or grinning at her with a face coated in ice cream, so she was confused even as Jon commented, 'Oh what a lovely picture of our Lucy, doesn't she look well.' Cath didn't think Lucy looked well at all. It was that bloody lilac colour again, taunting her from the photo, and all Cath could think was that this didn't look like their Lucy at all.

Jon was oblivious to Cath's reaction, scooping up the keys, proclaiming he was ready for that first pint. Cath slowly followed him to the door, remembering the last time Lucy changed her image.

TWENTY YEARS EARLIER

Everyone still looked at Lucy the following day, but this time it was the looks she had been hoping to get when she first decided to be like Kate. Over the next few weeks, she studied Kate as much as she could. She watched her throughout the lesson, noting how she would raise her right index finger to the corner of her mouth when she was concentrating and would then bite her lip if she was considering a point raised in the class. She monitored Kate as she stood on playground duty and noticed how she would throw her head back and laugh, and that when she was chatting with the other student teachers, she would casually touch their arm or shoulder. At night, in front of her mirror, Lucy would practice these mannerisms, at first noting that they looked stilted and wrong, but the more she repeated the motions, they slowly became a part of her new persona, until finally she felt she was ready.

On the last Wednesday of term, Lucy had volunteered to help out at the school open evening. Her job was to greet the parents of prospective pupils at the door and show them where to go to reception to register their details. To her delight, Kate was at the Reception Point and smiled warmly at Lucy and called out a cheery hello. Since Kate had come to Lucy's house, she had remained friendly at school, but Lucy was disappointed that really she didn't treat her any different to the rest of the class, other than the odd, 'I knew that outfit would look great on you,' and a smile and a wink. Lucy knew that Kate couldn't show her true feelings. Not only did they need to keep it a secret from the school, but Lucy was more and more certain that some of Kate's friends were attempting to keep the two of them apart. Lucy at times felt aggrieved that Kate didn't stand up for herself and tell her friends that Lucy was here to stay, but then, she reassured herself, they had plenty of time.

The open evening started at six-thirty, and the headmaster's address was an hour later. At that point, the crowd of parents suddenly eased off and there was just the odd straggler who was running late and arrived all flustered, muttering about it being impossible to park the car. Lucy wandered up towards the Reception Point, but as she neared the door, she could hear Kate talking to Mr Harris, the new teacher who had started at the school in September.

'Can't wait to break up on Friday. I've loved it, but I am exhausted.'

Lucy heard Mr Harris laugh and mumble something in response, and then heard the odd word from Kate as they moved away towards the main hall.

'Friday night…you should join us… The Duke's Arms in Town.'

Lucy stayed where she was. This was a message clearly meant for her. She knew that Kate couldn't ask her out outright, but she was telling Lucy to meet her this Friday. That night in bed, Lucy turned the invitation over and over in her head. Did Kate intend them to meet there alone? She decided, after much deliberation, that it would be best to organise a group night out. That way, her and Kate could slip away to spend time together once they were sure Kate was safe from spying eyes.

Lucy found it surprisingly easy to persuade her friends and Dan and his mates that they should go out Friday night to celebrate the end of term. Her suggestion of the Duke's Arms was met with some doubtful looks, but then Dan's mate Alex chipped in that his brother drank there, so they would be able to persuade him to get some drinks for them, and that was it sorted. Lucy ran from the bus stop home, hugging the knowledge of her special date close to her. Her heart was beating so loudly in her ears and seemed to echo the loop running through her brain, 'Finally she will see me, finally she will be with me'.

LUCY

When I opened my eyes the next day, I realised it was the first time in a week that I had not been woken by the sun streaming through the forgotten VELUX blind. I also had only a slight headache and had remembered to take my contact lenses out and my makeup off. In fact, I felt a little bit more like my normal self. Turning over, I saw that, again for the first time this holiday, Rob had got up before me and I could hear him and Milly pottering around in the kitchen, with lots of giggling and theatrical shushes. I lay in bed, savouring the sound of their joyful plotting, which I guessed was making breakfast, and then grabbed my phone and gasped as I saw it was gone ten. I was busting for the loo, which was no surprise as I had slept for nearly twelve hours; and as I washed my hands, I decided to give the 'Lucky' hand soap a miss this morning and grabbed a squirt of our shower gel instead. Looking in the mirror, I was pleasantly surprised to see my makeup-free face actually looked like we had spent a week outside at the beach, and somehow wasn't reflecting the ravages of a week of too much alcohol and too little sleep. 'You've still got it, Lucy' I whispered to my reflection, then smiled as I realised I had probably never had it!

Moving through to the kitchen, Milly hurled herself at me 'Mummy! You missed waving our friends off.'

I looked over at Rob, who smiled as he moved in for a kiss. 'Morning, sleepy-head.'

'Has everyone gone already?' I wasn't sure if I was relieved or gutted to have missed saying goodbye.

'They have literally just driven away. They sent their love

to you. Now it's peace at last and we can enjoy the second week just as you wanted.'

Rob turned to start dishing up the eggs and bacon, so I didn't need to hide the confusion on my face. 'Did they leave a contact number?' I asked, feigning a casualness that I did not feel.

'Well, I've got Steve's mobile obviously, as we are sorting that golf trip. Don't think I have a number for Andy. Have you not got Lydia and Jen's, then?'

Bending my head towards Milly and letting my hair cover my face to hide the two spots of red on each cheekbone I always got when I lied, I managed to casually state, 'Oh yes, I have their numbers, but I wondered if they'd written down their address or home number.'

For a moment Rob didn't say anything, and I could feel that he was looking at me, no doubt wondering what on earth I was on about, then he laughed, 'No one has a landline anymore Luce, you know that.' And then thankfully it was all forgotten with the bustle of dishing up and making plans for the day.

I joined in with the chatter, and chivvied Milly along to get ready for a boat trip, which was a bit of a holiday tradition for us. Milly was reluctant, wanting to head to the beach again, but soon cheered up with the promise of ice cream and a look round the novelty shop on the corner to part with some of her holiday spending money. But all the time my head was struggling to make sense of the stark fact that my holiday friends had not swapped numbers with me. Clearly, I had been endured rather than welcomed in their circle, and I couldn't help but feel that this was all Bella's fault.

As it turned out, we ended up having a really nice day. The boats weren't too busy, and Milly was fascinated watching the seals sunbathing on the rocks before slipping in the water to greet the boats with a bob of their heads. We laughed at the difference between their clumsy flopping about on land compared to their elegance in the water. There was little breeze, so the trip was smooth, and the sun warmed our skin and made the sea appear a deep blue, reflecting the colour of the clear sky above us. As the boat turned back towards the harbour, the people on the left shouted there were dolphins, and sure enough, we saw the pod slowly making their way along the coastline, before putting on a little show just for us. I sighed in contentment and squeezed Rob's hand. This was how the holiday was meant to be - enjoying the sea and the beach, the three of us happy with each other. I thought back to the churning disappointment of the night before and reflected it was probably the result of the hit-and-miss week with my tablets, coupled with drinking rather too much. I glanced at Rob but felt my stomach lurch as I noticed that his mouth was set in that too familiar straight line that had been eased away by the last week with our new friends. As he felt my eyes on him, I could see him make a conscious effort to smile, but I doubted the smile reached his eyes, that were hidden by the dark glasses.

'What a perfect trip,' he whispered to me, but his face didn't reflect the sentiment of his words; and poetically, at that point the sun went behind a fluffy white cloud, and I felt a chill. 'It was probably just the lingering effects of the tablets and booze,' I told myself as I watched Milly and Rob step off the boat and race along the harbour to buy ice creams. Back in the car heading to the cottage, I suggested we pick up fish and chips for tea, which was greeted enthusiastically by Milly and Rob who were excitedly making plans for a trip to Beadnell harbour the next day to try out the crabbing kit that Milly had eventually chosen from the shop on the roundabout. Returning to the cottage with the greasily wrapped packages, we set them out on the picnic table outside to eat so we could enjoy the evening sunshine. It was noticeably quieter back at the cottage; in fact it was the way I remembered it. As I was licking the salty residue from my fingers, the new people from next door headed out for an evening trip to the beach. A family of four: a mum and dad with two surly teenage sons who clearly wanted to be anywhere but at the seaside with their parents. They gave a polite nod and a 'Lovely evening' and moved on. I gave a sigh of relief that we wouldn't be embroiled in yet another group, though I could see that Milly was disappointed that she would have no new playmates.

As Rob seemed to have done the majority of the bedtimes - or at least I think he had - I volunteered for bath time with Milly, and she was soon smiling again as she revelled in the bubbles in the bath and chatted excitedly about the dolphins she had seen earlier. Realising I had pinned the bath towels out to air in the sunshine, I moved towards the open back door but stopped as I heard Rob on the phone.

'I don't know what the fuck you think you are playing at, but it has to stop. Do you get me?' He listened silently before interrupting, 'I don't care what story you have come up with. Just don't pull that sort of stunt again.'

I don't know why but I felt awkward hovering there in the kitchen, as if I had been eavesdropping on something very personal, which was just ridiculous. I could see that Rob was furious by the set of his shoulders, then he breathed out deeply, raising one hand to rub the back of his neck before he turned and saw me standing behind him.

'Bloody hell Luce, you made me jump. What are you doing loitering there in the doorway?'

'Towels,' I gestured towards the bath towels dancing on the line, and moved past him to collect what I needed, before asking as casually as I could, 'Everything OK?'

'Not really, bit of a balls up at work. Still, hopefully they will get it sorted now. Come on, let's get Milly to bed, then you and I can enjoy some time on our own.'

He took the towel from my hands, and I heard him move behind me towards Milly.

'I have heard there is a mermaid here that needs rescuing from the sea,' he said, and Milly dissolved into screams and giggles as I pictured him lifting her from the bath and tickling her as he enveloped her in the crusty air-dried bath towel.

I stood still for a moment, trying to pinpoint why I felt so uneasy. Rob often had to take the odd phone call from work whilst we were on holiday, and indeed Steve had good-naturedly moaned that they had been stuck at the fifth hole way too long one morning as Rob was on the phone. It wasn't his annoyance - I had heard Rob speaking to people at work before and had realised he could be quite forthright when things weren't going his way. But I had never heard Rob swear on a work call before. He always made a big deal about the importance of professionalism at all times, to the extent that he never participated in Dress-Down Friday, instead making the concession of wearing chinos with a shirt and tie, rather than his typical dark suit. And then I realised he had sounded annoyed, but in his voice had also been the hint of panic. And it was that which had tugged at my mind so that my stomach churned, and I felt that my feet were slipping off the edge of some precipice that had not been there before.

Shaking my head at the way my imagination was running riot, I realised that yet again I had forgotten the lunchtime tablet. I had meant to take it before we headed out on the boat trip, but with one thing and another, it was neglected again. I decided to take it now and then take my last one as late as I could. I really needed to get back in a rhythm tomorrow, as no doubt this change in my medication routine was allowing my mind to go to places that weren't real - to see danger and problems where there were none. Yes, that was it. I fixed a smile on my face, but as I joined Rob and Milly in the lounge, I couldn't clear the thought that was shouting for attention in my head; Rob had sounded afraid.

LUCY

The rest of the second week passed without incident. The days seemed to merge into each other, as they tend to do on holiday and at Christmas. Rob surprised me by declaring he had been lucky enough to have a great first week of golf, so his clubs would not be making an appearance for the rest of the holiday. That meant we were safe in our little family bubble, and we would head out to the beach for the morning, before walking over the fields to the next bay for lunch. We would take a trip to Seahouses in the afternoon for ice cream and crabbing, before collecting supplies for dinner to round off the day. It was perfect, just as I imagined it would be. The routine meant that I could get back to remembering all my medication, Rob had no more weird phone calls, and I convinced myself the unease I had felt the other night was simply the result of my mind missing whatever it was those tablets gave me.

I had been on the medication for years now. In the early days I would rebel against it, complaining that they made me stop feeling. And even though I was frightened to feel the way I did, I didn't want to be numb. I needed to feel alive. I needed something to help me, but the trouble was they seemed to deaden just everything, and at times I felt the cure was worse than whatever sickness burdened my mind. However, with the support of Mum and Dad, everything eventually got tweaked to be just right, and other than what I think of as a small bout of depression when Milly was born, which again Mum and Dad had supported me through, the medication seemed to be doing its job.

On the last day of the holiday, we woke to a black sky and

the sound of heavy rain battering against the glass windows of the conservatory. As I drank my coffee, I was tempted to suggest to Rob that we set off for home a day early. I could make a head start on all the washing and we might beat the worst of the traffic. But then I remembered we had ordered fresh mussels to collect from near the harbour and were planning a celebration last night meal. I didn't want to miss that, hoping that the dinner would let Rob and I return to the place we used to be, where affection and easy laughter were taken for granted and everything was going our way - the two of us winning against the world.

Looking at the forecast, I could see the rain looked to be set for the day, so I suggested a trip to Alnmouth to look round the shops and coffee and cake. Rob's face took on the now all too familiar set expression that I had seen far too often before we came away on this holiday, so, desperate to keep the mood light ready for this evening, I suggested Milly and I would take the trip and he could have some time to relax before he donned his chef's whites. This was clearly the right thing to say, and he was smiling again as he waved us off.

We struggled to find somewhere to park - obviously everyone had had the same idea as us as a way to pass a rainy day. Just as I was about to give up, someone reversed from a spot near the beach and I pulled in with a triumphant, 'Yes!'

Milly laughed at me, 'You are the best Mummy, and the best car driver.'

Yes I am, I thought to myself as I made sure she had her hood up as we faced the elements.

There was a gusty wind howling in from the sea, so I quickly abandoned the umbrella I had brought with me, and we dashed in the first little shop we came to. Milly was entranced by the pottery painting kits there, and I let her choose a set, figuring it would keep her occupied for the afternoon. There was a nice glass bowl that I knew Mum would love so I let Milly choose the colour, once I had angled the pretty lilac and pink one into her line of vision. I was also drawn to the selection of candles and chose a mixture of cream and purple swirls, optimistically named 'Love'. It would be perfect to light this evening when Rob and I got to recapture the feelings of our early days. Just as I was paying, my eye was drawn to the carousel of phone charms on display by the till. I wasn't aware I was holding my breath until I found myself breathing out deeply as I spotted the familiar silver star that had graced Lydia and Jen's (and presumably Bella's) phone. Without thinking, I added that to my haul and casually asked the lady behind the till, 'Do you engrave these?' She looked confused, before turning the charm over and showing me the words that were already on the back.

'Each time we look up and see the same star, we are together in our hearts.'

I smirked - seems like Bella wasn't so thoughtful after all. She had passed off a bulk-produced charm as something so special. Clearly her opinion of Jen and Lydia didn't run as deep as the adoration they felt for her.

'Do you still want it?' I realised the lady at the till was looking at me expectantly, and that there were a couple of people shifting impatiently behind me.

'Gosh, sorry yes, I was miles away then.' I smiled apologetically at the people behind me, noting that people were always in a much better mood when the sun was shining.

Taking my purchases, Milly and I moved to the doorway where I could see the rain was now bouncing off the pavement and small rivers were running across the cobbles, finding their way back to the sea. Even with the barrier of houses between us and the sea front, I could hear the groaning of the ocean as the waves crashed angrily against the sand. Suddenly, the thought of battling to find a seat in one of the small cafes, which were easily identifiable by the steamed-up windows, was just too much. Instead, I grabbed Milly's hand and we dashed over the street to the little bakery that we had often commented looked nice, but had never been into. We crashed, laughing, through the door and spent a pleasant five minutes choosing a selection of delights that didn't really go together and certainly didn't provide a balanced meal. But suddenly I felt a recklessness and could just imagine Bella doing the same on a grey rainy day like today. Pasties, sausage rolls, scotch eggs, a loaf of white crusty bread, chocolate eclairs, scones oozing with jam and cream, and Milly's choice of pretty pink iced fingers.

On impulse, on the way back I stopped off at the Co-op and bought lemonade and two bottles of champagne - the real stuff, rather than the prosecco we normally indulged in - and two bottles of Rob's favourite white, which would go beautifully with the mussels that evening. Feeling very pleased with my purchases, we headed back to the cottage with the windscreen wipers whizzing on full as I leaned forward and squinted in a battle to see through the deluge battering the glass.

Grabbing Milly, we ran from the car to the cottage but trying the door, I realised it was locked. Where the hell was Rob? I'd got the car and there was no way he would have gone for a walk on the beach or a game of golf in this weather. I ushered Milly back to the car and sat watching the windows steam up as I dialled Rob's number. Bloody voicemail, so he was either on the phone or in area with poor reception. Milly was starting to whinge that she was getting cold and needed a wee, so I punched out a text.

> *Where are you - we are back at the cottage and can't get in!!!*

'I really, really need a wee, Mummy,' said Milly in a small voice, and the fact that she was quietly asking made me realise she likely was desperate. I realised I was pretty desperate too, so we left the car again, planning to head to the games room where at least we could get a drink and use the toilet there whilst I figured out where Rob was. We'd only run halfway across the grass when I saw a figure dashing towards us and realised it was Rob.

'Sorry, sorry, sorry guys.' He scooped up Milly and ran her back to our cottage whilst I followed. Once inside we both dashed to the toilet, as I reflected that it was getting to be a sad state of affairs when my little girl had better bladder control than me. I heard Rob going out and was relieved to see he had collected the shopping in from the car. I really needed to carry on doing those pelvic floor exercises! Grabbing a towel to dry my hair, I went back to the lounge. Rob was stood in the doorway, and I laughed as he shook like a dog. 'I've got the shopping - looks like it was a successful morning. I've just dumped it on the side in the kitchen. Figured it would be best if you sorted it out.' He noticed that I was shivering. 'I know it's decadent, but seeing as we're not paying the bill, let's switch the fire on.'

The fire groaned and then settled into a grating rhythm as the fake embers took on an orange glow. Within minutes I could feel the warmth but also sniffed at that distinctive, not entirely unpleasant, smell that indicated it had not been used this summer. I edged away from the fire once I felt the familiar burn on the back of my legs that reminded me of my childhood friend's dog who always singed his fur by sitting too close to the fire; and I smiled at the artificial flames dancing on the backdrop. Rob followed my gaze. 'Welcome to the 70s eh!'

I laughed, 'We should be having prawn cocktail to start tonight.'

'Speaking of which, I need to go and collect our order for tonight. I'll only be half an hour or so.'

'OK, well if you do that, Milly and I will lay out our special party tea, which we are obviously having for lunch.'

Rob grinned. 'Perfect' and, dropping a kiss on the top of my head, he braved the deluge. It was only as I watched the car pull away that I realised he hadn't said what he had been doing over at the games room.

CATH

Cath was relieved that Lucy and her family were coming home tomorrow. She couldn't even say what it was, but there was a constant sense of unease that was worming in the pit of her stomach, and she had felt sick for days. It was like waiting for a dentist's appointment when you know that there is an unpleasant procedure ahead of you, except Cath wasn't aware of anything tangible that she needed to prepare herself for. Mind you, she reflected grimly, she had been completely oblivious last time too.

    She couldn't help it, but her resentment towards Jon had also increased as the days passed. The latest irritation was a delivery from Amazon that he had pounced on with a delighted 'Here we go', and Cath watched, bemused, as the package spilled open to reveal travel guides to Italy and Switzerland. Cath rolled her eyes. Normally she indulged him with his passions and the way he approached everything with such methodical enthusiasm, but this time all she could think was 'Silly old duffer, he could have found all that information online, and it would probably be more up to date.'

    As Jon took himself and his books off to the study to continue planning for a holiday that Cath wasn't sure would ever happen, Cath decided that she would make the effort to go for a swim in the outdoor pool. She normally avoided the pool during the day when it was school holidays, for whilst she liked children, she had no desire to be splashed in the face by them whilst she tried to get her lengths in. Cath preferred the lane swimming where she could lose herself in the monotony of counting her way to the minimum fifty lengths. But today she was desperate for something to ease her whirring mind, so the children and splashing would have to be endured; and she hoped the time in the water would bring her some clarity. Maybe if she switched off in the water, she would be able to pinpoint the cause of her disquiet.

Gathering her stuff together, she saw that Jon had been so keen to get at his Amazon package that he had discarded the junk mail on the hallway table. Tucked between the leaflet for a new pizza place and a voucher for ten percent off at the local garden centre, was the cheerful gold and blue of a seaside scene on a glossy postcard. Cath smiled - it would be from Lucy. Lucy had always laughed at her mum's love of the postcard, claiming that they were redundant in this age of mobile phones. But Cath loved a postcard. They reminded her of happy, carefree holidays when Lucy was young, sending postcards back to family that inevitably arrived way after they had returned home. Smiling at the fact that Lucy had taken the time to indulge her, Cath idly flipped it over and felt that knot in the pit of her stomach tighten its grip once more.

> *Having a great time. Milly made lots of new friends, and so have we. The sun is shining every day, but then the sun always shines on the righteous!*
> *Rob thinks he's improving his golf handicap.*
> *See you soon.*
> *Lots of love,*
> *Lucy, Milly and Rob*

The words were innocuous enough, and Cath would normally have been delighted that Lucy was allowing Milly to make new friends. The problem was not what the words said, but the way they looked. The handwriting was as familiar to Cath as her own. What was not familiar was the ink, which flamboyantly shouted Lucy's words in a vivid shade of lilac. Cath dropped the card and fled out the front door, desperate to feel the soothing envelopment of the water and block out that voice that was telling her things were going terribly wrong.

TWENTY YEARS EARLIER

Kate looked eagerly towards the door as it opened yet again, hearing the collective groan of those sat near the entrance as the cold air pierced the warm bubble of pre-Christmas cheer. Once again, she was disappointed when she saw that it wasn't Mark Harris arriving, and then cursed herself for not being bolder with him. She had been too nervous to ask him outright to go out with her, but she thought the casual invitation to join her and her friends for some end of term drinks was a rather large hint that he would surely catch the meaning of. The pub was busy but not packed, and they had managed to secure a large table and were already on their second round of drinks.

Her friends were busy swapping stories about the highs and horrors of their first school placement and Kate joined in with the expected laugh or grimace, whilst all the time keeping a close eye on the door. She was desperate for a wee, but didn't want to leave her seat in case he arrived when she wasn't there and she missed her chance.

As Kirsten was halfway through the story about the seven-year-old in her class who liked to eat all the paint, the door opened, once more letting in the outside chill. Kate whipped her head round expectantly, and her first emotion was disappointment that it wasn't Mark, followed by confusion as she was greeted by shy little Lucy and a bunch of her friends. The group bustled with bravado towards the bar, ordering cokes all round. Everyone that is except Lucy, who stayed where she was looking at Kate, and stood there for a few seconds longer than seemed necessary. Turning back to her friends, Kate shivered and recognised this wasn't a reaction to the draft dancing round her feet. She struggled to put her finger on what had made her feel so uncomfortable about Lucy's appearance. No teachers want to see their pupils when they are out socialising, but the disquiet Kate felt ran at a deeper level.

She was lost so deep in pondering this that she missed the arrival of Mark and jumped when a warm hand touched her shoulder. Spinning round, she grinned in delight to see him there, pint in hand, and shuffled along the bench seat to make room for him. A few of her group knew him already from the university, and after introductions had been made and more drinks purchased, the group settled into the easy conversation of good friends who are on their third round of drinks after a busy week.

LUCY

Milly and I had lots of fun setting out the table for our party lunch. Then Milly got the idea that she was going to draw a place setting for each of us. Rob was getting a crown as he apparently was King Daddy, I was getting a sparkling ring as I was like a princess, and she laughed as she declared she would be the banana as she was the little monkey. I felt a momentary pang of sadness as I realised next week would be her birthday and, as usual, it would just be the three of us with Mum and Dad calling round later for the traditional party tea. Milly would no doubt be spoiled and would be delighted with the pile of presents that had been chosen with such care, but she had never had a party with any of her friends or indeed attended a birthday party. Quite simply because she didn't really have any friends, which I reluctantly acknowledged was down to me. I realised that next year would have to be different, and I wasn't sure how I felt about that.

It was lovely to see her so relaxed and happy to spend time amusing herself. I realised I had always been afraid that if she made lots of friends, she wouldn't want to spend time with me. That I would somehow lose all relevance in her life; but I began to consider that maybe Mum had been right when she had told me it wouldn't be like that. Maybe I would share that with Mum when I got home as I knew it would make her happy, even if I did have to put up with the 'I told you so' that, although not spoken, would be implied in her smile.

I realised that Milly was tugging at my arm.

'Mummy, my yellow felt tip has run out and I need it for all the pictures.'

'Can't you use something else?'

'Don't be silly Mummy, when did you ever see a banana that wasn't yellow?'

I wasn't really sure what Milly expected me to do, but then I remembered the games room with the cupboard in the corner heaving with crafty things.

'Let's go and have a look in the games room,' I suggested. 'I bet there's some felt tips there you can use, and I think they had glue and glitter too, so you can really add some sparkle to Daddy's crown.'

Milly whooped with delight and, oblivious to the rain which was still in full force, dashed ahead of me to the games room. By the time I caught her up she was happily rooting in the cupboard, exclaiming with excitement at all the bits and pieces she could use to make her pictures just perfect. There was nothing for me to do but stand and watch her; and even though I knew it would be like poking a sore spot, I found myself wandering over to the photo board at the end of the room. I think maybe part of me hoped that one of the group had nipped in the morning they left to add 'the gang version two' to the wall. But as I looked, I could see that not only had that not happened, but the original picture, with the glowing Bella at the centre, was now nowhere to be seen. I flicked back a few photos, just in case they had been carelessly pinned on top of the photo I was seeking, though I honestly couldn't comprehend anyone wanting to cover up Bella. I checked on the floor and even contemplated looking under the sofas in case it had been kicked to one side. It was just odd.

'Are you ready to go back, Mummy? I've got lots to do.' I realised Milly was looking at me quizzically as I dragged my gaze from the photo board. 'What are you doing?'

I considered making up a story and then caught myself as I wondered why I felt odd looking for the photo of our friends.

'I was just wanting to look at the photo of all our friends that was up on the board but it's very strange, I can't find it now. Come on, let's get back and hopefully Daddy will be home so we can tuck into our party tea. I'm starving!'

As we got soaked again running back to the cottage, I couldn't help but think of Rob earlier heading back from the games room, and realised I hadn't asked him what he had been doing.

As if reading my mind, Milly piped up, 'Maybe Daddy got the photo and brought it to the cottage for us so we can see our friends all the time.' And with that pronouncement, she forgot all about it as she settled down with the glitter pens to complete her masterpieces. I was left with that seed firmly planted that Rob had indeed removed the photo from the wall; but why on earth would he do that and not even mention it? It was all very odd.

I was stopped from obsessing about it any longer by Rob's arrival. He was in a good mood, and we opened the champagne straight away to toast us and an excellent holiday.

'I really feel this holiday has done us the world of good, Luce. I know I can be snappy, but it really bothered me how...' At this, he glanced towards our daughter and, noting she was still engrossed in her artwork, continued quietly, 'you were really struggling to give Milly some freedom. And I know it sounds like madness, but maybe I was a little bit jealous that there didn't seem to be room for anyone else in your life apart from Milly.'

I could feel tears pricking at my eyes. 'Oh Rob, I have missed you.'

'I've missed us, Luce,' and, leaning in, Rob kissed me and handed me a glass of champagne.

I smiled. 'Here's to us,' and, as Milly bounded over with her glass of lemonade, we clinked glasses, 'the three musketeers.' And as we fell on the savoury and sweet delights laid out before us, laughing as Milly licked the pink icing off every bun, and Rob proved he could fit a scotch egg whole in his mouth, it seemed churlish to ask him what he had been doing in the games room. It obviously wasn't important.

The rest of the afternoon passed in a blur of laughter and giddiness. Rob kept topping up my champagne glass as we continued to nibble at the picnic, whilst screaming with frustration as we played, well Frustration! At around four the sky cleared and the rain finally stopped. Giddy on the bubbles from the champagne, and to Milly's delight, we all donned our swim stuff and raced barefooted through the dunes to dive in the waves. The shock of the cold sobered me up, but I turned my face towards the sky and laughed with the sheer joy of it all. What a truly perfect afternoon for my little family. We carried on, holding hands as we jumped the waves, the beach to ourselves, before Milly, despite the protestations that she was fine, couldn't hide her shivering. Rob scooped her up in his arms as we ran back to the cottage, just as the first of the thunder started to rumble around us.

Milly and I showered together and, once she was snuggled in her pyjamas, I set about making her the requested fish finger sandwich. Rob joined us, ruddy-faced from the hot water and the champagne, and poured us both a glass of wine as he started preparing our last night feast. After that I don't remember all the details. The images fade in and out when I try to remember the perfection of it all. I remember the crusty bread, dipped in the white wine sauce in which the mussels now swam. I remember my glass being never empty. I remember us talking until late into the night, the way we used to talk before things got so difficult. I remember a momentary pang of guilt as I realised Milly had fallen asleep in front of the film, and her sleepy 'I love you, Daddy' as Rob carried her safely to bed.

I remember waiting for Rob in the bedroom and kissing him deeply as we sank into the bed. And afterwards, I remember snuggling into his arms and feeling safe. It would be the last time I felt safe for quite a long time. And unfortunately, the one thing I didn't remember was to take my blasted little tablet.

TWENTY YEARS EARLIER

Lucy was drunk. In fact, Lucy was very drunk. As she sat in the corner of the pub with the haze of the smoke drifting around her, she was vaguely aware that her mum and dad, who would no doubt have waited up for her, would know that she hadn't been round at Anna's, making a start on the holiday homework. The scent of the pub seemed to cling to every inch of her, and she was starting to feel a bit sick. Actually, she was starting to feel a lot sick.

At the start of the evening her friends had been including her in the conversation, but soon ignored her, recognising that whilst she may be sat with them, she was not really *with* them. She kept moving over to the jukebox to punch in the numbers to play 'Lilac Wine' on repeat. Like the song, Lucy was feeling the heartache of losing a lover, and took solace, not in wine made from a lilac tree, but the steady stream of alarmingly blue drinks that were brought her way.

She was fixated on sneaking glances over at Kate's table, waiting for the signal that the two of them should move on, only to be disappointed that Kate had not acknowledged her when she arrived at the pub. She had half hoped that Kate would have the courage to defy the opinions of the so-called friends of hers, and would announce to them that her best friend had now arrived. That had been her fantasy anyway, but she had been gutted to not even receive a discreet wave. However, shortly after that she saw Mr Harris arrive and push his way in to sit next to poor Kate, leaving her trapped in the corner, and Lucy realised that Kate was having to work hard to protect their relationship from prying eyes. Feeling her stomach flip in anticipation, Lucy slipped her hand in her pocket, where she felt the reassuring shape of the square gift box she had wrapped so carefully before leaving the house. In it was a silver bracelet together with a delicate bee charm to match Kate's tights. It had cleared out her savings, but the minute she saw it she knew it was the perfect Christmas gift for her Kate. She had even allowed herself to dream that they would make the bee and the ladybird a theme around the home they would eventually have together. And when their friends asked about it, they would smile at each other and tell the story of how they had first met.

'Come on, dreamer.' Anna nudged her from the lovely world she was building and plonked a glass of Coke down in front of her. Lucy noted that Anna was looking at her with concern, and for a moment she was worried her friend would ask her what she was thinking. What a shock she would get if Lucy told her; but Anna instead just gave her a quick hug and turned to join in the debate over whether mushy peas went with Christmas dinner.

As the evening went on, Lucy determinedly drank each glass of alcohol that was placed in front of her, slowly becoming accustomed to the taste, and even when Anna suggested maybe they should slow down a bit or move on to get something to eat, Lucy shrugged off her concerns and rather abruptly told her, 'You can do what you want, I'm staying here.'

'Oh Lucy, I really think...'

'That's a novelty, you thinking! We're not joined at the hip, you know. I'm enjoying myself and intend to stay here until...'

Lucy trailed off. She had to keep the secret.

At some point in the evening Anna left, trying for a final time to persuade Lucy to come with her. 'Please, Lucy. My dad will give you a lift back to mine and you can stay the night, so your mum and dad don't see you like this.'

Lucy shrugged off her friend's hand and again wandered over to the jukebox to once more put on 'Lilac Wine' as a desperate plea to Kate, who must surely remember that this was their song. Lucy, rather like the singer, was well on her way to drunken blissful oblivion. A desperate reaction to the pain of losing love. Anna rolled her eyes, and with a sigh left behind the friend that she felt she no longer knew.

As the bell for last orders sounded, Lucy was unaware that her surreptitious glances towards Kate's table were not quite as subtle as she thought they had been. To her dismay, just as a final glass of something was plonked on the sticky table in front of her, Kate's group started to shuffle into coats and there was a flurry of cheek kissing and instructions to 'Enjoy the holidays' as they began to drift from the pub. Lucy expected at this point that Kate would signal her to make a move, but Kate was moving past her with Mr Harris gripping her arm, and as Lucy tried to catch her eye, Kate determinedly turned her head towards Mr Harris, pretending she hadn't seen the table of Sixth Formers. For a few seconds, Lucy was stuck to the seat, unsure what to do, then she grabbed her coat and chased after them into the street.

The high street was busy as customers high on Christmas cheer moved towards the bus stop and taxi rank, and Lucy frantically scanned the crowd to pick out Kate's distinctive jagged bob. As it was, it was Mr Harris she spotted first, jubilantly successful in hailing a cab. Lucy found that she could breathe again. Obviously, he was on his way home, and this would leave Kate free to come and find her. They would laugh about how hard it had been to meet up, and then they would probably go to Kate's flat where they could chat and make plans for their future. But as Lucy became lost in this fantasy of her future life, she was confused to see that Mr Harris was not getting in the cab alone. He stood back to let a laughing Kate get in first. As he slid in after her and the cab pulled away, Lucy saw Kate move towards him, and as the cab rounded the corner out of sight, the two were kissing with no idea that they had just shattered Lucy's life. She stood unmoving, oblivious to the people jostling past her, caught in the horror of watching Kate be snatched away from her. Once she could see the cab no more, she took the beautifully wrapped gift box and hurled it to the ground, where she promptly threw up all over it.

CATH

Cath returned to the house in a much better frame of mind than she had left. The pool, as expected, had been incredibly busy, and the sight of all the little ones and the hovering parents just reminded her of Lucy and Milly. She missed them desperately, even though it had only been a couple of weeks, and at first she thought she had made a mistake coming here. But then she found her rhythm and soon forgot everything other than concentrating on controlling her breathing as she ploughed her way through the water. Back and forth she went, not pausing to rest as she smoothly made a turn at each end, enjoying the glancing feel of the sun on her face as she turned her head sideways to take a breath of the air that always felt cleaner when she was in the pool. She relished the counting of the lengths in her head, as that left no room for any other thoughts. She knew that one of the ladies she often swam with said she used this time to think through anything in her life that was bothering her - Cath did not like that idea at all. Instead, she liked to count the strokes it took her to glide from one end to the other, then run a different counter alongside that to track the lengths she had completed. All that counting left very little room for her brain to think of anything else. She was on length forty-nine and deliberating whether to stop at fifty and see if she could get a seat at one of the bistro tables to enjoy a coffee and a slice of cake, when suddenly she felt the water directly in front of her explode and she was choking as she swallowed a mouthful of unpleasant chlorine cocktail. Spluttering, she floundered and for a moment thought she was going to sink under, an inelegant mess of thrashing limbs, before her instincts took over and she righted herself and was able to blindly grope for the side. She followed it along, eyes still shut tight, until she felt the familiar coolness of the metal of the handrail of the steps. Taking a shaky breath, she ripped the goggles from her face and blinked as her eyes attempted to focus through the uncomfortable burn of the chlorinated water. Breathing deeply, she looked around to where the rest of the pool seemed to be carrying on as normal. What on earth had just happened?

'Oh my God, oh my God, are you ok?'

Cath shook her head, attempting to clear the water from her ears, but slowly realised that she was being addressed by a woman who was crouched at the top of the steps and was holding out her hand to Cath, whilst looking at her with concern. At the side of her was a girl of about five, who was sobbing. Still feeling disorientated, Cath had taken the other woman's hand and allowed herself to be led up the steps until she was stood in the sunshine, dazed but feeling better now her feet were firmly on the warm tiles.

'I am so sorry, are you OK?' Cath realised the woman was still talking to her and for a moment was confused, until the woman continued, 'I've told her time and time again not to just jump in the pool without checking there is no one in her flight path.' She turned to the little girl who was still gulping back her tears. 'And you jumped in the lane swimming section. You know better than that. Now apologise to the lady.' The little girl attempted to stutter an apology, but was crying so hard she started to hiccup and turned to bury her face against her mum's legs.

Ah, it was all starting to make sense now. Cath realised she had been the victim of a rule breaker of the 'no dive bombing' instruction which was clearly posted round the pool. She should have been cross, but the little girl was clearly distraught and reminded her so much of Milly that she just wanted to envelop her in a hug. Cath took a deep breath and smiled at the young girl. 'I'm OK, so no harm done. No need to get so upset, but you do need to listen to what your mum tells you. You don't want to hurt someone, do you?' The young child gulped and shook her head vigorously.

'Let me get you a coffee and something to eat. The sugar will be good for the shock.' Cath realised the young woman was still talking to her. Her instinct was that she just wanted to get dressed and go home, but the woman continued. 'And it's the perfect excuse for us to have a huge slab of the carrot cake they have just put out.' And she grinned at Cath with such an open and captivating smile, that before she knew it, she was sat at a table being waited on with a mug of cappuccino and the promised slab of cake, which really did look good.

Once they had started on the sweet treat and Cath had warmed up after a few gulps of frothiness, they had settled back, relaxing in the sunshine, and Cath heard herself asking, 'So, do you come here often?' and then found herself blushing at the awfulness of the question. But her companion smiled and her eyes twinkled. She really did have the most extraordinary eyes, Cath noticed, and when she smiled it was like a light went on from deep inside and illuminated every part of her face. 'I like to swim every day, but it's a bit more of a trial at the moment with it being the school holidays. I'm sure you think that too, especially as my daughter just tried to capsize you.'

'Ah well, no harm done, and it means I get to eat cake and chat with someone new. I'm Cath, by the way.'

'Well, it's very nice to meet you Cath, even if the circumstances weren't the best. But they do say the best friendships start with a splash! I'm Izzy.'

'Do they say that?' queried Cath with a grin. 'That the best friendships start with a splash?'

'Well, they do now,' laughed Izzy. And that had been it for the rest of the afternoon. The two of them chatted as the pool gradually cleared, until Izzy declared she really must dash as she had to take her daughter over to her dad's. Cath couldn't believe it was nearly five o'clock; Jon would be wondering where she had got to.

As they made their way to the exit, Cath was surprised to find herself being drawn in for a hug as Izzy said, 'Thank you for being so understanding about your dunking, and I do hope we see you again.'

'Well, it was nearly worth drowning for - being treated to that lovely cake, and the lovely company too, of course. I do hope to see you here again.'

'You can count on it. See you tomorrow for the early morning adult swim?' And Cath, who disliked early mornings, found herself agreeing to be there at some ungodly hour, as somehow you just couldn't say no to Izzy.

TWENTY YEARS EARLIER

That Christmas was certainly not the season of goodwill to all men. Cath and Jon spent the days in a state of forced manic jollity as they dealt with this very quiet and subdued stranger who seemed to be living in their home. At night, they had long whispered conversations in the shrouding dark of the bedroom as they debated what could have possibly happened to bring about such a dramatic change in their Lucy. Jon seemed quite confident that it was just one of those phases that their daughter was going through - kicking off with the ridiculous change of image and the disturbing drunken night out. Whilst he struggled with the atmosphere in their home, feeling the change deeply as the three of them had always been so settled together, he assured Cath each night that they would soon be through this and would one day laugh with Lucy about the nightmare teenage times. Cath wished she could share his certainty, but she had a growing knot of anxiety in her stomach that told her something much more was going on than some typical teenage rebellion.

Lucy drifted around the house, barely speaking and barely eating. But her silence penetrated every inch of the house the same as if she was screaming at them. They could feel the weight of her sadness as if it had seeped into the heart of the house. Cath and Jon found there was no escaping it. Even if they were sat watching television, following the planned viewing from the Radio Times that Lucy had excitedly highlighted only two weeks ago, they were both aware that their daughter had chosen to sit alone in her room, listening to that bloody song over and over on repeat. In the meantime, Cath and Jon were unable to relax, unsettled as they strained to hear sounds of movement or the noise of Lucy coming downstairs, so they could paste the false smiles on their faces and pretend that this was a new normal for their family. A new normal that they were all happy with.

LUCY

This time I wasn't woken by the light streaming through the window, but rather woke sweating, with my heart pounding. With shaking hands I reached for my phone, groaning as I saw it was three am. Oh God, I needed water. I was wide awake and was in the grip of a real anxiety attack, no doubt brought on by last night's overindulgence. Beside me Rob slept peacefully - he never seemed to suffer with hangovers, and whilst he grumbled in his sleep as I slid back the duvet, he settled back to his peaceful rest whilst I once again tiptoed from the room. Being aware that I didn't want to wake Milly, I made my way down the hall using the light from my phone, then after grabbing a glass of water, I made my way to the conservatory, where I collapsed on the uncomfortable wicker sofa and tried to quieten the pounding of my heart. For a moment, I leant my head back and was content to feel the darkness wash over me, and I hoped that the sickness might start to ease. But after a few minutes, my mind took up the persistent beat of anxiety and I sighed as I looked for a distraction.

    I contemplated reading the guest book again, but knew I would be kidding myself if I pretended I wanted to read anything other than the lilac font that drew me like a siren. Instead, I reached for my phone and, after a moment of hesitation, opened the WhatsApp where I had muted the chat from the school parents' group. What the hell! Two hundred and twenty unread messages. In a week! What fresh torture was here? I knew I could simply switch my phone off and ignore it, but I also knew that now I had seen the notifications, their presence would be nagging away at my peace of mind until I read through the thread. I figured it was best to tackle it now and, reassuring myself that I only needed to skim through and that I didn't need to respond in any way, I scrolled back up to the last message I had read; an innocuous question about book bags.

As I started to read, I was momentarily confused. Whilst there was the odd flurry of messages and some self-important notifications from Heidi of things we needed to remember with the expected response of, 'Thank you that's so helpful,' on a repeat, nothing much had changed. As I scrolled, I was already down to two days ago and didn't seem to have missed much. Thankfully, the monotony was doing its job and a couple of times I felt my head nod and jerk as I drifted back to sleep. I scrolled past a panicked discussion on buying school shoes, relieved that Mum had persuaded me to let her sort out all the school wear shopping. I thought it was ridiculously early, and to be honest, hadn't wanted to think about or do anything which would make Milly starting school more of a reality, but it appeared Mum had been right again.

And then, dropped in the middle of the mundane, was the catalyst for the cork of the thread bottle finally popping and spewing forth some fizz. Unconsciously, I sat up straighter in order to concentrate better. It started off innocuous enough - in fact I nearly missed it.

Heidi added Izzy Watkins

This in itself wasn't that unusual - after all Heidi had added us all at some point and there had been little fanfare about the proceedings. Izzy however obviously saw the group thread as a different sort of platform.

Hi, my fellow warriors. Hope you are all enjoying the last weeks of freedom before we are tied to the school day regime and the politics of the school gate. I'm a bit late to the party, so I just thought I would jump on and introduce myself. I'm Izzy and my daughter is starting in Reception in September. Really looking forward to getting to know you better. Let's make a date! In the meantime, maybe you could let me know who you all are, to help ease this mum's new school nerves. Lots of love.

Something about the style of the text tugged at my consciousness, but was quickly replaced by a feeling of malicious glee. Heidi would not like this. She would not like this at all. I guessed that the flurry of messages had been Heidi putting the newcomer in her place and maybe it had then all kicked off. I needed a coffee for this, but as I moved through to the kitchen, I was pleased to find the banging in my head had subsided and the anxiety had been dampened down at the promise of a ringside seat at the online drama. Cradling my coffee mug and wrapping myself in one of the clean beach towels, I opened the thread again and settled in. But reading on, it wasn't at all what I expected.

Hi Izzy. Lovely to meet you. I'm Kate, mum to terrible twins, looking forward to school starting! And a date sounds perfect. Not had one of those for a while!

Hi Izzy. What a great introduction. Wonder why we never thought to do this before. I'm Alex, a mixture of worry and excitement for both me and my daughter Anna, starting this September. If there's a date, count me in.

Hi Izzy. Welcome to the group. I'm also keen to get to know everyone better, so thank you for breaking the ice! I'm excited to have a place here for my son, it's a great school.

And the messages rolled on, as all these people who up to now had just swapped fairly frantic messages about labelling uniform, the right type of plimsolls and snack etiquette, suddenly started to emerge from behind the shadow of their children and start tentative friendships. Nothing from Heidi yet. Izzy had taken the time to respond with a heart emoji to every single reply and then wrote.

> *Looks like a meet up would be popular. I don't want to tread on any toes here, being the newcomer, but why don't we get a date in the diary? I know how busy we all are. I vote Pizza and Prosecco!*

Now, what would Heidi make of this? I didn't have to scroll much further past the enthusiastic take up to a night out to see Heidi's contribution.

> *Hey Izzy, lovely to meet you. Love the idea of a night out and Pizza and Bubbles sounds just the job. Bit cheeky, but are you happy to organise this? I'm good at organising the practical things but not so good on the fun side of things!*

Well, this was a turn up for the books!

> *More than happy - fun is my middle name, so we are obviously yin and yang. Leave it with me!*

And Heidi - reserved, bossy, serious Heidi - responded with a face with love hearts emoji. What the hell was going on? I felt like I'd stumbled in a parallel universe.

Scrolling still further, I skipped past the logistics of the organisation, seeing that the Friday of the first school week had been agreed on and Marco's booked for seven thirty. There was then the typical show of hands and debate as to whether it would be better to pre-order. Heidi, proving she was indeed the practical organiser, shared the menu to the group and a link to a shared sheet where you could enter your food choices. Ridiculous! It was still weeks away, and how I hoped those weeks would pass slowly.

Once this was all in motion, I expected the thread would quieten down, but Izzy seemed to have broken the ice and all of a sudden there were plans to meet in the park, play dates being arranged and loose plans to meet for coffee after the first school drop off.

Though I might need something stronger and definitely tissues!

That was Izzy, somehow saying what all the mums were feeling, and they loved her for it.

Then Izzy posted again and fanned the flames further.

OK, so this is a bit odd seeing as we have never met, and your children have certainly never met Elizabeth, but I've been a bit spontaneous and, to make the most of the great weather forecast, wondered if you would like to come to a little party we are having at the outdoor pool, next Friday from eleven. No special occasion, just because the sun looks to be shining for the next couple of weeks and what better way to meet each other? Plus, I have an ulterior motive as I'm in charge of fundraising for the new Splash and Play area, so I may be shaking my donation bucket! I've booked it out until three and it would be so nice to see you all. Nothing fancy. Bring a picnic, or the cafe will be open. If you could let me know for numbers, that would be great.

Wow - with the excitement that greeted this, you would have sworn that Izzy had announced that Freddie Mercury had been reincarnated and Queen were going to perform a one-off concert for which we had front row tickets. OK, I smiled as realised this was a personal fantasy of mine, but that was the level of near-hysteria. Messages were flying about picnic choices and what to wear with the panic buying of a new swimsuit being quite a common theme. The other common theme was that, from what I could see, with the exception of a few sad faces as people were forced to decline as they were on holiday, the majority of the group were planning to attend.

Now I was in a quandary - I obviously hadn't responded to any of the thread. I had the perfect excuse that I had been away, but now I panicked that they would see that I had read the messages, and they would judge me for being rude in my silence.

Oh God, now the anxiety was back in full force. Would I be ostracised from the group and in turn, this would mean that Milly was never invited for tea and would be the only child not invited to birthday parties? I tried to breathe and put this in perspective - do people really look at who's online and who's responded? After all, I don't think I had posted anything on the thread at all so my name was just there, lost in the twenty-odd other names who were brought together simply by our children starting school at the same time.

Breathe in - it's fine.
Breathe out - Milly will be accepted.
Breathe in - it's fine.
Breathe out - people won't notice you've not replied.

I was nearly at the end of the chat now, when my breath caught in my throat at the last message Izzy had posted on the thread:

@Lucy, hope you are OK. Just wondered if you were planning to come to the pool party? Would be great if you can make it.

And after that there was silence. That message was sent yesterday just before lunch. It was the full stop to the flurry of activity, and it was all focused on me. Everyone would see that I hadn't responded. There was probably a separate thread already started where I was excluded and labelled as a misery. I staggered to the bathroom, where I stayed slumped on the floor until at last the dawn broke and I felt I could maybe breathe again.

TWENTY YEARS EARLIER

For her part, Lucy had thought the holidays would never come to an end. Christmas was normally her favourite time of year. She adored the time spent with her mum and dad, cocooned away from the world, following the traditions that had been a solid part of her life for as long as she could remember. She was vaguely aware that she had probably spoilt Christmas for her parents and that this was a precious time for them both, given they worked full-time. However, Lucy struggled to give this more than a passing thought, such was her obsession with the delightful Kate and the ongoing chatter in her mind as to just what had gone wrong between them. Had she been too forward? Maybe Kate had been jealous seeing her with her friends and so had tried to make her jealous with Mr Harris. The narrative in her mind was relentless, played out alongside the repeating lament of 'Lilac Wine', as Lucy started to feel maybe she was going a little crazy. It was all-encompassing and allowed no room for anything else. Lucy ignored her friends for the whole break, instead for the first days of the holiday wandering near the locations that she knew Kate often visited, and returning again and again to Myspace to try and glean any clues as to where Kate expected her to go.

And then on the day before Christmas Eve, Lucy searched Kate's name and saw she had been tagged in a post showing a grinning Kate surrounded by her family, with the caption 'Christmas can finally start now this one is home'.

Lucy was lost to the misery, knowing that Kate was now over two hundred miles away from her, and there would be no hoped-for chance encounter where the two of them could confess their deep feelings for each other. And so, each day after that had just been hours to be endured, time to waste until she could be back at school and see her beloved Kate again.

Cath had never been a parent to celebrate the end of the school holidays as she typically enjoyed her daughter being at home and the easy flow of the day with no timetable to adhere to. However, she was ashamed to find herself counting down the days until school started back, and when Lucy slammed out the door that morning, with something approaching a genuine smile on her face, Cath shouted her goodbyes and finally felt she could breathe again.

CATH

Cath had also been awake from the first light of dawn. She was surprised how well she had slept. Most nights, but particularly now that Lucy was so far away, Cath had a few hours in the lonely darkness to fret about her daughter; but she had sunk into a dreamless rest and was awake now with a sense of anticipation. Part of that was remembering that very soon Lucy would be home, but she was also excited to meet Izzy, her new friend, for that swim.

Izzy was already in the water when Cath arrived, effortlessly eating up the length of the pool, and for a moment Cath was quite transfixed by the younger woman's grace in the water. She hurriedly got changed and slipped into the pool, where Izzy acknowledged her with a grin and a wave, before they both started their swim. It was nice, Cath reflected, that they were both content to do their own thing - no need to make small talk if they happened to reach the end at the same time - both just concentrating on letting the activity in the water work its magic.

Cath finished her fifty lengths and smiled as she saw Izzy was still powering away. She signalled that she was getting out and mimed the action of drinking as a question, to which her new friend responded enthusiastically. She was a dab hand at changing quickly and was soon ordering drinks and took a chance on a bacon sandwich for them both. Just as the food and drinks were brought to the table, Izzy appeared.

Cath grinned at her new friend. 'Perfect timing. I've been a bit presumptuous on the food side; I do hope you're not vegetarian, but if you are I will eat them both.'

'You must have read my mind - I'm always starving after a swim.' Izzy leant forwards to give Cath a quick kiss on the cheek before flopping in the chair and giving a contented sigh as she picked up the sandwich in front of her. 'Yum, nice and crispy too.'

Cath couldn't help but feel a warm glow from Izzy's approval, and she realised the young woman was like that. At the same time as making you feel so comfortable, you also wanted to do your best to please her. And there was no doubt you felt really good once you earned that approval.

The two sat in companiable silence for a while, and then Cath asked, 'So, who's looking after your daughter whilst you're here?'

'Hah! Is that the subtle way of asking me if I'm married?'

Cath coloured but Izzy laughed and continued. 'I do have a husband, and he is indeed doing his share of the childcare. It's just that the husband and I no longer live together. Means I get plenty of time to indulge my passion for the pool. Helped by the fact that he feels such guilt we are no longer a couple!'

Cath nodded, dying to ask what he had done, but instead taking another bite of her sandwich. No doubt Izzy would tell her if she felt ready to share more of her story.

'What about you Cath. Do you have family?'

And before she knew it, Cath was chatting away about Jon and their dream holiday, their daughter Lucy and granddaughter Milly. As they ate and drank and felt the pleasant warmth of the early morning sun, Cath barely noticed that she was doing all the talking, with a few gentle prompts from her companion.

'And your family Cath, are they local?'

'Oh yes, five minutes away, which is nice as I get to see them regularly.'

'Family is so important I think, especially when you have little ones. And... Oh, hang on a minute. Just the person I need to speak to!'

Whatever Izzy was about to say, Cath didn't find out,

as the young woman jumped to her feet and suddenly waved frantically at a lady who had just entered the seating area. 'Excuse me Cath, I just need to catch up with Dawn about something.'

Cath watched as Izzy danced across the decking, moving as if the cafe floor was a stage and the people at the tables her adoring audience, which Cath reflected wryly, they certainly were. She'd noticed that about Izzy - she was a performer, a whirlwind, but her energy was contagious. She could see people at the tables smiling as Izzy, the star, whirled past them, a blur of colour. She watched as she reached Dawn and greeted her with her normal hug and kiss. 'How lovely and refreshing to be so free and unconcerned with what people thought of you,' reflected Cath as she watched the two women talking. How she wished her Lucy could be more like that, unencumbered by the worry of how other people might judge you. Dawn was smiling as Izzy animatedly regaled her, arms waving, and then both women laughed as Dawn walked away, still smiling, and Izzy made her way back to Cath.

'Sorry about that, I just needed to finalise the arrangements for the private hire of the pool I have next Friday.'

'Ooh very posh, private hire - is it for a special occasion?'

'Well, I may regret this, but I've organised for all the children who are starting school this September and their mums to meet here for a splash in the sun and a bit of a picnic. I just thought it would be nice to break the ice before the pressure of school begins, for the mums more than the kids to be honest.' Izzy grinned, showing perfect white teeth.

'Oh, what a nice idea. Milly starts school this time and I know Lucy is absolutely terrified. I'm sure that Milly is going to be just fine, but I can't help but worry about Lucy.' Cath surprised herself by opening up to this relative stranger. It was just that Izzy was so easy to talk to.

'It is tough. I know when my nephew started school, my sister cried for a week!'

Cath relaxed. At least Izzy understood.

The younger woman looked at her watch and stood. 'Whoops, look at the time - I've got to dash. Same time next week?'

Cath nodded, feeling a little like a giggly schoolgirl at the prospect of meeting up with this lovely woman again. She was relieved to find it wasn't just a one-off spurred by the guilt of her daughter's attempted drowning. Smiling, she watched Izzy sashay towards the exit before she suddenly stopped and pirouetted round and walked back.

'Which school is your granddaughter starting at?'

'St Wilfred's, you know, just on North Street.'

'No way! That's the same as Elizabeth. Which means your granddaughter is hopefully coming on Friday, which means that you of course must come too. See you Friday!'

Cath smiled. Maybe things were taking a turn for the better. She walked home feeling lighter than she had for some time. She couldn't wait for Friday now and would do everything she could to make sure that Lucy and Izzy, and of course their daughters, became the very best of friends.

LUCY

The journey home was relatively stress free, though silent. Rob was still recovering from his hangover but had perked up as we stopped off for breakfast at McDonald's. This time there was no suggestion from me that Milly should try and make a healthy choice, and she was delighted when I agreed a McFlurry for breakfast was indeed the only sensible option. I saw Rob wink at our daughter, and for the first time in a long time, I felt that we really were back to being 'The Three Musketeers'.

'Mummy should drink too much wine more often, don't you think Milly?'

As I responded with mock outrage, the two of them dissolved into easy laughter and before long I joined in, feeling that the holiday had done just the job that was needed. As we started to head South down the A1, I heard Rob's phone start to beep as the mobile signal strengthened. Shit, that meant I had signal too. I'd been enjoying the helplessness of not being able to look online to see if anything else had developed on the chats. In the back of the car, Milly had fallen asleep, the two weeks of late nights and full days on the beach finally catching up with her. Rob was listening to the radio and so I decided to sneak a look. Better to face it now than let it become some huge monster lurking in my subconsciousness.

Opening WhatsApp, I was relieved to see that there had at last been something posted on the group chat, which meant that Izzy's post naming me had been lost in the subsequent discussion of what people were planning to wear to the pool on Friday. I felt I could breathe again, and I was just about to shut off my phone and follow Milly's lead of a nap in the car, when

I saw I had a message request. Clicking on the chat, it was a message from Izzy.

> *Hi Lucy, I hope you don't mind me messaging like this, but turns out it's a small world! I have just been swimming with your mum and as we chatted, I suddenly realised that Cath's daughter Lucy was the elusive Lucy from our parents' group. Cath explained you have been away on holiday with rubbish reception so you might not have seen about the pool party on Friday. Don't get your hopes up. It's for the children, rather than something in the style of an Ibiza foam party. Anyway, I invited your mum along, so you have to come really. Let me know. Hope you've had a marvellous holiday xxx*

Like the first message Izzy had posted in the group chat, there was something about this message that was tingling the nerves of some memory, but I couldn't place it. Shaking my head, I smiled. Looked like my mum had inadvertently come to my rescue yet again. Well, I could reply to this message - that was easy - and it seemed my mum had given me the perfect excuse should I decide to finally pop my cherry on the parents' group.

'Come on, you can do this for Milly - time to put on the big girl pants.' I hadn't realised I had whispered the words aloud until Rob asked, 'Sorry, what did you say?'

'Nothing, just remembered I need to get Milly new pants for school.'

'The way your mind works, it's like a butterfly,' he said, but his smile and hand on my knee took any sting out of the words and I smiled affectionately, not feeling the judgement that I would have sensed two weeks ago.

As Rob concentrated on the driving, I spent far too long

debating which message to answer first. I decided I would go on the group chat first - that way I could pretend I had responded before I saw Izzy's message. Then I would accept her message and make some breezy reply. Yes, this was all perfect. My hands were shaking as I opened the parent group chat and I wasn't sure if it was from the waves of panic that were rolling over me, far more powerful than the waves we had left at the beach, or all a part of the dull hangover that promised to stay with me for the remainder of the day.

> *Hey, sorry I am late to the party! I'm Lucy, mum to Milly, and we are just on our way back from our holidays where signal was intermittent. We have had a magical time though and I thought I would have the holiday blues until I managed to read through this lovely thread. Love it! Milly and I are a definite yes for the pool party, and put me down for pizza night. Will be great to meet everyone.*

I hesitated for a moment then added:

> *And a big thank you to Heidi and Izzy for organising everything on here. So helpful and so nice to know it's not just me worrying xxx*

I read it through. It really didn't sound like me at all. I smiled to myself as I realised I probably sounded like Bella in her guest book entry. Well, that was perfect, as when I was home 'Be more Bella' was going to be my battle cry for the day. Smiling with satisfaction, I pressed send and then opened the message from Izzy. I liked this woman already, despite the fact I had never met her, and I just knew we were going to be friends. I needed friends, this holiday had taught me that. I had spent too long trapped in this bubble focused on Milly, and before that, centred on Rob. It was time for me now. And I felt reassured that Mum obviously liked her too. Mum was a great judge of character.

> *Izzy, a small world indeed. Thank you for your message and for organising the pool party. Maybe we can do Ibiza next year! Can't wait to meet you, and Milly is so excited to get an early intro to her new classmates - what a great idea! Let me know if you would like me to do anything to help.*

I hesitated over that bit. What if she did ask me to do anything? Then I decided I could always rope Mum in to support.

See you Friday! xxx

There, all done. I realised I felt better already. I hadn't understood that the niggle of not getting involved in the thread had been causing me such anxiety, and how easily it was sorted.

Rob glanced over at me. 'What are you looking so pleased about?'

'Milly and I have been invited to a pool party on Friday. Izzy, one of the mums, has organised it.'

'Bloody hell, we better turn round.' I looked at him puzzled as he continued. 'I seem to have left my wife back at Beach Cottage!'

'Very funny.' But again I felt the warm glow, realising that it had been a long time since Rob had teased me. It had been a long time since Rob and I had talked about anything other than Milly, and it felt good to feel like my own person again.

'Well, the woman who is an imposter for your wife has also agreed to attend a Pizza and Prosecco evening!'

'Careful, I'll crash the car. I'm getting on a bit you know. My heart can't take all these shocks.'

Although Rob's tone was light-hearted, I noticed he continued to smile for most of the journey home, and for the first time I realised how hard the last few years had been for him.

Turning back to my phone, I started to scroll through the photos of the holiday; and when I came to the selfie I had taken on the last night, I admired again how I had captured the spirit of Bella. I liked the fact that the photo didn't look like me at all. Quickly, I selected that as my new profile picture on Facebook. Clicking on WhatsApp I changed my profile there too. My old photo was one I had always loved of me and Mum at the outdoor pool. I felt a bit sad replacing it, but I wanted my new friends to see the new me.

Seeing that we were still nearly an hour away from home, I clicked on the messages from each of the mums in the group to see what they looked like. Most people had photos with a glass in their hand, dolled up for a night out. Heidi's photo was her with her two children, stood with the London Eye in the background. That was about right for Heidi I judged - the perfect family. Izzy was one of those annoying people who didn't have a photo uploaded, so I was left looking at a grey silhouette. In my imagination, Izzy was a bit of a party animal, but I decided that maybe she was a bit plump. I know I was being judgemental and locking her in a stereotypical box, but I had decided, by the time we made the final turning towards home, that Izzy was a larger-than-life character, a bit mumsy, probably did a lot of baking and then ate most of it. Oh yes, I built up quite a picture in my mind, and I had no idea how wrong I was.

CATH

Cath had been tracking Lucy's 'Find My' and breathed a sigh of relief when she saw that they had arrived home. Right on cue, her mobile rang.

'Hi, it's only me. We're back! Can Milly and I come round for lunch tomorrow? Rob needs to go through his work emails, so I thought we'd leave him in peace.'

Cath was delighted with this plan. She would get to see them without looking like she was fussing.

'Of course. Can't wait to see you and hear all about your holiday.'

'Brilliant, see you about eleven. And you can tell me all about blowsy Izzy. Love you.'

'Love you too.'

The line went dead, and Cath put her phone down and frowned. Blowsy Izzy. Where on earth had Lucy got that from? She was going to get quite a shock when she met her in person. Wandering through to the lounge, she found Jon on his iPad watching the YouTube channel of some people he had found touring Europe in a motorhome. He was completely obsessed with this and had started dropping hints about how they could have the freedom of 'van life' on their holiday. Cath had pointed out that if van life included emptying the toilet, then the money would be better spent on a nice hotel. Still, it was nice to see Jon so enthusiastic about something, and she noted the deep furrow between his eyes seemed to have softened over the last few days. Maybe she had done him a disservice thinking he didn't worry about Lucy. Maybe he was haunted the same way she was. They should talk about it more openly, but then she acknowledged maybe they both feared that speaking about it out loud would somehow conjure the trouble back to their lives.

'Pub for tea?' she suggested, and Jon grinned.

'You don't need to ask me twice. How soon can you be ready?'

They had a lovely evening. The usual crowd were in and as was the normal pattern, they ended up being there longer than they had intended. Giggling as they walked arm in arm a little unsteadily home. Watching the bats perform their swooping dance in the glow of the streetlight at the end of the road, Cath reflected that this had been a much better Saturday than two weeks ago. Since discovering the happy coincidence that her new swimming friend was in the same mums' group as Lucy, Cath had allowed herself to dream a little the same as Jon, and it felt good to feel they were finally moving towards the future they had always imagined.

Cath and Jon both slept well that night and were up early, looking forward to the arrival of their little family. Cath made an effort to get as much prepared for lunch as possible so that she could focus all her attention on hearing all about the holiday, and of course have lots of cuddles with Milly. By eleven o'clock she was stood in the lounge, pretending not to be looking for Lucy's car.

As she saw the familiar red mini pull in the drive, she rushed to the back door to scoop a laughing Milly in her arms and cover her in kisses whilst the little girl giggled and wriggled to be put down. Once back on her feet, Milly ran in the house in search of her beloved grandad, and Cath could turn her attention to Lucy.

Cath had fallen into a well-rehearsed routine when greeting Lucy. It was so normal to her now that she barely realised what she was doing: a sweep with the eye from Lucy's face down to her feet, looking all the time for something that might seem off. Moving towards her daughter to wrap her in her arms, Cath could only feel relief that Lucy was once more back in her normal world where Cath could keep her safe.

'Wow, you're a great colour - the sun obviously shone for you.'

Lucy laughed, 'Right until the last day, when we had a near biblical storm. It's been fantastic though. So much better than I expected.'

And Cath could not dispute that Lucy did look well. Her skin had that glow that told of long days outside and as ever, Cath was relieved to see Lucy had on a vest top, showing her unmarked arms.

'New outfit, Luce? That's not your normal style.'

And it wasn't. Lucy was a neutral tones sort of girl, in loose-fitting styles that covered more than they showed. Cath often thought she picked those colours and style in an effort to fade into the background - a desperation not to be noticed. Today the vest top Lucy was wearing showed off her toned arms and clung to her curves whilst highlighting her slim waist. The flowing skirt was a combination of vibrant, gorgeous colours, and whilst skimming the floor, Cath spotted a generous split which revealed a shapely golden freckled leg. And Lucy was wearing nail varnish. Pink nail varnish. Lucy never wore nail varnish.

'I bought some new stuff on holiday. Figured I was due a bit of a style overhaul, no big deal.'

Lucy was chattering away as they moved through the house to the back garden, and Cath trailed after her, reluctantly wondering if the problem was in fact all down to her. If she had lived like this for so long that she was starting to see problems when there were none. 'Come on Cath, time to get a grip girl.' Lucy looked really well, the brighter colours suited her; so why was she so disturbed by this slightly different version of her daughter? After all, she had been hoping for so long that Lucy would start to reclaim herself.

They settled in the sunshine and watched Milly tootling after her grandad to pick strawberries for pudding. The pair of them soon returned with a bowl full to brim of the luscious ruby jewels, Milly sporting a matching scarlet mouth, showing she had eaten as many as she had surrendered to the bowl.

Jon hugged Lucy and sank into his chair whilst Milly made a beeline for the slide and swing that her doting grandad had sacrificed his perfect lawn to install. For a moment the three adults sat in a comfortable silence, smiling at each other as they watched Milly's delight as she found ever more inventive positions to hurl herself down the slide. Glancing over at her beloved daughter, Cath noted that Lucy was still sitting relaxing in the chair, quietly watching, and felt that knot that had been present in her stomach for as long as she could remember loosen its grip slightly. Normally by this stage Lucy would be calling, in an increasingly frantic tone, for Milly to be careful before moving to hover by the slide, arms outstretched until Milly would stomp back to her grandparents in frustration. Well, this was a very welcome step forwards, although Cath noted the knuckles of Lucy's hands were white as they clenched the arm of her chair in what was clearly a monumental effort to give Milly her freedom. She was clearly not as relaxed as she was trying so hard to appear. Looking to ease the tension, Cath turned to Lucy.

'Come on, tell us everything. We have missed you.'

Lucy dragged her eyes away from her daughter and was soon in full flow about the holiday. Cath and Jon were content to just listen to her animated chatter. It was such a delight to hear Lucy talk about the friends they had made, though obviously she had been closer to one of the women in the group than the rest.

'So do you think you will keep in touch now you are all home?' asked Jon, once Lucy finally paused for breath.

'Well, Rob is planning a golf holiday with Steve, but whether we do anything else I'm not sure. After all, we have our lives at home, and it will be busy with Milly starting school.'

'I suppose so, but you seemed to really hit it off with Bella. It would be a shame not to stay in touch.'

Lucy hesitated just long enough for Cath to turn her eyes from watching Milly to focus on her daughter, who looked flustered as she said, 'Oh Bella wasn't there when we were. She was there the week before.'

'You're losing your marbles dear,' laughed Jon, who had only been half listening as he continued to look at motorhomes on the internet. Cath pondered whether to protest at the injustice of it all. After all, Lucy's tales of the holidays had included lots of mentions of Bella - her wonderful clothes, her dawn swims, the upset over her daughter's school place and how much the group missed her. She had just naturally assumed that Lucy had spent time with the woman, which had not seemed an unreasonable assumption in the slightest. Opening her mouth to share this, Cath glanced at Lucy and decided to let it go.

'Oh, how silly of me. I just get so confused with all these new names.' There was a slightly too long beat of silence, which put Cath back on high alert, before Lucy laughed and hugged her.

'Never change, Mum,' she said, which Cath reflected was rather ironic, as it wasn't her changing that had caused all the upset in the first place.

Lunch passed pleasantly enough, and both Lucy and Milly asked for seconds, which were willingly piled onto their plates. When everyone was full, Jon declared he was going to take the dog for a walk before he fell asleep and Milly begged to join him, clearly hoping the walk could take in a diversion to feed the ducks. Lucy and Cath moved back to the garden and for a while sat in quiet companionship before Cath broke the silence.

'How funny meeting Izzy at the pool and it turning out her daughter will be in the same class as Milly.'

'She messaged me yesterday to say she had met you. It was good really as I had been a bit worried about what to say in the parents' group, and Izzy's message gave me the push I needed.'

Cath smiled. 'Izzy's like that. She somehow says the right thing at just the right time. I do like her, and I think you will too. I've not seen that much of Elizabeth, but if she's like her mum she will be a lovely friend for Milly.'

'Come on then, tell me what she's like. I already have such a picture built up in my mind.'

Cath smiled. 'I don't think I can do Izzy justice, so best you find out for yourself on Friday.'

Afterwards, Cath wondered if she should have been less mysterious about Izzy. Had this sown the seed in Lucy's mind, planted the thought that started to draw her back to that dark place that she had been free of for so long?

TWENTY YEARS EARLIER

The bus journey to school seemed never-ending. Lucy tucked herself in the corner, ignoring the greetings of her friends and silently counted in her head the seconds, working out just how long it was until she would be in school and at least in the same location as her Kate. In her pocket she had the precious bee bracelet, retrieved from the pool of sick and carefully packaged in a new box and lovingly re-wrapped. She would give it to Kate at the earliest opportunity, and she smiled to herself as she wondered if Kate would have brought her gift into school or if she planned to pass it over when they met up later on. Lucy couldn't wait to hear all about how awful Mr Harris had been and how Kate had struggled to get rid of him.

'Come on dreamer, we're here,' Anna nudged Lucy as she passed her on her way off the bus. Lucy noticed Anna was looking at her a bit funny again and gave a bright smile. She supposed it was understandable that her close friends would start to feel threatened by this new and very important relationship that was bound to take centre stage in her life. She was sure things would settle once everything was out in the open and everyone could see just how right the two of them were for each other.

'I'll catch up with you in a bit,' smiled Lucy. 'Just got something I need do first.'

And she raced off, hearing Dan ask, 'What's up with the wicked witch?' and heard Anna muffling her laugh as she no doubt punched his arm and instructed him to behave. But the gentle mockery of her friends barely registered as Lucy hurried towards the English department, where she knew Kate would likely be setting up her room for first lesson. She wouldn't have long, but she didn't need long, and they would have plenty of time once things were out in the open.

Tapping on the door, she went in the classroom but halted awkwardly when she spotted Mr Harris was already there, trying to spoil her chances.

'Oh, hello Lucy, happy new year,' Kate smiled warmly. 'Come in. Is there something I can help you with?'

Lucy shuffled though the door and stood aside to let Mr Harris pass her, smiling as he wished Kate a good day. Suddenly, everything Lucy had planned to say to Kate slipped from her mind and she found all she could do was stare, drinking in the sight of her, knowing that she was finally where she needed to be.

'I really do need to get on - first day of term and all that. What can I help you with, or is it something that can wait for the lesson?'

Lucy was a little taken aback at the formality of Kate's tone now that they were alone in the room, but she figured that Kate needed to be wary as you never knew who could be lurking around doors. Rumours in the school could spread even when there was no basis for the stories circulating.

'I just got you this,' said Lucy quietly. 'And I wanted to give it to you before school started so you can wear it and know that I am thinking of you.' Shyly, she held out her hand with the beautifully wrapped gift, longing to see the light in Kate's eyes when she realised the care Lucy had put into finding this treasure. But instead of reaching for the present, Kate took a step back and Lucy was concerned to see a look of confusion, swiftly followed by panic, cross her face.

For a moment Lucy thought Kate was going to flee the room, but she took a deep breath and in a shaking voice replied, 'Lucy, you know I can't accept this. It's very kind of you, but it's really not appropriate.'

Lucy couldn't help herself. The two weeks of misery had built to this moment, and she felt pure anger burn through her as she struggled to stop the tears that were now pouring down her face, smudging the mascara and joining the ugly snot that she was failing to sniff away.

'Appropriate. Hah! What's not appropriate is you asking me out before Christmas and then ignoring me all night and leaving with Mr Harris.'

Kate's confusion increased. 'Lucy, I have no idea what you are...'

But Lucy wasn't going to be interrupted. 'No, let me finish. Well, if your aim was to make me feel bad and to ruin my Christmas, you will be happy to know that you succeeded.'

Kate stared, horrified at Lucy, and glanced at the door, as if hoping to summon anyone to come and help. 'Lucy, I have got no idea where this is coming from, but let's go and find your form teacher and we can get this sorted.'

'You are an absolute b-b-b-bitch!' Lucy could barely speak through the tears. 'I hate you!' She shoved Kate to the floor and fled the classroom, barely registering the sickening crack as Kate's head hit the corner of the desk.

PART TWO

Home

LUCY

Milly's birthday was a quiet affair, though as expected she was delighted with her gifts. It had always surprised me that Mum and Rob have never pushed me to throw more of a celebration or nagged me to invite a little group of friends round to play party games and spill lemonade on the carpet, but it seems we all recognise that not all the memories of this time are happy ones. So instead, we gather round Milly, who is beaming as she blows out the five candles on the birthday cake Mum collected from M&S, and breathe a collective sigh of relief that the day is done for another year.

The week leading up to the pool party flew by. You know what it's like when you get back from holiday - it's all endless washing and sorting until you feel like you've never been away. Rob had it worse as his work was manic, as usual, so his long days had stretched to be even longer as he tried to catch up. 'Makes you wonder if it's worth even trying to go away,' he grumbled as he fumbled to switch the alarm off on Thursday morning. Maybe it was because he was so tired that we had the row that night.

My day had been fraught. At the last minute, I had decided that I needed a new swimsuit for the party tomorrow. It was a sunny day, and Milly grumbled the whole time we were at the shops. I gradually got hotter and more flustered as we squeezed in the tiny changing rooms, and I tried to find something that I wouldn't feel horrific in meeting twenty-five strangers for the first time.

'Bloody stupid idea to have a pool party,' I grumbled as I dragged Milly into yet another shop, promising this was the last one and we could have an ice cream after. I saw the costume straight away, and I immediately recognised I had found *the one*. I knew it would look amazing on, because it had looked amazing on Bella as she had laughed at me from Lydia's phone, splashing in the shallow waves, a cocktail in hand. I didn't even need to try it on, and whilst the price tag made me flinch slightly, I felt I simply had no choice in the matter. As I made my way to the till, I passed the accessories and my breath caught as I spotted the perfect ankle bracelet which was an exact replica of the one I had spied on Bella. As I scanned the floor for the checkout, my eye was focused on yet more pieces that I had so lusted over as I had devoured the images of Bella on Lydia's phone, so naturally I wandered over for a look. Half an hour later, and delighted with my purchases, we emerged into the sunshine. I let Milly choose the biggest ice cream they sold, complete with the sweet, sticky pink sauce and sprinkles that I had always denied her, fearing for the damage they would do to her teeth.

As we waited to cross the road, Milly happily licking the dribbling mixture of pink and white leaving a sticky trail on her hands, I spotted a face in the crowd that didn't belong there. Rob was hurrying out of the Langdale Hotel, turning to wave to whoever was stood in the shelter of the doorway. I raised my hand to shout out to him, but he disappeared round the corner before the green man let us know it was safe for us to cross, and by the time we made it over the road there was no sign of him. I debated whether to nip in to his office to say hello, but told myself he had such a lot on, we would be an unwelcome distraction. He would already be cursing that he had been dragged out to lunch with clients. The truth was, I was keen to get home to try on my new swimsuit. A quick diversion into Waitrose to stock up on goodies for tomorrow's picnic, and we were soon back home.

Sitting Milly in front of the television with some toast and jam, I ruefully acknowledged I wasn't going to be winning any 'Mother of the Year' awards today. Never mind, it was just one day, and the start of a new life. Nodding vaguely in agreement to Milly's plea for chocolate, I left her to help herself and ran upstairs, closing the curtains, to try on my purchase. I was ridiculously excited and as I slipped on the costume, I felt the whisper of the fabric cling to my skin. This wasn't just about a new swimsuit and different clothes. It felt like I was slipping on a whole new person. Someone I liked a lot better than me.

Looking in the mirror in our ensuite was a bit of a shock. Whilst the costume looked nice, I had fully expected to see the reflection of Bella staring back, but instead, it was just me - Lucy, in a rather nice swimsuit, looking a little uncomfortable. Still, with the right bits of jewellery, I was confident I could pull it off, so removed the tags, discarding them and the packaging in the bathroom bin, and put the swimming costume with the rest of the things I had laid out ready for tomorrow.

Figuring Rob wouldn't want a great deal if he had eaten at lunchtime, Milly and I had fish finger sandwiches for tea, and Milly was already fast asleep in bed by the time I heard Rob's car pull in the drive. He was clearly in a grumpy mood as he walked through the door.

'Do you have to park your car like it's been abandoned in the middle of the drive? Makes it very difficult to get out of my car by the time I've squeezed in the ridiculously small space you've left.'

As he'd been grumbling, he had reached the fridge and popped the top off a cold beer, which was most unlike Rob, who prided himself for never drinking on a school night. Even at the client dinners he was often forced to attend, he would stick to sparkling water, using the excuse that he had the car. 'What's for dinner? I'm absolutely starving.'

'There's some pate and cheese in the fridge,' I offered, knowing this was a favourite, but my voice faltered as Rob whipped round. 'You've been at home all day and you tell me we are having pate and cheese. Unbelievable!'

'Well, I've already eaten. I had fish fingers with Milly.' My voice trailed off as Rob looked at me in disbelief. 'Look, you go and get changed and I'll nip out and get fish and chips. I won't be long.'

I was lucky - I found a parking space easily and the queue was short, so I was back home within half an hour. Remembering the recycling bin was due to be collected, I thought I'd get some brownie points by saving Rob a job; so, leaving the fish and chips in the car, I nipped through the back gate. Rob was out in the garden talking softly on the phone, and for some reason I stood still quietly listening.

'I know what you're saying, but we can't go on like this. I'm just not prepared to take the risk.'

There was silence whilst he listened. 'Well, I'm sorry for that obviously, but I don't think you can lay the blame for that at my door.' Silence again before he firmly spoke. 'No, I won't be able to do that again. Goodbye.'

I don't know why but I turned back to the car without letting him know I was there. I felt bad for listening in on his conversation and realised his work was obviously more stressful than usual. Grabbing the steaming fish and chips, I clattered through the front door, loudly announcing my presence with a cheery, 'I'm back.' Rob came to greet me, hair damp from the shower, and enveloped me in a hug.

'Thank you for going to get those for me, and I'm sorry I was such a grump earlier. I've had a bugger of a day. I got dragged out to a lunchtime meeting that I really didn't need to be at, and to add insult to injury, I wasn't even invited for the bit that involved food!'

I let out a breath, as relief flooded my body, and laughed. 'I thought I saw you in town, but you were in a rush, and we couldn't catch you.'

'Oh, I wish you had, that would have improved my day. Come on, let's sit and watch some TV and you can steal my chips.'

Rob dozed on the sofa, and I was content to watch the

mindless TV. It was funny thing waiting for the pool party. I felt a bit like a kid on Christmas Eve, longing for the next day to come, but relishing the anticipation which made me feel so alive.

I slept surprisingly well until the next morning that started with the rude awakening of, 'Fuck, we forgot to put the blue bin out!' As Rob dashed out to pull the bin out to join those of our better organised neighbours, I put on coffee. Rob emerged from the shower in his version of Dress-Down Friday and I nuzzled into him, 'Mm you smell nice, is that new?'

Rob hesitated. 'Shows how much notice you take - I got it before the holidays. Will you put my coffee in a cup to go? I've got a hell of a day again.' He dashed for the door before turning to blow me a kiss. 'Have a great time at the party. You're going to knock them dead in that new swimsuit, or you should do with the amount it cost!' And with a bang of the door, he was gone.

The house always seemed a little larger when Rob wasn't there. Often, I felt his absence sharply and would stick to the kitchen in an attempt to ward off the loneliness, but today both me and the house seemed to breathe a sigh of relief as the whirlwind of nervous tension departed for another day. I sat down to enjoy my coffee, reflecting how lucky I was with Rob. I hadn't told him I had been shopping in town yesterday, but he had clearly figured it out when he saw the suit and the labels that I had abandoned in our bedroom. He never moaned about the amount I spent or pointed out that I wasn't earning anything. I was very lucky, and I vowed to make sure Rob knew how much I appreciated him.

Mum picked me up at ten-thirty on the dot. That was the thing about Mum - she was dependable. I'd dug out the wicker picnic basket that we had received as a wedding present but never really used as it wasn't really practical to lug out on a hike; and somehow we never found the opportunity for the envisaged lazy afternoons lounging in a grassy meadow, feeding each other strawberries and sipping champagne. Mum had a more practical cool box and luckily had space for me to fit all our food too. I noticed a raised eye when I opened the door to her, but amazingly she refrained from making any comment, and normally I would have just let it pass. Instead, I gave an elaborate twirl, the sleeveless pink dress billowing around me as the gold thread pattern caught the sun, the same way as the dust on my sideboard did. 'Do you like?'

Mum considered, then smiled. 'I do like, but would never have picked that for you in a million years.'

I smiled. 'Well I figured it was time to live dangerously.' As Mum rushed to hug Milly, I whispered, 'To be more Bella.'

Mum has always had amazing hearing, unless it suits her not to have. 'What did you say?'

I smiled sweetly. 'I said that twirl made me dizzy.' Mum frowned but let it go.

We were soon parking up at the pool, and could see that there was already quite a crowd of mums congregating by the entrance, their accompanying children impatiently tugging at their hands, eager to feel the cool relief of the water. Suddenly, I felt foolish in my colourful dress and hippy-type jewellery. There was Heidi, immaculate in shorts and t-shirt following a nautical theme, and it seemed that most of the other mums were dressed in a similar fashion, just in various shades of colour. Milly was impatient to get out of the car, showing no fear at meeting her potential new friends for the first time, and I wished I was like her, eager to face the world head on. Mum, bless her, clearly knew how I was feeling and laid a reassuring hand over mine, giving it a quick squeeze and whispering, 'Into the fray, dear girl.'

Breathing a well-practiced calming meditation, I was able to step out onto the sizzling tarmac, collect our bags from the boot and, sending up silent thanks that Mum's there with me, I headed towards the entrance, just as the doors opened and the congregation moved inside. The three of us duly shuffled along behind them, and suddenly there was the pool, empty and inviting us to ruin the stillness of the top by leaping into the blue. Groups were already setting up picnic blankets and securing tables in the cafe area, and for a moment I felt the familiar wave of panic as I looked to Mum for guidance what to do now. But Mum was distracted, waving over at a lady with her young daughter, who had set up the most wonderful spot and was now beckoning Mum over to join her.

'Over here Cath, I bagged this spot for us all. It is so lovely to meet you in person Lucy. I'm Izzy. I feel like I know you already from everything your Mum has told me about you.'

I could only stand there completely dumb, because I certainly knew her already. Standing in front of me, in actual real life, was unmistakably Bella.

TWENTY YEARS EARLIER

Anna was concerned about Lucy. They hadn't really kept in touch at all over the holidays, and the couple of invitations Anna had made to come round for a sleepover or to go for a coffee in town to look at the sales had been ignored. At first Anna was convinced that this was all to do with the drinks they had out on the last night of term, but as she fretted about the situation, she realised there was something more going on. On the last Saturday of the holidays the 'Fabulous Five' had arranged to meet at Pizza Hut, but it soon became apparent to the group that this evening there would just be the four of them.

'I just can't understand it,' Lisa mused as she made her third trip to the salad bar. 'Lucy, out of all of us, was the one so upset when we all started going our separate ways.'

'And I won't be home again until the summer and I've not managed to catch up with her at all,' mused Jill, who had started to look quite tearful at missing her old friend.

'And to not even tell us she wasn't coming tonight,' offered Amy. 'It's just odd.'

And odd, thought Anna as she headed to form room, was really not a big enough word to describe the change in her friend. As if thinking about Lucy had somehow summoned her into the corridor, Anna was nearly knocked to the floor as a gasping Lucy pushed past her.

'Hey, Lucy wait,' shouted Anna after her friend as she

grabbed her arm, and Lucy finally stopped and then sank to the floor. Not crying, but shaking as if she had been pulled from an icy lake, before finally turning to look at Anna with a blank stare that told Anna that her friend wasn't really seeing her at all. Looking at her watch, Anna made a quick decision to lead Lucy to the bistro. It would be empty now as the rest of the year would be at morning registration and they could have some privacy to allow Lucy to gather herself together before lessons started.

Lucy trailed after Anna without saying a word, reminding Anna of the way her little sister would trustingly follow her around. But there was something in the way Lucy held herself that, when they arrived at the bistro and got settled in the corner, deterred Anna from giving her friend a hug, even though she desperately wanted to try and offer her friend some comfort. For a few minutes they sat in an uncomfortable silence and just as Anna was about to speak, Lucy gave a sob, and once her words started it seemed like they would never stop.

'I've been seeing someone, and they promised me that we would be together. That we were special together. I've changed everything to be the person they want me to be, but now they've decided they don't want me anymore.' As she spoke, Lucy was fiddling with the sleeves of her top and to Anna's horror, she could see what at first looked to be scratches, as if she had fallen into brambles like they used to when they went blackberry picking as kids. Anna was transfixed by the sight and struggled to drag her gaze from Lucy's wrists to look her friend in the face as she continued talking.

'They've been punishing over the holidays because I didn't do what they wanted me to do, and I'm just so sad I don't know what to do.'

Lucy raised her sleeve to wipe her nose and as she did so, Anna grabbed her hands and held them tight, looking at her friend as if trying to find the Lucy she knew.

'Oh Lucy, what have you done?' Anna was now also crying as she rolled up Lucy's sleeves and saw the tell-tale red lines that painted the picture of how Lucy had spent those desperate nights alone in her room, trying to release the hurt with the distraction of another type of pain. Pulling her friend close, she stroked Lucy's hair and did her best to offer some comfort in a situation that she knew was way beyond her control. 'But who have you been seeing? Was it someone you met that night in the pub?'

For a moment Anna thought Lucy wasn't going to tell her. Lucy's face became blank, and it seemed like her eyes lost all emotion. Then, taking a deep breath, she looked at her friend.

'You have to promise not to say anything. Promise?'

'I promise. You know you can trust me, we have always told each other everything. We can get through this.'

'It's Kate.'

'Kate?' Anna took some time to understand that her friend was in love with a woman, but she had no idea who this person was. She desperately shuffled faces of everyone they knew through her mind to pinpoint the elusive Kate.

Lucy sounded frustrated now. 'You know Kate,' and as Anna shook her head, 'Kate, you know, Miss Oxenham.'

And at that point Anna knew that, for the first time, she would not be keeping the promise she had just made to her friend.

JON

Jon hadn't said anything to Cath, but he was worried about Lucy. For once, it wasn't linked to things that had happened in the past, or a worry about her post-natal depression, or whatever label they had put on it, but was rather linked to Rob.

Once a month, Jon went to meet with the group that Cath had charmingly nicknamed 'The Old Gits Club' and yesterday had been a bit of a special get together to say goodbye to Dave, who was chasing sunnier climes by moving to Spain. To give fitting tribute to the occasion, they had booked lunch at the Langdale Hotel, and very nice it had been too. Well, it had been nice up to a point. Cath had dropped him and a couple of the other 'old gits' off in town and they had agreed to shell out for a taxi home. After all, it's not every day one of your best mates leaves the country, so a move like that deserved celebrating and, as they laughingly pointed out to Dave, 'Who knows when you'll next see a decent pint!' The fact that he had had quite a few of these decent pints meant that Jon was, once again, making his way across the lobby to the Gents, when he saw Rob emerge from the lift that went to the upper floors of the hotel. Jon didn't know why he didn't shout out a hello - Rob wasn't with anyone - but he suddenly felt uncomfortable and so ducked into the Gents and tried to put it from his mind.

Of course, that didn't work at all, and at three am when he was awake for another trip to the loo, he realised he was going to get no more restful sleep unless he did something. As soon as Cath set off to Lucy's to give her a lift to this blasted pool party, which Jon was sick to death of hearing about before it had even happened, Jon headed back to the Langdale and approached the reception desk.

'Excuse me, but could you let me know where your meeting rooms are please?'

'Certainly sir -they are all down the corridor to the left of the main staircase, in the business centre. Can you tell me which company you are with, and I can let you know which room you are in?'

'Oh no sorry, I'm just scoping out some locations for a course we are running in the future and well, a number of our attendees have mobility problems so would need easy access.' Jon was a little concerned how easily the lie fell from his lips. And the very helpful young man on reception had explained that all the meeting rooms were on the ground floor with excellent disabled access. Jon felt his stomach churn as he asked, 'So no chance we may be on one of the upper floors then?'

'Absolutely not sir, the upper floors just house the bedrooms for the hotel. Please take a brochure and let me know if there's anything else I can do to help you with your booking.'

Jon mumbled his thanks and emerged into the sunshine wishing he had never seen Rob yesterday. If only he had said hello to his son-in-law like he would normally have done, they would have had their banal chat and Jon would have shared why he was there, and Rob would have done the same and that would have been the end of it. Instead, it was now awkward to mention it - how could he explain why he had hidden from Lucy's husband in the Gents' toilets? It made him look a fool. What the hell was he going to do now?

LUCY

'Izzy, how lovely to meet you.' I'm not sure how I managed to speak. Izzy moved towards me and before I knew it, I was enveloped in a warm hug and my senses were suddenly assaulted by the familiar scent of 'Lucky', which smelt completely different on her than it did on me. The scent was a part of her, it was just somehow right. Mum was chatting away as we settled on the colourful rug that had been set out in clearly the prime spot, perfect for the pool and cafe area, getting the best of the sun but with a couple of stolen parasols from the cafe offering shade for the little ones.

'One of the perks of organising the event,' whispered Izzy rather gleefully in my ear. 'You can get in before the general masses, and hey presto!' I laughed and couldn't help but feel a bit smug to be seated with Izzy, who was clearly rather popular and somehow knew everyone there.

As Milly tugged at my arm, urging me to get ready to swim, and hassling Mum to sort her arm bands, I watched Izzy sorting Elizabeth and wondered if I was going a little bit crazy. Maybe I had spent so long thinking about Bella that I was starting to see her everywhere. Or I supposed Izzy could be Bella. Really, I just needed to ask her, but the longer I left it, the more awkward it felt until the moment was lost, and Mum was leading Milly to the pool and Izzy was following them wearing...

Shit! I wasn't going crazy. She had on Bella's swimsuit - well, rather the same swimsuit that I had. Looking around, I wondered if I could maybe stay on the rug, keep my dress on and not invite the scrutiny of comparison. But Mum was beckoning me over and Izzy was looking at me as if deciding whether I would be worth getting to know better, and I *so* wanted to get to know her better, so, closing my eyes, I tugged my dress over my head and walked to the edge of the pool.

'Oh wow, we are clearly destined to be friends Lucy as we share the same exquisite taste,' Izzy grinned at me.

Mum turned to look and smiled. 'Ah snap, well luckily you both wear it well!'

The ice was well and truly broken and I jumped in, making Milly squeal and Mum telling me off like I was thirteen again. As we splashed in the water and Milly and Elizabeth played together as if they had been friends all their lives, Izzy proved to be a magnet for all the other mums, and so I met everyone too, and as I was so clearly with Izzy, everyone seemed to want to be my friend as well. Izzy made sure that I was brought into every conversation, and Mum watched on like the proud parent she was. It was nice to see Mum looking so relaxed, and it made me feel happy to know that at last Mum could see that I was moving forward.

Milly suddenly declared she was starving, and her claim set up the general consensus to move from the water to start the picnics. Normally I hate the part of getting out of the pool. I dread the walk to the changing rooms and the slightly icky feel of the not quite clean tiled floor beneath my feet, shivering as I sort Milly out first and then pulling on clothes that have trailed in the slimy grey water that has pooled on the floor. But today the sun was shining so I followed Izzy's lead, who lay her towel on the rug and allowed the sun to do its work. Milly had grabbed a handful of cocktail sausages and then seemed to have forgotten she was hungry as she and Elizabeth linked hands and walked over to join a small group of girls sitting making daisy chains. I could feel Mum's eyes on me as she pondered if I would jump up to follow them, but I contented myself with grabbing my phone from my bag to get a snap of the blossoming of friendship. As I did so, Izzy's eye caught the glint of the silver star charm dangling from my phone.

'Oh my God,' she laughed. 'I don't believe it.' And, groping in her own bag, she produced a phone with a charm that mirrored my own. 'Twins!' I grinned back at her. We were definitely going to be best friends.

'How long have you had that on your phone?' The sharpness of Mum's tone as she spoke to me stopped Izzy's laughter. Mum must have realised that she had snapped louder than she intended as she laughed and rolled her eyes as she said, 'What am I like, acting like I should know everything you say and do. What a coincidence. Did you buy it locally?'

Izzy answered before I could. 'I'm sure you can get them everywhere, but I bought mine from a little shop in Alnmouth when I was there on holiday a few weeks ago.'

I could feel Mum staring at me before she asked me, 'Is that where you got yours Lucy, because that really is a coincidence.'

There was a silence that stretched a beat too long as I struggled to find the words to fill it.

'I've just got back from staying near Beadnell,' I explained to Izzy, who widened her eyes.

'No way twinnie! We stayed at a lovely place near there - Beach Cottage.'

I was vaguely aware that Milly was stood at the edge of the rug, quietly listening to the conversation in that way five-year-olds do when they sense there might be something worth hearing.

I tried to feign a look of surprise, but I could feel the tell-tale spots of pink spreading on my cheeks, and I knew Mum would have spotted them too. I wasn't sure why I felt as if I had somehow been caught out, but I really wished I had said something when we had first arrived and I recognised Bella. That wish intensified as Milly filled the silence with, 'I knew I recognised you. I saw your photo on Lydia's phone. But she called you Bella then.' Milly looked at me confused as she continued, 'You must recognise her Mummy, you looked at loads of photos of her on Lydia's phone and you brought that photo of her home with you. You know, the photo where she's wearing the same dress that you went and bought.' And on delivering that bombshell, Milly grabbed the tray of chocolate fingers and ran back to share them with her waiting friends, leaving me to face the questioning stares of Mum and Izzy.

The chatter of the groups around us seemed to fade as a voice in my head instructed. 'Act normal, you know how these things go, just act normal.' I realised that once again I had let the silence stretch a few seconds too long. Izzy's face simply registered a mild puzzlement, but Mum's stony face told me she was expecting the worst.

'Well, I feel a bit of a fool now,' I smiled at the pair of them. 'To think my five-year-old daughter recognised you before I did.' I held Mum's gaze and noted that the hunch of her shoulders was relaxing a bit, whilst Izzy remained with a quizzical tilt to her perfect eyebrows. 'Do you know I nearly said to Mum that I thought I knew you from somewhere, but it was the name that did it.' At this point I mirrored Izzy's facial expression. Finally, all that time practicing in front of the mirror at Beach Cottage was paying off. Whilst Mum continued to look completely lost, I saw the realisation dawn across Izzy's face.

'Ah, Milly mentioned Lydia, so I'm guessing you stayed after us in Beach Cottage and met my alter ego.'

'Well, if your holiday persona is Bella, then yes, that's who I'm talking about.'

'Ha! That's settled it Cath - your daughter and I will have to be best friends as she has uncovered my guilty secret, and will no doubt be able to regale you with tales of the shocking behaviour I indulge in when I'm away from home. I decided Beth starting school was the perfect time for me to shed that wayward woman and become Izzy the responsible mum! Now tell me! Did you get dragged in with the overbearing gang the same as we did? What a complete nightmare!'

Izzy settled down to gossip about the gang: Lydia a complete alcoholic, Jen just so two-faced, Andy the man child and Steve a complete lech. I could only listen as Izzy told a completely different narrative to the picture the gang had of their holiday. As she spoke, I felt simple relief that I hadn't swapped numbers with Lydia and Jen. Izzy clearly had no intention of keeping in touch with them, and I knew without doubt exactly who I wanted to be friends with. Funny how life has a way of working out just fine.

After the picnics had been packed away and everyone was settling in for a last play in the pool, Izzy beckoned me over to the cafe entrance. 'I hope you don't mind, but your mum mentioned it was Milly's birthday earlier this week, so I thought it would be nice to get a cake for her to share with the rest of the class.'

I really didn't know what to say and could feel the tears start to well in my eyes. I wasn't used to people being so kind to me and I really wasn't sure how to behave. Izzy handed over the cake to me, and what a cake it was. Designed to look like a swimming pool, it was even iced with Milly's name and five sparkly candles. 'Go on, you take it. Milly will be so excited.'

I hesitated, unsure of the right thing to do, but Izzy strode ahead of me clapping her hands. 'Gather round everyone, Milly's mum has something very special to share with us all.'

The children gathered in a group and Milly was at the centre, hopping from foot to foot in excitement. 'Oh Mummy, this is the best birthday party ever!' I was going to shush her as I could see a couple of the mums swapping disapproving looks, but then Izzy started the chorus of 'Happy Birthday' and then I was caught up with cutting the cake and dishing out the sticky treat to the steady stream of eager children. I heard one of the mums mutter something about being surprised there were no party bags, and I flushed, worrying that I had got something wrong. But that thought was soon banished by the sheer look of joy on Milly's face as she laughed with her new classmates, proudly showing off a 'Birthday Girl' tiara that I assume the pool staff had given her.

By the end of the afternoon Milly and Beth were firm friends, and I like to think that the same could be said for myself and Izzy. I hadn't spoken to so many people in one day since, well probably since I was at school, and I felt giddy on the high of it all. As people started to drift off, they all came to say goodbye to us both; and I liked the way our names sounded together - Izzy and Lucy. I reflected how it had taken just one afternoon for us to be accepted as a pair, and if it bothered me slightly that I couldn't escape the niggling thought that these mums only came to speak to me because I was with Izzy, I figured I would take what I could get and not stress about it. 'Be more Bella' I whispered to myself then giggled, *what would be my mantra now?*

As we packed up our stuff, Izzy casually asked, 'So will you be joining me and your mum on our early morning swims?' and I saw Mum stiffen at the side of her. I had a lot of sympathy for Mum - she clearly treasured this time she got to spend with Izzy and, feeling magnanimous, I decided it was only fair to allow her to continue with this treat. After all, Izzy was mine now, so I could afford to share her a little bit.

I smiled and shook my head. 'Sadly early mornings and swimming don't work for me.'

'That's a shame, but you're welcome to join us anytime. But I suppose I don't need to say that.'

We had moved out to the car park, and as Mum gave Izzy a swift goodbye hug, I stood awkwardly until Izzy once again swept me up in her warmth and whispered, 'Goodbye twinnie. We really are going to have the best of times.' And then she was dancing across the car park, turning for a final wave as she reached her car. It was funny, but Mum and I both let out a collective 'phew' as Izzy left us. It wasn't relief that she had gone, but almost like you had been whipped up in the air on the best ride of your life, and then were deposited down to earth with a bump as she left. I watched Izzy drive away and felt Mum's eyes on me.

'Well, that was quite a coincidence - Izzy staying at the

holiday cottage the week before you and you having no idea. We're not going to have any of that nonsense again, are we Lucy?'

I was hurt that Mum thought that I was so fragile that I would return to that place, and as Mum moved to give me a hug, I shrugged her off and bundled Milly in the car. Hesitating, Mum got in, started the car and negotiated the exit from the car park onto the main road before speaking again.

'I'm sorry to have to ask Lucy, and I know it was all so long ago, but you know how much we love you. If you tell us if there's a problem, we can help you.'

Feeling myself soften, I smiled over at her. 'Sorry Mum, I know you are looking after me. To be honest, it's all just been a bit of a shock and it did make me feel a bit weird, but only like anyone would feel. I promise I'm fine and I know the drill.' The rest of the drive passed in an easy silence, and I hoped Mum would relax now. I couldn't wait to get home and message Izzy.

Once in, Milly was happy to be allowed to watch TV, and I could see she was tired after her day at the pool and the excitement of meeting her new classmates. I poured myself a small glass of white wine, giggling like a naughty schoolgirl at the thought of Mum's face if she saw I was drinking alone before six. I was surprised when I saw that glass had gone, so I poured another one full to the brim and sat down to compose my message. I started and stopped several times as I just couldn't think of the right words, and then to my relief a message from Izzy appeared.

> *Hey twinnie. Great afternoon. Oh my God, Heidi! I'm sure she's nice but wow, she made me feel like I was somehow breaking all the rules. What's that all about? xxx*

I laughed, and it was easy to reply as there was an effortless back and forth before I took a deep breath and typed out the message I had been planning for days.

> *How do you fancy meeting on Monday with the girls? Maybe coffee and cake? xxx*

I waited for ages for the 3 bubbles to appear, and eventually they did.

> *Sorry, can't do Monday out as I have a man coming to give a price on a conservatory. A conservatory, we have really made it, eh!*

I felt close to tears. No kisses this time, and clearly Izzy didn't want to spend any time with me. I'd lost her before we had even properly begun. I went to the fridge and poured the remainder of the bottle in my glass. Funny, I thought that had been a new bottle and I seemed to vaguely remember opening it when I got home, but I must be muddled. There was no way I had drunk the whole thing. I have to be so careful drinking with my medication, as Mum constantly reminds me. When I sat back at the table, I saw there was another message from Izzy:

> *Just had a thought though - why don't you and Milly come round to my house? Sun looks set to shine next week and I'll get the paddling pool out for the girls, and we can talk about all the other mums!*

Oh, I knew my girl would come through for me!

> *Sounds like a plan. xxx*

Izzy replied immediately, almost as if she was as eager for my response as I was to hear from her.

> *Shall we say 12 o'clock? That way we can have lunch and it's late enough that we can drink*

wine! x

I know that lunchtime drinking is really not a good idea. After all, all my medications scream a warning about it, almost as frequently as Mum likes to remind me. But hell, it's only one day, so I tapped out a quick reply:

I'll bring a bottle! xxx

There were bubbles straight away as Izzy responded.

Best make it two! We have a lot to talk about. Got to go. I'll send over my address. Love ya! x

'Oh, I love you too Izzy,' I whispered to my phone. What a simply perfect day.

TWENTY YEARS EARLIER

Cath was just on her way out the door, running late for her shift, when the phone rang. She debated leaving it to ring, but then figured she was late anyway so another couple of minutes wouldn't make too much of a difference. It took her a while to understand what the person on the other end of the phone was saying - that it was the school, that there was something wrong with Lucy and they needed her to come in. As she drove the route she knew so well, Cath decided Lucy had maybe slipped on the icy paths near the school. She vaguely recalled there had been something in the newsletter about the maintenance team getting ready for winter and gritting the steps. Lucy had likely sprained a wrist, possibly even broken it. By the time she arrived at the school reception, Cath had convinced herself that this was the narrative and was already prepared for the inevitable long wait in A&E and the endless visits after to have the cast checked and removed. Cath really hoped it wasn't Lucy's right wrist, seeing as the A-Level work was ramping up and this was such an important term. Afterwards, Cath remembered these thoughts and would have given anything for it to be just that Lucy had broken her right arm.

The receptionist ushered Cath straight through to the Head's office and Cath barely had time to register that there seemed to be quite a few people in the room, and that Lucy was not among them. When she told the story afterwards to

Jon, she said that at that point she knew that something had happened which meant that things would never be the same again. But that wasn't the truth. That was a feeling she liked to think she had when she reflected on this meeting with the knowledge of everything that came after. In truth, Cath was mildly irritated that it appeared that she was going to be waiting for Lucy before they could set off to the hospital, and that no doubt there would be lots of forms to fill in so the school could absolve itself from any blame. This was all just such a nuisance.

As she was ushered to a chair, Cath was half thinking of the people she needed to let know that her plans for the next couple of days had changed. She supposed once Lucy was used to the cast she would be back at school and would be able to travel on the bus, but it might be wise to keep her at home for a day or so.

Her train of thought was interrupted by the Head. 'Mrs Weaver, are you happy for us to continue?'

Cath realised she hadn't actually heard a word that had been said to her for the last couple of minutes, and at the same time noted that the other people in the room were all looking very serious and expecting her to say something.

'I'm sorry, could you start again?'

'I understand this is all something of a shock, and there is no easy way to say this, but a friend of Lucy has come to see Miss Partridge,' at this the Head nodded towards Lucy's form tutor, 'to report that Lucy has admitted to self-harming.'

'No, that can't be right, I would have noticed.' But even as she spoke the words, Cath reluctantly thought of the difficult school holidays they had just had and all the time that Lucy had spent alone in her room. But then she shook her head. 'No, there's absolutely no reason for Lucy to have done that and she knows she can talk to me and her dad about anything.'

'Well, we think that there is unfortunately something very serious behind what we feel is a cry for help. It's very sensitive and maybe something that Lucy felt unable to share with you both.' At this Cath bristled in her chair, ready to put the Head right. After all, Lucy told her and Jon everything. Or rather, she used to.

'Lucy has also told Anna...' at this the Head shifted uncomfortably in his seat, 'that she has been having a relationship with someone and, well...' The Head cleared his throat and struggled to look Cath in the eye. 'Well, it would appear that she alleges that relationship was with a member of staff.'

Cath was unable to speak, but then felt the ball of protective fury start to build from the pit of her stomach.

'A member of staff? But how? What? I just don't understand?'

Cath was furious to find tears sliding down her face as she looked from the Head to Miss Partridge, begging them to make sense of all of this. 'Are you telling me that some pervert has taken advantage of my little girl, and no one has noticed?'

'Mrs Weaver, I have to say we are taking this very seriously but...'

'Seriously! Where are the police? This person, who you still have failed to tell me their name, has caused such damage to my little girl that she has started to harm herself. I don't want to hear anymore! I need to see her now! And again, where are the police?' Cath stood abruptly, knocking over the chair she had been sat in. For a moment she thought she really ought to pick it up, but then was distracted by the man speaking to her.

'We have reported the matter following the correct steps.' This was Mr Harris speaking, who Cath vaguely remembered from the newsletter was the school safeguarding lead - whatever that meant. She had paid little attention as she never imagined that safeguarding would be something that would ever be mentioned in a conversation she was having about Lucy. 'I will take you to Lucy now and you can sit with her in a private room whilst we wait for the police to arrive.'

'I just want to take her home. At least I know there she

will be safe.' Mr Harris flinched at this, but was firm in his reply.

'I think you will need to remain here just until the police arrive. We can bring you both warm drinks and it shouldn't be too long.'

Afterwards, Cath was pleased that she hadn't at that point realised just how long this nightmare would last, for if she had known she wouldn't have had the strength to mutely follow Mr Harris as he took her towards her darling Lucy.

CATH

Sat in her sunny back garden, Cath poured herself a large glass of wine. Jon raised an eyebrow, but knew better than to pass comment and instead poured himself a glass and joined her, enjoying the warmth of the sunshine now that it had lost its fierceness from earlier in the day. Then Cath was aware that Jon was shifting in his seat, clearing his throat. *Bloody man, why did he not just say what was on his mind?* She took another gulp of her drink, staring fixedly ahead until she could bear it no longer and eventually asked, 'Come on. What's up? You clearly have something to say.'

Jon opened his mouth and found he was racing through his garbled tale of seeing Rob, and his detective trip back to the Langdale Hotel, and how he didn't know what to do. Once he had finished, he sat back with a sigh and took a large gulp of his wine.

Well, thanks very much for that Jon, thought Cath. *As if I haven't got enough on my plate. Could you have not just sorted this out on your own for once?* And the two of them sat in a silence that wasn't companionable, and - at least on Cath's part - was filled with seething resentment.

So, Cath was more than ready for her swim with Izzy on Monday morning. Cath arrived first this time and was already on her third lap of the pool when she saw Izzy hurrying towards the changing area. She waved her hand in acknowledgement, but Izzy was squinting at her phone before tapping out a few words, frowning, and entering the changing rooms. Cath realised that she had never seen Izzy looking anything but sunny, so there was clearly something bothering the younger woman.

Izzy sank into the water and the two commenced their pattern of lengths in companionable silence until, after half an hour, Izzy caught her eye and gestured that she was getting out the pool. Cath nodded and carried on to reach her target before making her way to the changing rooms, seeing that Izzy was already ordering their breakfast in the cafe area.

'Morning Cath, I figured it was a bacon sandwich kind of morning.'

Cath laughed. 'Every morning is a bacon sandwich kind of morning.'

As they chatted about their weekends, Cath noted that Izzy looked tired; but before she could ask if everything was OK, the younger woman took the words right out of her mouth.

'You alright Cath, you seem a bit tense this morning?'

And that was all the prompt Cath needed to tell Izzy about Jon seeing Rob at the Langdale Hotel and how they just didn't know what to do about it.

Izzy listened, then smiled. 'Well, that's an easy one. I mean, the best thing is just ask him. You know, just a casual, *did I see you at the Langdale the other day Rob?* I'm sure there's a perfectly normal explanation and you are worrying about nothing.'

Cath noticed that as Izzy spoke, what she said suddenly made perfect sense. She supposed that her and Jon had been on high alert for so long that they were ultra-sensitive to every situation, seeing drama where there really was none. She felt a little foolish now.

'You are completely right Izzy. Anyway, you look tired too. All OK?'

'Hah! You have your daughter to blame for me feeling tired. I love her but wow, can that girl talk!'

'What do you mean?' Cath felt her heart go into free fall.

'Well, we have a WhatsApp chat going on and I feel like I'm being researched for a book. I reckon your Lucy knows as much about me as she does herself now. I bet you are never off the phone.'

Seeing Cath's face, Izzy hurriedly went on, 'Oh, please don't think I'm complaining, I love Lucy. It's quite flattering really. I don't usually get people who are interested in me and what makes me tick. Anyway, we are meeting for lunch today and she has messaged me already with a photo. I was going to reply but was running late to meet you.'

Laughing, Izzy passed her phone to Cath, who saw her daughter grinning back at her holding two bottles of rosé wine. But she also noticed with a sinking feeling, that the photo had been followed by a number of other messages, with Lucy seemingly undeterred that she had not received a reply. She was aware that her companion was speaking to her.

'Earth to Cath. I was saying I'm just so very glad I met you both.'

Cath smiled but couldn't help but hope that Izzy still felt the same way in a couple of weeks' time.

TWENTY YEARS EARLIER

Kate was sat in the office of the school nurse, holding an ice pack to her head. In her other hand she held the gift box that Lucy had flung at her as she had fled the classroom. She hadn't opened it, fearing it was like Pandora's box and opening it would unleash nothing good. She had a nasty gash above her eye, but that would heal. The thing that wouldn't heal was hearing Lucy's distress as she accused Kate of ruining her life. Kate really had no idea where this had come from. All she had done was help Lucy when she was so clearly struggling with the transition into Sixth Form and finding her 'look'. Other than that, Kate could barely remember seeing Lucy. There was that one weird time in the pub. She did remember how uncomfortable she had felt then, but it was a fleeting thought, quickly forgotten with the arrival of Mark Harris and the excitement of something new starting.

Kate was wrestling with her conscience. She knew she really needed to report the matter. So far, she had just told the nurse she had turned and walked into the open cupboard door. She was aware she had done the wrong thing as soon as the lie had slipped from her lips, but she felt bad getting Lucy into trouble when she was clearly so disturbed. Maybe she could have a quick word with Miss Partridge, and they could agree the way forward.

So, it seemed very fortunate when the very lady Kate had been thinking about appeared at the door, followed by the

Head.

'Kate, how are you feeling?' The right words were issued, but Kate looked up on alert as she realised there was some lack of care in the inflection of the question.

'I'm fine, I don't want to cause a fuss. But there is something I need to discuss with you when you have a moment.'

The Head took over the conversation at this point. 'I'm afraid there's been a rather serious allegation made against you.'

At that point Kate suddenly knew without doubt just what it was that the Head was going to say. She had been so silly to think this was something that could be managed discretely.

'I'm afraid a pupil has alleged that you have been engaged in an inappropriate relationship with them.'

Kate felt her world start to slip away from her. The Head was still speaking, and she caught words such as *the appropriate authorities have been informed, full investigation, until we sort this out, suspension, go home now, escort you from the premises.* Her head was now throbbing, and she realised that she had made a huge mistake telling that story to the nurse in a misguided attempt to protect Lucy. How would she explain that? She put her head in her hands and, mirroring Lucy from that fateful Friday night, threw up all over the beautifully wrapped gift box, that did indeed promise to wreak havoc in her life.

LUCY

I was ready by ten-thirty and didn't need to leave the house for at least another hour, so I dropped a quick message to Izzy, figuring she would be home from the pool by now.

> *Hope you had a good swim and Mum behaved herself!* xxx

I left it for a few minutes, but having not received a reply, I tapped out another quick note.

> *Can't wait to see you* xxx

I could see that Izzy was online, but still no response. *I'll leave it now* I promised myself, but five minutes later I lost the battle and tapped out a question. She would have to reply then.

> *What are you wearing?* xxx

At last, the three dots appeared.

> *Sorry. Stuck with the conservatory guy. Will tell you all about it when you get here.*

This was followed by a photo of her wearing cut off denim dungarees and a plain vest top.
Bugger! I looked at my floaty skirt and top. I was dressed completely wrong.
'Come on Milly, we're leaving in five minutes.'

Milly appeared grinning at me. 'Hurrah, I can't wait to see Beth!'

'Well, we just have to nip into town first. Won't take long, I promise.'

Thankfully Milly was so excited about the day to come that I didn't get the whinging that would normally have been the reaction to my announcement. Whilst Milly collected her toy puppy, which seemed to be the toy of the moment and had to go with her to meet Beth, I tapped out a quick message to Izzy.

Ha Twinnie, you're never going to believe this!
See you soon xxx

I saw the floating three dots appear but then stop and Izzy was offline. I was disappointed but figured I had lots to do, so ushered Milly out the door just as my phone started to ring. Mum! Bugger, I could do without this, but I knew if I didn't answer she would get herself in a bit of a state, so I picked up.

'Mum, I'm just getting in the car, give me two minutes and I'll call you back on the hands-free.'

I could hear Mum start to say something, but I put the phone down as I loaded the car with everything I needed. I was happy with the wine choice. I would have liked to have arrived with champagne, but at the same time didn't want to look like I was trying too hard. Once I was on the way, I took a deep breath and pressed the name that was always at the top of my recent calls.

'Hi Mum, sorry about that, I can't talk for long as I need to nip into town before we go to Izzy's.'

'Ah yes, Izzy mentioned you were going to hers later when we met for swimming. I hope you have a good time.' There was a pause, and I knew Mum had something else to say, so was glad I was able to divert the conversation.

'Is there any chance you could have Milly for a couple of hours tomorrow afternoon, Mum? Heidi has asked me to the

PTA meeting. I had mentioned to her that I used to do a bit of bookkeeping, and it seems they are after a treasurer. I thought it would do me good to put myself out there a bit.'

I could almost hear the relief in Mum's voice as she clocked I was socialising with other people and wasn't becoming too reliant on Izzy. Of course I had twisted the truth a little bit there. Izzy had told me Heidi had mentioned that she was looking for new members for the PTA and that she thought she might go along, so I had immediately messaged Heidi to ask if I could get involved too. I was surprised that Heidi hadn't replied, but had pushed the thought to the back of my mind. Heidi's friendship or approval wasn't something that really interested me at the moment. Of course, Mum didn't need to know any of these minor details. I stopped listening as I heard Mum prattle on about nothing, relief making her talk faster than usual. Eventually I was able to cut her off. 'I've got to go Mum, I need to nip to the shops. Love you.'

I found a short stay place easily enough in the car park and ran with Milly to the same shop where I had made my other purchases. Sure enough, there were the denim dungarees, an exact match to Izzy. I really wanted the same colour but thought that might be pushing it too far, so whereas Izzy was wearing a version in washed out blue, I went for the ink. Paying at the till, I asked the assistant to remove the labels and then made a detour via M&S so I could get changed in their toilets.

'What are you doing, Mummy?' Milly was looking at me, studying me as if I were a strange creature under the microscope.

I laughed. 'Can you keep a secret?'

Milly nodded her head furiously.

'Well, I suddenly realised that my skirt was completely see-through and you could see my pants!'

Milly frowned. 'I couldn't see your pants.'

'Well, it's a good job I noticed as I left the house, and as we had to come to town anyway, I thought I would try something a bit different. Please don't say anything, I've trusted you with this secret.'

Milly nodded solemnly. 'I'm five now. You can trust me.'

I realised I should have thought of a better story. I had been silly to think that Milly wouldn't notice, but it was too late now. I would have to do better in future.

Returning home, I parked my car carefully, ensuring I parked well to the side so as to not antagonise Rob. Then Milly and I set off on the twenty minute walk to Izzy's house, which was on the new estate on the far side of the village. I was already confident of the way as I had made a couple of detours past her house as I was running errands over the weekend, driving slowly by like some sort of Private Eye on a cheap 'made for TV' movie.

As we turned into her drive, Milly was jumping up and down in excitement and as soon Beth emerged from the back, they started to squeal their hellos and wave frantically at each other. The two of them hugged and Beth was leading Milly to the back, all thoughts of me forgotten. I stood for a moment, feeling a bit shy and unsure, and wishing I had the confidence of my daughter, before I followed with the wine and a bunch of flowers I had picked up in the store, to make me feel I was entitled to use the customer toilets. Following the direction the girls took, I followed the path round to the back of the house where Izzy was lounging in a hammock. She rolled rather inelegantly out of it when I appeared and jumped up and down laughing.

'Twinnie! No way, just no way!'

I cast a cautious glance at Milly, but she was enthralled with the white rabbit which was leisurely chewing on some lettuce in the corner of his run.

'Ha! I saw your photo and nearly went and changed into something else, but then I thought you would see the funny side of it!'

Izzy laughed and I felt a warm glow inside as I looked at my best friend, who grabbed her phone and insisted on a photo of the two of us, both grinning like idiots. We really were the perfect match. The wine was poured and drunk, and more wine was poured. Izzy had laid out a picnic lunch, so we were able to let the girls graze as we talked about everything. Before I drank anymore, I remembered I really should take my tablet, and popped the pack and swallowed the pill dry. After all, I had had plenty of practice. Taking another gulp of wine, I saw that Izzy was watching me intently. There was a lull in the conversation and then Izzy spoke.

'I hope you don't mind me asking, but is that lithium?'

I nodded. 'Been taking them for ages.' I could have elaborated about how they were part of a regime that had been agreed for me, how mixed with anti-depressants, these pills keep me under control. But I didn't want to be that person to Izzy - the person who needed help to stop her being her true self, which I now realised those around me didn't seem to like.

'My best friend from school was on those after her son was born.'

I didn't bother to correct her assumption that the medication was to help me after Milly's birth. It wasn't something I really wanted to think about, never mind have other people know.

'It's funny, she's recently moved out to France where her mum lives, and her next-door neighbour was horrified when she heard how long she had been on the tablets for. She found out that would never be allowed to happen in Europe. She decided she didn't like how she never felt quite right, so decided to just flush them away down the loo! I mean, quite irresponsible, but my friend says it's the best thing that ever happened to her.'

'I'm not sure I need them anymore. I mean, I missed loads on holiday and felt no different, but Mum would have a fit.' I did like that Izzy was so easy to confide in, that I didn't have to feel ashamed.

'Well, it's all personal choice. Maybe talk to the doctor, though my friends GP was very unsupportive. In the end she decided to just give it three months and see what happened. She didn't tell anyone, and at the end of the three months asked her husband if he'd noticed any difference and he was delighted when she told him what she'd done. Though he did say if she had told him beforehand, he would have tried to stop her.'

I was fascinated by this story and Izzy looked at me carefully. 'Not that I'm suggesting you do anything like that. Like I say, everyone is different.' She quickly changed the subject to start to moan about Heidi and the blasted PTA as she topped our glasses up. I had been going to tell her that I was going to the PTA meeting too, but instead I hugged the secret to me and figured it would be a nice surprise for her.

Wandering back to our house, I couldn't stop giggling, and also found I was struggling to walk in a straight line. We stopped off for ice cream as I was suddenly really hungry and Milly chatted away about her new friend, though she seemed far more taken with the rabbit, which was apparently the best thing ever. Reaching home, I put another couple of bottles in the fridge and dropped a text to Rob.

> *Any chance you can pick up pizza on the way home? I've got wine chilling in the fridge.*

I thought for a while before adding:

> *Cold wine and a hot wife are waiting for you x.*

I smiled again; I really was drunk.
Rob replied ten minutes later.

> *Well, how can I say no to that. I certainly won't be late home. The usual OK, and with or without anchovies?*

> *With. I feel like living dangerously tonight! xxx*

Your wish is my command x.

 I was tempted to pour a glass of wine but thought I might do better to sober up a bit first, so I opened a can of coke instead and grabbed a packet of crisps as I wandered upstairs to our ensuite and the cabinet where I kept my tablets, safely out of Milly's reach. Reaching for the first packet, I was about to pop the pills from the blister seal to start their journey to the sea, when I paused. Whilst it was only a remote possibility, there was a chance Rob, or more likely my mum, might just look in the cabinet and they would be bound to notice if the pills weren't there. I wanted this to be a secret, to be able to triumphantly proclaim in three months' time that I no longer needed the tablets. And when they told me that I must continue, I would reveal that I had already stopped, had done for a significant amount of time, and was absolutely fine. I couldn't wait to see their faces. A better plan was to flush the tablets every day, morning, noon and night, so that they were swallowed by the toilet rather than by me. I must admit I did congratulate myself on how clever I was.

 It was only later, as Rob raised his glass in a toast to me, accompanied by the now familiar cartoon-like lecherous wink, that I remembered his rule about no alcohol on a school night. It seemed he had also decided that rules are made to be broken.

TWENTY YEARS EARLIER

Looking back over that dreadful time, both Cath and Jon agreed that days seemed to both drag and fly by, until the weeks merged into one. An urgent call to Jon's work brought him pale-faced to the school, but Cath could see from the telltale red spot on each cheek that he was fighting to control his anger. She knew how he felt. She just wanted to kill the bastard who had so damaged their little girl.

Then they were at the police station, with kind-eyed and gentle-voiced officers speaking to a sobbing Lucy, who refused to say another word other than repeating Anna shouldn't have said anything. That it was not her secret to share. Days later the arrest of a teacher made the local news, and it was just before this that the officer in charge of the case had sat Jon and Cath down to tell them who it was that Lucy had confessed to an affair with. Cath was horrified to realise she knew the name. Not at first, as Miss Oxenham had not been someone Lucy had spoken about at home. But when the officer mentioned her first name of Kate, Cath felt her world tilt as she remembered the visit from a 'friend' and the time spent upstairs together whilst she consoled herself with the custard creams.

'Oh God, she's been to the house, spent time up in Lucy's room.'

Jon could only sit still, struggling to make any sense at all of, well, any of it.

And then things started to unravel still further. Miss

Oxenham's name was suddenly out in the open and they were informed that she had been bailed to her parents' house. She was denying that there had been any contact between the two which was inappropriate, but did admit that visiting Lucy at home had been an error of judgement.

In the meantime, Cath was discovering a patchwork of scars, not just on Lucy's arms, but on her back and tops of her thighs. Cleary, this had been going on for a great deal longer than the last two weeks. The scars almost looked beautiful as they waved across her youthful skin in various shades of silver and white, reminding Cath of a delicate spider's web. The recent scars were much deeper and reflected the state that Lucy was now in. She obviously wasn't in school and refused to see any of her friends. She wouldn't talk to her parents and Cath was afraid to leave her alone. They had a referral to a therapist, but Lucy refused to say anything and came back from the sessions tight-lipped and resentful.

Whilst Jon took Lucy to one of her sessions, Cath gave in to the temptation that had been haunting her since this whole thing began and searched through Lucy's things. She hated herself for doing so and knew that Lucy would never forgive her if she found out, but she needed to see if there was anything that may help her understand. Hidden at the back of Lucy's wardrobe was the savings book, which Cath swiftly saw had been pretty much emptied. It hardly seemed worth getting upset about this - there were bigger problems to face. But tucked along with it was a photo of Miss Oxenham which had clearly been cut out of the school newsletter; the newsletter issued at the start of term which had introduced new members of staff, and which Cath hadn't bothered to read. The photo had been stuck to a piece of card, around which Lucy had doodled hearts and both her and Kate's names. However, that was it. Cath had been hoping to find some letters from Kate which would tell the whole sordid tale. She wanted to be able to storm into the police station with this crucial evidence and see that dreadful woman get everything she deserved for damaging

Lucy so. Moving slowly downstairs, Cath pushed away that sneaky little voice that told her something was not quite right with this whole sorry drama.

And then the police were back, this time looking a bit sterner and asking to speak to Lucy again. And in that half hour, Lucy suddenly admitted that she had in fact killed Kate. Had slit her throat. Cath couldn't understand it. And then Lucy admitted that actually she was covering for Cath, who had stabbed Kate when she found out what had happened. She turned to her mum and urged her to, 'Run whilst you can, I'll take the blame.' The crisis team were called, Lucy was assessed and admitted to a secure ward, and Cath and Jon floundered. They had been floundering ever since.

JON

Jon was fretting; Cath had come back from her swim and had confidently informed him that he would just have to come out and straight up ask Rob what he was doing at the Langdale. Jon had noticed that Cath was always very confident about stuff that involved him having to do hard things, so he was in a pretty bad mood when his phone rang and he saw that it was Rob. It wasn't unusual for Rob to call his in-laws, usually when Lucy wasn't picking up, but with all things considered, Jon debated rejecting the call. Then he thought about what Cath would say and reluctantly answered.

'Hi Jon, I'm sorry to bother you, but I wonder if you could do me a bit of a favour?'

Jon noticed that Rob didn't wait for him to answer before pushing on with his request. 'You know Lucy's off to this pizza night the week Milly starts school? Is there any chance you could pick her up when it finishes? I don't really want to drag Milly out of bed.'

Jon readily agreed, as Rob elaborated, 'She's adamant she will get a taxi, but it's her first night out on her own since Milly was born and I know I'm fretting but, well, you know…' Rob's voice tailed off, but he didn't need to continue because Jon did indeed know.

'Tell you what…' Jon was pleased with this idea and thought it would lead him nicely into asking Rob that question that he had to ask, '…I'll tell her I'm at a do that night at the Langdale and if she calls when she's ready, it will give me the perfect excuse to get away early. I can make out that she's doing me a favour.'

'I really appreciate that. The Langdale - that reminds me, I meant to say, did I see you there the other day, hanging round the Gents' toilets? I was going to say hello but then you disappeared. I'm representing them in the small claims court, some pretty shoddy work done on some bathrooms they've had refurbished. I was inspecting the evidence - way below my pay grade, but the manager's a mate from the golf club so I felt I couldn't say no.'

Jon hoped that Rob didn't notice his overly hearty agreement that yes, it had indeed been him. As Rob said, 'Better go, work's manic. I won't tell Cath I caught you loitering round the Gents' toilets.'

Jon was aware he laughed far too loudly and for far too long, but God it was such a relief. He would never say this to Cath, but after everything that happened when Milly was born, Jon would have had some sympathy with Rob if his feelings for Lucy had changed. But their girl had got lucky and Rob had come through for her. Jon felt bad he had ever thought otherwise, and went off to tell Cath the good news.

TWENTY YEARS EARLIER

For six weeks Lucy continued to deteriorate, until Cath dreaded being buzzed through the locked doors to the ward where she would be greeted with the sound of Lucy screaming. There were fraught conversations with the consultant who warned there was a long road ahead of them. The police were very understanding and informed Cath and Jon that they would not be pressing any charges against Lucy as she was clearly very unwell. They debated whether they should try to write to Kate - attempt to make some sort of apology - but she had already left the school. Rumours were that she had left her teaching course at the university and had retreated back to her parents, where she had taken a job in the local supermarket.

  The papers reported on the whole sorry saga, and whilst no names were printed, it was a small community and everyone knew exactly who was involved. There was some unpleasant graffiti sprayed on the fence of their home, and whilst Jon told Cath to just ignore the whispers, she pointed out that it wasn't him who had to cope daily with people she had known for many years simply crossing the road to avoid speaking to her. Cath knew that a lot of this was embarrassment as they simply didn't know what to say. And after all, what was there to say? Lucy had woven a fantasy that had pretty much destroyed a woman's life. And now Lucy was severely unwell. Cath knew that if Lucy had been diagnosed with cancer, she would have been facing a very different reaction from those around her. But the stigma of mental illness, together with what most people perceived as the maliciousness of Lucy's actions, meant that any sympathy was in short supply.

Whilst Jon continued to go to work every day, Cath found she was becoming a virtual prisoner in her own home, counting down with dread the hours until she made her afternoon visit to the hospital. Jon came with her on the evening visit and that made things a little easier, though Cath was then faced with the task of consoling Jon as he sat with silent tears tracing down his cheeks, as he struggled to understand.

LUCY

Izzy was so surprised to see me at the PTA meeting that I laughed when I saw her face. The group had commandeered a large table in the coffee shop and there was plenty of room as most people chose to use the tables outside, making the most of the sunshine. Although there were a couple of seats free round the other side of the table, I grabbed a chair and nudged my way in so I could sit next to my best friend. I noticed Heidi roll her eyes and nudged Izzy, but she was playing the good girl and didn't nudge me back. I would rib her for that later.

Heidi chaired the meeting (well, of course she did) and as she started everyone took out pens and paper to make notes. It really was just like being back in school. Pleased that I had come prepared, I took out my little notebook and my beautiful fountain pen, writing the date carefully in the lilac ink. Listening to Heidi, I felt Izzy staring at me and, glancing over, I smiled as I saw her matching lilac entry in her own notebook. 'Snap!' I smiled gleefully, but Izzy just frowned slightly and didn't return my smile. They obviously didn't need a treasurer - I would tell Mum it looked like too much commitment - but each time Izzy volunteered for a job, I offered to help as well. In the end Heidi was quite rude when she suggested I maybe pick something I could do myself. Again, I nudged Izzy, but she half turned away from me, and I saw a couple of the other women shooting her sympathetic glances. Bitches! As the meeting drew to a close, Heidi made her final dig.

'What an unusual colour ink Izzy, not your normal blue or black and well Lucy, I see you have got exactly the same. What a surprise!'

At this a couple of the other women sniggered and Izzy shifted and looked uncomfortable. Glancing at me, she laughed. 'I love it, I take this pen everywhere I go, spreading the lilac love. Who wants boring blue or black when you can go distinctive.' Shooting me a sideways glance, she followed up with a rather cutting, 'Think it may be time for a change though.' This was greeted by laughter from the table, but they didn't see that Izzy gave my hand a reassuring squeeze to let me know it was me and her against the world. I understood she needed to be so careful when we were with other people.

The meeting stuttered to an end, and I saw I really needed to get back to collect Milly. But Izzy was chatting to, I think the lady was called Kirsten, and I didn't want to leave without saying goodbye to my friend. I sort of loitered awkwardly at the side of them until finally Izzy turned to me with a bit of a fixed smile, that to a stranger could be taken for a grimace, asking, 'Are you OK there, Lucy?'

I felt so sorry for her, stuck with Kirsten who was obviously trying to sort out a meet up, which Izzy was just too polite to be able to get out of, so I decided I could save the day.

'Izzy, don't forget we are meeting tomorrow with the girls. Don't want you to get double-booked when I know you're so busy. I'll message you later to confirm times.' Laughing to myself at the look on the faces of the women around me, I left the cafe, but not before I heard one of the women, Fiona I think she said her name was, say quite loudly, 'Honestly Izzy, you are far too nice, I would have told her it had to stop by now.' I worried a little bit that they were talking about me, and that Fiona had intended for me to hear what she said, but then they didn't understand me and Izzy.

TWENTY YEARS EARLIER

The whole time, Lucy screamed. And if she wasn't screaming, she was saying all sorts of nonsense. Terrible things that burned into Cath's mind as she struggled to decipher if any of these ramblings were real.

After two months the consultant told them that the situation was serious and that they were looking at electric shock therapy. Cath cried and Jon retreated further yet into himself, but they agreed to do what was best for their girl. And it was like a switch had been flicked, which Cath grimly reflected, was indeed what had happened. When they arrived to visit, Lucy was no longer screaming, and whilst she looked pale and tired, she was pleased to see them and asked when she would be able to go home. After that, Lucy improved practically daily. It was decided that she needed some extra support, so would continue to study for her A-Levels by attending lessons at the small unit attached to the ward, where they could continue to monitor the situation and adjust the medication as required. But the consultant agreed Lucy was now able to live at home. Cath and Jon were delighted with the news of course, but neither wanted to admit to the other the terror they felt that things could change in an instant. After all, they hadn't seen this episode coming and it had all happened so fast.

When it was time for Lucy to return home, they gently told her that they had decided to move house, to be nearer to the unit. Lucy accepted this and they didn't have the heart to tell her how shattered their old life had been. Cath had torn into pieces the picture of Kate she had found secreted away, saying nothing about this to Jon. Lucy never asked about it, for which Cath was relieved and grateful as she wasn't sure what she would have said. None of Lucy's friends tried to contact her and if Lucy thought this was strange, she didn't query this.

  They managed to make a new life. Lucy quietly studied and did pass her A-Levels, just a year later than the original plan. The three of them celebrated together, and Cath and Jon hugged each other in relief when it was agreed she would go to university locally, on a part time basis, and continue to live at home. If Cath had a niggle that it wasn't right that her and Jon were now Lucy's best friends – well, her only friends - she pushed this thought aside and concentrated on getting through each day without screaming. Cath started to envy that Lucy had been able to have that release whilst she was in the hospital.

  Lucy didn't want to attend her graduation, so Cath returned the outfit she had bought and swallowed her disappointment, trying to remember to be grateful for the normality they had managed to achieve. Lucy started work straight after her degree, at a local firm of accountants, and started to study for the qualifications she would need to progress. The three of them remained a tight unit, quietly existing for three years, with no room for anyone else; that was until Lucy met Rob, a bit of an up-and-coming star at the solicitors who were based in the same building as her work. Rob burst into their lives, swept Lucy off her feet, and went on to charm Cath and Jon so that any reservations they may have had were ignored. They agreed it was best all round not to mention to Rob the difficulties Lucy had experienced in her teenage years. After all, that was behind them now.

  There was a bit of a rocky patch when Milly was born, and Lucy got it in her head that the nurses were planning to snatch her baby from her, but Cath and Jon swooped in to promptly get her the help she needed, and an adjustment of her medication meant this small blip was just that: a very small bump in the road.

But at night Cath would try to block out the final words the consultant said to them all those years ago, as they were getting ready to take Lucy to their new home.

'Lucy is lucky - she doesn't remember any of this, and will have no recollection of the things she said when she was so poorly. You, on the other hand, will need to find a way to live with everything, to find a way to forget, because this is something you will never be able to make sense of.'

Cath feared that her and Jon would never be able to forget, and so would always be chasing that peace and clarity they so craved.

ROB

After speaking to Jon, Rob put the phone down and for a moment allowed his head to sink into his hands. The feeling of unease he'd had since the holiday just seemed to be growing, and even though he was making such an effort with Lucy, he just didn't know if it will be enough. When he first met Lucy, his ambitions for his career dominated his life and Lucy fitted in with that without complaint. He had been able to work evenings and weekends and spend time with his friends playing golf, all without complaint from Lucy who was just happy to go along with his plans. He was honest with himself and admitted that this was no overwhelming love match, but he cared for her deeply and would never want to hurt her. They had a tiny wedding with just their parents, which had suited Rob, although he had thought it a bit strange that Lucy didn't have a gaggle of friends for a hen do or parading as bridesmaids; but he soon found that Lucy was a loner - happy in her own company, happy to fit in with his plans, so really it was perfect.

They were both delighted when Lucy found she was pregnant, but he did remember the initial look of panic in Cath's eyes as they announced the happy news, before she covered it with a swift smile and enveloped them both in a huge hug. Lucy had blossomed whilst she was pregnant and he loved looking after her, rubbing her back in the evening whilst they planned the future they would have with their three children. When Lucy was six months pregnant, Rob was made partner in the firm of solicitors he had been with since he had finished law college, and he and Lucy agreed it would be best if she finished work so they wouldn't try to juggle the demands of childcare and both of them working. Rob felt the affection he had for Lucy deepen, and was very content with the life they had together.

And then Milly was born.

It had started off such a happy time. When Rob held Milly for the first time he was overwhelmed by the strength of his feelings, and looking at Lucy, he felt a deep affection for her too: the need to protect his little family from whatever may come their way. He hadn't realised he would be expected to act on that so soon.

When they had made their plans, Lucy had wanted to come home from the hospital as soon as possible, and with Cath and Jon living so close and clearly eager to support, it had seemed that there would be no reason why this plan wouldn't come to fruition. Unfortunately, Lucy had some tearing, which Rob still never liked to think about, and so needed to stay in for that night. It shouldn't have made a difference. Sure, they were disappointed that the new little family of three wouldn't be cosied safe in their home for their first night together, but these things happen. So, when Rob had arrived at the hospital the next day, feeling guiltily well rested after a perfect night's sleep, he had no idea of the nightmare that was about to start. Lucy was sat in the chair by the bed, already dressed and looking to Rob quite beautiful. Milly was sleeping peacefully in the funny little plastic cot and Rob truly felt like his heart would burst. When he looked back, he couldn't even remember what they talked about, it was all just so normal. And then Lucy said the strangest thing.

'See that nurse over there, Rob?'

Rob turned to look in the direction Lucy was indicating before she hissed at him, 'Don't make it obvious you're looking.' Rob let his eyes roam the small ward as if just looking around the general surroundings, and saw the nurse whom he assumed Lucy was referring to. She smiled at him, and Rob smiled back. He remembered her from when they had first brought Lucy to the ward. She had made him a cup of tea.

'Careful! She's seen you!'

Rob dragged his gaze back to Lucy, puzzled at her tone, and then she leant forward and whispered, 'That nurse there, she's stolen our baby. She thinks I don't know, but I'm on to her. They thought I was asleep last night, but I could hear them all talking about me. They don't think I'm fit to be a mother, so they've taken my baby from me.'

And as Rob was reeling, wondering whether he should laugh at this point as this was surely a joke, Lucy stood up and moved over to peer into the cot, with such a strange expression on her face that Rob felt truly afraid.

'Look Lucy, there's our Milly. No one has taken her from us. You must have been having a bad dream. You'll feel so much better after a good night's sleep in your own bed.'

Lucy looked around and Rob felt uncomfortable as he noticed a sly look come across her face. 'That's not our Milly. They swapped her you see, but I know. They are doing it to hurt me you see because they think I'm a bad person, but with your help we can get rid of this baby and escape. You do see don't you, I know you do. Tell me you see it.' For the first time in his adult life, Rob was desperate for his mum, but at that minute the next best thing arrived in the form of Cath and Jon.

They were carrying a pink balloon and looked so happy as they hugged Lucy and then drank in the sight of Milly, exclaiming how perfect she was, that for a second Rob wondered if maybe it was him that had the problem and that he had had some sort of brain haemorrhage. In fact, come to think of it, he did feel a bit odd, and he knew that the fear he felt was written all over his face. He couldn't hear what Lucy was urgently whispering to Cath, but as he watched he saw the same fear reflected on her face and then jump to Jon. Clearly something was dreadfully wrong.

Cath and Jon were marvellous. Rob would be forever in their debt for their help over the first few months of Milly's life. Everything happened very quickly. Cath went to find a doctor whilst Jon suggested Rob maybe take Milly for a walk to the nurse's station whilst he stayed with Lucy. Rob marvelled how calm they were given the circumstances, when he was paralysed with confusion. As different doctors and nurses came to see an increasingly agitated Lucy, Rob could only hold on tight to Milly whispering, 'It's going to be fine,' with no idea if he was telling the first lie his daughter would hear in her life.

In the end a tired-looking consultant sat with Cath, Jon and Rob and gently explained Lucy had something called postpartum psychosis. That scared Rob. He barely followed what the consultant was telling them but was roused from his inertia when it was mentioned that Lucy may have been more susceptible to the condition given her previous episode. He started to interrupt but Cath and Jon assured him not to worry, and so he sat back quietly as they took in all the details and somehow asked all the right questions. Afterwards, they took the time to sit Rob down and gently talk him through what was happening, and in the midst of all the information that was so overwhelming, Rob forgot that the consultant was confused about Lucy's medical history. Rob had never felt so helpless. Afterwards, he wanted to ask them how they had been so calm, how had they known the right questions to ask. But by then it was an unspoken agreement that this episode had taken enough of their emotional energy, and it would be best that it was never mentioned. Best if they pretended it had never happened.

At first, he visited every day. Lucy and Milly had been moved to a special mother and baby unit; but then Lucy continued to deteriorate so quickly that a case conference decided it was in Milly's best interest if she came home. Lucy refused her medication as she believed they were trying to control her thoughts. She screamed for most of the time Rob was visiting. And if she wasn't screaming, she was saying terrible things that Rob knew weren't true, but as he laid awake at night, he wondered how he would ever forget this version of his wife. Or if he could ever forgive her.

Milly was born at the beginning of August and Lucy finally came home in December. It was the Lucy from before, but a sort of faded version - quiet but prone to anxiety. Cath and Jon watched her closely and knew before she did if her medication might need a tweak, and Lucy went along with this. They settled into a routine that was so far removed from Rob's plan for family life that he wondered if he had somehow stumbled into a parallel universe. Rob fretted whether Lucy would love Milly, but she was devoted to her daughter, if anything a little obsessed, but Rob gradually came to realise that this was part of his wife's character, and he felt a bit aggrieved that it had been hidden from him for so long. Of course, Milly would be an only child. Whilst the medical professionals explained that they really didn't know why some people experienced this severe mental episode after giving birth, they did make it clear that the risks could be considered higher should Lucy give birth again, and everyone agreed that they would be grateful for the blessing of Milly and be satisfied with that. Rob and Lucy settled into their routine, though sometimes Rob felt so trapped that he wanted to scream, the same way Lucy had screamed at him on those endless visits. He began to tell her he was working late, when instead he would either sit alone in an anonymous pub nursing a double whisky, wishing he could escape in the bottle, or would pop into Paul and Lou's and just enjoy the happy chaos of their home. He never told Lucy any of this. How could he; because although she hadn't planned this, and he recognised she had been seriously ill, suddenly everything was all about Lucy and the constant fear that things could go wrong again.

The whole episode had strengthened the bond he had with Cath and Jon, but whilst it had brought them closer, Rob recognised that ultimately, whilst this had not affected the love they felt for their daughter, for him, things were forever changed. This weakness Lucy had shown, and though he knew he was wrong, Rob could only see this as a weakness and a character flaw; it would always be there - a shadow over every celebration, an added dimension of fear to every milestone that indicated change and the threat that Lucy wouldn't cope. Rob googled everything he could, and he had no doubt that Cath and Jon had done the same. He searched and searched for something to reassure him that Lucy's condition would never come back, but instead only found articles to suggest that they may be waiting for the inevitable. He could have talked about this with Cath and Jon, and maybe that would have helped all three of them if they had laid their fears out in the open; but instead he drank his whisky and sought escape for a few evenings a week in a fantasy life.

CATH

Cath was not powering through her normal lengths. Instead, she had moved to the main body of the pool and was floating on her back, lost in the thoughts that refused to let her rest. She had woken to a glorious day, and on impulse had taken herself down to the pool for an early dose of therapy. She was honest enough to admit that she was hoping Izzy would be there to catch up with, but after twenty minutes it was apparent her friend would not be making an appearance.

Cath had really enjoyed looking after Milly yesterday. She guiltily acknowledged that the primary source of this enjoyment was that she liked having Milly to herself. She could enjoy her granddaughter wholeheartedly, without a part of her being so invested in how Lucy was doing. It was a time to lose herself in the simple joy of the glorious uncomplicated companionship of sweet Milly, and be reminded of those carefree days of Lucy growing up, when it seemed the sun was always shining and there was no hint of the deluge that would later drown the life they had become so comfortable in.

This pleasure was enhanced by the fact Lucy had taken it upon herself to be involved in the PTA. Cath had worried that Lucy, having finally found a friend, was becoming too reliant on Izzy. So, she had welcomed the news that Lucy was branching out, becoming involved in school and hopefully establishing a wider friendship group.

Lucy had returned from the meeting a little flustered, and by the time Cath waved goodbye to her daughter and granddaughter, she was exhausted. Lucy had burst through the door, full of enthusiasm for the events she would be involved in and telling Cath the stories so rapidly that Cath's head had spun. Cath liked to hear Lucy chat about her day and was a good listener, but this rapid-fire bombardment had been rather overwhelming. She had tried to persuade Lucy to sit with her in the garden and enjoy a glass of the homemade lemonade that both she and Milly loved, but Lucy didn't want to sit down, choosing instead to race round the grass with Milly - even trying out the slide - before scooping her daughter up and throwing her in the air. As the sound of laughter and squeals echoed round the garden, Cath knew she should be happy that the two of them were playing so carefree. So why did it all feel so wrong? Cath had a fixed smile on her face as Lucy pulled away in the car, still waving frantically to her mum whilst talking and gesturing animatedly to Milly.

Hence this morning, Cath was floating on her back in the pool, attempting to quieten the churning panic in the pit of her stomach, gazing up at the perfectly blue sky which signalled they were to be treated to another gorgeous day. Dragging herself from the water, she pondered whether to have her normal coffee and bacon butty, but realised everything felt a bit flat without Izzy there to laugh with. However, the sun seemed to shine even brighter once she made her way from the changing rooms and her phone buzzed with a message from that very lady.

> *Me and Lucy are heading to Bolton Abbey for the day with the children and there's room in the car for a little one! I'll pick you up at 9.30, and I won't take no for an answer.*

Cath realised she was grinning as widely as the smiley face emoji she sent in response. Feeling lighter, Cath hurried home, excited for the unexpected treat of a day stretching before her. Once again, she sent up a silent thanks for Izzy coming into their lives. Izzy somehow just knew what they all needed.

LUCY

Although I'd been pleased with my exit from the PTA meeting, by the time I reached Mum's my insides were churning, and I was questioning whether that meeting had gone as well as I first thought it had. A little voice which had started as a quiet whisper, but which was now screaming for attention, was telling me that Izzy didn't like me at all and was not my friend. I chatted to Mum, but she was looking at me oddly and I was worried in case one of those bitches from the meeting had reported back on me already.

As soon as I was safely through the door, I poured myself a glass of wine. I was very happy to receive the message from Izzy confirming we were indeed meeting tomorrow and suggesting we make a day of it with a trip to Bolton Abbey. I love it there. Mum and I used to go there loads, but amazingly Izzy has never been. I felt very honoured that she had chosen that her first time there will be with me.

The day hadn't got off to the best of starts. When I told Milly what we had planned she was a little subdued and muttered about wanting to see some of her other friends from the pool party. I ignored her and finished off the picnic, fizzing with excitement at having Izzy all to myself. So I was gutted when her car pulled up and I heard Milly shout an excited 'Grandma!' and realised my mother had managed to wheedle herself an invitation. Izzy looked at me apologetically and shrugged with a rueful smile as I climbed in the back with the children and my mother monopolised Izzy for the whole journey, making no effort to include me in their conversation.

I stared sulkily out the window but then slowly realised

my mother's presence there just might be a blessing. I had a very special place I wanted to share with Izzy, so maybe my mother could be persuaded to look after the children for a while to give me the opportunity sneak off with Izzy and let her into the secret I had never shared with anyone. Yes, maybe this would turn out to be the best thing. I plastered a smile on my face and nodded along, biding my time until the day could give me what it had initially promised.

We parked up at the riverside car park and, leaving the picnic in the car, set off on the walk to the Valley of Desolation. Laughing at the mock horror on Izzy's face when she saw the ominous name on the way markers, the girls ran ahead as we meandered behind, enjoying the dappled shading of the woods. We made our way up the tranquil valley to be rewarded with the sight of the stunning waterfall, cascading down with the spray of droplets dancing in the sunshine. I looked to Izzy to see her reaction and she grabbed my hand and gave a sigh of contentment as she whispered, 'Just perfect.' We were able to enjoy a moment, just the two of us, before the bubble was burst by Beth grumbling that her tummy was empty. I had planned for us to carry on up to Simon's Seat, but Mum rather snappily pointed out that was too far for the little ones, and we should head back for our picnic.

As we trailed back, Izzy gave my hand another squeeze and winked at me before she moved ahead to join Mum. I appreciated Mum must feel very left out, but, she had no shame when it came to attempting to monopolise my friend.

As we reached the Priory Church and ruins, Milly picked up the pace, explaining to Beth about the stepping stones crossing the river. Mum volunteered to carry the picnic stuff across the bridge, whilst the rest of us danced our way across the sixty stones, daring the river to get our feet wet. Once on the other side, we settled on the small beach to enjoy the food and relax into the surroundings. Whilst the others devoured the picnic, I nibbled on a sandwich, realising I really wasn't hungry at all. Instead, I quietly plotted my next move, realising

I would have to be clever if I was to outwit Mum.

Normally Mum would be nagging me to eat more, but she was so obsessed with Izzy that I was forgotten. Occasionally Izzy threw me a smile, and I relaxed back into the warm sand, marvelling how a few weeks ago I had relaxed on different sand, dreaming of my Bella, and now she was actually here with me.

I might have dozed off - I haven't been sleeping well for a few days now and the caress of the sun's rays and the soft chatter and giggling of the children lulled me to oblivion. When I came to with a start, I realised I was alone on the beach. I could feel the panic start as I scanned the area, but there was no sign of the others. Was this all some sort of trap to lure me away from the places I was safe? But then I saw Mum coming towards me, smiling and holding out an ice cream, and my brain registered that the others were trailing behind, the girls greedily feasting on the chocolate flakes adorning their rapidly melting cones.

'Ah, you're awake,' smiled Mum. 'You looked so peaceful, we didn't want to wake you.' I smiled back at her, but I knew this wasn't true. Mum had obviously seized her opportunity to spend some time alone with Izzy. Well, two can play at that game.

Jumping up, I gave Mum a hug before casually asking, 'Do you mind watching the girls? I'd like to take Izzy to see The Strid and I think the girls would prefer to paddle and play here.'

To be fair to Mum, she readily agreed to my suggestion and Izzy and I made our way over the bridge towards the Cavendish Pavilion and on towards the woods. For half an hour we walked in an easy silence, with Izzy letting me grab her hand. Finally we neared the place, and I squeezed her hand tighter as we were suddenly greeted by the fearsome sight of The Strid.

Izzy looked at me quizzically as I urged her to sit down on the rocks which form the pinch point of the river. She gestured to the warning signs around and I explained.

'The Strid is the place of legends. The river is forced through this narrow gap and hundreds of people have died in this very spot.'

Izzy was wide-eyed as I gestured theatrically and then moved towards the edge.

'Come back Lucy, don't get too close!'

I liked the hint of fear in her voice, which showed me how much she cared. But something in me wanted to push it a little bit more, and I made a movement as if I was going to attempt to jump the gap. Obviously I wouldn't have, but my heart was pumping at the brush with danger, and I felt invincible. Laughing, I turned back towards Izzy, who grinned at me as I made my way back to safety.

'God Lucy, don't scare me like that again!'

I turned back to face the river and once again felt it's familiar pull. When my mind attempts to break free to drag me to the bad places, I often thought how I can bring myself the peace I so craved. I had read that drowning is a very serene way to leave this earth, though quite how anyone knows, I'm not really sure. There are lots of things I don't understand, but I'm pretty sure the dead can't come back to reassure us that their passing was peaceful. Hence, I'm fascinated, but at the same time repelled, with this stretch of water that promises to hold you in its beautiful green caress and adorn you with a crown of weeds as you sink at last to oblivion.

Turning towards my friend, this time I sank down next to her, stroking her cheek as I whispered, 'Can I tell you something I have never told anyone?'

Izzy pulled me close and the two of us became partners, exploring the dark place that was hidden deep in my mind.

CATH

Cath was happy to relax in the sunshine and watch the children. It was a lot easier than dealing with the bitter resentment to her presence that seemed to be rolling off Lucy. Cath couldn't understand it. Lucy had almost regressed to a surly teenager, and although it was bright sunshine, a very different season, her behaviour was a raw echo of the Christmas holidays all those years ago.

Lucy picked at her food which was just not like her, and whilst Cath tried to concentrate on what Izzy was saying, her mind was full of concern for her daughter who she loved so dearly. When Lucy fell asleep and Izzy suggested ice creams, Cath wanted to stay with her daughter. She needed to be there for her if she woke and didn't like the idea of leaving her out in the open, so vulnerable. But Izzy and the children dragged her along and then took ages in the gift shop, with Cath fretting all the time that Lucy would be panicking what had happened to them.

As she had hurried towards Lucy with the peace offering of the dripping ice cream, Cath almost recoiled at the bitterness that shone from her daughter's eyes. So, desperate to make amends for whatever wrong she had committed, she eagerly agreed to mind the children whilst the two adults went exploring. And once again, Izzy wove her magic spell, and Lucy returned serene and smiling, wearing a crown of daisies that she gleefully shared Izzy had woven for her.

That night in bed, Cath debated sharing her concerns with Jon, but she found her lips were almost paralysed. It was almost as if she didn't want to speak the words out loud.

Because once she voiced her concerns, that would mean they were real and not just a product of her over-vigilant mind. Tossing and turning whilst Jon snored peacefully beside her, Cath decided that maybe the best thing would be to have a quiet word with Izzy. And having decided on that positive course of action, Cath drifted off to sleep, happy she had someone else to confide in - another layer of protection to help keep Lucy safe.

CATH

Cath realised that she was coming to rely on the time she spent with Izzy during their morning swims. She had always loved the freedom and space that the time in the water gave her, but this blossoming friendship was quickly making this time at the pool the most precious part of her day. She enjoyed the early morning coolness of the water, reviving her from whatever dreams may have troubled her unguarded mind as she fell in a restless sleep; but the time afterwards as the two of them chatted over a coffee and the invariable bacon sandwich became her therapy, and she felt so much better for finally having someone to talk to.

The morning after the trip to the Abbey followed the same pattern as their normal meeting. Cath was worried that Izzy would have sensed the tension between mother and daughter and would feel awkward and pressured to pick a side, but the young woman was as open and friendly as normal as the two settled down after their swim, with Cath doing most of the talking. That was the thing about Izzy - she was more than happy to sit quietly, with no judgement, and allow her friend to unburden her fears. Of course, Cath didn't share with Izzy that terrible time that had prompted their relocation, but she had started to open up about the problems Lucy had experienced after Milly's birth and she found Izzy to be a compassionate listener. For the first time, Cath felt that someone cared about how all of this was affecting her, and it was a relief for those short periods not to be the strong one - to be able to unburden her worries to someone who wasn't really affected by the awfulness of it all.

Cath had been reluctant at first to share these hidden secrets with her new friend; she felt the stigma of mental health issues deeply. But she gradually began to question if this was a generational thing as Izzy seemed to take the story of what had happened as something that was a simple fact of life and, as she reassured Cath constantly, it was certainly nothing to be ashamed about. Cath hadn't meant to share quite as much with Izzy, but she did feel that maybe the younger woman judged her for being over-protective of Lucy and she felt compelled to justify her actions. Izzy quite simply understood and as her friendship with Lucy developed, Cath felt secure that in Izzy they had further support to keep Lucy safe.

This morning, as they sat in the sun, Cath was chatting about the plans her and Jon were making for their holiday. They had even set a tentative date of next May, and that way they would be back to help out over the summer holidays. Whilst it was still some months away, Cath felt that it was the closest it had ever been. Izzy asked lots of questions, seeming to be caught up in Cath's excitement, which was nice as Lucy was distinctly uninterested. Cath was used to that about her daughter, recognising that Lucy could be quite selfish, caring little for things that may be important to, or troubling others. Cath was shocked that this thought had come to her. She wasn't sure when her feelings towards Lucy had shifted slightly from unquestioning adoration, but there was no doubt she felt she was seeing her daughter the clearest she had in a good few years.

'Well, your timing will be perfect, Cath. You will be around to sell raffle tickets for the school Christmas hampers and back in time for me to rope you into manning a stall at the Summer Fair.'

Cath laughed. 'I think I've done my bit volunteering thank you, but I'll happily help out by spending my money, but only if you have a Pimm's stall there.'

Izzy grinned. 'I'll suggest that at the next PTA meeting.'

Cath smiled. 'Ah, did Lucy rope you into volunteering

too, then?' As she noted the confusion pass over the younger woman's face, Cath suddenly knew what Izzy was going to say.

'Well, Heidi asked me. She's the self-appointed leader of the Reception year group parents, and I know her from pilates. In fact, it was Heidi who recommended the school to me when I was looking for somewhere for Beth.'

'I know the name Heidi - I think Lucy has met up with her and it was Heidi who asked Lucy to join as well.'

Again, Cath noted that fleeting look of incomprehension before Izzy smiled, though it seemed a bit more forced than usual. 'Not sure how Lucy got involved to be honest. I know I mentioned it to her and then she turned up at the meeting. It's worked out well actually as the two of us have a number of things we are doing together, selling raffle tickets for the Christmas hamper being one of them. Hint hint!'

There was a small silence before Cath spoke slowly. 'I hope Lucy's not bothering you Izzy. She doesn't have many friends, and I do know she can sometimes be a bit much. I can speak to her if you want.'

Izzy looked horrified. 'Oh gosh, no Cath, it's absolutely fine. I appreciate Lucy may be worried about this new transition of the girls starting school and I'm happy to support her through this. The PTA is a great way to get involved and if she feels safer doing that with me, then I'm happy with that. I'm pretty sure she will soon be involved with the rest of the group and as her confidence grows, she will be less reliant on me.'

Cath thought she might cry, but she managed to blink back the tears and squeeze Izzy's hand. 'I'm just so very pleased we met you. You are so good to both of us.'

Izzy looked embarrassed but then smiled. 'I had a friend who suffered desperately with postnatal depression and I feel bad that I was so caught up in my own life that I didn't help as I should have done. To be honest, I got quite impatient with her and thought she just needed to get a grip, so maybe meeting you and Lucy is helping me to make peace with my past. I feel like I'm the lucky one.'

Afterwards, Cath looked back on this conversation and wondered if she should have been more honest with Izzy - warned her that things may be more complex than they appeared on the surface. Maybe that would have saved her and Lucy. But Cath smiled, content that Izzy was there to help shoulder the load, and allowed herself to dream of long holidays without a care in the world.

LUCY

The summer holidays raced towards their inevitable conclusion and whilst I knew I would miss Milly dreadfully, I was starting to believe that it would be good for me to regain some time back - to become Lucy rather than Milly's mum. It was funny how I never missed a dose with my new medication routine. Morning, noon and night, I religiously flushed those deadening pills down the toilet and obediently requested a repeat prescription that I never failed to pick up from the surgery.

And I felt fine. Free. I suddenly had a burning energy inside me that had been missing before; I felt truly alive. Sleep was starting to feel like something that wasted too much time, and I found I could function on very little rest, instead scrolling through the message thread between myself and Izzy and seeing the hidden messages that Izzy had conveyed. I would fire off my random thoughts to her in the night and would restlessly wait for her to wake and reply with her, 'Morning, you've been busy. I wish I had your energy.' Sometimes Izzy wouldn't reply and that would make me sad, but then I realised she might be being watched by people who didn't want us to be friends - shadowy figures who meant us harm. I loved her for that - my very special friend who sometimes had to put on an act to the rest of the world, just to make sure that I was safe.

We spent lots of time together, and Beth and Milly adored each other. Milly was delighted if I could manage to buy her the same outfit that Beth was wearing, though Beth could be a bit mean and was quite relentless with her, 'Stop copying me,' whinging. Izzy would laugh it off, but I could see her looking at Beth annoyed and worried. I would be worried too if Milly was such a rude little cow.

It even got that Milly would refuse to wear the outfits I laid out for her, which meant that for the first time, Milly and I started to argue. Milly could also be quite a nag, asking to meet up with some of the other children who she thought would be her friends. I couldn't understand why Milly didn't see that Izzy and Beth were the only people we needed.

Izzy, unlike her snotty daughter, didn't mind that we shared the same taste in clothes. In fact, she went with me shopping to pick an outfit for the Pizza and Prosecco night, and it was so funny when we both picked the same dress to try on. I suppose it wasn't really that much of a coincidence as I had seen Izzy pick it up as I was watching her from behind the gift card display. In the end Izzy persuaded me that I wore it better, so she would find something else. As she pointed out, the others would be jealous if we turned up wearing the same thing. It was enough for me that Izzy had said how much she loved me in the dress. I couldn't wait to wear it for her.

I learnt Izzy's routine. Three mornings a week were easy, as I knew that was when she met Mum for a swim. I was careful not to bump into her those mornings as I knew Mum was already suspicious, so I needed to tread carefully. I tried to meet up with Izzy as often as she was able, and noted down her reasons if she couldn't make it. It was quite straightforward to build up a timetable of her life and see how I could slot my comings and goings into that.

Rob was pleased that I was starting to take some time for myself on an evening, so was more than happy to make sure he was home on time on a Tuesday so I could go to pilates, and a Thursday, which was hot yoga. If he was curious as to my newfound interest in self-care, he never mentioned it. I know he had noticed that I was awake in the night, and I sometimes worried that he would hear me as I paced from room to room waiting for the green light to appear by Izzy's name to show me that she was back online. I had spotted that he had checked my tablets, as I had laid a single hair grip balanced against the corner and when I went to perform my ritual tablet disposal the next morning, I saw the hair grip lying on the floor. I wondered if he was checking for himself or if maybe he was working with the nurses who had been so cruel to me when Milly was born.

 I liked the hot yoga class the best. I always felt cleansed afterwards, as if any nastiness had been sweated from my core. Izzy had looked surprised when I turned up for the first session, and I had played the game and exclaimed shock on seeing her there and laughed again at my twin. The nice thing about the hot yoga was that afterwards I could normally persuade Izzy to go for a disgustingly healthy and revolting tasting green juice in the little cafe near the studio, and it meant I got to string a little more time out with her.

 Pilates was not as nice. It should have been, but Heidi went to that class too and I saw her whisper something to Izzy when I arrived for my first class, wearing an identical gym set as Izzy but obviously in a slightly different colour combination. I didn't want to be too obvious. It wasn't as easy to persuade Izzy out for extra time after pilates. Somehow Heidi, helped by a few of the other ladies, often managed to usher Izzy away from me. I heard Heidi say loudly, 'Really Izzy, I think you should report this to someone. It seems to be getting out of hand.' I think she was talking about me, and I didn't like it. I knew exactly who she would be reporting me to.

 It took me a little while to realise that there was something off with the parents' group chat. I was so caught up with my special message thread that I didn't notice how the group chat had gone quiet. It seemed that one minute the thread was a steady stream of silliness that I was happy to ignore, and in fact had muted notifications, to a resounding silence. Like everyone had just disappeared. Once I had noticed this, I couldn't quite forget about it. I asked Izzy if she had spotted anything weird, but she brushed me off and said she hadn't really noticed; she had been too busy reading my messages. She laughed as she said it, but I felt a little bit of a sting was in her words, so I vowed to maybe calm it down a little. On the last Friday before school was due to start on the Tuesday, I took Milly into town as Izzy had mentioned she needed to sort a couple of last-minute things for Beth so wouldn't be able to come round to mine for lunch. We had met for lunch on a Friday the previous week, so I thought that was a date set in stone, but I did understand that it was a bit of a frantic time with school starting so soon. Once again, I was so relieved that Mum had pushed me to get sorted before we went on holiday. I smiled as I thought how that holiday seemed so long ago, and how I would have never guessed as I envied the fantasy Bella, that I would one day be her very best friend.

Wandering through town, dragging a reluctant Milly behind, I failed to see the familiar figure of Izzy anywhere, and by our third circuit of the shops Milly was really starting to whinge. Sinking onto a bench whilst Milly continued to mutter and grumble, I logged onto Snap Maps and bingo! Izzy had shared her location settings, and I could see that she was in the nearby park. They must have finished their shopping early, and no doubt Beth would have nagged her to visit the park. Honestly, that child. Things would have to be very different when we all lived together. Better still, Beth could go and live with her dad.

I tried a casual message.

> *Hi, where are you? Had to pop into town, so wondered if you fancied meeting for lunch?*

I saw one blue tick emerge, then a second; but as hard as I stared at the phone, no bouncing bubbles appeared to herald a reply, and then the green dot disappeared to tell me she was gone. As I stared at my phone, willing Izzy to respond, I noticed that there was a new message in the parents' chat from Alex. I wasn't really sure who Alex was, and I scrolled up through the chat to see if I had missed something as the message didn't really make sense.

> *What time are we meeting at the park? I think we said 12 by the slides.*

This was followed by a message from Heidi, which I couldn't read as it had been deleted. I was confused now.

Not really stopping to think it through, I grabbed Milly's hand and suggested we head to the park for a play on the slides and the treat of an ice cream. The whinging stopped immediately as Milly's face brightened. 'Yes please! We might see Beth and the others there. She said they were going to the park for a picnic. Can we have a picnic too?'

I muttered something non-committal and followed the shady avenue of trees to the entrance to the park, and we skirted the duck pond with Milly running in front, knowing exactly where she was heading. My confidence dropped with every step I took, and for the first time I really hoped that I wasn't going to see Izzy in the park. I just had a feeling that what I was going to see was about to knock our friendship a little bit off-kilter. My heart sank as I saw Milly stop and wave her hand in a frantic gesture before she quickened her pace towards the group congregated by the slides. Even from this distance, the distinctive pattern of Izzy's rug, that I had settled on so happily at the pool party, jumped out at me to drill in my brain the fact that I didn't want to acknowledge: Izzy had arranged to meet other people and hadn't told me. Because, as I got closer, I could see that it wasn't just Izzy and Beth, but there were several other mums that I recognised from the pool party; and of course, sharing Izzy's rug was bloody Heidi. How I disliked that woman.

The easiest thing would have been to turn away, hope that no one had seen me and wait for Izzy to tell me all about her day, but Milly had already reached the group of children at the bottom of the slides, who were all delighted to welcome this new playmate to their gang. Sadly, I could see that the same welcome would not be applied to me.

Fiona spotted me first and she stared at me open-mouthed before nudging the woman next to her, before turning to watch Izzy. And so it began, a sort of nudge and notice dance until finally I reached the circle of the rugs, which reminded me of watching a film with my dad when I was very young. It was a Western, not the sort of thing I liked at all, but at one point there was some mention of 'circle the wagons', and I asked Dad what that meant. He explained that the group would gather together to protect themselves from a potential attack. It seemed to me that this group had formed a protective circle around my Izzy, and I didn't like the way that made me feel.

There was an awkward silence and Izzy was the first to break it, jumping to her feet and walking towards me. 'Lucy, you found us. Did you get my message telling you where I was?'

I made a show of taking out my phone. 'Oh, I haven't checked my messages recently, hold on. Nope nothing there.' Of course, I knew there was nothing there. I never stopped checking my phone, and I absolutely never missed a message from my Izzy. To the left of me I heard someone mutter, 'God, poor Izzy, just when she thought she had escaped for a bit. I have no idea why she is so nice about it.' I wanted to turn and confront whoever said that, but before I could do so we were joined by Heidi, who was struggling to meet my eye. However, she displayed the steely determination that had meant she was our unofficial leader and brightly addressed me.

'Thank goodness you found where we are. Obviously, we started the new group once Joanna decided that St Wilfred's wasn't good enough for her little ones - it seemed less antagonistic than removing her from the group. We set up the new chat, but it was only when we arrived at the park that we realised there was a few of us missing and saw that somehow not everyone had been transferred over. I feel dreadful about it, and we are just trying to get in touch with the others now, so I am so pleased that you found us.' She smiled and I smiled back, confused, and the moment of awkwardness was gone.

We had a pleasant afternoon, and I actually made the effort to try and talk to a few of the other mums, though they all seemed wary of me. Everyone was sharing their summer activities and I half listened, relaxing in the warm caress of the sun, until I heard Kirsten mention she had been walking in Malham with her sister.

I sat bolt upright and managed to knock over a tray of juice as I stared at her. 'Oh, I hate Malham. It's the drop above the cove, you see. I'm just drawn to the edge. Every time I go, I'm afraid something will force me to take that step into nothingness and then I'll be lost forever.'

The whole group fell silent and then a couple of the women gave a nervous laugh, which trailed off as I stared at them. 'Don't you feel it too? That sense of evil that chases you up the steps, that wants to wipe you away from face of the earth?' I knew I was talking far too fast, but my heart was pounding, and I was concerned to see a couple of nurses from the Mother and Baby Unit were stood over by the swings, monitoring my actions. I bet they were going to report back on me. I knew the medication allowed them to monitor my thoughts, so maybe they had somehow discovered that I had started to escape their control.

There was a long silence and then Heidi started talking loudly about setting up the picnic, and this was greeted with enthusiastic agreement, as people took the chance to shift away from me. Clearly, they sensed the darkness that threatened me, and felt they needed to keep a safe distance. All around me people were talking nonsense, with their voices somehow too high to be comforting, and I found I couldn't relax in the sunshine as all I could hear was the frantic pounding of my heart in my ears that drowned out the chatter around me, though I caught the odd snippet of, 'Really, needs help' and, 'Thank goodness none of the children were listening,' and I was pretty sure they were talking about me.

Eventually, I moved back to the safety of Izzy and tugged on her arm frantically, interrupting her conversation. The group of people surrounding her, because of course Izzy was always surrounded by a group of people, glared at me. Heidi looked as if she was going to lead Izzy away from me, but Izzy gave them a reassuring smile and, putting her arm round me gently, led me to one side.

'What's up Lucy? You don't seem right. Shall I call your mum for you?'

I looked at her confused, why was she speaking so loudly? I turned to look at the group behind us and saw they were hanging on her every word, like we were actors performing a play for them. 'Izzy, you see those two women over there? I think they have followed me from the hospital where I had Milly.'

Izzy followed the direction of my gaze and smiled at me. 'I think they do work at the hospital, but I'm sure they are not here for you. However, just to be safe, why don't we head back to my place and that should throw them off the scent. You wait here and I'll just get the children and my stuff then we can get away. I'll be pleased to escape this lot anyway, and we can have a good catch up.'

Turning away from me, I saw her conferring with the watching group, and they all stared over in my direction. Then Milly and Beth were with us, and we turned and left the park.

As we made our way to Izzy's house and she talked to me about her day, I felt my heartbeat slow, and the jumbled chaos of my mind started to ease. I found this was happening more and more - that I had periods when I felt I was in control, that I was in charge and safe, and then the panic would engulf me, and I needed someone to throw me a lifebelt. Thank God Izzy was there for me.

Once we were settled in her garden, she unpacked the picnic she had obviously made for the park and the girls pounced on the food. I felt bad. It was gone two now and poor Milly hadn't had anything to eat since breakfast, and come to think of it neither had I. My sense of self-preservation told me that I needed to eat and then I probably needed to seek some medical help. However, Izzy then appeared with a cold bottle of wine and poured me a large glass, and as I gulped at the wine and listened to Izzy talking to me, I started to feel better.

Looking back, that afternoon was probably the last time I felt truly safe with Izzy. The last time before my mind started to tell me that something was wrong, that Izzy might mean me harm. But that afternoon, I relaxed as Izzy told me how proud she was of me, to keep going because I was becoming exactly who I was meant to be. At least I think that's what she said; to my shame I can't really remember. I don't remember getting home either. It was lucky that Rob was out at some sort of awards dinner, so I just heated up some chicken nuggets and oven chips and Milly ate those whilst watching something on the Disney Channel that I don't really remember. I wasn't hungry at all. I was tempted to have another drink, but a part of me knew that would not be safe for me, so instead I went to bed at the same time as Milly and hoped that sleep would cure my fuzzy brain.

I heard Rob come in and, grabbing my phone, saw it was nearly three in the morning. I heard the sound of the shower running in the family bathroom before the creak of the floorboards told me he was checking on Milly before he headed to the spare room, closing the door firmly behind him. I was now wide awake and, as was habit, checked online and was delighted to see the green dot by Izzy's name.

> Hey, what are you doing still awake? Thanks for everything you did for me today. You're right. I just need to keep going and I will be victorious!

Although Izzy remained online, the second blue tick failed to appear to show she had read my message. Hoping to lull myself back to sleep, I opened the parent group and had another nosey at the group members. Oh my, Heidi had changed her photo to one of her on her wedding day. That woman was so sad. I couldn't wait to tell Izzy. I was just about to message her when I remembered something. Scrolling through the names, I checked once, then read through a second time more slowly, but there was no Joanna there. So why had Heidi lied to me?

CATH

When Cath took a seat opposite Izzy, she was concerned to see that her friend looked to have been crying. Cath knew better than to ask outright if there was anything wrong. Izzy would open up in her own time and Cath would be ready to listen. The two of them sat in a comfortable silence until Izzy suddenly blurted out, 'Cath, I'm really worried about Lucy.' And all Cath remembered afterwards about that moment was that, like some melodramatic film, the clouds moved to block out the sun, and it really did feel like the end of summer.

'I really like Lucy, you know I do, and I really don't want you to think I'm complaining about her because I'm really not, but, well, Lucy seems to be very dependent on me and I'm worried I won't be able to give her everything she needs.' Izzy sank back in her chair now and took a deep breath after managing to get the words out that had clearly been causing her such concern. Cath nodded and she hoped her face didn't display the devastation that she felt inside.

'Oh Izzy, I am sorry. I feel dreadful about this. Lucy can be needy and I'm afraid I sort of assumed all was well, so I've sort of neglected her a bit.'

Izzy touched Cath's hand and quickly interrupted.

'No! Please don't get me wrong, I'm not telling you this because I want you to do something. I just thought that maybe we could work together to help Lucy. This is what I think we should do.'

Cath listened as Izzy detailed how she would continue to spend time with Lucy but encourage her to seek help, and would update Cath daily so that between them they could decide whether they needed to seek further intervention. Driving home from the pool, Cath was surprised that she had found herself agreeing to this plan when her initial thought was that she needed to contact the GP immediately. But then Izzy had pointed out that Lucy would respond so much better if she felt she was the one to decide she needed help. After all, what difference would a few more days make?

As she walked in through the door, she saw Jon was engrossed in watching his favourite YouTubers explore Switzerland, and she decided to keep the news of Lucy's deterioration to herself for the moment. After all, they might get it sorted and Jon, and indeed Rob, need never know of this little problem.

But as she waited for the kettle to boil, Cath couldn't stop the silent tears that rolled down her cheeks and she wondered if this nightmare they had found themselves in would ever stop. And even though Cath knew Lucy wasn't well, at that point she was furious with her and allowed herself to wish, just for a second, that Izzy was her daughter.

ROB

Rob felt bad. In fact, he felt very bad. When he and Lucy had left for their holiday, he had vowed that this would be a new start for them both. He was irritated by Lucy's complete over the top anxiety about Milly starting school, but he decided he needed to be more understanding, show a little more compassion. He was also very aware that he was reacting as badly as he was because he felt guilty. Part of him felt his behaviour could be justified. After all, he had heard his wife say things that he had found truly damaging. He couldn't reason with himself that these things were likely hallucinations caused by her illness. Hearing Lucy rant about the love of her life, who was clearly not him, had torn away at him, bit by bit and fuelled the resentment even further.

When he was sat alone in the bar, drinking his double whisky, he spoke to no one and instead replayed Lucy's words over and over, trying to make something rational out of something that was anything but. One minute she would be talking gibberish about being ripped away from her lost love, and then she would be calling for Kate, and Rob really couldn't get his head round how the two fitted together. Or rather, he could but really didn't want to, so chose to try and figure out something that was a more palatable reason. Sometimes he would regret that Lucy had ever got pregnant, and then his thoughts would stray to the idea that maybe Milly was to blame for everything that had happened. Then he would hate himself even more; and on those nights, he would have a second double and get a taxi home.

When he went round to Paul and Lou's house, he found

he could forget. For a while he could pretend that Lucy, with all her neediness, wasn't waiting for him at home, and to his shame, he would try to forget about Milly too. He could pretend to himself he was still single. Maybe it was because he was so invested in this internal fantasy that he acted so out of character. Just after Easter, he had dropped in on his sanctuary as normal, but the door was opened by a stranger. He had forgotten that his friends were away. They had mentioned their dog walker was popping in to feed the cat and sort the post.

'Hi, can I help you?'

'Sorry, I forgot Paul and Lou are away. I'm not a burglar scoping the place out, I promise you!'

'No problem.' She smiled at him, and he felt a bit strange. 'I'm pleased you knocked. Brightened up my evening.' Rob didn't know what to say, unsure if the woman was flirting with him. So he said nothing, just gave a stupid grin and walked away. He turned as she called after him, 'Hopefully I'll see you around again.'

He wished now he had just kept on walking - taken a detour to that bar and maybe this time ordered a treble - but instead he had turned and replied, 'I hope so too.'

And after that, as if the universe had heard his wish and decided to grant it for him, he had suddenly seen her everywhere. Maybe she had always been in the background, but he had just never been aware of her. One thing was for sure: he was very aware of her now.

First of all, they bumped into each other at the golf club. It was just a quick chat. All completely innocent, so Rob couldn't explain why he was relieved no one saw them together, and he didn't mention to Paul he had bumped into his dog walker. Then as he nipped out for a sandwich one lunch, she was passing, so it made sense that they go and grab a bit of lunch together. Again, nothing wrong with that, except he didn't mention it to Lucy when she asked him how his day had been. And he normally would have mentioned that as it would have been something to say, something to fill the long, awkward silences as they sat together once Milly had gone to bed.

And well, everything after that just seemed inevitable. Rob absolved himself of any responsibility, figuring that fate had brought them together and it was no use fighting it. He had however been honest from the start, explaining he was married with a daughter, and also explaining that he would never leave Lucy. 'She's just too fragile.'

After the holiday, he was determined that the affair had to stop. He had been a coward and broken the news in the middle of his holiday, and the relief he had felt had taken him by surprise. It also seemed that by deciding to focus on his family, things with his wife started to improve and indeed, he started to see glimmers of the Lucy he had first known. Rob began to hope that maybe the three of them could make a decent life together. 'The Three Musketeers' ready for adventures and celebrating their little girl as she made her way in the world.

Obviously, he wasn't going to get off that lightly, and a few tearful phone calls and messages caused him some discomfort. But then there was the threat to come round to his house if he wouldn't meet and give a proper explanation. And that was how they had ended up at the Langdale. As usual, he didn't think straight, and they'd ended up in bed. It had almost led to disaster, being spotted by Jon, and it scared him into cutting all contact.

But she was there at the awards dinner and too many whiskeys, plus feeling a bit neglected now Lucy was spending all her time with this new friend, Izzy, who she seemed to be completely obsessed with, meant that he reverted to a behaviour which he knew had the potential to tear his life apart. He wasn't being fair on anyone, but he felt hopelessly stuck. And then this morning he had received a message which just simply stated that she could see that the whole thing was making him miserable and that whilst she cared for him deeply, she thought it best if they ended it now before too many people got hurt. And Rob was shocked that rather than relief, the overwhelming feeling was that he had been punched in the gut. Rather than being able to look to the future with his little family, he was struck by just sheer desolation at what his life looked like stretched out before him. What a mess.

LUCY

Suddenly it was Milly's first day at school. The day that I had been dreading before the start of the holidays was now here, and I welcomed it. I was looking forward to seeing Izzy every morning and then I thought we would probably end up spending the day together before we collected the children mid-afternoon. I was disappointed that I hadn't heard from Izzy since I had been round at her house, but I sent lots of chatty messages just so she knew I was thinking of her. Milly was so excited that first morning and I was so proud to see her dressed in her little school uniform as she insisted on carrying her own book bag. I had deliberated on my outfit, but went with cut off dungarees again, seeing as we were in the last gasp of summer, before autumn overtook us and the weather, as well as the nights, turned darker.

    Just as we were about to set off I saw Mum's car pull up, and for a minute I worried that something was wrong, until I remembered that months ago, before I found Izzy, I had asked Mum to be there for me on Milly's first day. I opened the door and Milly pushed past me, doing a pretty twirl, book bag flying out to the side. Mum stood still for a moment, obviously lost in a world of her own, and then I realised she had tears in her eyes.

    'Oh Milly, you look wonderful. You are so like your mum was when she was a little girl. Quick, let me take a photo to send to Grandad.' Milly was more than happy to oblige, and then Mum turned to me and gave me a hug. 'Oh, enjoy this Lucy, it seems no time at all that I was taking you to school for your first day.'

I hugged her back, noticing that she had lost weight. Must be all that swimming she was doing.

'Mum, we've got to dash. Can't be late on the first day.' Milly was already fidgeting, hopping from foot to foot, impatient to get the day started.

'Of course.' Mum turned to the car but simply clicked the fob to lock the doors; then, giving my hand a squeeze, she started to walk with us to the path.

Oh, bugger! I was hoping Mum might see we were fine, but she'd clearly not forgotten that I'd practically begged her to come with me on Milly's first day all those weeks ago when I had been so afraid. I'd forgotten to tell her that I didn't need her anymore, that I had Izzy now. But looking at the proud smile adorning her face, I didn't have the heart to tell her that I didn't want her, and so we linked arms and I resolved to make the best of it. I could soon get rid of her once I met up with Izzy.

I enjoyed the walk to school that day. The world felt normal - the colours not as sharp and jagged as they had been for the last week or so, everything was softer, gentler, not so confrontational. Maybe I had turned a corner. Thinking back, I could see that I had allowed myself to get overwhelmed with it all since I had stopped the tablets. I still wasn't sleeping, probably because I spent endless hours scrolling on my phone and drinking too much.

'I like September,' Mum's voice broke into my thoughts. 'Lots of people make New Year's Resolutions, but I think September is a time for new beginnings. A time to let go of things that no longer serve you and move forward.'

I smiled at Mum. I liked that idea; and squeezed Mum's hand three times - my way of letting her know I loved her. I hoped she understood. From the smile she gave me and her bright eyes, I think she did.

And then we were turning the corner and were assaulted by the noise of over-excited children all heading towards the gates. Milly hung back for a second, for the first time looking a little unsure, and I felt some of the old panic start to resurface.

At that point I was so glad to have Mum with me, giving me a little nudge in the back to prompt me to go forward with a confidence I did not feel, to show Milly that we could do hard things.

'I'll wait here love, you don't want me getting in the way whilst you settle Milly in. Milly, come and give Grandma a hug; and I can't wait to hear all about it when you get home. Especially what's for lunch. I hope it's not cold boiled socks.'

Milly laughed, launching herself into Mum's arms, all the earlier trepidation forgotten. I wished I could do the same, but Milly was already leading me into the crowd, where she had spotted Beth. And if Beth was there, I thought with relief, that meant that Izzy would be there too.

And it seemed that the crowd parted in front of me so that at last I saw Izzy, laughing and joking with a group of mums from the Reception year. Heidi was there of course, and she was the first to spot me heading towards them, and she gave Izzy a very obvious nudge. I decided I really didn't like Heidi. As I reached them, I saw the way Milly was embraced into the group of children, which was a little different to the rather frosty welcome I was given. Then I decided I was being silly. I have always worried too much what other people think, always been afraid that they don't like me. But like Mum had said, this was a time for new beginnings, so I smiled widely at the group and gave a cheery 'Good morning!' There were a few mumbled responses and then an awkward silence. Izzy looked uncomfortable and I could see that she was struggling to meet my eye, but as I pushed in the circle to stand next to her, she gave my arm a light touch - her way of showing me how special I was to her.

'Izzy, shall we go for coffee afterwards, and then you can come to mine until it's time to pick the girls up?' Although I had addressed the question to Izzy, I could feel the eyes of every woman in the little group swivel first to me, then to her. I really hoped the others didn't expect to get the same invite. Izzy shifted uncomfortably and took her time answering, and

I can't bear silence, so I blurted out, 'No need to look so scared, I won't bite you. Well, unless you want me to.' I followed this with a laugh, which even to my ears sounded a little manic, and I wished I had not made such a stupid joke. What was wrong with me? I noticed the group move a little closer to Izzy, as if acting as a shield, but they must know that Izzy didn't need any protection from me.

After what seemed an age, Izzy raised her eyes from the floor. 'Lucy, we went through this the other day. I have my new job to go to as soon as I've done the school drop off. I'm sorry, but I did explain this when you turned up at my house.' I was very confused. The last time I had been at Izzy's house was when she had taken me home with her after the upset in the park. The way she was speaking, it was if I had called in uninvited, hassling her to spend time with me. And although I was getting muddled with the days, I was pretty sure I hadn't called in since, limiting myself to just walking past when I paced the streets, unable to sleep. And I couldn't remember anything about any job, but then again, the whole of that afternoon had been a bit of a blur. Izzy did have very large wine glasses and I couldn't really remember a great deal between arriving and stumbling home. I realised that I was just staring at her, and then jumped as the bell rang to herald the opening of the gates.

'Saved by the bell,' muttered Heidi, and I wanted to give her a pinch.

Milly was already storming ahead of me, so I ran to catch her up, helping her find her peg and handing her over to the care of Miss Murray, who was obviously surprised that I deposited my daughter with very little fuss. *Well, you won't be the last person I prove wrong,* I thought to myself as I loitered at the gate, waiting to see if I could catch Izzy on the way out.

'You're wasting your time hanging around there.' I turned towards the voice and recognised Fiona. 'Izzy asked to be let out the front entrance. Honestly, you need to get some self-respect. It's really not on. She won't tell you, but you need to hear it.' I wanted to reply, to ask her what she meant - Izzy was my friend whatever they thought - but then I saw Mum walking towards me, and I decided to leave the battle for another day. I reasoned that maybe there was a touch of jealousy from the others. Ah yes, that made perfect sense, and Izzy was trying to show me less attention to protect me from any nasty comments. Feeling much happier, and suddenly ravenously hungry, I linked arms with Mum.

'Come on, let's go get a coffee and cake. Lots of cake.'

LUCY

That first week flew by. I missed Milly, but I missed Izzy more. I got no more than a quick wave at pick up and drop off, and there was always one of the other mums with her, acting as if she needed a bodyguard. I was looking forward to Friday night though. A whole evening with Izzy, and maybe I could persuade her to come home with me afterwards for a few drinks. Dad had offered to act as a taxi service, so I knew he wouldn't mind the extra passenger. I'd obviously messaged Izzy every day. Well, several times actually, but had received few responses other than the odd thumbs up. I did hope they weren't monitoring her phone, and I thought I must remember to ask her on Friday.

As I was getting ready my phone buzzed, and I felt my heart leap as I saw it was a message from Izzy.

> *Thanks for all your messages, sorry I haven't been able to get back to you. It's been that sort of week. Looking forward to tonight. See you later. x*

I tapped a reply straight back.

> *Can't wait to see you. Save me a seat next to you. I love the outfit we picked out, can't wait for you to see it xxx*

Rob gave a whistle once I came downstairs. I had fully expected him to be late home and was ready to call Mum to come and babysit, but he was home for five and was now sat in the lounge with Milly, tapping away on his laptop.

'Wow! It's not your normal style but I really, really like it.'

I smiled as I gave a twirl, loving the way the dress made me feel. Sleeveless, the top of the dress was fitted and cut with a deep V-neck that made me feel slightly reckless. I loved the pattern of pink and black that nipped in at my waist, before a plain black skirt fell to my ankles, with a simple pink border skirting my feet. I wore gladiator sandals, showing off painted pink toenails and felt like I should be heading off to meet a young lover on a beach in Greece, rather than heading into town to meet a group of mums. Still, Izzy would be there, and that was all that mattered. As I moved towards Rob for a hug, he seemed to recoil as he inhaled the scent of 'Lucky' that I had rather drenched myself with.

'I wish you wouldn't wear that. I really don't like it on you.'

'Well, luckily I'm not wearing it for you,' I smiled. 'I'm wearing it for me.'

And Izzy, a voice in my head followed up.

We were late setting off to the restaurant, as I had messaged Izzy to see if she wanted a lift and had been reluctant to leave until I had received a reply. Rob muttered about never getting to meet the mysterious Izzy, and 'was I sure she wasn't an imaginary friend?' His remarks hurt me more than I let him see. Rob, still grinning at his witty jibe, dropped me off.

I checked my reflection in the window of the shop next to the restaurant to reassure myself that I looked just perfect. Pushing open the door, I could see our group had taken over the long table at the back of the dining space and most people were already there, chatting and drinking. As I made my way over, I once again got the feeling that people were staring at me, as if I'd already done something wrong. I couldn't see Izzy anywhere. Oh God, maybe she'd replied and was impatiently waiting for the lift I had offered. I reached for my bag to check my phone, but then I saw Izzy stood at the bar with Heidi. I frowned; something was definitely wrong here. Heidi and Izzy turned to make their way back to the table with their drinks and I saw Izzy freeze as she spotted me. Heidi put a hand on her shoulder, and I heard her say, 'Oh my God, I don't believe it!'

Izzy and I were dressed identically. I could see that Izzy was annoyed but as she reached me, she smiled and said, 'Nice dress, Lucy. Looks like we match again.' I couldn't smile back as my head felt all fuzzy. I was sure we had agreed that I would wear the dress. Izzy had clearly said I should have it as it looked better on me, though looking at Izzy tonight I could see that she had not been truthful when she had told me that. She looked completely stunning, and I suddenly felt very much like a pale and rather cheap imitation.

Izzy slipped into her seat in the middle of the table and there was no room for me to sit by her. I considered trying to pull a chair over, but Heidi rather loudly told me, 'There's a seat for you there at the end, Lucy,' and I had no option but to take the place offered. I sat, struggling not to cry, and barely remembered ordering the food, preferring instead to take advantage of the prosecco on the table as I reached over yet again to fill my glass. All around me, people were chatting and laughing and, whilst it may not have been intentional, I felt excluded from pretty much every conversation. I sat feeling awkward and concentrated on refilling my glass.

When the pizzas arrived I tried to force myself to eat, aware that I had drunk too much too quickly. But by then I had lost my appetite for any food and all I wanted to do was to drink some more. Struggling to my feet, I stumbled across the restaurant to the Ladies, feeling that everyone was watching me and judging me. As I stood waiting for a cubicle to become free, the voice of Fiona rang out as she spoke to the next-door cubicle.

'I mean, it's just getting ridiculous. Izzy really needs to do something, but she's far too nice.'

'Oh, I agree. I mean, these things can end up escalating and can become so unpleasant.'

I didn't recognise the voice shouting back over the cubicle divide and I felt vaguely uncomfortable listening, but they had mentioned Izzy, and I was concerned that there was something wrong with my best friend. There was a flush and Fiona emerged, stopping as she saw me standing there.

'Ah, Lucy,' she said loudly. 'Are you having a nice time?'

I ignored her question. 'Is there something wrong with Izzy?'

Fiona gave a sort of snort as the second toilet flushed and the other woman emerged. My heart sank as I recognised Kirsten from the PTA meeting. She had obviously been hitting the prosecco nearly as hard as I had, and her eyes had an unpleasant glint as she looked to be relishing some sort of confrontation. I took an involuntary step backwards as I recognised she had been looking for the chance to hurt me ever since she had noticed that I was Izzy's favourite.

'You turn up, wearing the same outfit as Izzy, yet again, after hounding her all summer and you ask if she's alright? Of course she's not alright. You had a nerve turning up here tonight after everything you've put her through and to be honest, the best thing would be if you gathered what little remains of your self-respect and fuck off home.'

I stumbled back against the wall as if she had slapped me and was furious to feel tears pricking at my eyes.

'You have no idea what you're talking about. Izzy is my best friend.'

Fiona gave a snort then instructed her friend to, 'Leave it, you're talking to a brick wall.' They both left me stood like a fool in the middle of the Ladies, wondering what the hell was going on. Sitting in the cubicle, I realised I just wanted to stay there, hidden from the world, but I needed to see Izzy.

As I stood, washing my hands, I could see that my mascara had smudged and my eyes remained slightly unfocused from the glasses of prosecco I had downed to drown my misery. I looked, I thought, slightly mad and a little bit frightening. I didn't like it - it felt like someone else was fighting to take control of my body and mind.

Taking a deep breath, I emerged from the safe cocoon of the toilets and swayed back to the table and stopped by Izzy. I really had to concentrate to speak the few words clearly, as my mouth seemed to have stopped working properly.

'Could I have a word Izzy, in private?' There was a sort of collective gasp round the table which I wanted to giggle at, but the look on Izzy's face stole the joy before it could break free from my mouth.

'I don't think so, Lucy. Look, you've had quite a bit to drink. Why don't you go home and then later in the week, when you are feeling a bit better, we can sit somewhere safe, maybe with your mum, and talk about this.' I wanted to stand my ground but out of the corner of my eye I could see more staff from the Mother and Baby Unit watching me, and I suddenly felt afraid that they had come to take me away. As I hesitated, Heidi stood up and tried to take my arm to guide me towards the door and I felt the fury that had grown from the deep hurt of Izzy's rejection, rise to the surface.

'Don't you touch me!' I screamed and gave her a shove. She stumbled and fell against the table, knocking plates of pizzas and a couple of full bottles of bubbles to the floor. As people leapt to their feet and waiters rushed to stem the flow of liquid snaking across the floor, I caught Izzy's eye and, making sure no one was watching, she smirked at me and blew me a kiss, before dissolving in a flood of tears in Fiona's arms. Turning, I fled, knowing I had somehow got something terribly wrong.

I knew I could ring Dad at any time, but I decided to walk around town for a while, just to try and get things straight in my head. The streets were busy with couples and groups heading out for the start of their evening. Everywhere I looked, people were smiling and laughing as they greeted old friends with hugs and excitedly shared their news of the week. It wasn't that long ago that I had been so excited to be going out, to spend time with Izzy, but now everything was ruined. As I passed a few groups, I could sense they were looking at me, and I realised all these people were probably talking about what I had just done.

As I walked, I made sudden turns and crossed the road, just in case the nurses had decided to follow me. Though I was starting to believe that maybe the person I should be fearing was actually a little closer to home. I needed to think, but my brain wasn't working properly and everything seemed so muddled. It had started with that entry in the guest book: my first introduction to Bella who turned out to be Izzy, but who was she really? Did she work for the hospital and had she befriended me so they could trap me and take me back there? I just couldn't make sense of it. She said she was my friend, and I had showered her with love and attention and instead of us growing closer, we just seemed to lurch further apart.

It was clear now that all the other mums hated me, and they were plotting to take Izzy away from me. And judging from the events of tonight, it seemed that Izzy was only too happy to let that happen. Just as I had when I had arrived at the restaurant, I caught a glimpse of myself in the shop window. I moved in for a closer look, lost in my own reflection, because the person staring back at me was not the same woman who had walked into that restaurant an hour or so earlier. Wiping my eyes, I opened my phone to call Dad. I just wanted to go home.

CATH

Cath woke up on Saturday morning with the familiar churning in her stomach. Jon had been home way before she expected last night, and he had some story about Lucy needing to be picked up early as she had an upset stomach. Cath had messaged Lucy straight away.

Hope you are Ok. Let me know if we can do anything.

There had been no reply and Cath tried to tell herself that Lucy had probably gone straight to bed to try and sleep off whatever had struck her so quickly. But Cath knew she was buying into a fantasy, so she headed off to the pool, determined to see if she could get to the bottom of things with a little help from Izzy. She'd already messaged her young friend:

Can we meet at the pool this morning?

Izzy had replied immediately.

We do need to meet. See you there in an hour xx

Cath hoped that Izzy was keen to meet because she enjoyed the time they spent together, but she feared she was bound for disappointment. Grabbing her stuff, she shouted her goodbyes to Jon and, unable to wait around any longer, headed straight to the pool. By the time she saw Izzy, she was already breathing hard and feeling an ache in her arms and neck.

Rather than head to the changing rooms, Izzy gestured that she would meet her in the cafe and Cath reluctantly completed her length and hauled herself from the safety of the water, recognising that even up to the point of seeing Izzy, she had been clinging to the small hope that all might still be well. She normally semi-dried herself, throwing her clothes on, eager to make the most of the time they had to chat. But today she found herself taking her time, standing in front of the mirror to moisturise her face, surprised to see the elderly woman with haunted eyes looking back at her. On impulse, she scrambled in her handbag until triumphantly she located the old lipstick that she knew was hidden somewhere amongst the used tissues and sweet wrappers, and, adding the slash of bright pink to her mouth, she somehow felt she had armed herself the best she could for whatever was about to be unleashed.

As she made her way to the table to join Izzy, she noted that there was a drink waiting for her but no bacon sandwich. Clearly things were a bit different this morning, and this was further highlighted by the fact Izzy greeted her with an almost forced smile, rather than enveloping her in a warm hug. Cath took a seat and, struggling to know what to say, she took a gulp go her coffee and then spluttered as she burnt her mouth. At least this seemed to break the ice, and Izzy could at last meet her eye as she started to speak.

'I really hate to have to say this Cath.' Izzy's eyes were already filling with tears. 'But this thing with Lucy is now a real problem.' Cath nodded, disappointed but not surprised that this was the direction the conversation was going. She had had such high hopes for this friendship, praying that it would bring Lucy out of herself, but it seemed that it was following a pattern that was frighteningly familiar. Once Izzy started talking, it seemed she couldn't stop and Cath could only listen, increasingly horrified at what she was hearing. It was a story of a tentative friendship that quickly escalated to messages at all hours of the day and night. A casual invitation to lunch, leading to Izzy 'bumping' into Lucy most days, before it gradually dawned on her that maybe these meetings weren't accidental; Lucy copying every outfit that Izzy wore and showing unreasonable possessiveness if Izzy tried to socialise with other people, before things had come to a head the previous night.

'Cath, it was just awful and I'm ashamed to say that I don't think I handled it very well. I've been trying to tell everyone that Lucy is just a bit insecure and will settle down once she relaxes into Milly starting school. I so wanted this to be the case as I value our friendship Cath; I love this time we spend together after our swim. You're like a second mum to me and, knowing how you worry about Lucy, I wanted to help as much as I could. But last night I was frightened. Lucy was out of control and could have really hurt Heidi. I feel dreadful about this, but I'm asking if you can persuade Lucy to see a professional because everyone is telling me I need to report her behaviour to the police. I don't want to do that as I think she needs help, not punishing, but I am frightened and I'm afraid she might end up hurting someone or herself.' Izzy sat back, breathless after the release of the jumble of words.

'Oh God Izzy, I am so, so sorry. I had no idea that things had got so bad. Lucy has been well for so long that maybe I have got complacent.'

'Cath, please don't blame yourself. I love Lucy, you know I do, and I thought maybe I could help her, but I am completely out of my depth on this one. I feel bad, but I've blocked her on social media. I just need a break from all the messages, but I am really concerned how she will react to this. I think for Lucy's safety, we need to do something.'

Cath could feel the tears starting and was so grateful as Izzy reached over and squeezed her hand.

'Cath, don't cry, we will get Lucy through this.'

'But poor Milly, all her friends' mums will think Lucy is just dreadful. She won't get party invites and will never be able to ask friends over for tea. I know she's poorly, but Lucy has ruined everything for Milly.'

Izzy smiled for the first time the morning. 'Right Cath, enough! You need to get a grip. I will never let Milly suffer because her mum is poorly. Once I have spoken to the other mums, I am sure they will be nothing but understanding. We will get Lucy well, and you and me will look after Milly.'

As the two hugged their goodbyes, with Cath once again apologising for all the upset, she thought how fortunate she was that Izzy had come into their lives when she did.

LUCY

Yet again I had struggled to sleep, my mind whirring. Had I really got Izzy so wrong, and rather than my friend, had she been working against me all this time? Exhausted, I dropped off to sleep just before five, curling up on the downstairs sofa where I felt safe, knowing I had an easy escape route out of the back door. And that's where Rob and Milly found me as they made their way noisily downstairs with plans of making pancakes in celebration of the completion of Milly's first week of school. Rob looked at me in a way I didn't like at all. Had they managed to get to him too? I hated this feeling that I was surrounded by people who meant me harm.

Refusing pancakes, I went upstairs for a shower, hugging my phone to me, hoping but also fearing a message from Izzy. The phone stayed resolutely silent but the hot water of the shower, followed by a burst of cold water, helped me gain some clarity. Picking up the phone, I took a deep breath and typed out a message to Izzy.

> *I'm really sorry about last night. I'm not sure how the mix-up happened with the outfits. I'm so confused, and to be honest I don't feel well at all. I'm frightened. Please can we meet?*

I saw the one tick appear but then no more. Sitting staring at the phone, I slowly noticed that something was wrong with my WhatsApp screen. Did this mean they had got into my phone somehow and were diverting my messages? Izzy's picture had disappeared, and the one tick stubbornly remained. When I clicked onto the parents' group, I gasped as I read the notification.

Heidi has removed you from the group.

It was the word 'removed' that did it, that set my heart pounding. It felt as if I was being erased, piece by piece, from my own life. As I sat there, wondering whether I was safer in my own home, or if I should try and run, I heard Rob calling me.

'Lucy, your mum just rang and as it's such a lovely day, I've invited them round for a BBQ. I'll take Milly to pick up what we need. Can you have a quick tidy up downstairs?'

I felt overwhelmed with relief. Mum and Dad had always kept me safe; they would help me sort this all out.

I'd decided in the early hours of the morning, when I battled a pounding head and gut-wrenching nausea, that I needed to stop with the alcohol. A voice buried deep inside was telling me that my mind wasn't really behaving itself. Part of me was afraid it might be stopping the medication. But the medication was exerting control over me - a weapon of those shadowy figures that I kept glimpsing. I had so many thoughts crowding in my mind, and they weren't kind thoughts. I was feeling very afraid. I wanted my mum.

Mum looked ill, and she held me so close when she arrived that I had to wriggle free, complaining she was suffocating me. I had some understanding then for Milly, who would grumble as I held her that I was crushing the life from her. For the final time, in the sunshine of that Saturday afternoon, with Mum and Dad watching over me as we all teased Rob being bossy in his chef's apron, I was able to banish some of the darkness and tell myself I just needed to get through this. What I was feeling wasn't real. I just needed to breathe. It would be worth it when I emerged through the other side, completely free.

The afternoon went well and then Dad persuaded Rob

to walk to the local for a pint, whilst, Mum and I chatted as the sun disappeared below the houses opposite and we moved inside as it was chilly. Mum was cold, so I told her to go and grab one of my fleeces whilst I made us coffee. As I waited for the kettle to boil, watching Milly colouring at the kitchen table, I reflected that this had been a good day. I was feeling much better, and when I took Milly to school on Monday I would apologise to Heidi - maybe explain that I hadn't been well. I would have a quiet word with Mum and ask her if she would come with me to see the GP, and decided I would come clean and admit that I hadn't been taking my medication. I knew Mum would be cross and it would take hard work to build bridges with Heidi and the rest of the group, but I had to do this for Milly. And for me, Lucy, because I was learning that I was worth looking after and feeling valued too. It was all going to work out just fine.

For a while I didn't notice Mum stood in the doorway. She was stood so still and just looking at me, and as I turned, I jumped.

'God Mum, you scared me half to death sneaking up on me like that.'

Mum didn't say anything, and then I saw that she looked to be crying.

'Mum, what is it, what's happened?'

Mum hesitated for a moment and then reached for me, trying hold my trembling hands, and said, 'Why don't *you* tell me what's happening Lucy?'

I was aware that Milly had stopped colouring and was staring at us, obviously alerted by the tone of our voices that something wasn't right. But I forgot all about Milly as I saw what Mum was holding in her hand. It was the photo of the gang on our holiday that had disappeared from the photo board.

'Where did you get that?' I asked and Mum's voice cracked as she told me.

'I found it hidden in your wardrobe upstairs. I wasn't

snooping, it was just there tucked under all the jumpers at the top of the wardrobe. Why are you hiding a picture of Izzy? And if that's not bad enough, you have got the same outfit. This has to stop, Lucy.'

I couldn't actually say anything, but Milly broke the silence. 'That's the photo that was on the wall on holiday Mummy, you know the one that you thought had gone missing. You must have taken it, because you know how much you liked Bella. You loved looking at photos of her.'

My brain refused to allow my mouth to say anything, and I stood silently whilst Mum ushered Milly off to watch some telly. Coming back, she tried to put her arm round me, but I shrugged her off.

'I see you are doing your best to turn my own daughter against me now.'

'Oh Lucy.' I could feel the tears start in my own eyes as I heard the hurt in Mum's voice. 'I think we maybe need to get some help for you. Will you agree to see the GP?'

I knew there was no point in fighting Mum over this, she would only take it further and I knew where that would lead. I couldn't believe that only minutes earlier I had nearly fallen into the trap they had set for me. I knew that once I willingly walked into the Medical Centre, that would be the end of it for me. But I needed to think quickly; they were already watching me, so I need to tread very carefully.

I nodded in agreement. 'Please don't say anything to Rob. We can sort it out Mum, just me and you. I'm not feeling so good - to be honest it will be a relief to get some extra help.'

I saw the relief spread over Mum's face. She had clearly been expecting a battle. 'Of course love, don't worry, we can get you better in no time.'

I was struggling to stay silent at that point, and I bit my lip so hard I tasted the metallic tang of blood. It reminded me of the hated side effects of one of those tablets that always left such an unpleasant taste in my mouth, spoiling any other flavour I wanted to relish. I wanted to tell Mum that I knew that she had planted Milly to spy on me and that I knew she was working with the nurses to try and get me back under their control. But I was saved by the noisy arrival of Dad and Rob, who had clearly enjoyed more than just the one. Then there was the flurry of reluctant goodbyes as Mum took the keys from Dad and finally, they were gone. For the time being, I was safe.

I wouldn't sleep that night. I was too afraid to even try, so I found myself wandering from room to room. I wrote some little notes in that fateful lilac ink and hid them in secret places. That way, if they eventually overpowered me, someone might come across my cries for help and I could be rescued. I went over and over the last day of our holiday, but I had no memory of taking that photo. Had Milly taken it as she had enjoyed that time making friends so much? But then I reasoned Milly was too small to have reached it from the wall. Then I remembered Rob walking through the rain, making his way back to the cottage from the games room. Had he taken the photo and hidden it? After all, we share a wardrobe, so it could have been him. Except he had no reason to do so. It must have been me, when my mind was being controlled by the medication. I spent the rest of the night plotting, knowing I had no one I could trust, and by morning I was ready to move forward.

ROB

Rob had enjoyed the BBQ, particularly the few beers he had enjoyed with Jon at the pub. His father-in-law was relaxed and chatting about his planned trip to Europe, and Rob was relieved that his explanation of why he had been at the Langdale had been accepted without question. But as he sat drinking his coffee in the conservatory, enjoying the peace of the Sunday morning stillness of the house, listening to the comforting drum of the rain droplets on the glass roof, he was unsettled.

First of all, he had slept badly, hearing Lucy prowling the rooms of the house. He was on high alert, especially when he heard her open the door to Milly's room, but thankfully she had then moved downstairs, and he had drifted off to oblivion. When he had slept, he had dreamt of the woman he missed so much.

He so wanted to move on from the way he had acted, which was not the man he had thought he was, and he remained hugely ashamed of his behaviour. But at the same time, he was desperate to reach out, even knowing that if he did, he would be right back in the midst of things again. Rob recognised that, despite his intentions, he was simply powerless to resist her. Despite this, it wasn't any noble behaviour that prevented him contacting her again. More shamefully, the only thing that stopped him sending the message he had drafted so many times, was the fear that she may refuse to meet, or even worse, simply not respond, and he didn't think he could bear that. He preferred to live with the hope that she was there, just waiting for him to contact her.

And then, as he went to open a new bag of coffee, tucked behind it he found a note in the familiar, yet different, lilac writing, and he realised it had been written by Lucy.

> *Help me. They are plotting to make me disappear. No one is who they say they are.*

Now Rob sat at the table, dreading hearing Lucy come down the stairs. He had noticed his wife was behaving differently - of course he had. She would wait for him to come home and gabble about her day, not allowing him a moment to speak, and he couldn't fail to notice this obsession with her new friend Izzy. He had been worried that she might be slipping back into the grips of the illness that had claimed her after Milly was born, but when he checked he could see that she was taking her medication, and so he told himself that this was just maybe Lucy starting to emerge from the shell she had hidden herself in. After all, he had been so relieved with the way she had coped with Milly starting school and he had been pleased that she looked like she was starting to make friends. Selfishly, he realised that this was because it meant he could share the burden of being responsible for her happiness. But the tone of the note reminded him of those dark days when she was in the hospital, and he once again felt the fear in his stomach that had been so familiar to him as he had walked down the corridor to visit his wife all those years ago.

He jumped as the scream of the smoke alarm jolted him to the present, and cursed as he realised he had burnt his toast. Right, that settled it. It was no good ignoring it. Something would have to be done; and he stepped out of the shelter of the house into the damp garden to make a call. Cath and Jon would know exactly what to do.

LUCY

The bleeping of the smoke alarm woke me up and as I lay there, I noticed the blinking eye of the burglar alarm sensors. Of course, that made sense - that was how they were watching me, through the little sensors in my house. Rob was in a strange mood all that Sunday. He didn't go to his normal golf game in the morning, making the excuse that it was raining. Rob played golf in all weathers, so I knew he was plotting something.

    Just after lunch, Mum and Dad popped in with cake, claiming they had been out to the garden centre and thought they would drop in for a coffee. I knew they were lying as they never visited the garden centre without filling the back seat of their car with new plants which they would force into the tiniest gaps in their pristine flower beds. This time, I could see that the car was empty.

    It was all very awkward, and I noticed as they moved around the house, the sensors on the alarms blinked furiously. Were they passing secret signals? My thoughts were racing, and I wasn't really sure if any of this was real. I went to join Milly, who was happily scoffing chocolate cake whilst completely engrossed watching the film 'Dumbo'. Sitting down next to her, I flitted between watching the film and studying my daughter. Milly giggled as the film moved to the dream scene, and she clapped as the pink elephants began to sing and dance across the TV screen. It was the giggle that first alerted me. It did not sound like Milly, and as I watched the little girl sitting beside me, I had the horrific realisation that this person beside me was not my daughter. But what had they done with

Milly? Grabbing her head, I forced my fingers into her mouth and held her jaw open as wide as I could. Was Milly somehow trapped in there?

'Lucy, what the hell are you doing?' Rob pulled the crying creature from me, and she ran to Mum, who scooped her up and took her out of the room.

'Rob, you have to listen - that's not Milly. They've taken Milly.' I saw the colour drain from his face as he realised what I was saying. And then as the awfulness of the situation dawned on him, Rob began to cry, and I reached out to comfort him. He jerked away from me, and I saw Dad was stood listening in the doorway, an equally terrified look on his face. Then the two of them left the room.

I tried to think how this could have happened, and I realised the switch must have been made when Milly was at school. Which meant that all the parents must have been in on it too; and with sudden clarity I realised that the instigator of all this must be Izzy. I had trusted her, loved her, and all the time she was plotting against me. At that point my mind stopped racing and I felt a sudden calm as I followed Rob through to the kitchen, where I could see Mum was sat quietly crying.

'Mum, you have to help me. It's Izzy. She has done all this to drive me mad and steal my Milly.'

Mum looked at me horrified, and I wondered if she too was regretting how easily she had been deceived. All those mornings she had met with the woman - Izzy probably took the chance to pollute her mind against me. I had no idea why. Was she working with the nurses from the Mother and Baby Unit to try and imprison me there again? Well, I was stronger this time and I wouldn't allow that to happen.

Mum simply looked at me. 'Oh, Lucy.'

'Don't worry Mum, I'm going to sort this out.' I turned and fled into the rain to confront the woman I had only a few days ago thought was my saviour. I had been weak before, but this time I was going to fight back - after all, it was a battle for my family.

Although it was still only four in the afternoon, the rain made the day somehow seem darker and was an indication of the shorter days to come. I had left the house with no shoes on, but I barely noticed the tearing of the pavement at my feet as I ran towards the woman who was the cause of all this. My feet knew the route - I had walked it so many times. Sometimes with my Milly in the bright sunshine, often in the night when I couldn't sleep and I just wanted to be closer to Izzy. When being stood outside her house had been enough to keep me satisfied until the light of the next day began.

I passed a couple out walking their dog, who both stopped and stared as I ran towards them and then huddled themselves against the hedge, as if seeking its protection. Did they sense the darkness that was chasing me, that meant me such harm? Seeing them made me run faster as I realised that Mum would surely come after me. And then I was stood outside her house, and Izzy was stood in the door as if I was expected. She smiled at me and beckoned for me to come in. And that's the last thing I remember.

CATH

Cath was immobile as Lucy fled the house - for that blessed moment feeling only relief that she was free from the crushing responsibility of her daughter. Then she shouted for Rob and called Izzy.

'Izzy darling, I'm so sorry but Lucy is on her way to yours. We will be there as soon as we can - but please try and keep her with you.'

Afterwards Cath wondered why she didn't warn Izzy just how poorly Lucy was. Why she didn't beg her to be careful. If she had spoken those words out loud - would things be different? But she didn't speak the warning and so they were set on the path to the end. Leaving Jon to comfort a sobbing Milly, Cath left with Rob, who looked as if he may fall down at any moment.

'Come on Rob, we have to hold it together.'

'Where do we start looking Cath? She could be anywhere. Oh God, what if she harms herself? I'll never forgive myself for not realising there was a problem.'

'You mustn't think like that, Rob. I know where she's gone. She has headed round to Izzy's. We can pick her up from there, and then I think its best if we go straight to A&E.'

Rob nodded in agreement as he reversed the car from the drive and the two sat in silence, other than Cath giving directions. Pulling up, Cath was out the car before Rob had switched off the engine, and she raced ahead of him, towards the front door, which was standing ominously open, spilling a faint light from the hallway onto the puddles on the path. For a moment Rob sat frozen, seemingly incapable of making his legs take him from the car, and he realised he didn't want to leave this cocoon of safety. He wanted to drive home, collect Milly and then keep driving. Even better if the car was a TARDIS and he could drive them back to the start of the summer and do it all again, but different.

Cath beckoned him frantically from the door and as he stepped from the car, he could already hear the high-pitched voice of his wife as she screamed incoherent words at whoever was inside the house. Rob found that he was unable to take another step. This had happened to him before when he had gone to visit Lucy at the hospital. As the doors opened and he had heard the screaming he would freeze, and it would take Jon or Cath to give him a gentle nudge to move him forward towards his wife.

Cath didn't hesitate. Running into the house, she froze as she saw Izzy backed into the corner of the room and her dearest Lucy stood over her, holding a broken wine bottle as she screamed in Izzy's face - just a jumble of words that clearly made sense in Lucy's head, but to everyone else were simply nonsense. It was only a matter of seconds, but for Cath it seemed that time stopped, and everything happened in glorious slow motion. That had happened to her once before when she had been in a car crash. She had seen that the car coming towards her was going to hit her, she looked in her rear-view mirror and saw that the lady in the car behind was screaming and she remembered thinking, 'Why are you screaming? It's me that's going to be hit.' It seemed to take forever, but it happened too quickly for her to take any evasive action. And it was the same now.

She saw that her daughter was going to lunge for Izzy; she turned and saw Rob frozen in the doorway, staring at Izzy in horror, and they all seemed to be stuck in this moment - the last moment before their lives would change forever.

Lucy took a step forward, her arm raised, and Cath shouted her name. Lucy hesitated, and that moment allowed Cath to fling herself in front of Izzy, holding up her arm as Lucy slashed at her with the jagged bottle. Afterwards, Cath didn't know if she had acted to save Izzy or her daughter, but she felt the pain of the glass as it gouged her arm before making its way with deadly precision towards her stomach, and her last thought before she sank to the floor was, *how awful that Izzy would have all this mess to clear up.*

Cath was vaguely aware that Rob and Izzy were stood over her, and Izzy appeared to be saying something, but her mind couldn't make any sense of it. Frantically, she searched for Lucy and tried to say her name, before a kinder darkness took her.

ROB

Rob was so terrified he didn't think he would be able to breathe. Lucy's friend Izzy had made the frantic call for an ambulance, followed by a request for the police. And all the time he had just sat there. It was as if his mind had started to shut down, unable to make sense of everything, or indeed anything, so instead it had just given up, protecting itself at all costs. He had barely registered that Lucy had taken the car, and he couldn't seem to care enough to wonder where she may be heading. Instead, he tried to keep focused on Cath, though recognised he was being of no use to anyone - rather was one more person who really needed to be looked after, simply getting in the way. Rob and Izzy didn't speak whilst they waited for help to arrive, and Rob only moved when he heard the siren of the ambulance approaching, and finally he was able to rouse himself to run out to direct them to help Cath. He hoped they could help Cath. It looked like she was dead. Izzy had held her hand and kept talking to her, making false promises that everything was going to be alright when it so very clearly wasn't.

    There was a flurry of activity as the paramedics started work, and Rob was vaguely aware of more flashing lights and sirens as the police came to take charge. He was conscious that the neighbours all along the avenue were staring at the house, roused from their Sunday evening boredom by the commotion outside. This would keep them going for weeks, if not months. Normally so concerned with appearances, Rob found he was oblivious to the interest generated by the drama he was an unwelcome participant in. He shrugged away the concern of the immediate neighbours who were trying to persuade him to come with them, away from the horror being played out in front of the chattering audience. Instead, Rob sat helplessly until eventually he was roused by a steady, and somehow comforting, hand on his shoulder and a calm voice of authority asking him if he knew where Lucy might have gone. He was aware that he wasn't able to make his mind and mouth formulate a response, and the questions grew more urgent.

'Do you think your wife means to harm herself?'

Izzy interrupted, 'Oh God, Lucy would talk about this - I know exactly where she will have gone.'

Then thankfully Rob was left alone again until a different policeman ushered him to a waiting car and drove him back to his house, where he had had to break the dreadful news to Jon.

And now they sat, Jon and him, on uncomfortable orange plastic chairs, both anxiously waiting for news on their wives - Milly asleep on a couple of the chairs pushed together. They took it in turns to fetch hot drinks that neither of them wanted, and looked up with a mixture of fear and hope every time the double doors swung open. Finally, the doctor came and spoke to Jon, who collapsed in tears of relief as he processed the news that Cath had made it through surgery and was in recovery.

Rob found he felt better for the news; there really would be no way back from this if Lucy had killed her mother. Rob couldn't believe he was rationalising this, and almost smiled. It was all just so bizarre. For the second time whilst in a hospital with Lucy's family, Rob found himself wondering if maybe he had suffered some sort of breakdown and none of this was real. And then the doors swung open and two policemen entered, and Rob knew, without them needing to say a word, that there really was no way back from this.

CATH

Cath was pleased that it was raining on the day of Lucy's funeral. It would have somehow been unbearable if they had had to bury their girl whilst the sun was shining. Jon was silent most of the time; Cath found she just cried. She hadn't been aware that her girl had died. She had always imagined that she would know, instinctively recognise that a part of her was gone, but when she woke in the hospital bed and managed to focus on Jon, she had thought the tears on his cheeks were for her. For a moment that made her feel very cherished, knowing how adored she was, and then gradually she remembered and urgently gripped Jon's hand as she whispered, 'Lucy'. And that was when she knew.

Lucy had made her way to The Strid and had stepped out into oblivion. Sinking down into the caress of the water, even if she had changed her mind, from the minute she had given herself up to the churning river and the clinging weeds, they were never going to give her back. Maybe someone could have talked her out of it, but there was no one there, the police having dashed to Malham Cove, hoping to coax Lucy to safety from the edge of an abyss that had not proven to be her final destination. Of course, everyone was distraught and living with a lot of guilt. The whole village had rallied round, the house was filled with cards and flowers, and Cath reflected bitterly that this time she had the support of all her friends but had lost her daughter.

"Be careful what you wish for,' she would mutter endless times as the doorbell rang to herald yet another visitor or delivery.

To be honest, Cath hadn't known how any of them would have got through those first days if it had not been for Izzy who cooked, made drinks, looked after a totally withdrawn Milly and simply listened. Cath noticed that about Izzy. She really was a good listener.

Cath was interrupted from her vigil by the window by Jon touching her on the shoulder.

'The cars are here Cath, it's time to go.'

All Cath could think was, 'She's gone, she's gone, she's gone. I've lost her. How will I ever go on?'

But, emerging from the room, she saw Milly leaning into her dad - a very solemn and reserved Milly who had the rest of her life ahead of her, and Cath knew that would be her reason to keep living. Cath anxiously scanned the room and felt relief as she spotted Izzy, who moved towards her and held her hand. 'Come on Cath, I've got you.' And the little group left to say their final goodbyes.

TWELVE MONTHS LATER

Cath dashed back to the house yet again, just to check they really had got all the bags. Jon tooted the horn impatiently, and she smiled as she walked out into the spring sunshine and saw him proudly sat at the wheel of the much too large motorhome that he had bought ready for their six-week adventure.

'Come on woman, let's get this party started.'

Cath gestured for him to wait as she turned to give a final goodbye hug to Milly and Rob. Just a year ago, Cath had not been able to imagine how the world could go on, but it had, and she had Izzy to thank for that. Smiling, she moved to hug Izzy and whispered, 'Behave,' and then gave a wink to show she was joking.

Izzy had come through for her family and Cath would have had to be blind to not notice the way things were changing between Izzy and her son-in-law. Rob was starting to smile again, and Milly adored Izzy. Cath felt guilty realising that at times it felt natural that Lucy was no longer there. She hadn't realised that for so many years she had been holding her breath, waiting for disaster to strike, so that when the worst happened, it was almost a relief.

As they pulled away, Cath glanced behind her to see Rob pulling Izzy in towards him for a hug, Beth and Milly jumping at the two adults, desperate to be involved, before the four of them started to walk back home. Things were exactly as they should be.

PART THREE
When The Hunter Becomes The Hunted

BELLA

I wanted Rob from the very first time I saw him, stood in the doorway, looking confused. Just to be clear, that's not the time he was stood in the doorway looking confused whilst his wife screamed obscenities at me whilst threatening to kill me with a smashed wine bottle. No, the first time I saw him, I was just finishing off my second visit to check on my client's cats; I opened the door and well, there he was. And as he babbled his apologies, all I could think was, 'what a lovely looking man'.

It helped, of course, that I quickly worked out that this must be Rob, the friend who was a partner in a firm of Solicitors in town - the friend who was unfortunately very married. I knew all this because, as well as being their trusted dog walker, I was also quite friendly with Lou and was more than happy to lend a sympathetic ear as she had a grumble about Paul's friend, who was lovely, but seemed to be always round at their house. It's amazing what you can find out by being a good listener. It seemed that Rob played golf at a weekend, 'I mean they see each other every Sunday at the golf course, why does he need to pop round during the week as well, just as I'm trying to get the kids to bed?' I made the appropriate sympathetic noises and filed that away just in case I ever needed that knowledge. I like to do that - collect information.

And then I met him, and everything changed for me. I couldn't stop thinking about him and it was easy to be at the golf club, enjoying a drink on the decking on a fresh spring Sunday morning. The sun was shining brightly but there was still the chill in the air that meant you need to wrap up warm, and I was shivering by the time I finally saw Rob and Paul heading towards the clubhouse. Rob had his head thrown back laughing at something Paul said, and then they were joined by two more golfers and started to head to the bar. I thought I had missed my chance, all that time sat there freezing for nothing, but then Rob called that he would catch them up and headed for his car for a forgotten wallet. I waited a few beats and then walked after him, pretending to be studying my phone until he practically bumped into me.

'Sorry, I should look where I'm going.' I looked up apologetically and then allowed myself a large smile of surprise. 'Well, well, hello Rob. I hoped I'd see you around.'

Rob smiled back and I noticed he looked a bit flustered. 'Hello again. Not seen you here before. Do you play golf?'

'Oh, no.' I gave what I hoped was a casual laugh. 'I was just dropping off my bill for the owner here. I walk his dogs.' Of course, I didn't, but how was Rob ever going to find that out? That's the thing with a lie - you can normally get away with it as long as it's nearly the truth. Rob knew I was a dog walker, so why would he ever question that what I was saying was true? And that was it. I didn't want to push it any further at that point, just imprint myself on Rob's mind.

The second encounter proved more difficult. It had been easy to find where Rob worked (LinkedIn is a wonderful thing) and I had originally thought that I could maybe make an appointment on the pretext of needing some legal advice. However, not only did this look a little calculated, but it also soon became apparent that the firm Rob worked for didn't generally offer their services to the likes of me. They were so called corporate lawyers and somehow, I didn't think my business as a dog walker quite fitted into their client base. The best option seemed to be to loiter around there at lunch time. I would have preferred to have tried for an evening encounter - meeting for drinks early evening offered so much more promise - but I had to collect Beth from nursery at five-thirty so that wasn't really an option.

I lost count of the number of lunch times I aimlessly

walked up and down outside Rob's offices. Did the man never eat? I'd been at it for about two weeks when I finally saw him leave through the revolving door and stand blinking into the weak sunshine as he looked at his watch, then set off purposefully in my direction. Although I had planned this meticulously, and had had two weeks to finesse the details, my hands were shaking and I felt dreadfully unprepared. And then Rob was in front of me, a smile spreading over his face as he greeted me. 'Well, hello again, we really must stop meeting like this.' And I laughed, and after that it was easy.

I could have moved it on to an affair much quicker than I did. Rob was more than willing, and whilst he didn't come out with, 'My wife doesn't understand me,' it was clear he was terribly unhappy. Like I say, I'm a very good listener. So, I was able to find out quite a lot about Lucy before I had to do any deeper research. Rob talked about the terrible time they had gone through after the birth of Milly. He talked about post-natal depression, but there was clearly something a bit more concerning going on there. A quick consult with Dr Google led me to the conclusion that Lucy had suffered a form of postpartum psychosis. I paid particular attention to the information about future outcomes and was drawn to the many references to how the condition can affect a person's sense of reality. Sadly, the patient may attempt suicide or even attempt to harm their child. The articles also warned that whilst sufferers can go on to make a full recovery, they may develop further mental health problems further down the line. It was frightening reading, and my heart went out to Rob, living with this hanging over his happy little family. No wonder he sought escape wherever he could.

When I judged it was time to move our meetings to the next stage, I realised I was entering quite a dangerous phase. Rob was a decent man, and I was worried that he would suffer such guilt over his actions that we would be finished before I had managed to get him completely hooked. It proved that my concerns were well-founded, but not in the way I had expected. Rob was more than happy to carry on seeing me, but he sat me down and very gently explained the reality of our situation. 'Before this goes any further, I need to let you know that I will never leave Lucy. She's just too fragile.'

I nodded understandingly, whilst thinking that I had obviously underestimated Lucy, who I had, quite frankly, labelled as being a bit of a dreary mouse. Rob mentioned she spent a lot of time with her mum, so I figured she could go back home to live once Rob told her that he had found someone new.

Clearly Rob took my nod as encouragement to continue to tell me how difficult things were. 'I just feel like she is so reliant on me. I mean she has her mum, Cath, but we really are her total support system.'

I filed away the name of Lucy's mum, Cath, and asked, 'Does she not have friends that can help shoulder the load?'

'Lucy doesn't really have friends. She doesn't keep in touch with anyone from school, was a bit of a loner when she was at work, and since she has had Milly, well, she doesn't get out much.'

Again, I nodded sympathetically, but my brain had selected one piece of vital information there. I mean, who doesn't keep in touch with a least one friend from childhood. Clearly this was an area that offered possibilities.

I was able to compose my face into sympathetic understanding, 'Of course, and Rob, I do admire you for the devotion you show to Lucy. I would never want to affect that.' I thought Rob was going to cry; he looked so pathetically grateful and as he pulled me close, he inhaled the scent of me as if I was filling his lungs with the breath he needed to make it through another day.

'God, you smell so good,' he muttered, as I pulled him close to me and pulled his hand downwards to show just how much I wanted him.

'It's my favourite scent, 'Lucky'.'

Rob groaned, and at that moment I knew he was lost to me as he whispered, 'How lucky am I to have met you.'

BELLA

So, Lucy is too fragile to leave. This was a slight bump in the road, but I was more sure than ever that Rob was my future, and I've always been very good at getting what I want. I sat night after night, waiting to see if Rob would message me to meet, and plotting how I could bring this to the correct conclusion. To be fair to me, my first plan was actually quite magnanimous. If Lucy was too fragile to leave, I would find a way to build her up, make her strong. In fact, I reasoned, I would be doing her a favour – the power of sisterhood. Rather than stealing her husband, I was giving her back her independence. That felt good.

    But curiosity got the better of me, and I felt compelled to get to know Lucy better. It was so easy to find out such a lot about people through social media. Even if you think you have kept your own musings private, you can't stop what's out there that other people have posted. And once it's out there, it's swirling round forever, ripe for the picking by people like me. Lucy was relatively easy to find on Facebook. After all, I knew where she lived, and thankfully Blythe is not too common a name in the area. And there she was, smiling back at me from my laptop screen. I could only see her profile picture as she had locked her privacy settings down quite hard, but I clicked on the photo to get an idea of the woman I was dealing with. Predictably, the picture was of her with Milly, a hand protectively on her daughter's shoulder as they looked at the camera. Lucy was smiling shyly, peering through a riot of curls that she had let fall to shield her eyes, using her hair as protection against the world. Pale skin with a smattering of freckles. I suppose you could say she was cute, but the overwhelming impression I got was that she was, well, a bit wet.

In stark comparison, Milly looked to be bundle of fire. She had the same halo of curls as her mum, but this girl was definitely no angel. She was grinning at the camera and had her arms flung out wide, as if inviting the world to throw every bit of life at her. I liked Milly immediately - no doubt that the two of us would get along just great. Plus she would be a nice companion for my own daughter, and having the two of them would mean they could entertain each other and allow me to concentrate on Rob, once we were a family. But I was getting ahead of myself - there was work to be done first.

I turned my attention back to the screen and saw that Lucy had kept her friends list private. How very annoying; instead I was forced to have a nosey of the people who had liked the recent profile picture. It didn't take long. Lucy obviously had very few friends, but I was able to click through each one, and when pulling up the profiles of one of these friends, Rachel, I could see that she too had a daughter of Milly's age, who would soon be starting at St Wilfred's. Bingo! I noted this down. Now I knew where Milly would be in September. Scrolling through the rest, there was no Cath, so it would seem that Lucy's mum was not a fan of social media.

Closing down Lucy's profile page, I searched her name again to pick up any mentions of her from other pages. There were lots of entries, but none for the Lucy I was looking for. I was getting frustrated as I reached the bottom of the first page and saw a familiar open grin peering at me from the page. No doubt that this was Milly. Clicking on the post, I saw it was from the open-air pool and was captioned:

> Enjoying the first day of the summer season with her mum Lucy Blythe and Grandma Cath. Milly, we hope you take after your grandma and become a regular. The pool really is for all

ages. Come along and find out for yourself.

The photo featured Milly in between two women, and from the way they both gazed at her adoringly, you could see she was the centre of their world. Lucy was smiling and Cath sported the same grin as her granddaughter. I zoomed in on Cath to get a better look. Looking to be in her mid-sixties, Cath sported the familiar curls, but hers were tamed in a shorter cut. Lines around her eyes told of lots of laughter, but the furrow between her brow hinted that there had been plenty of stress too. So, Cath was a regular at the pool. I noted that down and used that as the starting point to dig about further into the life of this woman who so far was oblivious of my interest in her.

The Facebook page of the pool yielded no new information. I sat irritated at Cath and her aversion to social media. So very inconsiderate. Still, there's always a way, and I clicked on the website for the pool and methodically investigated the details. And there was Cath, in the minutes of the last committee meeting, asking a question about family membership. Now I had her - Cath Weaver - which meant that Lucy was originally Lucy Weaver. Now I could delve back a bit further. But at this point I ground to a halt. There was no hint of a Lucy Weaver at school in this area, and Cath continued to be a digital blackout. Frustrated, I shut up the laptop and plotted my next move.

BELLA

The next day, lying in bed early afternoon with Rob at our usual meeting of the Langdale, I started the after-sex chat in a slightly different direction. Usually, I let Rob witter on about dreams for the future, figuring if I let him share these dreams he might start to include me in them, see our future.

'Oh God, you'll never guess what I've got on tonight.'

Rob smiled. 'Do I get a prize if I guess right?'

I laughed, feigning casualness. 'I can guess what prize you'd pick, and you can have that anytime with me.' To reinforce the point, I kissed him on his chest and then started to make my way down his body. 'To save time, I'll tell you. It's a school reunion.'

'You're right. I would have never guessed that.' Then a gasped, 'Don't stop, and please tell me you're going to be dressed in your old school uniform.'

It's quite easy to play people when they run so true to type. Rolling my eyes, I gave a suggestive wink, bending to resume my task before suddenly sitting up faking a sudden panic.

'Oh God Rob, there's no chance your Lucy could be there is there? After all, it was a big school and there were a few Lucy's in the year above, and I know she wouldn't know me, but if I was introduced and saw your surname on her name tag, well I would just lose it completely.' I gabbled on as if I'd been overtaken by an irrational fear. My story was shaky at best and if Rob had been thinking straight, he might have figured it was a ridiculous thing to say as surely coincidences like this would be stretching things a bit. Happily, Rob was too busy pushing my head back down to think straight, but as I resisted, he finally said, 'No chance of that, unless your school reunion is in Boston Spa. That's where Lucy grew up, she moved here with her parents nearly twenty years ago.'

Satisfied that I had got what I wanted, I set about making sure Rob got the same, knowing that he would be thinking about me for the rest of the day. I was feeling a bit of pressure as Rob had mentioned his upcoming holiday to the Northeast coast, and I was concerned that in his head he might be seeing that as the perfect time to draw a natural line to draw under our relationship. Two weeks with Lucy and Milly posed the real threat that he might wake up and realise just what he was risking losing.

It was much later in the evening before I had chance to investigate further. I had a number of dog walks booked in for the afternoon, then Beth had her swimming lesson at the outdoor pool. Obviously, I had only booked this course of lessons once I figured this would be a great place to bump into Cath. So, by the time Beth was settled in bed it was nine o'clock, and I poured myself a large glass of wine and started to hunt. Boston Spa isn't that big a place and there was only one high school; making the assumption that Lucy had not been to private school, this seemed the best place to start. Sure enough, there was a 'High School Remembered' page for ex-pupils; but I couldn't see much. It was easy to click on a request to join and put in dates of attending twenty years ago, hoping I wouldn't be unlucky enough for the admin to have been there at the same time. It seemed that no one really bothered to check, as I had only had time to refill my wine glass before the 'request accepted' popped onto my screen and the world of Lucy's school days opened up before me.

Group pages are easy to search. You just put in the name you're looking for and, as long as you have the patience to search through the apparently random crap that is also thrown out, you can normally find what you need. There she was - an old class photo posted from when they were fourteen.

The poster had filled in most of the names, Lucy's included, but there were a few gaps which other members of the group eagerly helped to fill in:

> *I think that's David Soames second from left at the back row.*

> *Agreed*

> *Front row middle is Abigail Green. I don't think she's a member of this group so if anyone knows her can you get her to join.*

And the comments went on as I scrolled down the page, eyes glazing over:

> *Third from right is Anna Morris. Best friends with Lucy Wheeler, who I'm pretty certain isn't in the group. Lucy if you are, please don't kill me.*

This was followed by a number of laughing face emojis from a number of people, until someone called Lisa Thornton commented:

> *I think that comment is in rather poor taste. You know Lucy and I were good friends before everything that happened and whilst I'm not defending Lucy, it was dreadfully sad what happened, and she was very ill.*

There were a couple more comments along the same lines and a couple of comments that had been deleted. How very strange. Was this why Lucy kept in touch with no one from her school days? I really needed to find out more information, but how to do this without people clamming up and getting me thrown out the group? I pondered that overnight, clicking to find the main profile of Lisa Thornton, and a gem of an idea struck me. Whilst I couldn't see a lot about Lisa, I could see that all her profile pictures involved her holding a glass of something alcoholic. As I moved down the timeline to ten years ago, I could see that Lisa was a bit of a party animal. Clearly things were a little different now as the pictures showed the addition of a daughter, and then two years later, a son. But my gut told me that Saturday night would still be party night for Lisa. Even if that was a party for one with her phone and virtual friends.

That Saturday night, I forced myself to wait until just after half nine. I figured that was enough time for her to get the children to bed and then get tipsy, and I typed out the message I had been constructing all day.

> *Hey Lisa, apologies if I have the wrong person, but I'm trying to trace friends who were at school with Lucy Wheeler. Lucy is my future sister-in-law and I'm trying to surprise her with a bit of a red book 'This Is Your Life' moment, and would love to have someone from the dim and distant past to be my final reveal.*

And then I waited to see if my message request would be accepted. I expected this to take a while. If there was a story to be told here, Lisa would read and re-read my message and ponder her reply. I had no doubt she would drink a large glass of wine and then probably another before deciding whether to delete the request, and that would be the end of that. But I was pretty confident I knew Lisa, well, her type anyway.

By nearly eleven I was starting to think maybe I had read her wrong when my phone buzzed to let me know I had a new message:

> *Hey Bella, I wasn't sure how to respond as*

> *this is a little awkward. I was very good friends with Lucy at school, but after the unpleasantness with Kate Oxenham and Lucy being so ill, she cut contact with all her friends and moved away with her parents. I have thought to look her up a number of times, but I wasn't sure any approach would be welcomed. I am pleased that life is going well for her, but I think at this stage you would be best to maybe not remind Lucy of this very difficult period. I'm sure you understand xx*

Well, I didn't understand, but I was starting to get an inkling. I responded with a quick heart emoji, not wanting to waste any more time on Lisa now I had as much as I would get from her. Lisa had proved to be far more discrete than I had given her credit for. What a pity she hadn't reached out to Lucy in the past - that could have made such a difference.

Clicking back to the group, I decided I would try someone who maybe had less fonder memories of Lucy. Now, where was the person who had begged Lucy not to kill them? I tapped out a very different message to Dan Tilburn:

> *Hey Dan, long time no see. Not sure you'll remember me, but just wanted to say I still smile when I think about our crazy school days. I bet you knew I always had a crush on you. My God though, do you remember mad Lucy and Kate Oxenham? What a drama! I often wonder what happened to them both. Do you know? Gosh, I'm a nosey cow - no change there then! Lots of love xx*

This time I didn't have to wait that long at all.

> *Hey, of course I remember you! Gosh, yes, what*

excitement. I have kept the cuttings from the papers, so how sad does that make me? No one has heard from Lucy since she moved away, and I wouldn't be surprised if she ended up committed. Yes, she was ill, but God, she made Kate Oxenham's life a misery. I mean, not just at the end when she turned on her with all the allegations, but the weeks of mooning around after her, copying everything she did. And that night in the pub! Pretty sure you were there. Bloody 'Lilac Wine' on the jukebox on repeat. No idea what that was all about. Complete nutter! Let me know if you are ever around and we should meet up xxx

Now this was very promising.

No way you kept the clipping! Can you send me a photo? Would love to see it. I've been trying to tell my husband about it, and he doesn't believe me. So please let me know everything you are up to. Married? Kids? Go on, break my heart all over!

The scan of the newspaper articles came through first and once I saw, it gave me everything I needed. I quickly blocked Dan and Lisa and quietly left the group. Sadly, I never got to find out what happened in Dan's boring little life, but it just goes to show how gullible people are on faceless Facebook when they are embarrassed to admit they don't have a clue who you are. No doubt it will keep him going on a few lonely nights - the predictable little fantasy of the girl from high school who had a crush on him. See, I'm not all bad.

The first article noted that a teacher from the school had been arrested and brought in for questioning following allegations made by a pupil. The article had very few details other than that the teacher had been suspended, and a statement from the school which simply read, 'We have no comment to make at this time other than to confirm we have passed a matter on to the police, and a member of staff has been suspended on full pay whilst the appropriate investigations are completed'.

A month or so later, there was an update detailing that police had confirmed that the allegation had been of a malicious nature but that no charges were to be brought against the pupil, who was receiving treatment at a mental health facility. The school statement this time was, 'We have no comment to make at this time'.

Well, well, well - seems like there was a very good reason why Lucy hadn't kept in touch with her school friends. I seriously doubted Rob was aware of any of this, as the one thing I knew about Rob was that appearances really did matter, and a woman with a history of mental health problems would never have made the first cut of future wife material. I still wasn't sure what I was going to do with this; and then on the Sunday afternoon, a bit of mindless TV-watching whilst Beth was at her dad's gave me the perfect plan. It was a pretty crappy American 'made for TV' mystery adaptation of Agatha Christie's 'A Caribbean Mystery'. I wasn't really watching, but started to pay attention when I got the gist that the scoundrel husband was trying to frame his wife by slowly driving her mad. Belladonna in the drink or some such nonsense. Now the whole plot there was just too fantastical for words but with a bit of adaptation, I saw it was a plan that could work for me.

Instead of making Lucy strong enough so that Rob could leave, how about I make her just too fragile to stay with?

BELLA

Lady Luck was smiling on me the next day as well. When I arrived at Paul and Lou's to take the dogs out for their morning walk, Lou was still at home, full of cold and generally very grumpy. Evidently Rob was expected to 'just pop in' again that night. Obviously, I didn't let on that Rob and I were rather friendly.

'The thing is Bella, we are due to the holiday cottage for a week at the start of July and Rob and Lucy take the two weeks after. On change over day, we all play happy families, and I don't think I can face it this year. Lucy is apparently a nervous wreck with this Milly starting school thing, so I will spend the whole week dreading the one day I will be forced to spend with them.'

I was probably not very sympathetic with my, 'Just don't do it, then,' and started to make my way to the door when Lou replied, 'Oh, I wish it was that simple. My sister has made a last-minute offer to go and stay with them at a villa they have rented in Tuscany, but we won't be able to get a refund on Beach Cottage at this late stage, and we can't afford both.'

Walking the dogs, I rather grumbled to myself about first world problems, whilst still mulling over how I could start to get to Lucy. And then the most marvellous peach of an idea just popped into my head. The poor dogs were practically dragged home, and I tried to appear casual as I dropped them off and turned to say my goodbyes, adding as a careless afterthought, 'Look you might not want to do this, but if you are considering Tuscany, is there any chance I could buy the Beach Cottage holiday off you? Jules and I need somewhere to go with this co-parenting lark and whenever you have talked about it, I think how great it would be. As I say, probably a daft idea, but let me know.'

As Lou started stuttering about not being sure, I gave a cheery wave. 'Got to dash - as I say, just bear me in mind if you decide to head to sunny climes and drink wine. Or alternatively I'm happy to go to Tuscany with your sister!' We both laughed and I gave a casual, 'See you Wednesday,' as I headed to the car.

There was absolutely nothing casual about the way I watched my phone, waiting to see if Lou took the bait. And I heard nothing, not a damn thing. So, on Tuesday Beth and I headed to the pool and signed up our membership for operation 'Meet Cath'. It looked like I would have to fall back on Plan B. It was irritating, but I've always been good at adapting to circumstances. Just like I had to adapt when Jules and I split up. That actually was a curveball that I hadn't seen flying my way. Jules was OK, steady and he was a great dad to Beth. He just lacked my ambition. But the fury with which he reacted when he found all the loans I had taken out in joint names was something I had never expected. I actually liked him a bit more when he showed that bit of backbone. There was no talking him round and we agreed to sell the family home, and I moved to the smaller semi I live in now. Obviously though this was very much a temporary home until I could get myself settled in a finer feathered nest. Jules works away a lot, so as part of the agreement we decided to co-parent one holiday a year. We'd successfully managed two of these holidays, so I wasn't lying when I said Beach Cottage would be good for us.

Shivering slightly, Beth and I splashed around for twenty minutes or so in the pool before retreating for a hot chocolate, with no sign of Cath at all. It seemed that Plan B was a bit of a slow burn as well. But good things come to those who wait, and as I arrived to collect the dogs on Wednesday, I could see that Lou was looking for me from the window, trying to appear casual.

'Hey Bella, you know what you said about Beach Cottage?'

'Oh, ignore me, it was a daft idea.' I saw her face fall. Well, I wasn't going to make it easy for her after she had made me wait. 'I spoke to Jules, and he wasn't sure. He's worried about the cost.' I relented slightly, 'Though Beth and I would have loved it.'

I saw the relief wash over Lou's face. 'Right, let's do it then. And you can have it for a discount on what we paid.' She named a figure that was still eye-wateringly expensive for a potentially wet week in the Northeast, but I nodded enthusiastically. Plan A was a go.

I already felt that I had got inside Lucy's head. I had already suspected that the postpartum psychosis Lucy had experienced may not have been her first brush with mental health problems. Clearly, she had stalked this Kate woman and when things hadn't worked, had reacted very badly. All I needed to do was encourage Lucy to be obsessed with me. And Bella was going to be the start of this obsession. I would be inside Lucy's head before she realised. I almost felt sorry for her - she didn't stand a chance.

BELLA

Beach Cottage was OK. I mean, I'm sure if I had been there with anyone other than Jules, we could have had a good time, but I kept in mind that I was there for a reason. The minute I met Lydia and Steve, I knew they were exactly the people I was looking for, and Jen and Andy were just an added bonus. I quickly established they would be there for the second week. The 'gang' were a nightmare. Hard drinking, loud, dreadful gossips and very easily influenced. It took me no time at all to become Queen Bee, and I made sure there were lots of photos taken. I just knew they wouldn't be able to resist talking about me to whoever came along after me. And I didn't lie to Lucy when I said Steve was a lech. Any chance to get himself alone with me, he did, and so I used his schoolboy crush to my advantage. On the last morning, I went for my usual early morning swim, knowing that yet again he would just happen to be down on the beach, desperate to snatch a few minutes alone with me and ogle at me in my swimsuit without Lydia spotting him. As I strode from the waves and made my way towards him, I almost felt sorry how easy it had been to manipulate these people. It had made the holiday rather boring.

 Reaching Steve, I touched his arm and moved in closer. 'I shall miss our early morning time together, Steve,' I whispered, and he blushed and coughed and mumbled his agreement.

 'Steve, I feel I can ask you a favour.'
 'Oh God Izzy, anything for you.'
 'Well, my dear friend Lucy and her husband are taking

the cottage after us and Lucy really wants Rob to be able to switch off. He has a hugely pressured job. He loves his golf but refuses to play on holiday, worrying about Lucy and their little girl Milly being left alone. I sort of wondered if there's any chance…' I let my voice tail off. 'Sorry, that's a silly idea. It's too much to ask of you.'

'Shall I invite him for a game with me?'

'Oh, would you? I would really appreciate it. But is there any chance you could keep this to yourself? They are a very private couple and would be horrified if they thought I had been talking about them.'

Steve nodded in enthusiastic understanding, and I looked at him shyly from under my fringe as I whispered, 'If I give you my number, maybe you could let me know how it's going? And really, that is the perfect excuse for us to keep in touch.' He eagerly handed over his phone whilst I tapped in my number and saved it under 'Golf Club'. Then I leaned in for a quick kiss on the lips that I knew would have him dreaming about me long after I had left.

It was annoying to leave the 'Lucky' hand soap behind as that was expensive, but I remembered how Rob loved the scent of me, and I had figured the soap might just mean he didn't find me so easy to put to the back of his mind. It was such a stroke of luck that Lucy became so taken with it and bought the perfume too. When I smelt it on her I thought I really was being blessed, even though it didn't smell quite right on her. Perfume is like that: you need to find your own scent. But I'm getting ahead of myself.

The entry in the guest book was another master stroke. I had racked my brains all week to think how I could invoke those unhappy memories of 'Lilac Wine'. I'd thought of ever more bizarre plans to get the song played, and they all were just unworkable. That's the key with a plan like this: keep it subtle and simple. I wanted Lucy's mind to do all the hard work for me. Nipping into Alnmouth to buy those silly phone charms, I spotted the fountain pen with choice of a rainbow variety of ink, and it was just perfect. The lilac entry in the guest book was left as my calling card. We made an early departure the next day; and phase one was complete.

I could have moped about for the two weeks Rob was away - he had already told me there would be strictly no contact - but thankfully I could use this time to befriend Cath. I mean really, how unlikely would it be that the woman Lucy would end up obsessed with, would just have happen to meet her mother at the pool? Of course, it was all part of the plan. I liked Cath. I actually liked her a lot, and we got very close very quickly. She liked mothering people and I'd never been close to my own mother. She really would be the perfect mother and grandmother figure in our lives. I was also very busy getting Beth transferred to St Wilfred's. I was right on the edge of the catchment area and had already opted for the school with the better after school provision, but I needed to get into Lucy's life in more ways than through her mum. I mean, there was the danger that if Milly settled at school, Lucy might come out of her self-imposed solitary confinement and make friends, and the whole thing would be so much harder if she had a support system around her.

Again, Lady Luck was shining on me. Heidi, a very annoying woman who insisted on talking to me at pilates, mentioned she was some driving force of the PTA there and was 'rather friendly' with the Head. I gave some sob story about really wanting Beth to have a place there, but I had made the wrong choice; and a few phone calls later I had the place secured. It was as easy as that.

The parents' group chat was also a godsend, though I was disappointed Lucy, whilst in the group, didn't appear to have made any contribution. I would have to give her a gentle shove in the right direction.

Of course, there was the very unpleasant phone call I received from Rob when he spied me in the photo on the games room wall. I wish I had been there to see his face. I was already prepared for this and cried as I told him Lou had sorted it with

Jules without me knowing, and I hadn't really twigged until I saw the name of the cottage as I arrived. For the first time, I wasn't sure he believed I was as innocent as my story portrayed me. Never mind, he would soon have much bigger things to worry about.

IZZY

Rising like a phoenix from the ashes of Bella, Izzy was born. Izzy - the swimming, laughing, helpful, friendly mum to Beth. The perfect friend for Lucy.

I decided I would have to lead Cath to the realisation Beth and her granddaughter were going to be in the same class, and the pool party seemed the perfect opportunity. It was a bit of a pain to organise - never mind the cost - but I figured it was an investment in my future. It also gave me the perfect excuse to message Lucy directly; and suddenly we ramped up a notch. In the meantime, I was able to casually mention to Heidi that a couple of people in the WhatsApp group were a bit full-on. I ruefully explained that I had been forced to put my phone on silent as I couldn't sleep with all the messages coming through. Of course, this was a total fabrication, but I had no doubt that the 'harassment' would start very soon. Heidi had tutted and had been dying to know who the culprit was, but obviously I didn't want to say. I'm too nice like that.

Of course, Heidi clocked straight away who the perpetrator was likely to be as soon as Lucy arrived with the identical swimsuit to mine. It was just so distinctive, and I had made sure I was wearing it in nearly every photo that Lydia took. I was able to flash Heidi an exasperated eye roll and thought I could leave her to start to get to work on the other mums. It's so much better when you can get other people to do some of your dirty work for you.

The phone charm was an absolute gift as well. I'd hung the tacky thing on my phone just to please Lydia and Jen and with one thing and another, hadn't got round to taking it off. When Lucy had the identical charm, well it was the perfect way to explain away my holiday persona. To be honest I thought she would say something the minute she was introduced to me at the pool - I saw the clear recognition in her eyes - but she kept silent. So when Milly blurted out that of course her mum must recognise me as she was 'always staring' at pictures of Bella, Cath was put on high alert, obviously concerned that a familiar pattern was about to repeat itself. I actually couldn't have planned it any better.

And the birthday cake. Oh, what a pure stroke of genius that was. My gentle suggestion to Lucy to produce the cake, as if it had been all her idea. I smiled at Cath and Lucy, but managed to make my smile very obviously forced as I joined in the 'Happy Birthday' song with all the children.

When I got home from the pool, there was a flurry of messages from Heidi:

> *OK, you have to spill the beans. Is it Lucy who has been messaging you?*
> *Surely it's no coincidence she had the same costume as you.*
> *I have to say she seemed quite captivated by you. Be careful!*

I thought for a while to get the tone just right, then sent my reply.

> *Heidi, yes, it is Lucy who has been messaging me, but you have to absolutely promise me not to say anything to anyone. You are right that the costume clash was no coincidence. We both holiday at the same cottage and some friends of mine had warned me that Lucy had taken a bit of an unhealthy interest in me. I will be careful, obviously, given Lucy's history of forming obsessive fixations, but I really don't*

want to be unkind to her. I am very good friends with her mum, Cath, and I want to support her as much as I can.

Now, I never said that I had known Cath more than a couple of weeks, so it's not my fault if Heidi inferred from this that I was some sort of long-term family friend, but there you go. Lucy had also messaged with an invite to meet up. It was just perfect, but I forced myself to come up with an excuse. Waiting a while, I knew Lucy would be fretting, before I finally put her out of her misery and invited her for lunch. I couldn't have predicted that Lucy would be curious to see where I lived and drive by a few times, and I know she thought no one saw her. Unfortunately for Lucy and rather fortunately for me, Heidi had dropped in to ask me to come on board with the PTA, so I was more than happy to point out Lucy cruising by. I threw in a few tears as well but again begged Heidi not to say a word, secure in the knowledge that once she left me, she would tell pretty much everyone.

It was easy to shed the tears. Whilst 'Operation Lucy' was going well, Rob was proving to be rather difficult. He was adamant he wanted to call things to a halt and for a while refused contact. I didn't like having to threaten him, but I think I managed to hide it under the guise of broken-hearted hysteria. We met back at the Langdale, and of course we had sex. It was good sex, but I could see that part of Rob wasn't with me and I know as soon as we were finished, he couldn't wait to get away from me. I recognised I would have to put that part on a hold for a while and concentrate on his wife.

I had planned the lunch meticulously and was careful to ensure there was lots of alcohol involved. From my research, I could see that it was likely that any medication Lucy was on wouldn't mix well with alcohol. More importantly, when we spent time alone together, I wanted her memory to be fuzzy enough that she couldn't remember who said what, or even if things were actually said at all. Thankfully Lucy asked me what I was wearing, and I happily sent a photo of an outfit I knew would be easy to buy in town. If she hadn't messaged, I would have sent the photo anyway. As soon as Lucy arrived, I acted thrilled and took a selfie of us both, grinning at the camera and sharing that with Lucy. She didn't even notice I'd snapped a second picture of the two of us, this time when I looked rather glum. This pic I sent off to Heidi with the caption:

> I'm getting a bit worried now. Not sure what I should do.

Of course, I don't have a friend who flushed her tablets down the toilet, but Lucy listened, fascinated, and I knew my work was done.

Now it was time to upset Cath a little bit more. However, before I got chance Cath dropped the bombshell that Jon had spotted Rob at the Langdale. Thankfully, I dropped a message to Rob to warn him, knowing that he was clever enough to come up with a plausible story. When Cath reported back later that all was well, I was impressed with Rob's deception. It really did reinforce my belief that the two of us should be together.

I didn't really need to say much to Cath. Her fear was so close to the surface that it took very little to convince her that things were going wrong. I debated sharing my concerns that Lucy had stopped her medication, but then worried she may intervene too soon, so I continued with the death by a thousand cuts.

I didn't mention to Cath or Heidi that I instigated a lot of the meetings. I took Lucy shopping and encouraged her to dress the same as me. It was an added bonus when Milly started wearing the same as Beth. That was a joyous photo to share with Heidi. I told Lucy about pilates and hot yoga and when she mentioned it wasn't her sort of thing, stressed how helpful these things had been to my friend as she came off her medication. As predicted, Lucy turned up to class. Heidi was horrified. I remained stony-faced but 'not wanting to make a fuss', whilst privately telling Lucy how nice it was to see her there.

And really at that point I had done enough. I didn't intend for Lucy to come to the PTA meeting. I had told her about it, but intended to use it as a stage to dissolve into tears and share with a wider audience the difficult circumstances I was dealing with. As it was, I only got as far as mentioning that I had found it a bit weird that Lucy had hijacked the pool party to turn it into a birthday party for Milly. 'I mean, who would do that'; and the other mums all nodded in agreement, clearly realising that Lucy was a difficult character to be avoided. But before I could share some more of my concerns, Lucy turned up and did much better than I could have hoped for. It was as if I had given her the script and she followed it without fault.

After the meeting, I gave Lucy a quick call and apologised if I was quiet but confirmed she was my best friend, but that the others could be quite jealous. I then sent a private message to Heidi:

> *Hi Heidi, I know you were thinking of organising a picnic in the park to celebrate the end of the summer holidays. I'm sorry, but I think its best if Beth and I don't attend. This thing with Lucy is actually getting quite frightening, and I don't want to make things awkward for people. Obviously, we are both so disappointed, but I think it's for the best. Please keep this to yourself.*

Of course, Heidi flew into action, and all of a sudden there was a second group chat, to which Lucy definitely wasn't invited.

Nonsense, Izzy. I'm afraid I'm not as soft-

hearted as you. New group set up for the picnic and I'm afraid I have had to share some of the details. Please think, we don't want someone else to be targeted the same as you.

I reluctantly agreed to go along; and if Lucy hadn't found me, I would have messaged her with my location. The look on everyone's faces when Lucy turned up - it was perfection. And I couldn't have planned for Kirsten sharing about her day walking with her sister at Malham Tarn. When Lucy blurted out about stepping into oblivion and feeling like she could fly, well it really was like I had been sent a gift. Taking the poor girl home, I made sure Lucy drank wine whilst I pretended to join her, and when she was very drunk, I whispered all sorts of nonsense in her ear. And she told me some of her deepest fears, and I felt a bit bad, because in her mind sounded like a terrifying place to be.

In the meantime, I had broken it off with Rob. It was a risky move, but I was pretty sure that Rob is a man who most desires the thing he can't have. And I continued to reluctantly confide in Cath, share in confidence with Heidi - who I knew, in turn, whispered the details to everyone else in the group. I watched as, little by little, Lucy lost that fragile grip on reality. Until, at last, I didn't need to do any more.

I could have left it, probably should have left it. I could see that Lucy was spiralling - she didn't need any more pushing - but if I'm honest with myself, I was quite enjoying it all. The playing of the victim, the care the others showed me, I didn't want to give it up. Pizza night though was the perfect final act. I'd dressed with care in the dress I had encouraged Lucy was just perfect for her. I only had to sit back and wait, and poor Lucy had a terrible time that evening. Maybe I should have felt worse, but quite simply I didn't. I returned home, blocked her, shared my fears with Cath and thought no more about it. I was ready to be there as the supportive friend once Lucy was sectioned again, and things would take their natural course.

When Lucy turned up at my house, emerging from the rain, she really did take the chance to fight back. I'd invited her in, noting her bare feet, and thought I could discreetly text Cath to let her know Lucy was with me. Obviously, I opened a bottle of wine - it would be perfect if Lucy was drunk when help arrived. But I didn't expect her to grab the bottle, smashing it on the corner of the counter, before moving in towards me. She was quite deranged, convinced she was being hunted, but she was very clear as she screamed, that I was trying to steal her life. I wasn't really afraid. I didn't think Lucy had it in her - after all, she was a nice person. Then everything happened all at once: Cath rushing in, the shock on Rob's face, not so much caused by seeing his wife brandishing a broken wine bottle as a weapon as his ex-mistress turning out to be his wife's new friend. Cath bless her made a choice, and she chose to save me. I am thankful for that.

And that was as far as I had intended to take it - Lucy could be sectioned, and I would help Rob and Cath rebuild their lives. Rob would realise I was the woman for him, sympathetic as I explained I had no idea until it was too late, that Lucy was his wife. My story to him would be that she must have found out and targeted me to take revenge. Rob would never share that with anyone as he would be overwhelmed by guilt that his behaviour had led to this destruction of his wife, and he also would want to maintain the appearance of a devoted family man. I would be completely safe.

It was only when the policeman asked if anyone knew where Lucy had gone, that I thought ahead. We would be forever tied to Lucy. Visiting times, maybe home visits, Milly wanting to see her mum, Cath having no time for me as she cared for her daughter. I knew where Lucy had gone. She had shown me, and spoken how, when it was her time, she would allow the water to take her to a place where she could taste the sweet release from the pain she was in. So when I volunteered the information that would have saved Lucy, I found myself whispering instead, 'She will have definitely gone to Malham.'

EPILOGUE

IZZY

I love my new life: an adoring husband, two beautiful girls and a 'mum' who would do anything for me. I've deleted all my presence from social media. Of course, there will be a trace of me floating somewhere out there - I won't have captured everything - but I've done as much as I can. I worry there is something out there that could one day destroy me, that could mean those close to me see that I have blood on my hands, but I think I covered every eventuality. I just have to hope my luck holds.

  I miss Lucy. It's almost like she was the better half of me and that if we had been friends, she could have brought some light to the darkness inside that sometimes threatens to take me over. In town I catch glimpses of her, just a fleeting ghost in the corner of my vision, but I know she's there. Sometimes I dream about her, and I beg forgiveness and promise to look after Milly. I say I dream about her - sleep often evades me and then I sit in the kitchen and listen to that bloody 'Lilac Wine' on a loop, until sometimes I think I might be losing my mind.

MILLY

I do miss Mummy, but not the Mummy from the end. She was quite frightening, and I'm pleased she has gone. Good Mummy, who loved me so much, was able reach me one last time. The night before she had her accident, she crept in my room and left me a note, hidden away in my dolls house. I pretended to be asleep because I wasn't sure which version of Mummy had come to see me; but this Mummy stroked my hair, told me she loved me and that she would always protect me. So I'm pretty sure this was the Mummy I loved.

I am doing well with my reading at school - I'm starting to recognise more difficult words but I'm struggling to understand the long letter she left me. Theres just so many pages and all written in that nasty lilac ink that she liked so much. There are some other things too. It looks like pictures of the sort of things that used to be on her phone. Mummy's phone fell in the water and was never found. Maybe she was trying to get her phone when she had her accident, because she did love her phone and all the messages Izzy used to send her. I can't really make sense of it, but I can see her face and Izzy's face too in little circles by the side of pages and pages of words. There are some photos too: Izzy wearing cut off dungarees in one nice photo. I remember that afternoon - it was before Mummy started acting odd, and the day Izzy told her to stop taking the tablets. I think maybe the tablets were making Mummy poorly, just like too much chocolate gives me a tummy ache, so I'm guessing Izzy was trying to make sure Mummy was OK. My favourite photo is one of Mummy in the pretty dress she wore when she went out for pizza. She looked very beautiful, and Izzy must have thought so too as she sent Mummy lots of hearts.

Mummy sent Izzy pictures of a river too, and a signpost which reads 'DANGER'. I could spell that out, and I'm frightened it could be a picture of the place where Mummy had her accident. I'm not sure it is though as Izzy has sent lots of hearts to that picture too. And it's not a nice place, so I don't see why you would love it.

We have been there once since the accident. We went back to lay some flowers. Just me and Daddy. Daddy cried a lot, and I just wanted him to be happy again. I think Izzy makes him happy, though he drinks a lot of his whisky and cries more than he used to, especially if he hears Izzy playing that tune that Mummy used to play towards the end. I like the song. I don't know why it makes people sad. After all, the lady takes the magic potion and is able to be with her love. I hope Mummy is with someone she loves and isn't too sad without the rest of us.

I haven't shown anyone Mummy's last gift to me yet because for now, it's something special for just the two of us. But soon I'll share it with Daddy, after I've shown Grandma. Maybe at the ceremony we are going to for the opening of Mummy's area at the pool. I think they will like this last message that Good Mummy was able to leave for me. I just need to pick the right moment.

ACKNOWLEDGEMENT

I owe thanks to many people, but first of all thank you to you, the reader, for giving my book your time.

Thank you Mary Hoyle for your hard work on the proof copy. It was a pleasure to work with you.

Thank you to my husband, Ian, who always believes in me more than I believe in myself, and has put up with me talking about writing, and book covers and plot twists without complaint. I'm excited for our next adventure which we can now class as research for a book. I am lucky to share my life, and my dreams, with you, Ben and Charlotte.

The book is dedicated to my mum, who would have been so thrilled I wrote a book. She inspired some of Lucy's story, but thankfully not her ending!

ABOUT THE AUTHOR

Sarah Jones

Following a degree in Theology from Durham University and a successful career in the world of finance, Sarah saw the opportunity to take early retirement and fulfil her lifelong ambition to write a book.

Fascinated by people watching and amateur detective work via social media, these pastimes form the basis of the unsettling stories Sarah writes.

Sarah lives with her family and dogs in rural North Yorkshire and completed her debut psychological thriller, A False Reflection, in 2024. Her second novel, Family Traits, is due out late 2025.

Instagram:

@sarahjoneswrites

BOOKS BY THIS AUTHOR

A False Reflection

Family Traits

Coming Autumn 2025